PROVENANCE OF ASHES

A MARRIED INTO THE MOSSAD THRILLER

JEFFREY ULIN

Black Rose Writing | Texas

ISBN: 978-1-68513-583-6
PUBLISHED BY BLACK ROSE WRITING
www.blackrosewriting.com

Printed in the United States of America
Suggested Retail Price (SRP) $24.95

Provenance of Ashes is printed in Book Antiqua

*As a planet-friendly publisher, Black Rose Writing does its best to eliminate unnecessary waste to reduce paper usage and energy costs, while never compromising the reading experience. As a result, the final word count vs. page count may not meet common expectations.

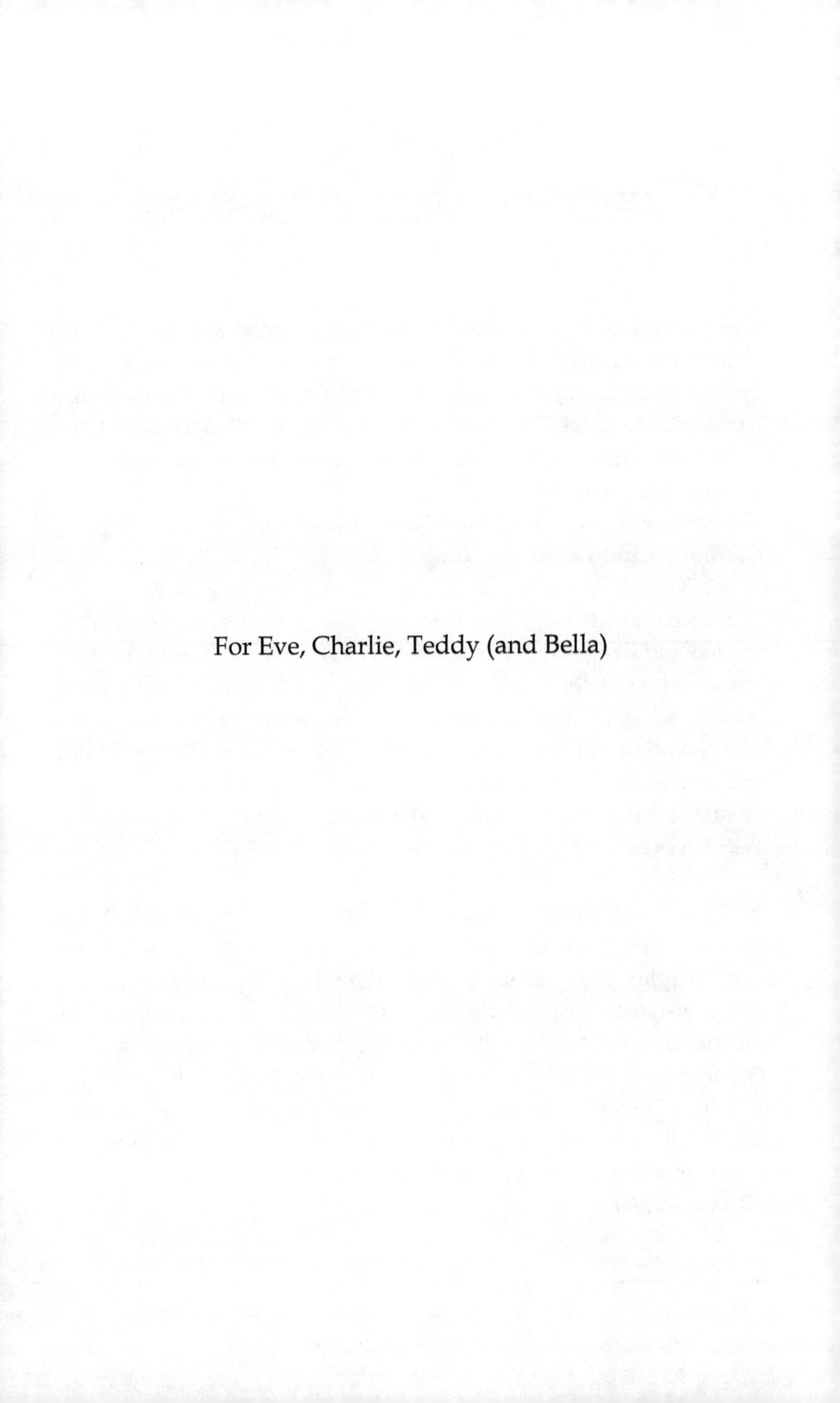

For Eve, Charlie, Teddy (and Bella)

PRAISE FOR
PROVENANCE OF ASHES

"Jeff Ulin is a writer you MUST be reading. He creates detailed worlds of moral complexity which will have you racing to the next chapter. From a Bruce Springsteen concert behind the Iron Curtain, to a poker game with ex-Nazis that goes horribly wrong, to stolen Jewish art, this thriller set in the world of the Israeli Mossad will have you on the edge of your seat. Five stars!"
–Kent Heckenlively, *New York Times* bestselling author of *Plague of Corruption* and *The King of Italy*

"Rapid-paced action burns from the pages where no one can be trusted and danger lurks around every turn. This well-written story, strewn with vividly detailed scenes and impeccable historical aspects, wastes no time drawing the reader in, never letting up, never disappointing. A talented wordsmith, Ulin crafts a multilayered plot and read to be remembered long after the last page is shut."
–Paulette Mahurin, international best-selling author of *The Seven Year Dress*

"…Ulin's historical epic emphasizes the pros and cons of surveillance, curiosity, and following one's instinct in a story that spans decades. The complex plot, which is intercut with narration from a Nazi antagonist, features meticulous attention to detail, with aspects based on true events. It all results in an exciting read that will have the threatening note's words ("Do not think you got away. We are always watching.") echoing in readers' minds until the very last page. Overall, Ulin's skill at drawing on aspects of the past to question the present is impressive. A page-turning, wide-ranging espionage tale. "
–Kirkus Reviews

"I was immediately swept up by *Provenance of Ashes*, a smart thriller that explores the way privilege and lineage both expand and limit a person's fate. Commencing in Soviet-era East Germany, it weaves a tale of modern espionage and deceit, family truths and secrets, art and finance, across Europe and into the 21st Century. Jeff Ulin's book is a reminder that the truth has many layers—and that it can be both fun and fascinating to uncover them."
–Philip Reari, author *The Earth Jumped Back*

"*Provenance of Ashes* by Jeffry Ulin is a meticulously researched historical novel, starting with art stolen in the waning days of WWII and spanning the period from the fall of the Berlin Wall to modern times. Ulin's engrossing characters, which include menacing ex-Nazis, in confrontation with a beautiful and deadly Mossad agent and her financial wizard husband, are drawn with scrupulous attention to detail. The story is deliciously complex, but Ulin's careful research and skillful narration make it both enthralling and believable. This multi-faceted novel is certain to make you a Ulin devotee—you'll want to grab a copy right away."
–Bill Schweitzer, author of *Doves in a Tempest*

"Jeffrey Ulin's new novel has all the ingredients sure to please lovers of contemporary spy fiction-a thoughtful, well- written book with believable characters and a cracking plot written with pace and verve. Having both protagonist and antagonist alternately tell their story through their own prisms is a unique and highly engaging style of writing and Mr. Ulin pulls it off very well. If ever a novel deserves a sequel, it is *Provenance of Ashes*. Highly recommended.
–David Philips, author of Amazon #1 bestseller
The Errol Flynn Conspiracy

PROVENANCE OF ASHES

PROLOGUE

Munich, Germany—1944

Allied bombs fell mercilessly, each impact cratering the earth and spewing out shockwaves and debris. Dieter struggled to hold his balance, surprised at how the ground shuddered. He was ready for the rumble and the spray but had not expected to lose his footing as the earth lurched upwards. Fearing another blast, Dieter ran toward the back of the renowned museum he was in charge of protecting. The Alte Pinakothek was one of the grandest museums in Europe, commissioned by King Ludwig of Bavaria more than a hundred years before the Nazis marched to war. The ornate galleries held treasures of the centuries, from a staggering collection of Peter Paul Rubens' murals to masterpieces by Bruegel, Durer, Rembrandt, and countless more. Some of the paintings were iconic, including Renaissance masters Leonardo da Vinci's *Virgin and Child* and Raphael's *Canigiani Holy Family*. The building predated and probably served as a model for St. Petersburg's Hermitage and stood with the Louvre as among the world's greatest museums. And today, it was crumbling beneath the bombs, the massive colonnades and timeless marble no match.

Obersturmbannfuhrer Dieter Mullenhauer, a tall man whose party-approved nose was so perfectly proportioned a compass should have been screwed to its bridge, foresaw the assault and had stored most of the treasures in a bunker. Given the pace of the attack, though, it was clear he had not moved quickly enough. He barked orders above the chorus of booms, urging his men to haul faster. In an hour, there might be nothing left. Mullenhauer was not a particular fan of art. Fate simply tasked him with the job of protecting the museum, and he faithfully carried out the packing and inventorying of paintings amassed over centuries. Of course, the German masters were the priority, yet he understood the value stored in the landmark building and pushed on duty-bound, if not for posterity. This was a heritage and collection built and bequeathed to the German people. He took pride in helping the curator augment the collection with so many paintings coming on the market over the last few years. Damned Jews hoarded too many works and, even in the face of the inevitable, had the impertinence to haggle when offered fair prices. How could they be so ungrateful when they should have been paid with a bullet rather than a few hundred Deutsche Marks? A fabled collection that under his auspices had blossomed into something even more acclaimed must be saved. He would not let the motherland down.

"Schneller!" Dieter urged on his men, ripples of fleshy muscles in old-world oils mirroring the muscles of soldiers heaving boxes and crates onto lorries. The bunker was only a few hundred meters away, burrowed into a shallow hillside, already reinforced with steel doors and archways.

By daylight, the convoy had finished its work, sheltering the cultural jewels of the past as collateral for the Reich's future. Mullenhauer breathed more easily, confident he had done his best. It was time to dismiss the bulk of the men, keeping four of his most trusted soldiers behind for the phase he would keep secret for a generation.

The bunker had been hastily constructed, and toward the front, the tunnel split in two. He told the engineers to abandon the fork to the right, with its large hollowed-out chamber dug but not completed, when the first waves of bombs started to fall near Munich. However, his private crew constructed a supporting arch and installed a secret door set back into the shadows to the right. His whispered instructions were to line the chamber with concrete and create a concealed vault to hold special treasures at the instruction of the Fuhrer himself. Now Dieter worked with his men to stockpile the room with paintings he had hand-selected. Not the most famous paintings, in fact, but treasures, nonetheless. Finally done, they sealed the door and covered up the entry with dirt and mud. Within two hours, it was undetectable, a slight dent to the right along a passage that appeared to curve to the left. He marked the spot by creating his initials out of stone pebbles embedded into the clay walls, placing the letters backward and at two spots equidistant from the joints of the hidden arch.

The men moved outside into the morning's drizzle, adrenaline-buzzed by their feats. Dieter clapped his hand on each of their backs, lauding their achievement in saving the museum's pieces from the enemy and fulfilling the Fuhrer's wishes. These were men who followed orders, hard men who would not take pride in viewing, let alone saving, artwork under any other circumstance. Today, though, they took pride in their extraordinary mission. They may even be hailed as heroes.

Dieter told them to get his jeep ready; he would join them in a minute. The men piled in and started the engine. In the distance, past a tree line shorn by misguided bombs, they could make out the cratered left front of what used to be part of the

Alte Pinakothek's portico. No bombs fell now, no sound of planes, just the patter of rain and the banter of soldiers singing the Reich's praises.

Dieter lifted his arm as if to signal his crew then tossed a grenade into the jeep, blowing up his men. For good measure, seeing one of them still alive, he drew close and shot him in the head. It was not to put him out of his pain, for Dieter was not a merciful man. But he was excellent at covering his tracks.

CHAPTER 1

East Berlin, East Germany (German Democratic Republic)—1988

I am more than ten years younger than my brother, Gunther, and only ten and a handful of years older than his children. That gap cast me in an awkward middle, neither close to my brother nor sibling to my nephews. My strongest family bond always was, and always will be, to my father. He was a great man. Perhaps a bit evil, but great. Sometimes you have to be strong to get ahead. It was part of his race, his blood. My bloodline. How can we compare the comforts of today to the war? It could have ended so differently. I knew my generation was supposed to be ashamed. But I, Werner Boesseneker, have never been ashamed. Think about what the Nazis accomplished in such a short span of time! Amazing. My father thought his grandchildren, my nephews, could help carry the torch for those who had come so close. For a time, I was charged with watching over them. A kind of guardian angel. Gunther strove to direct his sons, but he was too soft. Too traumatized, perhaps. My father and I tried to start them on a path over the Berlin Wall, but there were some difficulties — major ones, to be fair.

Berlin was another beginning and downfall all in one. It would take a while before we could overcome yet another setback. To me, though, my childhood Berlin, the Berlin where my father hibernated, was all I had known in flesh and muted color. The other pieces of history were drawn only by stories. Yet, most of the stories proved true, and what lay hidden would help fund our future. My father taught me to be patient. My turn would come. His turn promised to come again.

The Netherlands—1988

The Dutch tulip fields were in vibrant bloom, perfect rows of pink and yellow stretching toward infinity from the still canal, as Beryl and I pedaled through the small town of Lisse. It was a month before graduation, and life was carefree. She called to me, "Marco, hurry up!" and I nearly ran into an elderly couple leisurely riding down the bike lane as I wove around them to come alongside her.

We had set off from our homes in Wassenaar, an elite village bordering The Hague, cycling past mansions topped with thatched roofs. I always wondered how someone maintained thatching nowadays. My mother refused to live in one of those traps, as she called them, fearing fire and rats in no particular order. I remember when she was upset with me, she used to call me by my whole name, and I imagined her shouting, "Marco Bellagio, watch where you're riding. If you keep staring at that girl, next time you'll crash into that old pair or run your bike right into a canal." I pushed my mother's voice away and sprinted ahead of Beryl.

The lush woods and tree-lined streets gave way to open fields with windmills popping up beside canals, their lazy rotation belying the smooth generation of energy. The grist of productivity had powered the land since Holland's Golden Age and remarkably still fed the local bakeries. Mostly, though, these marvels from the 1600s had become picturesque landmarks, whirling in an arc reaching out to the past and beckoning a return to a cleaner future. As I pumped my legs in a smaller circle, I thought of my father, a prominent banker in Rotterdam whose varied portfolio of loans included financing futuristic wind farms. A group of Dutch entrepreneurs was preaching how windmills could once again rule the landscape. Giant metallic arms generating clean power would soon replace wooden slats and sails. And he would provide the money and guarantees to build these great new towers. No Don Quixote fantasies: Tony Bellagio would become an insanely wealthy banker, and I was destined to follow in his footsteps.

First, I needed enough energy to power my tiring body to our destination. My legs were cramping after riding more than an hour, the day unusually hot for a spring normally yoked to winter by the bite of the nearby North Sea. I slowed and let Beryl pass me as she laughed, calling me slowpoke and whizzing ahead. I lowered a gear, content to drop back and watch the sway of her body straddling the frame, a gentle lean countering the angle of her bicycle. A poet might have commented on the lovely arch of her back masking my view of the handlebars or her jet-black hair flicking back in the wind, filtering the light and animating the shadows in the field beyond. About to graduate from high school and hormonally driven, I focused on her skirt, waiting for a gust to billow the folds and give me a cheap sneak. I always tried to be honest with myself. What a shame so many of my adventures would thrust denial into a dogfight with honesty. The trifling sins of a boy's lustful thoughts were literal child's play compared to what I would soon face.

"How much farther?" Beryl called, snapping me back to a different vista.

"Not too much more, I think. The gardens are just past the town. I think we turn by that next stand of trees."

"Good, my legs are killing me. I shouldn't have bullied you setting the pace," she mocked, turning toward me and smiling widely.

"I know. You warned me about dating a girl from a military family."

"Ha. Come on, pick up the pace so we can have our picnic."

Within fifteen minutes, we arrived at the Keukenhof gardens, the most famous tulip fields in Holland. Manicured to perfection, the grounds undulated with colored patterns. Atop a lake, a burst of white and pink curled along the bank. We walked on steppingstones to a bridge, crossing to a display of royal blue and lavender, the petals melding into the shape of a drawbridge leading to a gold turreted flower castle. Beryl took my hand and led me to a blanket of grass beside the castle overlooking our pretend moat. Ducks floated past, and a pair of swans paddled toward us, completing the fantasy. The scene felt lifted from one of those Monet paintings Beryl could talk about forever. Who knew her knowledge of impressionist masters would prove so useful later?

As we spread a blanket and unpacked sandwiches, passersby hardly noticed the couple we had become. We stared out silently, transfixed by the hues and breathing in the fragrances. The rainbow of colors trumpeted the arrival of a new season, new beginnings. In retrospect, the bloom should have caused me to reflect on my own passage of time, that I was on the cusp of a seminal transition.

I was too naïve to realize that Shangri-La moment in time would not last. The Dutch Golden Age of Rembrandt, Vermeer, and Hals had been buoyed by exploration and wealth acquired from bartering across the seas. The fabled East India Company traded spices and other goods, growing so large it printed its own coins. The riches helped dredge Amsterdam and Haarlem's grand canals and build gabled rows of townhomes that stood testament today to the ingenuity of architecture and design. I knew we were perched on the threshold of a new golden age, one that would be driven by technology and the arc of limitless flight. I stood witness to the first generation of human beings that could truly see the world. Not part of the world—the whole world! My father used to say, twelve hours to anywhere. And it was true. The age of jet travel made mincemeat of old wooden

Dutch sailing ships. I could be in New York today and Tokyo tomorrow. I could see more of the world than Marco Polo, Christopher Columbus, and Lewis and Clark combined!

Parking those thoughts on the horizon, I returned to the temporal game of seducing a beautiful girl, musing whether one day she would become my bride. I calculated my odds should improve basking amidst a field of flowers with swans breaking the mirrored reflections of a blaze of red tulips from the far bank. Beryl's blue-green eyes, raven hair, and pink skirt teased more kaleidoscope hues. Life couldn't be this perfect, could it? History, if nothing else, guaranteed the illusion must be broken. Struggling to bury my wayward thoughts, I let my eyes follow the swans toward the far side of the lake. Beryl was holding my hand, the sun was shining, and in a few weeks, I would be in East Berlin. Unimaginable.

"Are your parents okay with you going to the concert?" I asked.

"Absolutely."

"Good. I can't believe we're going to see Springsteen. And in East Germany. Should be a bit of history. The wall can't last that much longer."

"I don't know about that. They still shoot people trying to escape. But should be safe enough to go—I hope."

"Thanks for that reassuring image…It will be all right. Plus, you're connected, and Dirk's dad will watch out for us. Can't believe he managed to score those tickets."

The Iron Curtain had been showing signs of relaxing—even if just a bit—and Bruce Springsteen was planning a show in East Berlin, oddly billed as a concert for Nicaragua. I wondered if they had told Bruce that yet (doubted it). Hard to believe they were going to let him sing "Born to Run." Could that cause a riot? Maybe. A bunch of us in world government class had heard about the concert, and then Dirk (Dirk van Dijksen to be proper) asked if we wanted to go. I could remember the conversation vividly.

"Shouldn't be a problem. Let me ask my dad," Dirk boasted.

"What, no way!" Beryl said. "How can he do that?"

"He's the Dutch Ambassador to East Germany. What good is that if he can't even get us some Springsteen tickets? And free, of course. Do you want to go?" he said, winking at Beryl.

"If all of us go. Marco, you, me," turning around, adding, "plus Bryan, Amanda, Tessa, and Hamid."

"I don't know. What's that, nearly ten tickets?"

"Thought you claimed that wasn't a problem," Beryl said, quickly making eye contact with me. *Good girl.*

She continued, turning back to Dirk, "It will be our graduation trip. We'll never forget it."

"Let me see what I can do. I'm sure some parents won't allow it. Maybe a few tickets will be enough."

"Everyone," Beryl said flatly, closing the argument. She had a way of doing that.

Our lives would have been so different if Dirk had ignored his crush and foolish dreams of wrestling Beryl away from me. It would have been infinitely easier not asking his dad for those tickets. My God, Springsteen behind the Iron Curtain! The very idea was hard to imagine. Well, not only were we imagining, but we went. With twenty-twenty hindsight, listening on the radio would have been much less life-threatening. That, though, was never an option. Hell, if I would have let Dirk lead the way.

That beautiful day picnicking in the tulips seems ages ago. I cannot remember the bike ride home, but I can still feel the sun on my back as we stopped talking about the concert and kissed until we feared having to cycle back in the dark.

***

Before our concert trip, there was the small matter of graduating. The American School of The Hague (or ASH as we often called it) provided a privileged bubble for sons and daughters of business expatriates, military families, diplomats, and wealthy local Dutch. Occasionally, there were even the kids of royalty and the new type of royalty — sports stars. The school was akin to a mini–United Nations, which I suppose was not surprising given the multinational institutions scattered nearby. Among the most famous was the International Court of Justice, established just after WW II in the Peace Palace. At the time, being dragged to visit the august chambers was a field trip I could have missed. *Hindsight again. Would I have admitted to saying privileged?*

At graduation, flags identifying each student's nationality graced the auditorium. The program took the added step of listing where all the seniors' parents hailed from. Matched sets were much less fashionable, and those kids lucky enough to benefit from divorced upbringings could boast of head-spinning continental mixtures. If you only had one passport, or could not claim polyglot roots, you were nobody. Those in my clique were a who's who of who's who.

I had a great group of friends, but even back then Beryl was first among not quite equals. I tried to call her Luziy until she browbeat me to stop. Her dad was named Uzi, and I thought the nickname, for little Uzi, would be cute, even though I had more than a letter off, and it never fit. Coming up with a letter off is no big deal and almost a prerequisite when every one of your classmates grew up speaking a different language. Beryl's was Hebrew. Her father did something tied to the Israeli government and some European command. She was never that clear about it, which told everyone paying attention all about it. Maybe I should have called her LoMo for little Mossad. Oh, and how I was taken by Beryl's bewitching walk, her hips undulating with a pivot so perfect it should have been patented.

Thinking about Dirk, that boastful son of an ambassador, always broke the spell cast by Beryl's sway. Same could be said about Hamid, the type of exotic kid that would stand out anywhere other than ASH. Hamid was half Pakistani, half Iraqi, and his dad was a bigwig at Shell Oil. I think his mom worked there too. Back then, engineers were not as sexy a topic, but she was a looker and a genius, passing along both traits to her only son. Shell happened to be headquartered in The Hague and threw around a lot of money. Sometimes it even felt like a company town. Nice for an endowment when one of the world's largest corporations had its base just past the next canal.

Rounding out my rat pack was Bryan Anderson—because an American school ought to have at least one American. Bryan had moved to the Netherlands from Chicago, another town known for its beer. Guess Bryan's dad realized Heineken beat the shit out of Midwest brew and took the leap.

When I first moved to Holland, I only knew about the beer. I soon learned that Heineken was a family name and that the heir to the beer empire, Freddy Heineken, had been kidnapped and released after a ransom was paid, all just a few years before I started high school. ASH not only had riches from Shell, but now world-class security. That was my high school.

I fit right in hobnobbing with this group. My last name, Bellagio, bespoke acceptance, but more simply marked where I was born. Not the hotel in Las Vegas; I cringed at that association. Generations of my family hailed from the real Bellagio, a beautiful little town on the shores of Italy's Lake Como. Guess that was what attracted my mother, Claire, a product of an American father and French-Canadian mother.

My mother moved to New York as a teenager, eager to cloak herself in an air of sophistication and forget the perceived wilds of moose and Mounties. In her marital reinvention, she relished putting down knockoffs and loved talking about the real Bellagio, the real Venice, the real Amsterdam, not New Amsterdam. Marrying into a banking dynasty also probably had some sway.

My dad came from a line of bankers and was an executive at a private bank just over the border from Italy into Switzerland. Travel took him all over the world, including often to New York where he met my mother at some party where she was set at discovering more than wine and cheese. Years later, just when I was old enough to begin idolizing the football stars on Inter-Milan, he was recruited to a major Dutch bank's executive committee, and we moved to the Netherlands. While he would be working out of Rotterdam, my parents bought a house in The Hague to be closer to my campus. Luckily, for the summers I always returned to the Bellagio family's villa on Lake Como where I could follow my football heroes on TV. I guess that made me part Italian, American, Canadian, Dutch with a bit of Swiss rubbing off. Maybe all those nationalities made up for being an only child. I spoke five languages fluently, which I doubt I would have mastered without the simplicity of dinner-table banter. I flaunted that prowess — just a bit too much — and hardly hid that I expected to become one of the richest men in the world. *Had I only known my boasting would prove true and I would marry a beautiful Mossad agent.*

Everyone dreams, and before I set to scaling financial heights my cadre of friends and I needed to graduate from ASH. And there was nothing like a graduation built for nostalgia. Not the ceremony. Yes, that had its expected pomp and projected slides of flags and countries and trophies. I took home the math cup, which was a good harbinger of banking success. My trophy denoted an era well past the abacus and slide rule, when Hewlett Packard calculators were novel, and well before apps and algorithms became common parlance. I had to write out equations by hand and perform calculations and proofs the hard way — leading to a type of absolute confidence that tasks with only one right answer can breed. I was smug and winning that cup gave me confidence at the time. Today, I probably couldn't win a thimble.

What I remember most about graduation were the parties, like Great Gatsby on a canal. Beryl's friend Amanda hosted a soiree on a grand estate in Wassenaar, not too far from the Dutch royal family. We arrived by following a couple canals and thickets of woods darkening streets from overhanging branches to the third thatched mansion on the right. Someone told me the building used to be the Argentinian embassy before Amanda's parents bought it; crests still adorned the gates and a couple arches. In the backyard's sprawling grounds was a two-tiered garden, replete with a pond and oddly an archery range. Given all the alcohol provided by our Heineken friends, arrows were prohibited for the day. Good idea. I was on the cusp of seeing double before dinner was served, and the best I would have done was skewering someone in the ass.

There must have been well over one hundred people there, not enough to crowd the estate yet enough to mingle and distance as you fancied. Walking with a flute of champagne, I found Amanda wearing bright pink lipstick matching her body-hugging dress. I tried not to focus on the plunging neckline, failing miserably — a mix of averting and gawking, which I suspect she wholeheartedly appreciated. No, I was not looking for the heart, couldn't seem to find it.

"Did you grow up here?" I asked Amanda, trying to divert my thoughts.

"Yeah, you know, Shell brat."

"Ah, I know your dad worked there, but didn't realize he was such a big shot."

"Oil makes the world go round, they say. I wish he were home more. Seems he's always in the Mideast. Dubai, Qatar, you know."

"I kind of do. My dad travels a lot. Twelve hours to anywhere, he says. Singapore, New York, Tokyo, Geneva, London, Cape Town. Even Abu Dhabi. Ever think of going to visit Beryl's family if your dad's always in the Mideast?"

"Yes, I'd love to go. I've never been to Israel, and she's invited me to Jerusalem. We've been plotting my visiting next year. Just need to convince my dad, who's not too keen on my traveling to the Mideast alone. I think he'll give in, though. A couple years ago he surprised us, and we all went to the

Emirates. It was beautiful. The sand dunes were right out of *Lawrence of Arabia*. We had dinner out in the desert, rode camels. Camels actually break the spell a bit. They're pretty gross. Smelly, ornery. Spit. I much prefer riding horses."

"I know Beryl loves to go riding with you." Looking around, "Are your horses here?"

"No, we have a stable a few minutes toward The Hague where we keep a few horses. Easy cycle there. There's also a small guest house, so we can change into riding clothes and get cleaned up. I love it over there."

Amanda flicked her bleach-blond hair, twisting her skinny torso and sucking in my gaze. I remember thinking, *Careful, boy. This is one of Beryl's best friends. Horses, champagne, country garden, secluded guest house. Get a grip. Normal conversation.* "What are your plans after graduation—still planning on grad school in London?"

"No, changed my mind. Going to get an economics degree at Edinburgh. Scotland for me. Rolling hills, just not sand! But first, looking forward to Springsteen. Can't believe we're going to East Germany. My parents are not keen, giving me lots of trouble."

"Everybody's. I know. But I think I've finally convinced my folks. Played up Dirk's dad's diplomatic credentials. I mean, we're going under the protection of the Dutch ambassador, for Christ's sake. We'll be okay."

Beryl walked up as Amanda mulled over the risks of traveling to East Germany for the umpteenth time. "Mind if I take him away?" Beryl asked.

"Always spoiling my chances. Marco, you know where to find me," drawing her head up towards a window.

Was that her bedroom? Jesus. I hoped to get laid that night, but not there, not with Amanda. Prom and spring and graduation and plunging necklines notwithstanding. Beryl led me off toward the lower garden's archery range, grabbing a fresh flute of champagne. We snogged behind a tree, a bit drunk, enjoying the slight danger of being discovered.

When we walked back toward the house, Beryl's parents caught sight of us, and there was nowhere to hide. Uzi probably had me bugged anyway. The two managed to look casual and elegant, Uzi in jeans, blazer, and polo shirt, and Beryl's mom in a salmon-colored cotton skirt, Moroccan patterned blouse, and simple jewelry. A model of blending in without the pomp fussed over by the bankers and oil barons.

"Mr. Jaffe, nice to see you. And Mrs. Jaffe, exciting day, huh?"

"Marco, call me Anna. No reason to be that formal." She leaned over and hugged me. "Yes, can't believe the two of you are done with high school. And it's a new chapter for us as well. At the end of the summer, we move back to Israel. I'll miss it here."

"I think we all will," Beryl said.

"Marco, can you tell me more about this concert?" Uzi asked, casual, though I never believed anything he said was truly casual.

"It's a Springsteen concert. That's really all there is to it. Other than it's taking place in East Berlin, which is cool and a bit weird, and maybe means they're starting to open up a bit. How many times do you get to visit behind the Iron Curtain? We thought it would be a once in a lifetime experience."

"But will you be safe? This is East Germany. It's a big deal, not like going to London. What kind of security will you have?"

"Security? Uh, I don't think any. Everything is being arranged by Dirk's dad, who's the Dutch ambassador over there. I'm sure he wouldn't get us the tickets and let us go if he didn't think it was safe. I assume he'll look out for us."

Uzi looked unhappy but fought to put on a smile in front of Anna and Beryl. He was a master at appearing at ease, yet I had spent enough time around him that I could sense restrained energy coursing below the surface. His nonchalant air and professorial wavy gray hair were cultivated to misdirect others away from his perpetual vigilance; Uzi's wiry frame waited in a constant state of readiness. Sighing, he answered, "Okay. But I am concerned about it. You know we Israelis take security pretty seriously. Before I let Beryl go, I am going to have a word with Dirk's father, if that's okay. And I might want to put a couple people on notice just in case you get into any trouble. I've got some connections at the local embassy too. Can't be careful enough."

"Sure. I mean that would be fine. Great. Last thing we want is to get into any trouble or be stranded over there."

"Good. I'll look into it," he said, clasping me on the shoulder then walking away.

I imagined that within an hour, he would call someone and sort out a team to watch over us. Would he allow his daughter to go to East Berlin without an escort? Springsteen concert or not, he would worry. I wondered if Uzi was packing at the party. Not an Uzi submachine gun, of course; that would have been over the top. A nice gun hidden beneath his sport coat, however? Probably just like Anna putting on a necklace. Belt, shoes, underwear, gun. I wanted to ask Beryl, but that was not the best opening line when I was hoping to sleep with her that night. Still, kind of sexy to think about. What if she was packing a gun? Now that would be something.

I asked Beryl if she had ever been to Amanda's stables and dropped a hint about the guest house. Maybe she had been thinking the same thing. To my amazement, Beryl had a key. The mind can play tricks, and I thought what I most remembered about graduation were the parties. Guess I lied.

***

Berlin, Germany- A Few Weeks Later
Only five of us made the trip, and ultimately, only three of us made it to East Berlin. Amanda's parents put the kibosh on things right after the party. Her dad had toured enough hot spots with Shell to know danger when he smelled it. The

Mideast had been among his safer postings. Jaunts to Africa had hardened his outlook. Bribing dictators and staving off kidnappings were all part of drilling in rough neighborhoods. Oil respected neither borders nor civility, and those sitting on black gold usually expropriated special kinds of tolls.

Dirk, Beryl, and I were all given reluctant approvals. Although, I wasn't quite sure about Beryl—the reluctant part. Maybe she was already being groomed, and this posed a good test. I remember thinking, if you grew up in a Mossad family, split time in Europe, and were fluent in Dutch and German, wouldn't a little weekend trip to East Berlin be almost too good to be true? We were talking about a Springsteen concert and passes from a Dutch diplomat—stuff you couldn't make up. What a cover. I bet old Uzi jumped at the opportunity, feigning his disapproval, fretting for my amusement. I asked her, of course. She said something about the separation of church and state, which struck me as kind of funny her being a Jew from Israel. Even couples keep some secrets from each other. Especially when one of them is Mossad. *I think.*

While Dirk boasted about obtaining tickets, the truth was he found convincing his father quite a challenge. A key obstacle was his father had to attend a conference and could not be in East Berlin when we were traveling. Dirk ultimately succeeded, though, the force of a graduation trip plea trumping the risks. Winning that argument was critical, of course; without him, there was no trip. I worried the plans might still fall apart because Dirk's girlfriend, Tessa, backed out. Her parents freaked and said absolutely no. She was Dutch too, but unlike Dirk's father, Tessa's parents still held overt prejudices from the war. They did not want her going to West Germany, let alone East Berlin. Sadly, Tessa didn't seem to have issues with her family's perspective. That type of inflexibility did not bode well for a relationship in a diplomatic family. I wondered if Dirk sensed his relationship was in peril and was searching for new horizons when I fended off his flirtations with Beryl at Amanda's party. No. Dirk was a good kid, and he was probably drunk and upset, realizing he might not be able to convince Tessa to join the trip.

That left just two more who managed to manipulate and secure a thumbs-up from their folks. Bryan was a bit of a surprise, as his dad had also been to plenty of tough spots with Heineken around the globe. In the end, he was a sucker for beer, and Germany was the promised land. Lots of jokes there at his expense. The other comrade was Hamid, yet another surprise given his dad also worked for Shell. I would have handicapped him a definite no. What I had not counted on was the force of relativity. I suppose being part Pakistani and part Iraqi, danger was viewed through a different lens. Even long before the Iraq war, one always watched the crossroads in that neighborhood. And who in East Germany would care about Hamid? The struggle was East-West, and Hamid was from a compass bearing that hardly registered. He was as good as from Mars.

That was how the five of us ended up in a guest house in Kreuzberg, West Berlin, en route to the concert. We had flown into Berlin's Tegel airport on a KLM flight, five recent graduates out for an adventure. The plan was to stay two nights in East Berlin, possibly only one. We would cross over the border to East Berlin and stay there the night of the concert. Hopefully, we would stay one more evening to experience the city but could always return to West Berlin the morning after the concert if we felt in danger. Five days total in Germany.

Kreuzberg was in the American zone, an upscale section of Berlin with wide boulevards, tree-lined streets, and plenty of parks. The houses were not as grand as Charlottenburg in the British zone, but Kreuzberg had the advantage of being right on the border. In fact, it was only a short walk to the Berlin Wall from our hotel. We set out that night to behold the landmark. The first time I saw it, I froze. The Wall stretched as far as I could see in both directions, barbed wire at the top ominously signaling this was no ordinary cement barrier. The graffiti was spectacular, a dazzling splash of defiance. Random, ugly, beautiful, scary all at once. We all held our breath. We then walked what we thought was north—we were pretty sure we were not walking east anymore—until we saw a guard post in the distance. A spotlight circled out, and we froze, not wanting to come under its glare. I was confident bullets could fly farther than the light's reach. It was a somber walk back to the hotel. Bars were still hopping, and some soldiers walked nearby joking and taking drags on their cigarettes. Normal was not normal. Shit, was this really a good idea? It would be a lot simpler to buy Springsteen's new album.

***

The next morning, we grabbed our backpacks, checked out of the hotel, and confirmed our reservation to return in two nights. The checkpoint to enter East Berlin turned out to be the opposite direction from the walk we had taken the night before. We climbed into two taxis traversing Yorckstrasse, driving past a large park, and within five minutes, we were on Friedrichstrasse and at the infamous Checkpoint Charlie. There wasn't much to it on the American side—merely a shed with an American flag and an ominous sign reading, "You are leaving the American Sector," repeated in several languages.

"Okay guys, just like we practiced," Dirk reminded us. "Take out your passports, and if they ask questions, tell them you're going to the Springsteen concert and show your reservation back here in two nights. Let's go. I'll pass first, should be easier with my diplomatic visa, and I'll tell them we're all together."

"Viel glück," good luck in German, Beryl called out, and off Dirk strolled toward the guards. A Dutch giraffe, awkwardly tall, Dirk stuck out his chin which cleaved the slopes of his jaw more diplomatically than the haphazard boundaries we were set to traverse.

I went next, opting to use a Canadian passport I had procured thanks to the roots my mother too often tried to deny. That day, those innocuous papers came in more than handy, and the conversation went mostly to script. Still, my heart was pounding, and I struggled to control my breathing. I failed miserably at trying to appear composed, feeling seasick on land, the cobblestones undulating like waves beneath my soles. The guards probably took side bets on who would wretch passing through the border post. I was hardly the first person unable to hide their anxiety. In the end, all the drama was my psychosomatic doing. In retrospect, I was disappointed not to harbor a better story to tell for the ages. It made me wonder how many historical accounts are embellished. I could undoubtedly feign bravado, scoffing at the process, strutting through with a disdainful smirk, but the reality was I nearly pissed my pants as opposed to passing with a James Bond swagger. Given a body that looked like it should ooze musk, capped with dark unruly hair and accented with curated stubble and my mother's perfect teeth, I really did not have much to fake.

I waited to walk to the East Germany side with Dirk while the others were processed. Beryl came next, using a Dutch passport Uzi procured; no reason to tempt fate using an Israeli one. The contrast of her composure to mine was stunning, and even years later I felt embarrassed by my weakness. I guess courage was not something I could fake. I managed to improve with my baptism over the next couple days, but none of it came naturally. Nature versus nurture? Was there something to growing up along the idyllic shores of Lake Como, the greatest danger being an odd spray from a speedboat coming too nearby? Would I have shown more mettle growing up in Jerusalem, preparing for the next war, exercising daily vigilance against a car bomb? My veins pulsed.

Next up was Bryan. We were a bit concerned about how he would fare handing over a US passport, given the obvious tensions. At least his name wasn't Charlie. Well, maybe that would have helped. Whether mere bureaucracy or some other obstacle, he was not allowed to pass and started arguing with the guard. Dirk walked back but was told not to proceed further, a guard commanding that he turn around. Jesus. Everything had begun to fall apart.

"Hey, just go ahead," Bryan yelled. "I'll go back to the hotel and wait for you. Don't worry about it. Better not to make waves. Will be fun to check out Berlin."

I felt horrible and knew he was taking one for the team when Hamid said, "I'll hang back too so Bryan isn't alone."

I never thought Hamid was that keen on going anyway, and I was not surprised he jumped at the chance to back out. He probably wanted to look cool to all of us, but that was his golden ticket—out. Beryl, Dirk, and I huddled, debating what to do. I thought the decent thing was to abort and forget the trip. How could we ditch Bryan and Hamid?

Dirk, though, wanted to press ahead, and said, "I think we should keep going. My dad had to pull a lot of strings to get the tickets and make all the arrangements. It's not like you can call a travel agent to cross over. I'm not sure what I'd say to him if we just turned around."

How about they wouldn't let us through, I thought. I couldn't believe his indulgent logic, bending facts to appease his father who likely didn't care. Maybe being a natural chameleon was in character for growing up a diplomat's son. I was halfway to hitting him when Beryl put her hand on my arm and quietly took Dirk's side. This was no place for a public argument; a shake of her head and her eyes said it all.

That was the first time I realized she probably was Mossad, or at least a recruit. She wanted to go. I knew it. I had never heard her talk about Springsteen or listen to his music the whole time we had been dating. Without much further debate—we were stranded between East and West Berlin with guards and now a few others looking at us from both directions—we waved goodbye to Hamid and Bryan, promised we would see them in a couple days, and told them to enjoy the beer halls. The last thing we wanted was to make a scene entering East Berlin.

With Dirk's urging and Beryl silently nudging me, hooking her arm in mine, we turned around and walked toward East Germany as if it was the most natural stroll anyone had ever taken. What do they say, a walk in the park? Or, in this instance, a walk in the shadow of a wall under gunpoint trying to find a park holding an impromptu concert for the biggest rock star in the world. Oh, and a Mossad recruit on my arm. Shit, what was I doing?

CHAPTER 2

East Berlin, East Germany (German Democratic Republic)—1988

My father was initially reluctant to sanction my joining the Stasi, but living in East Germany, career options were limited. He came from power and guided me how to leverage the petty authority granted from bureaucratic cravings into more productive pursuits. He remained a proud Nazi, superior to the rabble proletariats in suits slavishly beholden to the Reds. Time would need to skip a generation for opportunities to rise again. Panic was for the weak. He had kept a secret for years that would be my key, our key, to a better future.

Officially, I worked for the Ministry of State Security although everyone called it the Stasi. My training was routine, schooled in wiretapping, tailing and other spying techniques — and of course the arts of persuasion. The Stasi was ahead of its time in perfecting surveillance state skills, for all East Germans learned how to watch and report. The Stasi simply sat atop the pyramid of thousands of civilian informants. Instead of love thy neighbor we preached watch thy neighbor. Perhaps preached is too tame a word. Enforced, threatened, beat might be more apropos. Fear is an amazing motivator. Sadly, the East Germans relied solely on fear, devoid of the type of glory the Nazis offered. My only inspiration came from my father and his stories of days past. I struggled to imagine what it felt like to work driven by pride and purpose. When I planted bugs and listened to lovers daring to betray the monotonous order, I dutifully reported transgressions or doled out whippings. We all did. Except my fidelity to the state was largely a charade, an act to put food on the table and buy time. My father had plans for me, for us — and we would overcome that belittling existence. Our opportunities were near.

***

The concert was in Weissensee, but it was only midday, and we had plenty of time to find our guesthouse and make the concert that evening. Dirk's dad had arranged a simple place to stay. A family someone in the embassy knew was renting out rooms in a large house. Western currency was at a premium, and we hoped they would keep quiet, estimating money from the couple of nights may be more than they could otherwise save in a few months. We talked about the dilemma of booking five rooms, with only three of us making it past the checkpoint. We would pay for all of them — better to keep to the plan, Dirk counseled. I decided not to point out we only needed two rooms, Beryl and I could share. The sacrifices we make.

The guest house was along a road that led to a lake, with deep woodlands beyond. It was a stark contrast to the apartment blocks we passed making our way from the Wall to the Weissensee district. The streets were drab gray, rows of utilitarian apartment blocks rising around a few individual homes spared by the war's bombs. I thought back to the *Wizard of Oz* and how the scenes in Kansas were in black and white; the world burst into vibrant color only when Dorothy dropped into Oz. The contrast between West and East Berlin was nearly as dramatic. I was happy to make it to the lake, the tranquility easing our nerves. I was still second-guessing leaving Hamid and Bryan behind, but it was now too late for what-ifs — make the best of it, enjoy the concert, and tell the tale of crossing to the other side of the Wall. Taking in the contrasts, I thought back to my childhood lake, Lake Como, and how lucky I had been growing up amidst peace and opulence.

The innkeepers, if that's what I should call them, were an older German couple who did not speak English. No better time to practice my German. I apologized that it was only the three of us, explaining we would still pay for all the rooms. They visibly relaxed, though it became clear they were worried about how they would report all their guests. It had not occurred to me they were being watched, which realization heightened my alertness that we too were almost certainly under surveillance. What would it mean that their records did not match? Five reservations, only three occupants? Should they report all the rooms? The husband, Martin, a graying man defined by a drooping mustache and beer-belly stretching worn suspenders, took each of our passports, dutifully entering the key details into his logbook. After a sidebar with his wife, he told us they were only recording the three of us, but we would need to pay cash for five. Probably a smart move; no doubt the GDR authorities knew only three of us had crossed and were staying here. How they reported or hid the money was not my problem.

The house itself was unremarkable. High ceilings and grand moldings topped the walls, with faded wallpaper hinting of better days past. Only one bedroom had an en suite bath, which we both offered to Beryl. It was easier for me to be magnanimous, privately fantasizing how the large tub would fit two. The beds themselves were creaky, the comforters a bit musty. I doubted they had many guests. Martin had held the register close, but I noticed he did not flip many pages when opening it. These were the type of details spies probably covet. I wondered if Beryl had caught that too.

Once in the room, Beryl leaned over and whispered in my ear, "I assume the room is bugged."

"Out here? The house isn't in the heart of the city," I kept my voice low.

She shot me a withering look. "Don't be stupid. Of course it's bugged. My dad warned me to be careful of what we say. If people aren't part of the Stasi, then they're informants for them. Especially ones that have contacts with the West. Don't be fooled by Martin and Christina's looks."

"Really, that old couple?"

"Yes, that old couple. This state runs on fear. Everything is rationed. Food is hard to afford and sometimes find. If they didn't volunteer, then they were probably coerced — bribed with access to some privilege, threatened about one of their kids. Or a more direct message. Watch and report, or we'll throw you in jail. And from what I hear, jail usually involves torture."

"Jesus."

"So, keep your mouth shut, and watch what we say. All of this is an illusion." She swept her arms in a circle around the room.

The painting on the wall, birds flitting about trees beyond the window, a neat dresser for our clothes: it all looked real to me. Were they merely set dressings? Were Martin in his suspenders and Christina, her wide berth and fading blond hair neatly stacked in a bun, actors in our drama? Did the toilet flush with actual water? I went and checked, pulling the cord. Paranoia could be a funny emotion. What would they want with us, a few kids from ASH carrying backpacks, excited about seeing Springsteen?

I whispered back, "What should we talk about?"

"Talk about the concert. What songs you hope Bruce'll play. Let's just not talk about leaving Hamid and Bryan, thoughts about what we see on the street, whether Bruce will talk about the Wall or freedom. About being listened to! Keep it boring. You can use your charm to impress me later," she said with a bat of her eyes.

I nodded and smiled back, puckering my lips in a mock kiss. I looked around the room, now wondering if there were cameras. Beryl had only talked about people listening, but could they be watching too? Maybe? I'd ask later when we were on the street. Cameras would present a different type of problem. Obviously, from our passports, we were not married. Would that be an issue? Surely East Germans had sex too. Probably more, I thought. Entertainment options here were limited. Still, I felt exposed.

Maybe that was precisely how it worked. I had only been in the house half an hour, and already they had compromising information on me. Separately registered, sharing a room. The pillow talk and next level of exposure would complete my file. *Mr. Bellagio, is this your signature on the registration, noting room 2? And is this a picture of you in room 3 with Ms. Jaffe, an unmarried Dutch woman? Did you know cohabitating is illegal in the GDR? You are not married, are you Mr. Bellagio?* My mother's recriminations paled. *Get hold of yourself,* I chided. So, what if they were watching? Jealous I got the hot girl? I was only there a couple days to see a concert. What could happen? I needed to relish the experience, not be drawn into the paranoid stupor paralyzing the natives. I closed my eyes and took a nap, enervated from the day not yet half over.

We woke towards dinnertime, able to smell Christina's cooking downstairs. Breakfast and dinner were included with the room. It was early, not even 6:00, and the three of us wolfed down the meal. Nothing fancy. A plain soup, the ingredients of which taxed what I thought was my fluent German. I made a note to consult my dictionary when back home. Could that be a weird type of bean? The main course was a stereotype come alive, consisting of bread and boiled sausage. I dowsed mine in the horseradish laden mustard, chasing bites with local beer. We were anxious to leave, so bid our thanks, and headed out toward the event of the season.

***

It was still early, and we stopped en route when two guys standing outside a cafe bar beckoned us.

"Hey, are you going to the concert?" one of the men asked.

"Yes, can't wait," Beryl answered in flawless German.

"Any extra tickets?"

"Actually, yes. I was going to sell them in front of the concert," Beryl teased, remembering Dirk was carrying all five tickets and realizing we had two extras.

"Oh my God, anything. Please. Rolfe, come here. This is my brother, Rolfe. I'm Florian. Rolfe, they have two extra tickets!"

"You're kidding," Rolfe said, suddenly alert. "I'm the biggest fan. I would do anything." He then broke into a tragic version of the chorus from "Born to Run."

I whispered to Beryl, "Maybe we should give him the tickets to shut him up. His singing's awful!"

"How much," Florian chimed in. "We'll go anyway, but it would be nice to have tickets. What a souvenir."

"What do you mean you'll go anyway?" I asked, it being an odd statement.

"Haven't you heard? The government has lost control of the situation. Everyone wants to go, and nobody has tickets. A crowd is storming one of the gates, and it's only a matter of time before they break through. No way they can hold people back. Everyone is going."

"That's crazy," Dirk said. "I wonder if we'll have problems getting in."

Rolfe said, "Don't worry. We know a back way around the crowds. You can follow us. We have a cousin that helped set up the site."

Florian added, "How about we buy you some beers, show you the back way in, and you give us one of the tickets? Sorry, we can't afford much. I don't know what you were planning to ask. How did you even get them? One of your fathers a major in the Stasi or something?"

I backed up a bit and called Dirk and Beryl over, asking Florian and Rolfe to give us a minute. Were they bullshitting us? Dirk figured probably a bit, though he was concerned about their insight into the tickets. Tickets were tightly controlled, and just having them legitimately was a bit suspicious. We should be careful about divulging our source. Dirk was also skeptical about their other claims, scoffing at the notion there would be a crash at the gates. This was the GDR. People would be shot before a mass push at a concert. What were these guys talking about?

Beryl, her instincts for dealing with unusual circumstances the best among us, disagreed. She argued this concert was unprecedented, and who knew what would unfold. Anything from orderly to riots was possible. She also posited we would hardly make money scalping the tickets. The economy there hung by a thread. Having some locals buy us beers might be the best offer we could expect. We had an hour to kill, it would probably be chaos, and if these jokers really could lead us to a back way, what did we have to lose? We wouldn't give them the tickets until we were at the gate. We held all the leverage — in theory. What the hell did we know about scalping tickets versus avoiding a riot in the GDR?

Beryl said let's do it, Dirk voted no, and I became the tiebreaker. Well, I wasn't sleeping with Dirk: the choice was obvious. We shook hands with Florian and Rolfe and walked inside to have a beer. Our second crazy split-second decision of the day. Would that mean two strikes against us?

The cafe was teeming, assuredly more packed than usual given the buzz around the concert. Florian and Rolfe led us to a table in the corner, away from a group playing darts. They didn't bother to ask our orders, carrying over five brimming steins of local brew.

"To the boss!" cheered Florian.

"*Prost!*" followed Rolfe.

We all clinked glasses, splashing a bit of beer on the table, grabbing at a basket of brown bread placed in the middle. After a few minutes, it was hard to hide our accents—that plus the tickets blew our cover as locals. We copped to coming over for the concert, telling them we were all friends living in the Netherlands. Holland was a relatively neutral country, and admitting to living there was as safe an option as we could muster. Did we really need to be so cautious? Dirk had counseled us to be careful, and Uzi's warning bells were not far from my mind. We were prepared but had hardly rehearsed. Beryl, probably already in training, advised to stick close to the truth; that was always the best cover story.

Rolfe and Florian appeared to be two local lads, excited to celebrate what promised to become one of the most memorable evenings in recent memory in East Berlin. The Boss did not drop in every day. Mass rock concerts did not happen here. *Ever.* Some kids out for a bit of adventure, crashing over the border wall to join in the fun, was no more out of character than everything else happening. *Prost!*

"But come on," pressed Rolfe, "how did you get tickets? I mean, that's impossible. You must be connected."

Now a few beers into the evening and loosening up, Dirk admitted, "My dad's with the diplomatic corps in Holland. He knew I was a big fan and pulled some strings. Kind of a graduation present. A bunch of us were supposed to come but getting visas and more tickets was harder than we thought. The three of us ended up being the lucky ones. Glad I made it," he said, lifting his glass in yet another toast.

"Cool," Florian said. "I wanted to be in the foreign service, but the Stasi here. I don't know. Not the career I dream of. But you, free, in the West. Are you going to be like your father?"

"Maybe, definitely thinking about it. I like traveling. I'm going to study international law next year, and from there we'll see. Foreign service would be great if I can get in. Step at a time, you know."

"You're lucky, getting to choose your career like that."

"I guess so," Dirk hesitated, suddenly conscious of his privilege. All of us thought those poor two probably would be lucky to get jobs and would do what they were told. "Well, who knows, maybe you'll change your mind and join the Stasi after all. Then I can join the Dutch foreign service, and we'll be each other's informants," he teased.

"Fantastic," replied Florian. "Who would ever believe we met at a Springsteen concert crashing a back gate in Weissensee? I'll have to give you my address!"

Dirk, Beryl, and I looked at each other, but the joking was still harmless. When in Rome, or rather East Berlin…That was before Rolfe's next offer. He pulled Florian aside, and they excused themselves briefly, standing and leaning against a nearby wall. We all watched them argue a bit, gesturing, nodding, talking animatedly. Taking a big swig of beer on returning to the table, Rolfe sat down and looked at us, a serious expression hushing us to hang on to his words.

Rolfe was blunt. "We want to get out. Go to the West. Can you help us?"

If there had been a camera, I'm sure it would have caught Beryl and my expression and cataloged it for future licensing: deer in headlights. Nobody moved or responded, all eyes on Dirk, who was facing Rolfe. The lack of foreplay, and the directness, had shaken us. I had no idea how Dirk would deflect this plea.

"I, I don't think so. I just graduated high school. Way out of my league. All of our leagues. I'm sorry. I wish I could help, but I wouldn't even know where to start."

"You said your father was a diplomat. If he could get you here, and these tickets, he has the connections."

"Yeah, but that's him, not me. And I don't even know you guys," he stammered, seemingly looking for a way out. Eventually, he fell back on what must have been standard diplomatic table talk: dangle hope without commitment. "Look, when I get home, maybe I can ask. But I can't make any promises," obviously eager to leave and get out of the mess. I knew he would never ask his dad to help two random beer-guzzling East Germans he made the mistake of talking to en route to a concert. A concert Dirk probably realized he should never have tried to see, and which we ought to leave for soon—in fact right then. Maybe Tessa had been right—this had been a crazy idea, and Dirk should have stayed in Holland with her. Enough potential self-recriminations. Dirk followed another diplomatic rule: cut your losses and move forward. "Okay? Hey, shouldn't we be leaving soon for the concert?"

"In a few minutes, we've got plenty of time," Florian said. "I know this must sound crazy to all of you. But you're not from here. You don't know what it's like. We'd do anything to get out of here, you randomly show up, and it's like the ticket we've been dreaming of. And not a concert ticket. The real thing."

"I'm sorry," Dirk repeated.

Florian continued, "We can offer something that might change your mind."

"What are you talking about?" I blurted, my mouth moving faster than my senses, a habit accompanying large beers. I looked more closely at the brothers, my senses heightened and cataloguing their features. They could easily have been twins, but for Florian's hair unnaturally parted by a slight white streak as if lightening had branded him just off center. Rolfe's eyes were also a bit wider, creating an awkward intimacy to his stare. Both boys were handsome, the type of blond-haired blue-eyed sturdy specimens that a generation before would have made ideal Hitler youths.

"We know you wouldn't just help us like that. Maybe you feel sorry for us, maybe you like us, but we understand. Too sudden, don't know us, too risky, whatever." Watching us all shake our heads, seeing shades of relief in our expressions that there may be a way out, Florian looked directly at Dirk and asked, "What if we could give you something that would make your diplomatic career. Not your father's, I mean your future?"

Now Dirk's mouth was out in front of his senses. "What, what in the world are you implying?"

I was about to say something similar until I felt Beryl's hand on my thigh, signaling to keep still. Beryl had switched into full operational mode, sensing a secret, waiting to play her cards. This was better than any simulation drill. We all waited, confused, wanting to leave. Beryl simply paused, eyes slightly downcast in a show of sympathy, disguising her intrigue.

"You know the Nazis didn't just all go away after the war. There are a lot of them proud of the party, frustrated by Hitler's strategy, but not his dreams. But it's too late, so they just reminisce."

My blood went cold. No doubt so did Beryl's, but her training kept the pressure even, and her nose inhaled opportunity like a cheetah stalking the savanna. "Tell us more," she said so softly it was more a whisper.

"There are rumors these guys are hunted, but here they're protected. Live normal lives, hang out in plain sight. As long as they don't cause problems, they feel untouchable. I'm not sure what the arrangements are, but the rich ones pay off the Stasi. The police are desperate for money, and Nazis who were clever enough stashed money in Switzerland or Monte Carlo…I don't know, they probably have some of it hidden here. I'm not sure, but I know it happens."

"What does this have to do with us, with you?" Dirk asked, shocked and still looking for a way out. "I mean, it's not like some big surprise there are ex-Nazi's living in Germany."

"No," Florian continued, "but a lot of them changed their identities, are still cautious, not stupid enough to expose themselves and be captured. And I bet it would be a career-maker to expose a bunch of them, figure out a way to bring them to the West for trial. If you managed to get them to Israel, it would be front-page news around the world. How often does that happen?"

Beryl remained calm, not biting at the Israel lure, even leaning back relaxed. Fucking impressive. I could barely hold my bladder. And it wasn't from the steins of beer. She slowly leaned forward, "And what makes you so sure about all this? I mean, that you know who these guys are and that anyone would be interested? As Dirk said, not exactly front-page news that ex-Nazis live in Germany."

Rolfe cut in, "We can't give you all the details. Not now. But we can show you, and then you can decide for yourselves. A bunch of them get together for a poker game every week. Talk about the good old days. We've overheard things. A couple of them were ranking officers. The type of people that would be, let's just say, of interest. See for yourselves. Then you can decide."

I butted in, once again losing control. "What, you just want us to walk into a poker game with a bunch of ex-Nazis and introduce ourselves? Are you out of your fucking mind?"

"No, of course not. We would set it up. We know one of the regulars. I haven't thought through all the details—it's not like we were planning this, planning to meet you. I guess we would tell them we met you at the concert and invited you by. We can make it work."

Florian added, "Yeah, we know one of the regulars pretty well. We could find an excuse for dropping by, just quickly introduce you. Say we met at the concert and went out for a beer. They won't think anything about it. We will give you a photo and some names to take home, and then you can check it all out. Quick ID, no risk. You wouldn't have anything to lose."

Dirk lost his patience, the bizarre ambush clearly having gone too far. Grabbing his coat, he patronized, "Look, we'll think about it. You do know this all sounds crazy? And I don't see how we can help you…," pausing a moment. "We really need to go to the concert before it's too late…." Standing up, he said, "Sorry, this is too risky for me. Good luck. We'll find our own way to the concert. That's why we're here, not for some cockamamie spy mission tracking down old Nazis playing poker." He reached into his wallet and pulled out two concert tickets, dropping them on the table. That should get rid of them. "Thanks for the beers. Beryl, Marco, let's go. We don't need some back way. Let's just get there in time." Turning back to Florian and Rolfe, "Good luck, guys."

Beryl and I stood up, nodding to them. Florian reached out his hand, and I shook it then turned to leave. Dirk's lanky frame was already out the door. As I turned, with Beryl following, Florian came close to us. "Think about it. This is all real. No bullshit. If you're interested, we'll be here tomorrow night by seven o'clock. Come by. We'll take you to the game. You would only be there a few minutes, long enough to confirm you saw the men in the picture we'll give you. If you're interested, then we'll give you further details, names, a way to contact us. If it checks out and you're interested, then help us get out. That's the deal."

I stared at the brothers, speechless. This time even Beryl looked a bit unnerved.

"Enjoy the concert. Maybe see you there," Rolfe said.

We quickly left to join Dirk. At least I thought we had both walked out. Once outside, I realized Beryl had hung back a moment. "I need more than that. How are you so sure one of these guys was a bigshot Nazi?" I heard Beryl say to Florian, who was closest to her.

"Because he's our grandfather."

***

Talk about taking the excitement out of a concert. What the hell had just happened? Once Beryl caught up with us and filled us in on her sidebar, we raced away from the bar. We shared our different levels of shock, debating the possibility of their story being true. After we put sufficient distance between us and the tavern and felt the adrenaline rush of our exit ebbing, we agreed to put the surreal encounter aside and try to focus on the concert. It became easier to forget Florian and Rolfe's bizarre proposal as we came closer to the concert grounds. Hordes of people were descending on the site. We saw a ticket booth being overrun as a group pushed through. No more finger in the dike—the converted cycling track was flooded with people. I thought back to Florian's warning. Christ, he was right. We wondered if—not if, when—the shooting would start. I recalled Dirk's promise that the guards would never let this get out of control. However, in front of us, right in front of us, it was already out of control. The guards stepped to the side and, tickets or not, whoever was there pushed forward. The three of us included. I joked, "Who's the boss?" and Beryl punched me in the arm. I needed to watch my puns. That girl could hit.

We had no idea where our seats were and just sat down amidst the wave. We had made it. Our hands were above our heads, swaying with the crowd, trying to conjure the band to appear. Finally, Bruce came on stage, and the day's drama disappeared with his first chord. Ditching our friends at the Wall, wondering if the room was bugged, running from Florian and Rolfe—all forgotten in the music. The acoustics were horrible, and we struggled to hear what he said when talking to the crowd between songs. But who cared? The place was rocking. We sang along at the top of our lungs, belting out "Born in the USA" … Must have been for hours, Bruce famously playing a long set, earning his fans' adoration. Everyone got their money's worth. Funny, I thought to myself. I wondered if anyone here had paid.

Reports later suggested that nearly half a million people crowded the grounds where a stage had been erected at one end. Virtually every East Berliner living then could tell you where they were and what they remembered. Some later even claimed the concert galvanized confidence in people to buck authority and sparked the beginning of the end. Around a year later, the Berlin Wall fell. Back then, though, it was very much real, and even in my delirium at the concert, I remained acutely aware I was singing on the wrong side. Bruce's lyrics were not particularly comforting. Trapped in death, needing to get out while young, tramps having to run. Did he know something I didn't? I could not shake the memory of Florian and Rolfe. Baby, it was time to run.

I hardly remember stumbling back to the guest house in the middle of the night. By the time I woke, my head splitting, it was nearly midday. The lady running the inn, Christina, gave me a scolding about missing breakfast. Bacon was not something to waste in those parts. Martin watched me in a way that confirmed he was indeed watching me. No doubt his logbook would be turned over. The same certainty applied to concealing the extra two rooms' rent. Black markets can be quite efficient in their own ways.

Beryl, Dirk, and I decided to take a walk down to the lake, hoping to gain a bit of circulation back in our limbs while plotting the rest of our day. Should we cut bait and head for the West or take advantage of our second night? We briefly talked about whether Hamid and Bryan would be worried but knew that diversionary tactic was futile. We leaned toward staying another night. That was the easier decision. However, everyone was reluctant to raise the question on all our minds. The stench or glory of Florian and Rolfe's offer hung in the mist over the lake. If we waited long enough, it would all disappear. Inaction is sometimes the best of actions. We had come for Springsteen, and the concert was the event of a lifetime — a dream fulfilled, a cocktail conversation filler for decades to come. Did you know I saw Bruce in East Berlin? With a half-million people when the government blinked and opened up the party to all, card-carrying or not? Fucking amazing. Why should any of us want more?

Because the offer was equally incredible. What if it was true? What if we just had a couple more beers, walked not-so-innocently into a room with a bunch of old men playing cards, and continued outside for a smoke? I came to hate these votes. Déjà vu. Dirk had the most to gain yet voted no. He would attend law school, and his dad could help secure him a posting to launch a diplomatic career; no Nazi accelerator needed. For Beryl, a Mossad family product, future prospects were more likely reporting on skinhead scum, checking out the tip more a duty than a choice. Come on, high-level ex-Nazis delivered in your lap? She could no more embarrass Simon Wiesenthal than her father. She argued we had to see for ourselves. We could grab our stuff and check out of the guest house straight after meeting Florian and Rolfe. We would be back in West Berlin that night and didn't have to commit to anything. It was not as if they could follow us there. We would take a peek at the game, knowing that whatever happened we held all the cards. Shit. I wanted no part of it. But as I said before, I was not sleeping with Dirk. Strike three.

CHAPTER 3

**East Berlin, East Germany (German Democratic Republic) —
1988**

*My mother was a secretary. She was a typical Aryan beauty with bright
blue eyes that bedazzled men. I inherited her looks, but my blue eyes
have a milky tinge, a gift from my father, mixing a type of purity found
in different Great White species. Her name was Astrid, and I the
product of their long affair.*

*People took comfort when and where they could during the war,
and afterwards to drown haunting memories. My father's lawful wife,
Ute, died in a random bombing raid, leaving him with two legitimate
children and a legacy requiring constant denial. My mother was not
ashamed, and my father took care of me as the son I was. Awkwardly,
my mother was nearly the same age as his legitimate children, making
me a bastard uncle to my father's grandchildren. That proved a
convenience for all of us — distant but linked, family but not, known
but unknown. My father raised me to watch the next generations, a
still-close link to his past that could look beyond the guilt-hampered
meekness of his first progeny.*

*At the time, it was inconceivable that the GDR's stifling
atmosphere would hold back the aspirations for my half-brother's life
while imbuing me with the skills to build vast future riches. Perhaps it
was my father's hatred of the suffocating grip and foolish economics*

propounded by the puppet government that drove him to school me in skills both nefarious and legitimate. While Gunther would struggle navigating the current system, he fixed my eyes toward an unleashed future; a future where I would leverage the lessons of spymasters and Nazi mentors. Imagine that mindset in environments where others were strictly taught to follow the rules? While the Wall still loomed, though, I struggled to appreciate how I was being molded to seize extraordinary opportunities when the tides shifted. My father knew he could wait out the current regime and would then tap hidden resources to fuel our rise. Even Hitler had to wait his turn. My mother would have been so proud.

***

"I can't believe we're doing this," I said, hoping for a chink in Beryl's resolve as we made our way back to the cafe bar where we had met Rolfe and Florian the evening before.

"Come on. It will be, I don't know…interesting. What do you think a Nazi looks like?" she asked, a hypothetical none of us were that particularly keen on resolving.

"Like in the movies. Tall, blond-haired, wearing one of those uniforms with eagles on the shoulders, jackboots. Bold red swastika emblazoned on the arm, maybe another pin for show. What the hell do you think they look like?"

"Stop glorifying them. Remember, they lost. *Badly.* Look around. What do you see? Glittering high rises? No. Barren streets, bombed-out blocks. Monotonous ugly architecture."

She had a point. East Germany was hardly a tourist attraction minus Bruce. The food was bad to scarce, clothes bland to threadbare. I recalled my initial impression about color draining past the Wall, people and buildings filtered literally in shades of gray. Men and women on the street had a defeated look if they looked at you. Most turned away. I suppose that was how you could identify the spies. They were the ones that stared back.

Sometimes their eyes would literally look left then right, head still as if pupils shifting like a metronome could hide their intention. The place was institutionally creepy. Why the hell were we going to this meet? I could have been in a Berlin nightclub on the other side, trying to find the next big act from Liverpool. Wouldn't that be something after seeing the Boss?

Beryl continued, "All you're going to see is a bunch of down on their luck old men. Men who were high on ghastly propaganda. Men who have had the weight of history judge their heinous acts every waking moment, knowing it will not get any better for the rest of their lives. And if they have any religious beliefs, not much to look forward to in the afterlife." She stopped and spat.

Would I marry a woman who could spit in public? She continued her cathartic rant. I tried not to judge. We all needed a pep talk before coming face-to-face with the unimaginable. We rounded the corner, and across the street stood the cafe bar. With few people hanging about, the pub was now quiet and barely beckoning guests, its exterior looking as mundane as the night before. We paused, our feet stuck in dry cement, each successive step feeling ominous.

"Let's go," Beryl said. She crossed the street and walked right in, no Bruce tonight animating crowds to spill outside and pack corners. Dirk and I followed, knowing that time still remained to abort and by walking inside we were crossing multiple thresholds. As opposed to the last evening's raucous crowd, the tired cafe was mostly empty. Faded paint around the dartboard suddenly seemed in need of more repair. Our eyes fell on Florian and Rolfe sitting at the same table. They rose, smiling and extending their hands as we walked over to join them.

"I didn't think you would come," Florian began. "I'm glad you did."

"We almost didn't," I said. "This is all a bit crazy."

"And we don't have much time," Dirk added. "We have some other people we promised to meet," not mentioning they were on the other side of the Wall and blessedly had not been here the night before to be seduced into this…what was it? An adventure at best. Something unspeakable at worst.

"Don't worry," Rolfe tried to calm our trio's not well-concealed anxiety. "We'll head over to the card game just like we described. I promise. Five minutes. Enough information so you know we're telling you the truth. Then we give you a couple of pictures, and you can go." He paused and reached into his pocket, pulling out a sheet of paper. "Here are our names and how to contact us." And as goodwill, he reached into his jacket and pulled out a folded photo, sliding it over. "We're the ones taking the risk. You can go back to Holland and just forget about us. We're the ones trying to escape, not you. Our lives are in your hands. Help us. Please."

The three of us looked at each other, searching for telepathic assurance. I could tell Dirk was still not moved, but my empathy needle moved just past neutral. Beryl continued to take the lead when the moment should have paralyzed. "Who's in the picture. Is that him, your grandfather?"

"No, that's Karl Becker, his friend. Former SS. I've written his name on the back. We'll give you the other photo after meeting them."

"He's one of the regulars? At the card game, I mean?" Beryl asked.

"Yes."

"And what else can you tell us about him? I mean, about his past. Are we talking major war crimes? Worked in a concentration camp? How bad a guy was he? Is he?" pausing, worried she had pushed too far. "Has he changed? Sorry, I don't believe people who did what they did, deep down, have changed that much. Maybe I'm wrong. I don't know."

"I hope you're wrong," Florian said. "They're not all monsters. A lot of them were just following orders."

Beryl shot him a conscience-searing look. "You said he was SS. That defines monster. And I doubt you'd be ratting out these guys—your own family—if you weren't sickened in some way…What else do you know?"

"Not much from the war. I heard rumors he coordinated the running of some of the trains. I once heard a mention of Buchenwald. He now owns an appliance store, refrigerators, and things like that. Seems to have a lot of money."

Everyone was silent. Buchenwald was one of the Nazis' concentration camps. The name said everything. I felt wobbly, grateful not to be standing. Images quickly raced through my mind at speeds like in a movie when someone's life flashes before their eyes. These were different images of death and ragged lives.

"Okay," said Beryl. "And this is his real name?" holding the picture in her hand and flipping to the writing on the back.

"I think so," answered Florian. "That's all we've ever known. He was in the war with our grandfather. I don't think he changed it for us. He goes by Oscar, but we call him Uncle Karl, so I assume he changed his first name, and his real name is Karl. That's all we know."

"Okay," Beryl sighed, clearly starting to believe the tale. If not, these guys were good liars. "You're sure about the last name? Nothing changed?"

"Maybe, we don't know. Could have been shortened. But I don't think so."

I wondered what it could have been shorted from, names of infamous Nazis filling my thoughts, coming to me like sick words on a scrabble board emblazoned with a Swastika in the center. Goebbels, Himmler, Mengele. What the hell would triple points signify?

Beryl then asked Florian if he knew the other men's ranks. "If you want us to go, better tell us." Her stare broke him down, and he took the picture and scribbled down more notes on the back.

Although I didn't understand the meaning of all the titles, the words themselves looked ominous; anything ending in fuhrer was not good. "I don't want to go. Sorry, this is just too...sick. I can't be in a room with people like you're describing," I said.

Beryl put her hand on my arm, calming, not romantic. "Marco, that's exactly why we're going to go. These monsters have been hiding from justice for decades. It's our duty."

"Why ours?"

"Sometimes we don't get to choose. Do you believe in fate?"

"Funny choice of words."

She smiled, knowing I would come along. Damn my sarcasm. I needed to disguise my emotions better. Good luck, I thought, still competent at self-flagellation.

"Let's go."

***

I had not known what to expect when we knocked on the door. A voice called out, "Wait, our hand's almost over," as I peeked inside and saw five old men seated around a table. I watched a regular poker game unfolding not much differently than one anywhere else in the world. Beers in hand, a couple guys dragged on cigarettes, while players either stacked their different colored chips in neat towers or let them spread before them haphazardly.

Rolfe identified the men in a whisper, first pointing out his grandfather who eyed his cards furtively. To his right sat Uncle Karl, or Oscar, Becker, depending on whom you believed. One thing that never changed was prior rank: strumbannfuhrer. The title sounded appropriately ominous. Across from the two old friends, stroking his chin, watched one-time squad leader Scharfuhrer Thomas Mainz. Next to him sat former Ortsgruppenleilter Frank Krueshof and, rounding out the table, Reiner Schlempburger. Reiner had been merely an accountant, but they needed to fill the table, and any available non-denying Nazi was apparently welcome.

The most unusual part of the scene was the glittering gold pieces scattered amidst the poker chips. Missing a full complement of chips, they included real money, the equivalent of tossing $100 bills on the table along with markers. By contrast, East German Deutsche Mark were of limited value, their exchange rate a depressing reminder of the hyperinflation and worthless currency fostering the rise of the Third Reich. All these men had heard the stories of wheelbarrows full of worthless money, money devaluing by the day if not the hour. More than the ignominy of defeat and terms imposed by the allied victors following WWI, it was the deep economic depression and collapse of the currency that helped fuel the rhetoric of the Nazis ascent. The glorious master race would no longer rut about looking for scraps, the value of its Marks not even worthy of beggars' hoarding. The stench of the gutters would be for the rats and Jews.

The gold coins before them were Krugerrands. Issued during apartheid by South Africa, the gold pieces came to represent the majority of gold coins in global circulation. Each weighed an ounce and bore an image of a springbok on the tail side. The front depicted a former South African president, Paul Kruger, whose name became associated with the money and the country's most famed game park. While protests against the South African regime would soon temper their use, and the coins would decline in the West, the Krugerrand remained a useful ingot in neighborhoods more focused on dirty exchanges than politics. Gold was gold. A small fortune in gold littered the table. This was no penny ante game.

When the hand finished, Uncle Karl got up and waved to the boys he treated as real nephews. "Come in. Sorry to keep you waiting. I had a hot hand and didn't want to interrupt the flow."

"Hi, Uncle Karl," Florian said, making Karl wince.

"Funny boy," Karl said, looking at the three newcomers and extending a pudgy hand. "Call me Oscar. Karl's a nickname that Florian and Rolfe use. Those two mentioned they might be stopping by with some friends."

I walked into the house, shaking hands with a Nazi. Did I just say that? Fuck. How could I imagine such a thing? Karl or Oscar or whatever his name was—fortunately, he was not introduced as Strumbannfuhrer Becker—motioned us to follow, and we made our way inside. There was nothing remarkable about Karl, his slight gut and rippling chins suggesting he had the means to supplement government-imposed rationing. The house too had an air of normalcy, save, of course, that four old fugitives stood up as we entered a parlor. I half expected them to give us the Nazi salute, shooting out their right arms and shouting *Sieg Heil!* Instead, a tall balding gentleman with slightly milky-white, blue eyes and a chiseled nose that defied the effect of aging stepped forward.

"I'm Florian and Rolfe's grandfather, Herr Mullen." He offered his hand in greeting, but I was certain he was no more honest with his name than Karl. Later, I would learn my hunch was right.

I was unsure what to do and shook his hand more in reflex than meaning. Now I had touched two Nazis. Touched the hand that had…Jesus, I didn't want to think about what that hand had shot, or ordered, or saluted.

"I hear you are going to help Florian and Rolfe cross over to the West," he continued, a slight got-you-sucker grin flashing across his face.

Florian cut in quickly, "Sorry, guys, when I mentioned we were coming by, Opa and Karl …sorry, I mean Oscar, didn't want anyone seeing the game. They sort of squeezed it out of me. I wasn't planning on saying anything, but don't worry. You can trust them."

"Trust them? After what you told us?" I blurted before realizing I had revealed too much.

Florian and Rolfe's grandfather, Mr. Mullen to us, snapped at his wayward grandkids, "What did you tell them? Don't lie to me, boys."

"Nothing," cowered Rolfe. "We were working on a scheme to go over to the West. Just as we talked about. We could smuggle goods back over here to you."

"That's enough," Karl broke in, appearing alarmed at how open the conversation had become in an environment otherwise shrouded in hushed tones and half-truths.

Herr Mullen brushed him off, asking, "And why would they help you? These three schoolchildren stupid enough to cross the Wall for that concert, thinking they could skip over here and just go back?"

"We were going to pay them," Florian said, jumping in to help his brother. He reached over to the table and let a fistful of Krugerrands drip through his fingers. The room was quiet as the coins dropped, a waterfall of gold clinking to a halt.

"Ha." Karl glared at Florian. "I doubt a bunch of rich kids from the West would be interested in helping you get across for a handful of coins." Turning to Beryl, Dirk, and me, he continued, "I don't know what Florian and Rolfe told you. They want to cross over to West Berlin? That's true. We have dreams. Plans if we're lucky. Not unlike most of us stuck over here. But that's all you need to know."

He scowled at Rolfe and Florian. "What did you tell them about our plans? This is a private matter."

"Nothing! I swear," Florian answered.

"I believe them," Grampa Mullen said. "But I don't believe this story about paying for the help. Boys, this is no joke. The

Stasi could even be listening in now. I want to know exactly what you told them." Pausing, first turning to Karl then looking at the table full of Krugerrands, he continued, "I think we need to…up the ante."

Karl nodded, walked over to the cabinet, and came back. He was pointing a gun at us. "Shit," I yelled before catching myself.

"Shut up!" Karl barked as Beryl, Dirk, and I backed against the wall. What the hell was going on? First, hearing about Nazis, then shaking hands, now a gun pointed at me! I started to say something and felt Beryl's elbow jab me in the ribs. She flashed me a look that took no interpreting. I probably could not muster words anyway. My breathing was fast, and I tried to steady myself. I was so out of my league. I was a great poker player and could best anyone if numbers and odds were the variables. Bullets represented an entirely different dimension. This was Beryl's game. I tried to spin the scene in my head, deflecting nervous energy. How could she be so cool? Was this Uzi's training?

Karl turned his gun toward Florian, asking, "Last time, the truth. What did you tell them about the plans? I'm not taking any stupid risks."

"Nothing. We were just arranging for them to help us get out. Really, we were going to bribe them."

"Bullshit," Reiner said, drawing an angry look from Karl Becker.

"I told you not to speak," Uncle Karl said. With only the slightest hesitation, Karl turned and shot toward Reiner, grazing his leg and drawing blood. Reiner screamed, grasping his calf, cursing in German. "Frank, take him in the other room. Bandage him and stop the bleeding." Looking at his other comrade, "Thomas, go with him. *Schnell!*"

Before Karl pulled the gun, I had been calculating how we could help Florian and Rolfe, pledging anything to get out of this mess. We were connected, could get them fake passports, help them move fluidly back and forth across the border. Whatever they wanted. We had banking and diplomatic connections. No problem. I had the goods to bargain for our lives. I would give an Oscar-winning speech, promise the world, then figure out a way to betray them as soon as we were away. Fuck these assholes. But then, huddled with Dirk and Beryl, I crouched in shock. I remember thinking, *Am I going to die here? Is this it?* In some dingy house in East Berlin where no one in the world knew where I was? Or would the Mossad come rushing in to rescue us? Uzi had been right, but had he sent a team to watch us? Where were they now? *Fuck, Fuck, Fuck!*

"Get up," Grandpa Mullen commanded. "Stop sniveling like cowards. What did you think was going to happen here? Reiner is expendable. Not really one of us. We just needed someone else to fill out the table for our game. We won't hesitate to do what's needed." He nodded to Karl, who still held the gun, now pointed back at us.

Karl said, "I trust you now understand the seriousness of my questions."

Definition of an understatement. At first, I had no idea why Karl had shot one of their friends, whoever Reiner was. Uttering a word, stating the obvious, was hardly justification. Then I realized they were making a point: if they could shoot one of their own, they would not hesitate to shoot us. I noticed a small Nazi flag in the corner of the room that I missed before. Evil incarnate. Looking at the balding man holding a gun at me, it all seemed impossible. Five old men playing poker. What kind of retirees were they? Would they really shoot me?

No matter how much I tried to rationalize and search for hope, there was an undeniable truth blocking that rescue. These were never nice guys — another understatement.

"What do you want from us?" Beryl asked.

"It's the girl that has balls," Grandpa Mullen snickered. "We want to know what Florian and Rolfe told you. That's all. Simple question."

"They wanted us to help them get across the Wall, to West Berlin. We hear so many stories like that, it didn't shock me. That's all."

Grampa and Karl exchanged looks, with Karl taking over the interrogation, "And they asked you to come here tonight? Why? You just took up some stranger's invitation?"

"It was kind of spontaneous. I thought, why not? They seemed desperate. We liked them. I guess we were thinking of it as an adventure. Stupid." Beryl looked directly at Karl and his gun. "Really stupid."

Karl glanced at Herr Mullen, who now turned to Florian and Rolfe. He turned his grandparental-tell-me-the-truth eye on them. "Karl, point the gun at Florian, please."

"You'd shoot your own grandson?" Karl asked, apparently not alarmed but to make sure he had interpreted the instruction correctly.

Mullen simply nodded, looking directly at Rolfe and Florian. Karl aimed the gun at Florian, the white streak parting his hair creating a convenient bullseye. The two brothers now joined their new friends in shock.

"Why are you doing this?" Beryl interrupted. "We haven't done anything. We even offered to help Florian and Rolfe. And we meant it. Why else would we be here? What's going on? Why did you shoot… I don't even know his name. If I'm going to die, if you're going to shoot Florian, at least let me know why."

"Reiner, Reiner's his name," Karl said, deflecting her other questions. "I still want to know why you were willing to help Florian and Rolfe. I don't believe you were doing it for adventure or took pity on two strangers. Too risky, too fast."

Dirk mumbled, "It was like they said, for the money. Gold is gold, even in the West," thinking Beryl's explanation had failed and trying another tact.

Herr Mullen started to lose his patience as Karl now pointed the gun toward Beryl. He said, "I've had enough of these lies."

"Please put the gun down. Please! The money wasn't it," I stepped in. I might have lacked natural courage, but I was not going to have them shoot Beryl and then me. I had to try something. Anything to buy time. Then we could figure out something to bargain. "They told us you were former Nazis," the words slipped out as if taking on a life of their own. I realized I had gone too far and wanted to suck my sentence back in, but it was too late. Self-preservation won. "They would have us see you, give us your pictures and names, and then trade that for helping us get them across. You were worth more than tables of gold coins."

Herr Mullen now nodded, smiling slightly. "I see. That makes more sense. Just Nazis, nothing more sinister?"

"That's all they said," Beryl whispered, willing me to ignore the taunt. "We don't know anything about your backgrounds, not even names. They promised to give us your names and pictures, and then when we verified who you were, we'd make the trade."

"I see," he said again, seeming pleased, turning to Florian and Rolfe. "Is she telling the truth?"

"Yes, Opa," Florian answered, cowering.

"Good. Florian, Rolfe, leave us. Go to the kitchen and check on Reiner." The two boys rushed to get away, disappearing into another part of the house, leaving the three of us with Herr Mullen and Karl. And, of course, the gun.

"Since you agreed to help Florian and Rolfe," Mullen said, "I am going to let you finish what you promised. We're just going to change the rules."

I had no idea where he was heading, but if they would let us live, maybe we could escape from this nightmare. I started to wonder if we could overpower them. It was now three against two, and we were two decent-sized young men and a Mossad agent in training against a couple flabby octogenarians. I heard Springsteen going through my head. Death traps, suicide raps, running. Nice tune and running was a thought, but one of them did have a gun pointed at us. And they had given us a demo. Even in crisis, it seemed I had not lost my gift for calculating odds.

"You will help Florian and Rolfe get papers to freely travel across to West Berlin. We'll start there. We'll keep the girl here while you sort that out. And if you don't cooperate, we can make it look like baby ambassador here shot Reiner."

"What?" my brain again failing to filter my words before they slipped out. "Are you insane? You can't do that."

"Why not?"

Because you're out of your fucking mind? Probably not a good response, my brain cooperating this time, my mouth not moving. What could I say? His question, in all fairness rhetorical. Leaving Beryl in the grasp of these geriatric goons was not an option I would consider. I couldn't even fathom the rest of the threats. I looked over at Dirk who was staring at the ground. I sensed he was barely processing the current debate. Whatever happened next was in my and Beryl's hands.

"Nobody would believe that. And there's no way we're leaving Beryl behind. You expect us to trust you?"

Beryl looked at me, probably wondering if I was finally being chivalrous or merely buying time. Or was there something else? Did she have a plan? Beryl glanced over toward the Nazi flag in the corner and gave me a nod. What was she signaling? I didn't understand. Then she crooked her neck back over toward the flag again. I was missing something and sensed it was vital. It was something about the flag.

"That flag, how can you keep it?" I asked, knowing it was a stupid question. No matter, buy time. "Was that yours, a souvenir of the good old days?"

"What?" Karl asked, turning to look at the flag in the corner.

As soon as he turned, Beryl shot out and karate kicked his hand holding the gun, the gun flying out of his grasp. Karl screamed, his wrist likely broken. Beryl ran toward where the gun clattered and yelled, "Grab Gramps!" Dirk and I tackled Gramps, and Dirk clocked him in the face. I looked around for something to tie him up. I saw a threadbare blanket over a chair and grabbed it. The seams split easily, and I tore it in half. Not ideal, but it would work for the moment. Dirk held him down as I twisted his arms behind his back and tied his hands together. The old geezer was struggling and yelling. Somehow looking across his body, I saw the Nazi flag in the corner, reminding me this was not some kindly grandpa. I was wrestling a former ranking Nazi. My sense of dread flooded back: these guys would not hesitate to kill us. I held his arms as he tried to wriggle free, and then Dirk, suddenly wild-eyed, slammed the Nazi's head against the ground. Not hard enough to kill, but it stunned him, and he shut up. A gash opened over an eye, blood oozing onto the floor.

While that was happening, Beryl had run back over to Karl and delivered another couple kicks. A vicious elbow to the head knocked him out. We were dealing with elderly men. The fight, if you could call three fit teenagers hyped up on rage unleashing wild punches and kicks against defenseless old men a fight, lasted less than a minute.

The commotion drew Florian and Rolfe, together with Thomas, back into the room. The boys froze seeing their grandfather, together with Karl, buckled on the ground. If that was not enough, Beryl standing over Karl, pointing a gun at the two old men, steeled all of them in their place.

"Down, on your stomachs, hands behind your back. Now! *Schnell!*" she ordered.

Beryl handed me the gun, "Cover me. Keep it on them. If they try anything, shoot them." She walked over to Florian and kicked him in the head. He immediately went limp. Rolfe was next.

"Jesus, did you kill him?" I cried, still holding the gun, shaking, and moving it to point at Rolfe.

"No. I know what I'm doing. He could have a concussion. Hopefully a bad one. But he'll be all right. Dirk, get over here, take that other strip of blanket and tie up his hands in case he comes out of it."

She moved over to Thomas, twisting his arm behind his back. I heard something snap as he screamed. "Jesus," I said again. Vocabulary choices tend to narrow in these types of circumstances. I watched her deliver a blow to his head, his body convulsing against the floor. Confident he was not fighting back, she grabbed two threadbare scarves hanging on a coat rack, wound them to form an improvised rope, and used them to gag Florian and Rolfe.

"Don't worry, they're not too tight. They can breathe," she said, not waiting for my question.

Hearing the carnage, no doubt, Frank entered the room. I had forgotten about him, tending to his bleeding compatriot.

"What the hell," or the equivalent of that I translated from his German. He started to rush Beryl, who was adjusting Florian's gag, and I yelled for him to stop. At the sound, Frank turned toward me and saw my gun leveled at him. I'm not sure why, but he failed to stop. He flew at me in a rage. Maybe it was pent-up anger sitting with Reiner in the other room. Maybe it was seeing Gramps, Karl, and Thomas in a heap on the ground, or the two kids gagged. Maybe it was the former soldier in him. I would have loved to attribute it to his Nazi past. No matter. He was coming for me.

Despite his age, he moved quickly. Beryl, kneeling on the ground, could not spring fast enough to stop him, adrenaline briefly imbuing former officer Frank Krueshof with the speed of youth.

What was that law of physics? For every action, there is an equal and opposite reaction. Something like that. I pulled the trigger.

Frank stopped and lurched backward, the bullet piercing his lung, blood splattering from his chest. His body twisted, and he fell over with a heavy thud, body first then head banging like a muted double clap–a sound I am not sure I had ever heard before and which would haunt me. There it was again, "Jesus," I said involuntarily. I guess that was a good time for someone to pray. Forgiveness was a different story. One step at a time.

The gun's recoil had been sharp, and my fingers stung. No one warned me that about shooting a gun. TV detective shows focus on powder burns and residue. In fact, shooting creates a kick. What was it I thought before? Oh yeah, every action has a reaction. All these crazy thoughts flew through my head as my hand pulsed and I stared at Frank limp on the ground. Dead.

I had just killed him. Was I a criminal or a hero? Was this self-defense? Were all Nazi killings justified? Did it matter if he was an ex-Nazi? How many Nazis were you allowed to kill? Should I turn the gun on Grandpa Mullen, or would that be cold-blooded murder? Was there such a thing as cold-blooded murder when shooting a former Nazi? I didn't even realize Beryl had come over and was gently prying the gun from my hand. She took it and put it in the back waistband of her pants.

"It's okay, you had no choice," she said.

I just nodded, happy to relinquish the gun. She was good. Mossad had a winner. No hesitation, no arrogance, all business. I wondered if I was less in shock, a bit braver, if we would have shared a high-five. Shit, I just killed a Nazi!

"Wait here a minute." Beryl put her hand on my shoulder. "Keep an eye on them," glancing toward the breathing bodies lying on the ground. "I want to go check the guy in the other room."

A minute later, I heard a short yell, and soon she returned. I didn't ask; she didn't offer.

"We need to get out of here," Beryl stated the obvious.

Dirk spoke up, the shock of the beatings and shootings somehow jolting him into practicality, "What should we do? I mean, do we need to wipe things down, cover ourselves?"

"You're forgetting there are four people here who saw what happened. Florian and Rolfe can identify us. Probably the others. Wiping things down isn't going to help."

"Are you suggesting we need to kill them all?" Dirk recoiled.

"No. We're not murderers. Karl pulled the gun. This was all self-defense."

"Nobody will believe us," I said.

"Of course not. We just need to get the hell out of here. Run," Beryl said.

"Run where?"

"Back to West Berlin. We can sort the rest out later. We just need to get away. Now."

Dirk and I agreed. "How long do we have?" I asked, looking down at Florian and Rolfe.

"You mean until they come to?"

"Yes."

"I don't know. We can make sure they're all knocked out before we leave. That should give us at least a couple hours. Plus, they'll be in shock. They didn't see that guy die. Remember, this is East Berlin. This is not something that will be easy to report, for them to explain. Anyway, that's not our biggest worry."

"What do you mean?"

"This is East Germany. For all we know, this house is bugged. Someone could be listening. The police could be on their way right now. We've got to go."

"Shit," Dirk said, then fetched his small backpack from near the doorway. "Let's take the gold."

"What?" I said.

"The gold coins. Could be handy if we have to bribe anyone to get out. Back, I mean. Must we worth a fortune."

"Are you mad?" I was the banker and should have been the one urging everyone to scoop up the Krugerrands. This was crazy.

"Come on!" Beryl cut short the debate.

One by one, she checked the pulses of Rolfe, Florian, Karl, Thomas, and Herr Mullen, bending toward their heads to listen for breaths. I could hardly watch. I went to the table and helped Dirk fill up his backpack, shoveling in coins. A box sat on the table which we opened: a mini treasure chest. I put the box into my backpack, and we hurried outside, following Beryl. Everything was quiet. Without a word, she pulled the gun from her pants, used the edge of her shirt to wipe it down and casually tossed it into the bushes while whispering instructions for us to move. We started jogging down the street until we found the intersection where we had left a tram — our first break of the day. A tram was coming down the street, and we hopped on board.

"Any idea where we're heading?" Dirk asked.

I pulled out a map from my backpack and tried to find landmarks as the tram swayed and clacked along its route. I was able to make out a street sign and located the boulevard on the map. We were heading in the right direction. Like a ship captain without his compass yet able to follow the sun, I had similar simplicity in taking bearings. Head west.

After ten minutes, the tram started to turn, and I told everyone, "Let's jump off. I'm not sure where we are, but I think if we keep heading this way, we'll eventually hit the Wall. Then if we just head south a bit, we ought to come back toward Checkpoint Charlie."

"Should we try to get to the Dutch embassy instead? Maybe that would be safer," Dirk asked.

"I don't think it's as close. If it looks like trouble at the checkpoint, then we can double back and try to get there," Beryl said, more aware of the embassy's location than I had realized. *Definitely in training.*

I thought about Uzi and wondered if he had followed through and put people on alert. Probably, but that would not help us in the next hour. I asked Beryl, "Hey, what about your dad—did he give you a local safe-house or anything?"

She ignored my question and simply took charge, walking toward the street's vanishing point. "Let's get to the Wall. Our best bet is crossing quickly. I don't think we want to be answering questions. This is still East Berlin. Who knows what side someone's on."

I could tell her mind was spinning and later learned she had indeed been provided local contacts for an emergency. Much like getting to the Dutch consulate, though, she judged crossing back to the West before it grew too late as the better plan. We should pass as kids returning from the concert.

The streets were quiet, and it had now turned dark. It was still early evening, yet our footsteps on the cobblestones had the foreboding sound of sneaking around in the wee hours. At the next intersection, we saw a couple smoking outside a small cafe. Beryl casually walked ahead and approached them. She asked to bum a cigarette, smiling, and the girl pulled one out. We hung back, and in a few minutes, Beryl left them, shouting *"Danke!"* and waving goodbye. *Unfuckingbelievable.* How could she remain so cool?

"They said continue up this way about ten minutes then take a left, and in a couple blocks, we should hit Mauerstrasse. That runs right into Checkpoint Charlie. If we find Mauerstrasse, we can't miss it."

Within fifteen minutes, we saw the guard posts in the distance. We hoped we could simply walk across, no appointment, in the middle of the evening. A car passed us, and a couple people got out, then walked toward the gate. Good sign.

I was acutely aware of what I was wearing and had checked for blood stains. A tiny bit, but not too noticeable, especially if I could keep wearing my coat. We had not been able to return to the guest house for our luggage. Beryl had her purse, and Dirk and I each carried small backpacks. Fortunately, we had been smart enough to bring our passports and visas.

Before advancing, we paused and rehearsed our story. We pledged to stick together, this time not leaving anyone behind. The thought of what would happen if caught and interrogated by the police was horrific. We came to see Springsteen, beginning and end; stick to that script. We debated who should go first. Would Dirk, with diplomatic papers, be the most or least scrutinized? We decided he should grease the path, and with that, he strode ahead.

Dirk made it through with little difficulty, and I went next. Odds were that Beryl's passport would also be perceived as neutral, and they were less likely to hassle a pretty girl. Even if they grilled her, we theorized the guards were ultimately less likely to forbid her passing. I walked forward.

The guard took my passport and visa, carefully thumbing through each page. "Mr. Dubois, why were you visiting the German Democratic Republic?"

I paused, not expecting to be called by my mother's maiden name, then quickly remembered I had used my Canadian passport which listed me as Marco Dubois. Recovering, I said, "I came to see the Springsteen concert. I thought it would be an event here in East Germany." So far, all true.

"Did you come alone?"

"No, I came with a couple of friends. My friend Dirk," whom I pointed to, safely on the West German side now staring back at me, "and my girlfriend," pivoting and looking back toward the east to Beryl waiting next in line. I hoped the ring of girlfriend would make me appear more benign. The label was undoubtedly safer than Israeli Mossad agent.

The guard paused, looking back and forth to Dirk and Beryl, both close enough to identify. I fidgeted in place, worried that I was being questioned, whereas Dirk had breezed through the checkpoint. "And you were here only one night, is that correct?"

"Yes, just for the concert."

"Where did you stay?"

"At a guest house my friend arranged. Up by Wanassee. It was by a lake, but I don't remember the name."

"And where is your luggage?"

"Luggage?"

"Yes, I don't see any luggage," he reiterated, peering now toward Beryl and undoubtedly seeing her standing with just a purse over her shoulder.

We had not been smart enough to anticipate that question. Stupid! We had fled the Nazi lair and were only focused on running, making it to the checkpoint before being hunted. What should I say? Two obvious choices as I desperately tried to salvage a scenario. We could have been robbed—a simple and plausible answer. Beryl counseled stick to uncomplicated answers. Straightforward. But if I had been robbed, would we have reported it to the police? I could have also lost my bag—another plausible reason, relatively simple. Maybe I lost it on a bus or tram, excited and tired, and just got off without it; dumb move, but I could play the dumb kid. What to pick? The guard had looked at Beryl, and what was the chance we would both lose our bags? If I chose that excuse, would it doom her? Time to pick.

"It was stolen," I answered.

The guard looked at me suspiciously. "Stolen? Our crime rate is extremely low. We are an orderly country."

"I don't know what to say. It was stolen. I suspect there were a lot of strangers that came for the concert. We went to a cafe today at lunch and left all our bags together. We had a beer, and guess didn't keep an eye on them. All of a sudden, they were gone. We talked to the bartender, the waitress. Nobody saw anything."

"Do you know where this was?"

"Um, no, it was back closer to where the concert was. I've never been here before. I'm not sure what the neighborhood was called. Maybe my friend who went ahead remembers."

I was starting to believe my own tale. This sounded altogether possible. Could it have happened? What were Martin and Christina back at the guest house planning to do with our luggage? We had not brought much. They were still waiting for us to return tonight. I expect they were angry we had not come back for dinner. Hopefully, they chalked it up to reckless Western kids with no manners. Depending on your perspective, it is always sunnier on the other side of the street or full of riffraff. Whatever they thought, I prayed they had not yet reported our absence. Even if the house was being watched—check that thought. Whoever was watching the house would probably wait a bit too. With a bunch of kids who trekked here for Springsteen, they ought to hold off until closer to midnight. Too early to call in the dogs. Dogs. I felt a chill thinking about bloodhounds trying to track down whoever fled the other house. My story about the bags being stolen should be safe for a while.

The guard continued to press, "Did you report this robbery?"

"Uh, no," I stammered a little. "We were only here a night. It was just a small duffle bag with some clothes. Nothing valuable. I just didn't think it was worth the hassle."

"Reporting a crime a hassle? Is that what you think?"

"No, I didn't mean it that way. I thought the chances of ever getting my things back was small. We'd already asked at the cafe, and nobody had seen anything. And like I said, there was hardly anything in my bag. Just some clothes. Nothing special."

"You give your possessions such little value? People here do not have so many clothes they can just give away or lose what they have. This is why the decadent West is falling apart," he said, more like a scolding than a question. I was happy to take the beating if he would let me pass. "Please wait here a minute," he instructed as he walked over to a colleague and had a brief discussion. That was not good. My mind started to race. What did the basement of a gulag look like?

I realized I better alert Beryl. How could I warn her of the questioning? Our stories needed to sync. She looked to be within earshot, so while the guard continued his conversation, I took a step back and called out to Beryl, cupping my hands, hoping the sound would carry far enough. "No worries, just telling them how our luggage was stolen at the cafe."

The guard returned, and I tensed, expecting a chastisement for calling out to Beryl. Instead, he handed me a piece of paper. "Please complete this form."

"What is this for?"

"To report your stolen luggage. If we find the thief and your belongings, we can arrange to return them."

I looked back, stunned. Bureaucracy at its finest. I completed the form, described my underwear, signed, and handed it back. "Thank you. Maybe I'll be lucky, and someone finds my clothes."

The guard took my form, stamped it, and walked back over to his colleague. Unfortunately, when he returned, I was not yet done: "May I please inspect your bag?"

The innocent response would have been sure, no problem, sir. Immediately I needed to concoct another story. This one would be more difficult: I had the box of Krugerrands. How the hell would I explain that? No luggage, but a pound of gold? Dirk had already gone ahead, and Beryl did not have any Krugerrands, so at least my story could stand on its own. Not much solace. The gold I was carrying probably tallied more than this guy earned in a year, maybe a few years. Shit. Jesus. There were those words again. Praying was not going to solve this dilemma. I needed to fabricate a story and fast. Again, I raced through my options. Plan A: I won them in a poker game. Forget it. Plan B. I didn't have a plan B. Shit. Time to dance.

The guard went through my pack, immediately found the box, and opened it on the table. His reaction was as if a genie had materialized. I doubt he had ever laid eyes on anything that valuable. What would he do? I had already reconciled forfeiting the loot as a bribe if necessary. Never mind paying a bribe to get past the checkpoint was why we scooped up the coins in the first place; missed gaming this implication. I could have used a crash course in bribing border officials. Too aggressive and I would be back to images of the gulag basement. I waited for him to make the first move.

"Why are you carrying these gold coins?"

"They're Krugerrands. South African gold pieces."

"I know. They are used here often on the black market."

Shit. "I didn't know that. I just thought they worked as universal currency." Shit, that's code for black market. Better backtrack fast. "I didn't know how difficult it might be to exchange money, so I brought them with me. I would have done anything to see Springsteen, and we didn't have tickets. We had no idea what it would cost. Springsteen in West Berlin would be a fortune." Good choice of words, fortune. Why else would I be carrying a box of Krugerrands? Indeed. There was no good story for the box.

The guard looked confused. My story was on the edge of plausible and yet not likely. It would not have been extraordinary to bring something to exchange on the black market; in fact, that was normal. Just happened to be illegal. I was in possession of a mini chest of gold.

"This seems unusual," he said, my hope deflating.

"I'm sorry. That's why I have them." Maybe mix in a red herring to make him wonder. "I didn't have to use any of the money to buy tickets. That's why I still have so much. When we got there, the crowds had broken down a barrier. Everyone was just walking in. It turned into a free concert."

Everyone had heard what happened, and the guard paused. My threadbare story had a tad more credibility. The concert had been an unprecedented event, in fact shaking the foundations of the state. My account was probably no less crazy than a lot of what the guards were hearing, and three kids from the West crashing a concert was hopefully a trivial concern. I waited.

He looked at me and, without taking his eyes off me, fingered a few coins. I expected him to pocket a handful and tell me it was a tax or a toll. Instead, he simply put his hand back into his pocket then zipped up my backpack. He waved me forward, and the next moment I was back in the West. Shit. That was close. I never knew if he took a few coins. I speculated that if he reported me, he would have had to divulge the gold; maybe he decided it was too much of a hassle. Or perhaps he stole away a handful and would keep it quiet. Why enrich his boss? While not the dictionary definition of win-win, it was good enough for me. Beryl would later tell me these guys were straight—no games. She didn't buy my hide-it-from-the-boss theory. I suppose all stories about crossing the Wall have a touch of gray. I anxiously shuffled on, craving not clarity but just making it home.

I looked back toward Beryl, who was now with the same guard. No suitcase, but thankfully no gold. I watched from a distance, straining to glimpse the interaction. He appeared to be flipping through her papers, followed by some questions. I could see him go through her purse. No idea what was in there, nor did I care so long as she hadn't thrown in a fistful of

Krugerrands that I had missed. Beryl's posture remained upright and confident, even relaxed as she shifted her weight onto one leg, a contrapposto pose worthy of a Roman statue. What a pro. Within a few minutes, she slung her purse over her shoulder and sauntered over to us.

Once all past the gate, we gathered in a group hug, followed by a tighter hug where I squeezed Beryl. There were no shouts of joy, just a collective exhale of relief. I didn't even realize I had been holding my breath, releasing it in a spasm. Beryl, of course, looked like she didn't have a care in the world. Whether she had just passed an unplanned initiation or was merely a high-school graduate back from a concert, she already masked her feelings like a pro.

CHAPTER 4

East Berlin, Germany — 1988

My illustrious father had fallen from his pinnacle of power and spent the first years after the war securing his son Gunther's schooling and scheming about the rise of the next generation. His daughter, Angelica, died young. I hardly remember her, and these things were common during wartime. Perhaps such tragedy drove him to nurture a back-up family, a Plan B in the shadows. I, the bastard result.

My father wanted nothing of the bureaucratic toady administration that rose in East Germany, a fall so far from Nazi grace that he redoubled efforts not to let his firstborn toil in Stasi games. He forced Gunther to become an accountant, believing expertise in numbers could be used to help conceal a stashed fortune — a trade he would also demand I learn. Mostly, though, he reckoned it was time to hibernate and plot. The time would come to rise again, and he had the foresight and patience to realize it could take a generation. Perhaps two. His time was sadly done, and the realization hollowed him, an old piece of wood fighting the termites trying to burrow into and expose its rotting past. Despite his losing battle, he believed in destiny and vowed to groom Gunther and me for the next march. It would take money and education, and he would ensure we rose above the dreary limits of the communist East. His resources were beyond what I could have imagined, and his connections deep and compromising.

I was never competition yet not concealed. In retrospect, perhaps I was the benefit of an experiment. If something failed with Gunther, my father would learn and try a different tack with me. We were both being groomed, Gunther for the real world and me for the underground that propped up that other world.

Gunther, true to plan, became an accountant and soon had former Nazi elite among his clients. He knew who they were, and I always sensed he was ashamed. His job was to filter dirt, sprinkle it on new fields, decide how long to leave the new land fallow, and then help plant fresh harvests. He was never happy, moving through life with a methodical gloom not unlike much of the new East German proletariat.

Although I too became a product of the system, my life was at least sprinkled with a bit of daring — or at least that's how being recruited into the Stasi was supposed to feel. My formal schooling in accounting quickly became augmented with tradecraft on exploiting secrets. In retrospect, I realize my father relented to my service because he understood the training would prove useful, recognizing that Gunther was incapable of shepherding his plans. His forlorn son had the misfortune of growing up in a historical pall, spirits and drive suppressed.

While I, too, had spent my life in East Germany, my soul came into being on the other side of 1950, an imaginary line of hope. I may have had Nazi heritage, but my birth was somehow free of the shackles which bound Gunther. I became the son my father wanted, and I grew up with the privilege usually bestowed on the firstborn, the legitimately born. Although I grew up in the darkness, I was raised with the confidence that I would rise above it and become a bridge to a glorious future. With that hope, I was taken into my father's confidence — well, at least in part — about the source of his fortune and his ambitions for its management.

My father, though, harbored concerns about the pace of achieving our goals. As talented and devoted as I was, I was still perhaps born too early. The gloom of East Germany persisted longer than he predicted, the Wall casting a shadow over all our dreams. And yet, he could see light. The new leader in Moscow started his experiments with Glasnost's concept of openness, and the economic restructuring ushered in via perestroika. The failed Marxist strategies, political and economic, were waning. Gunther's children would come of age at the threshold of opportunity. His boys, Florian and Rolfe, and his daughter Sophie, would be young men and women at the most opportune moment, poised to leverage their family trust. And I would be their guardian of sorts, a peer and an uncle, their partner in our family's next chapter.

West Berlin, Germany—1988

The elation of escaping back across the Wall quickly ebbed. Dirk tried lightening the mood, "Bet you a thousand pounds you'll never see your luggage again."

"Ha, I wouldn't even bet ten Krugerrands."

Then suddenly serious, Dirk asked, "What do we tell Hamid and Bryan about what happened? You know, at the house, with Florian and Rolfe."

It had only been a couple hours since we left the…what to call it? Crime scene? Was it a crime? Murder? I made a mental note to think of it as the poker game; maybe I would add the word massacre later. Standing just outside the barrier, in the free air west of Checkpoint Charlie, less than two days since we had crossed over waving reluctantly to our stranded friends, I needed to start making up my umpteenth cover story of the day. Except this one would not be fleeting. This story needed to be good. Great even. Bulletproof shrouding the real bullets. The bullet I had shot, which killed a man that same evening.

"Let's go find Bryan and Hamid first. Not say anything. Say we were up all night and then figure it out tomorrow," I suggested, bone-tired and wanting to settle down in a safe hotel, yearning to sleep off the nightmare.

"No," Beryl said. "We need to get our story straight first. We can't talk to them, to anyone. Let's think about the angles. Come on, let's catch a taxi. We need to find a bar or someplace to talk quietly."

Dirk and I agreed, knowing she was correct. The last thing we wanted was to relive any part of today. Even though we were safely in the West, we were still on the run. For all we knew, we were fugitives. By now, surely someone had alerted the police. Perhaps they were already at the house. Had they been watching us? Would they connect us with Florian and Rolfe? Would they be interviewing Martin and Christina at the guest house near the lake, finding our not stolen luggage, and reviewing the ledger showing us supposedly checking in for a second night? Were they staking out the house waiting for us to return and arrest us? Or had they found our names in the ledger and connected the dots to our having crossed back over to West Berlin? Would they be alerting the local police here? Shit. Again. I then remembered I had smartly used my Canadian passport, which benignly listed my mother's maiden name as my surname. Marco Dubois from Canada should give me a bit of breathing room. Uzi would have been proud of us, Beryl the Israeli masquerading as Dutch, me a Canadian with an accidental false name, and Dirk under diplomatic cover — not bad for three dumb kids, and yet crazily not atypical for the melting pot of ASH.

Since we were not heading straight back to the hotel, we decided to experience the freedom of being back in the West. We all jumped at the respite. I thought about the tranquility of Berlin's grand parks, the boisterous youth spilling out of beer gardens. I asked the driver to take us toward the Tiergarten district, driving along the park and then toward leafy Charlottenburg. From there, we could walk back toward the park and find a restaurant along one of the boulevards. We glided north, almost along the Wall, the imperious Brandenburg Gate forbidden to us, hidden only a few minutes stroll to the east. Twenty minutes later, we were seated in a smoky bar with enough noise that nobody would overhear us. We moved to a corner table for caution, at least a few meters from the nearest patron.

I started the conversation. "We need to consider different scenarios, one pretty bad. What do we say if someone finds out and tracks us down? What if we were watched or they were watching us and saw us with Florian and Rolfe? They could connect us. Also, I said my luggage was stolen, and even filled out a form at the checkpoint. If they connect the dots, they'll find my duffle at the guest house. They'll know I was lying. Everything will look bad. Florian and Rolfe will rat us out, blame us. We could be accused of murder."

"I hope this is the bad scenario," Dirk said.

"Yes, I think this one is as bad as it gets. International fugitives from a shooting. We'd probably be okay. The truth happens to be on our side. We were accosted by ex-Nazis, held at gunpoint, and managed to escape."

"After killing one and beating the others. Who knows if they lived with those gags on or if the guy shot in the leg will make it."

Beryl said, "They'll be okay. No one else will die as long as someone comes by before too long. Somebody will expect at least one of them home later. With all the watchers and people bribed to snitch over there, and that gunshot, someone will check. I'd be shocked if someone wasn't there already. And I checked them all carefully before we left. They'll be fine. Well, maybe not fine. But alive."

"Great," Dirk said, "then we only have one murder to worry about."

"Not murder," I corrected. "It was self-defense. And I think that is our best story if we're caught." Caught? Wrong connotation. "I mean questioned, if they connect us. We won't be able to deny we were there. I guess we could, but I'm sure someone will vouch for seeing us with Florian and Rolfe in that cafe. We were there two nights in a row. And the local police are going to believe their story first. I don't know what we left there. I just don't think we'd get away with a complete denial. Florian who? Do you guys think we could get away saying we went to the concert, don't have any idea what they're talking about?"

"Probably not," Beryl said. "I agree. If they connect us, we go with the truth. They'll separate us, and it's the only way our stories will dovetail. And the truth is a good defense here. My God. Held at gunpoint by ex-Nazis? Who would believe that? And what authority in West Berlin would arrest us? We'd never be turned over. In fact, we'd probably be heroes. If you want, I can talk to my dad and tell him what happened, get his advice. He can figure out diplomatic cover for us if things go badly. The only thing we'd be criticized for is not coming forward sooner. Who would blame us? And I can cover that by telling my dad. We reported it to the Israeli government, and they told us to keep quiet. I think that's safer than seeking protection from the Dutch consulate—not sure how to put this, but the Israelis are used to being discreet about these types of things."

"I like it," I said. "Dirk?"

"Okay. It makes sense, and I can't think of anything better right now. Plus, I'm not exactly jumping to tell my dad. Beryl, you really trust your dad if you confess all this to him?"

"Yes. He'll believe me. And he'll protect me. Us. What's he going to do, turn in his daughter as an accomplice to a shooting in East Berlin? The whole Nazi thing—he may want to report that, but he won't for now. And he'll agree it more than exonerates us. Who wouldn't freak out confronted like that?"

"Okay. So, Marco, what's your other scenario? And remember, you promised it wasn't as bad."

"No, not nearly as bad. The other possibility is they never report it, never connect us. Honestly, I think that's pretty likely. Remember, the Stasi are in bed with Moscow. There is no love lost for ex-Nazis. They'll find the flag. And do you think they want to publicize what happened? Doesn't look good for them. For anyone. They may take the remaining Krugerrands, lock up some of the guys, and tell them if they ever open their mouths, they'll find themselves in a ditch."

Everyone sat quietly, contemplating that outcome, hopeful in a sick sort of way. I continued, "So, the second scenario is the whole thing never comes out. Nobody comes after us. Buried like a bad dream. In that case, our best option is to do the same. Never say a word about this to anyone. Ever. We need to trust each other for the rest of our lives."

Quiet again, except for the background chatter of the bar. Both contingencies were sobering. I tended to opt for the truth, yet in this dilemma, I prayed for lying. Some lies could be justified, right? The expression white lie? Bad pun given Aryan overtones? This was no white lie. A bald, pre-meditated mother of lies. And without a doubt the best possible choice.

"I agree," offered Beryl. "If nothing comes out, we pretend it never happened. No one knows beyond us. We keep it that way. Like Marco said. Forever."

"If we ever get married, can I add that to our future vows?" I tried to lighten the mood.

"Shut up, Marco. Not the time."

I looked down sheepishly. Why couldn't I help myself?

"I'm in," Dirk joined. "I don't think we have a choice. Anything else is too risky. I'd rather we don't tell anyone. Beryl, are you sure it's a good idea to tell your dad? Can't we just claim we were scared to tell anyone, afraid no one would believe us? Is it really worth it, just in case we're questioned, to have the defense we reported it?"

"You have a good point," I said. We both looked at Beryl.

"Let's sleep on it. For now, we say nothing. I won't see my dad for a day or two, and no way I'd tell him about this on the phone. I still trust him. And there are still reasonable odds they may question us, at least connect us, and we would appear a lot less guilty if we had reported what happened. But we don't have to make that decision right now. Let's agree for tonight that we say nothing, and if we get caught, we tell the truth. Agreed?"

"Yes."

"Yes," Dirk said. After a pause, he added, "What do we say to Bryan and Hamid? And how do we explain the Krugerrands?"

Beryl jumped in, "The Krugerrands are easy. Say you won them in a poker game. The concert was out of control, met a bunch of people at a bar later. Ended up in an all-night poker game. Who's going to challenge that? Where else would you get them? Not as if Bryan's gonna concoct you stole them from some Nazis you came across and killed. Or maybe, we just never mention the coins. That's probably the better option."

Wow, she could be cold. The arguments, though, were solid. I liked it. And, so did Dirk. Nods all around.

Beryl continued, "As for Bryan and Hamid, we tell them everything that happened — well almost — except for tonight. We went to the guest house, met a couple of people at a cafe on the way to the concert, had a couple of beers. Scene was out of control and ended up a free concert, everyone crashing the gates. Craziest concert ever. Then we ended up at a bar, joined an all-night poker game, slept until this afternoon. Just decided to come straight back, still guilty we abandoned them. Drank so much our memory is hazy after the concert. That's why we forgot and left our luggage behind. Stick close to the truth. It will be easier to pass off. What do you think?"

"I like it," Dirk said, the edge of his lips starting to form the slightest smile. A smile of relief, of light at the end of the tunnel.

I was not so sure. I thought about the angles. I was so tired of making up lies on the fly today, split-second judgments of permutations and risks. Beryl was right about sticking as close to the truth as feasible. A bit of omission — I happened to shoot and kill someone — at the end of the tale. Still, I could think of no better spin.

I looked at Beryl, jealous of her composure, now not merely in love with her but needing her. I had sided with her on every significant decision since heading to Berlin; no time or reason to change my stripes. Stripes, I thought. Shit. I didn't want to go to jail. This was the best plan. Most importantly, who was I to question a budding Mossad agent? I thought back to Uzi's warnings about the trip. I should have listened then. I was going to listen now. This time, my decision had nothing to do with sleeping with her.

We hailed another taxi and headed to the hotel. The clerk handed us our keys, massive clunky brass batons to much-needed privacy, without questioning anything. It was as if nothing had transpired. *"Gute nacht,"* the pretty braided girl wished us, oblivious to the truth. Maybe we would all get away. Maybe we could forget.

***

The Netherlands — 1989

By New Year's my paranoia abated. Our return to Holland had proven uneventful, Hamid and Bryan no wiser. They wanted to hear about the concert, which grew in lore with the weeks. Reportedly, half a million people attended, the largest concert ever in East Germany. It turned out to be one of those flashbulb moments, an evergreen conversation starter. A Woodstock of other sorts. Every East German citizen could answer: where were you for the Springsteen concert? The three of us became quasi-legends in our graduating class for the sole reason of attending. Everyone wanted to talk to us about it.

For all the wrong reasons, I had to make up yet another story. The concert being a mere footnote to my trip, I needed to build up the moment. "Oh yeah, the concert was awesome," did not suffice for boasting and buttressing fantasy. Beryl and I agreed that we needed to drop all mention of Florian and Rolfe; in fact, the cafe needed to be wiped from the history books. Too many traumatic memories. Too many complications. We set about building a new myth. Sometimes I told the story with seven books, sometimes condensed into four.

Genesis always needs to start the same way. Hence, Book One, Chapter One, in the beginning: we were distraught leaving Bryan and Hamid at the threshold of Checkpoint Charlie. How different the rest of their lives would have been if the guards simply let them pass. The thrills, the multitudes, the booming bass, and feedback from a speaker blowing, as loud as the shot of a gun. Never a day passed when we failed to reflect on what it meant to them to be stopped at the infamous Berlin Wall. But the disciples of Springsteen carried on, crossing the Wall and trekking toward the hallowed concert grounds. Along their journey, the trio worried would they be welcomed as followers, or as strangers should they conceal their identities? Would they find shelter or be cast out to fend amongst other invaders? With only the stars to guide them and already heading east, they followed the North Star, soon finding thickening crowds as they neared the pilgrimage site.

Book Two announced our arrival, packing into the vast lawn. The city on the hill, or in this instance a constructed stage buttressed by scaffolding and banks of speakers, loomed on the horizon. Sound checks reverberated across the expanse, electricity literally passing through and exciting the crowd. And then The Boss, his hallowed presence, rocked onto the stage. We screamed in adulation. We hung on every word, the poet laureate of our generation speaking to our yearnings and fears. The haunting reach of a saxophone lifted our souls like a modern forged shofar, a siren calling. When the preacher ended his sermon, the lyrics and memories were imprinted forever in the hearts of those attending. He would go forth to other crowds, repeating the songs and poems for believers and newcomers to recite in unison. When they had memorized the verses, they could sing along, a chorus of voices uplifting the makeshift cathedral. He had been everything we imagined and more. I had come for the fascination and left a follower. I would buy books with his words, search for recordings of his voice. Originals, if they could ever be found, would be considered priceless. Anything touching the prophet's hand would be considered by many invaluable.

Book Three recounts the newborn disciples dispersing, going forth their separate ways. Most went back home, some exhausted from the gyrations, and others buoyed with emotions virtually floating toward random destinations. The next day was a blur, people I never saw before and will not again greeting me, asking me strange questions; perhaps there were even some untoward demands. I was, after all, a foreigner in a strange land, not aware of their customs. Away from the concert congregation's embrace, people were wary, and at one point, I needed to pay a toll to cross a bridge. Fortunately, I had brought some dollars, a universal currency. At one point, though, I became concerned, surrounded by a few loitering men. When a man reached into his coat, I feared he would pull out a gun— would I need to run, beg for my life, defend myself? I professed to be a member of the flock, but without the power of the masses around me, I was suddenly alone. How would I fare, not hailing from a local tribe, an interloper with riches from afar? I needed to stay true to my faith.

Book Four. I made it away safely. "Born to Run." I crossed the Wall without incident (that part I always struggled with). There was always a price to pay on a pilgrimage, hardships to bear. The trip was a true adventure. How could it be any other way? I had crossed the Berlin Wall and seen Bruce Springsteen. The Boss behind the Iron Curtain.

The story played brilliantly then became enshrined in my personal mythology about a year later with an unimaginable turn of history. Without forewarning, the Berlin Wall came down. Confusion at a press conference, unclear instructions about whether border checks were still required, and throngs pressed through the barriers. Guards confronted with masses of their citizens refused to fire, and suddenly young and old were partying atop the Wall. Global news networks descended, East and West embracing, freedom dancing. The night marked a seminal moment in history, catapulting a shift in political thinking and, on an individual scale, reuniting families separated by political will. Beryl and I watched on television, sharing the ecstasy with the world, more acutely sensitive to the moment than the global voyeurs.

For me, for us, though, the evening was not all revelry. The scene dredged up haunting memories and sparked fresh fears. Despite our anxiety, we were never contacted after that horrid night. No messages from Florian, Rolfe, or Gramps, and no inquiries from the police — East or West. The innkeepers had our names, but perhaps our Dutch and Canadian passports threw off the scent. If anyone wanted to search deeply, however, we had visas arranged through Dirk's father at the embassy. How hard would it be to learn I was truly Marco Bellagio from Italy rather than Marco Dubois from Quebec? Anyone wanting to track us down would have been able to piece together our whereabouts. For whatever reason, they had not, and enough time had passed that we felt safe. But after the Wall's dismantling, would it be different?

I asked Beryl, "Did you ever tell your father about what happened? You were going to talk to him in case it ever came up. Remember, our backup plan?"

"Of course, and don't you remember what I told you?"

"Yes. You told me, don't ask. You'd figure it out. And if you did speak to him, it would remain between the two of you."

"That's right."

"So. Now I'm asking again. New circumstances. Did you talk to him or not?"

"Same as I told you before, don't ask."

"Really? Come on."

"Yes, really. If I didn't tell him, I didn't tell him. And if I did, it's buried. So, forget about it."

How could I forget about it? I was left to wonder. Unfortunately, I didn't have many options. In fact, as I pondered what may or may not have transpired, I realized I had no options. I could piss off my girlfriend, arguing we should have no secrets and we needed to trust each other absolutely. Good luck. My life was not a daytime soap opera. Being romantically involved with a Mossad agent—especially one where it was the family business—had its issues. I reconciled it was better to keep my mouth shut and leave questions lingering.

What I was not privy to until years later was that shortly after the Berlin Wall was breached with open arms, a clandestine operation was launched at Uzi Jaffe's behest. Of course, he knew what happened. East Germany had now fallen apart, politics moving toward reunification. The pace was breathtaking, and the West was eager to cement its bloodless victory. Former Stasi agents and informants were scrambling, their power lost and discovery of their not-so-benign eavesdropping inevitable. Some fled to Mother Russia, and others tried to slither into respectable positions. In the chaos, files were exposed, and those most fearful dedicated themselves to destroying incriminating dossiers.

Uzi's sources had discovered which directorate investigated the carnage from that evening. They did not care what happened to Florian and Rolfe, though it would still be a nice coup to track down Gramps and the other poker-playing Nazis. The priority, instead, was expunging Beryl's involvement. Deleting my participation would be a bonus, almost like collateral clean-up, if such a term existed. Even years later, I didn't know the details of the operation. All I gleaned was that the team infiltrated a branch of the Stasi, its former security gutted, and found a trove of records. Whether they existed in a vault in the vicinity of Tel Aviv or were destroyed was need-to-know information. None of that mattered as much as what we learned years later: not all traces of that evening were secured.

***

Germany became reunified several months later, October third now German Unity Day and a national holiday. Springsteen continued touring, his legend secure, working as hard as ever to rock adoring crowds. Beryl and I started university, reconciled to the challenge that we would be apart. At first, we spoke often and tried to avoid talking about what had happened. Eventually, a comfortable silence about it took over. Berlin was in our past, and we were content to let it stay there. The distance—from Germany and from each other—helped.

As we moved on with our lives, not quite sure whether our relationship would stand the test of long distance or shared trauma, I dove into my business studies while Beryl pursued a master's in art and economics. One of my classes was about investing, and we were given ten thousand pounds sterling in hypothetical money to test theories. We were to analyze certain stocks, make theoretical purchases, and manage our portfolio. I did exceptionally well, especially with my shadow investment. I guess I should say, our shadow investment. You see, I had a small chest of Krugerrands that needed laundering. If only that small chest had been the end of it, then we could have lived our lives in peace. If only.

CHAPTER 5

Berlin and Munich- 1989

The fall of the Berlin Wall was both unthinkable and easily imaginable. It was all we had dreamt about for years. I had been seconded to the Stasi in part to pass time, perfecting nefarious skills yet truly schooled in waiting for our chance to break free. My father was never a believer in the puppet communist malarky. We recited what we must and feigned party loyalty to curry favor and not draw attention. Funny, that was probably not much different than Jew-lovers trying to avoid my father's suspicion before the Wall cast a different pall. Circle of life? No, for most of my life, it was more a circle of oppression. And now in one evening it was lifted, a freeing of our yoke with disorienting speed.

Nobody really understood what happened, but any effort to grasp causes was swept away by the tidal wave of euphoria. People were dancing on the Wall, streaming into the West, hugging each other and crying—and not really processing how to shed years of fear and ducking in a matter of hours. Everyone was at a crossroads, and I did not realize how much was at stake in the next twenty-four hours until my father berated me for joining the circus and drinking to a new day.

"What are you doing celebrating?! And get out of that uniform! Don't you understand what that means now?"

"I know I don't have to go to work tomorrow. Hopefully won't have to take orders from that asshole Fritz anymore," I said, the priorities of youth blinding me.

"Werner, the Stasi are dead. Tomorrow you'll be hunted. People will be looking to drag you through the streets. They'll be looking for vengeance. I know. I've been there. Not long ago…," his tone somber. "Get rid of anything connecting you to the Stasi."

"Okay," I said, trying to imagine my new life. I had thought about the West, and we had talked about the future, but more in terms of dreams and grand plans. I had not plotted details which would define the intimacy of a new identity.

"Hurry. We need to get to your office. We need to destroy any files connecting you. Us. Tomorrow, we vanish. Into my past and your future. I've started a fire in the hearth — throw everything in there and then let's go."

In an hour, we were in front of my office, a utilitarian building that was already buzzing with activity. We were not the only ones to realize our predicament. Because colleagues recognized me, we were allowed to pass without inspection. I wondered whether chains-of-command still applied, whether anyone was in control.

"Over here," I ushered Dieter, walking to a room with seemingly endless filing cabinets. "You look for personnel files. Under my name. That will be easier for you. I need to go in the other room and find reports I filed. Anything with my name. That's going to be harder."

"Go!" Dieter said, intuitively understanding the forks of a proper cover-up.

I ran to another room and found two other men — was I still supposed to consider them colleagues? — rifling through cabinets. Files and paper already littered the corridors. We had shredders, but they were clunky and not fit for industrial-level obliteration. Someone had started a fire in a waste bin in the corner, and anything remotely noteworthy was being thrown into the flames. Smoke began choking the room, windows in another room providing a draft, but not enough air. I thought about my mundane reports, snooping and idly *condemning, affixed with my name. Fortunately, I was merely a junior functionary and rarely signed papers. I made a mental checklist of my biggest cases and hoped that burning four or five files would char most trails. In half an hour, I managed to rummage through enough, satisfied I had a decent chance of becoming a ghost. Thank God our files were so well organized. At least there was something positive about pedantic oversight.*

My eyes smarting from the smoke, I found my father still pulling at files. "Haven't you found my files?" I asked.

"Yes, found your personnel file. Burned it right away."

"Then what are you doing?"

"Looking for files on your bosses, high-ranking officers."

"Why?"

"Blackmail. Information. Could come in useful. Ammunition for the new toadies in the West looking for former agents. They'll need sacrificial lambs. These files will be gold. Think how we can compromise agents who believe they've gotten away, changed their identities, and feel they're free. This is the new currency. More valuable than Deutsche Marks. For once, Stasi tactics can be useful."

Again, my father was steps ahead of me.

Dieter continued, "Where will they keep files on me? We need to find them. Get rid of the Nazi reports. Of any reports about that night when those kids shot Frank. The last thing we need is blackmail material on us."

Luckily, that was one contingency I had thought about. I knew — hoped — one day we would be free and that I would need to expunge any records about my father as well as that night. I knew where they were, but I did not have access. However, in the confusion of that day, there were no guards. Access would be as easy as walking through the door.

"Let's go, Papa. We need to get to the U-bahn. It's only a couple of stops away. Hopefully, it will be as chaotic as here and we can just walk in."

In under an hour, we were breaching another precinct headquarters. Same type of drab building, smoke billowing out signaling a cleansing bonfire. Except here I was not recognized, and a guard tried to block our way.

"Stop, you're not allowed in here."

"I'm an officer. Werner Bosseneker, District 7."

"Then what are you doing here? Get to your district and help get rid of the records. There'll be hell to pay if the pigs from the West get hold of them."

"I know. We were just there. Finished, and thought I'd come here to help. I worked on a couple of cases with Otto Scheiner that were delicate that need to be burned," I said, glad I remembered the name of one of the officers there.

The guard paused, everyone unsure of protocol that day. "Show me your ID."

"I burned it."

Dieter stood behind me, listening to the conversation, then moved over to the wall. He picked up a fire extinguisher by the door and walked back toward us.

"What are you doing?" the guard asked. "Last thing we want to do is put out the fire. Probably best if we just burn the whole fucking building down."

"I agree," Dieter said. "But just in case, we want to make sure a few things are not spared." He then aimed the hose at the guard and blasted him in the face with foam. The man was taken completely by surprise and screamed, his hands flailing around his engulfed eyes.

Dieter kicked the guard's legs out from under him, then brought the cannister crashing down on his head. A pool of red blood spread amidst the white lather. Dieter then kicked him in the head before dropping the extinguisher. "Let's go," he said to me, stepping over the body and searching for the file room. I followed, thinking that if we hadn't beaten the asshole, someone else would have gladly obliged.

We put faith in the guard's prophecy. What files we didn't find and destroy we hoped would burn when we put the room and building to flames. Back home, we packed, gathered the rest of our family, and *plotted our disappearance. The Wall's fall brought many types of new beginnings. Sadly, it brought an end for my brother.*

***

My half-brother Gunther was set to turn a half-century just as the Wall was turning into splintered pieces of graffiti destined for museums and fireplace mantles. Most of his life was bleak, and on reflection, I realized Gunther never had a chance. Born at the height of the war, swaddled in swastikas, he was branded before he could grow. Imagine being a fair-haired Nazi child of five in 1944, losing your mother in a crater caused by allied bombs, everything you had ever known burning and crumbling. Gunther clung to my father's wishes, eager to please, craving shelter. As a teenager, he realized his privilege studying rather than scavenging; it was not a time of rebellion and choice of profession, let alone plentiful food.

He lived virtually his entire life in East Germany, never setting foot in the West. He died literally on his 50th birthday, the dual milestones of life half fulfilled and the Wall coming down collectively too much for his heart. A child who had to change from a Nazi toddler to an East German humdrum worker was too old to start again in a united Germany.

Little was holding us in Berlin, and after the Wall's fall and Gunther's passing, my father was ready to move permanently. He was still undecided where to settle, but he knew the first big trip we would take was to Munich. We traveled with Uncle Karl, though by then I was well aware it was a kindly title, and he was not truly family. Some may say that does not matter, but to those hailing from the Third Reich or trying to rise from its ashes, blood lineage remained a litmus test. Tracing roots and proving ancestry was a life-defining line when my father, the once Obersturmbannfuhrer Dieter Mullenhauer, oversaw a team of men protecting one of Germany's most famous museums. I suspected that my father had long dreamed of taking Gunther to

Munich, but fate cast me as the son that stood beside him looking at the repaired portico of the Alte Pinakothek.

"It's hard to believe," my father said to me.

"What is?"

"Everything that's happened. That it's almost fifty years since I was here. That we were trapped in that shithole of East Berlin for so long. That Gunther never saw this, never traveled to Munich…That we lost."

"Do you want to go in?"

"No. Not now. I've walked those halls a hundred times." He turned his head to a hillside in the distance before saying, "Why don't you go inside, take a tour. I hear most of the works survived. Another day, I'll tell you more about my part in preserving some of the treasures…. I may be awhile. I want to take a walk around the neighborhood, relive some memories…Think about if there is time left for revenge." He was still staring at a small hillside when he waved Karl over to him.

"Karl, why don't you take a walk with me," and I sensed his spirits rise. "There's something I want to show you. At least I hope there's something still there I can show you. Let's go. I've been waiting a long time."

***

A few weeks later, I sat with my father in an oak-paneled room at the law offices of Bauer & Hoffstein. The firm was of modest size but apparently catered to clients like former Obersturmbannfuhrer Dieter Mullenhauer. The brochure I perused in the lobby advised the firm was nearly seventy years old; quick math dated its founding to the 1920s. Pompous language described how the original Herrs Bauer and Hoffstein helped some of the industrial giants grow. Glaring omissions shrouded how they likely helped dirtier titans pillage and shelter other fortunes. I wondered how a firm like this had managed to survive wars, walls, and diplomatic reckonings.

When a man looking just the part, sporting a close-cropped salt and pepper beard and round spectacles, walked in, we both stood up. I was briefly flustered by the unexpected coupling of his blue silk tie and absent suit coat, a disarming combination no doubt designed to exude wealth while casting a more welcoming air. "Herr Mullenhauer, and I understand you must be Mr. Boesseneker, so nice to see you," Jurgen Kranz extended his hand.

"Jurgen, nice to see you again," Dieter said, never explaining to me how the two of them knew each other or when they first met. The subliminal jousting was supposed to convey some level of trust, and I was not one to second guess my father on such relationships. I was impressed he had so skillfully dodged the lawyer's wardrobe ploy to take a measure of control. The posturing complete, he turned to business: "I assume you have the papers drawn up we discussed?"

"Yes, the formation of the new company, Mullenboess Ventures GmbH. You are to be Geschaftsfurer [managing director], and I understand Werner is to be given signing authority, subject to certain items requiring your joint signature."

"Exactly. The annex will include the table of authorities."

I smiled, proud of the incorporation of Mullenboess, an abridged hybrid of my parent's names, Dieter Mullenhauer and Astrid Boesseneker. In a small way, it was to become a verbal brick, repeated on mastheads rather than rooted underfoot in an entryway, the firm hopefully destined to live on, cementing their memory.

"There is one significant gap in the document, though, I'm sure you realize," Jurgen continued.

"I assume you mean the funding schedule."

"Yes. I don't mean to be impolite, but the incorporation calls for five million Deutsche Marks in contributed capital. That's quite a significant sum. Do you plan to fund via a bank transfer? I can set up an escrow account, or we can go straight into setting up a corporate account under the venture's name. I will just need instructions, and then I can finalize the documents."

"*Actually, I need you to handle a somewhat delicate transfer.*" *My father reached into his briefcase and pulled out two photographs, sliding them across the conference table. I was no art expert, but I could tell they looked like museum-quality paintings.* "*I'd like you to sell them and use the funds to capitalize Mullenboess. I suspect they will clear more than the number I slotted in.*"

Jurgen stared at the photographs, picking them up and scrutinizing the detail. "*These could be worth a fortune. Where did you get them?*"

"*I was a collector in the War. My wife, Ute, had some masterpieces in the family and got me hooked.*"

Jurgen raised an eyebrow yet remained silent for a beat. "*Why not sell them yourself?*"

"*The provenance is a bit shaky. And I want a new start. After East Berlin. Mullenboess is just the beginning. I would prefer a quiet sale. I need this to be clean. No questions.*"

I held my breath and looked back and forth between my father and Jurgen. Or should I call this lawyer my father's new broker?

"*I can't promise perfectly clean. If there's no paperwork, we'll have to...let's say imagine something. The auction houses will demand something. But there are a lot of gaps for older works coming on the market. Not all that uncommon, I suspect.*"

"*Twenty percent. Your fee, I mean,*" *Dieter said.* "*I understand the challenges. That's why I brought this to you.*"

Jurgen nodded and shuffled the photographs into his briefcase, taking longer than necessary. It was clear he wanted to ask more questions but was wrestling with what to say. "*I'll give you a call. I assume you have the paintings stored safely.*"

"*Yes. These and some others...I'm working on sorting out a more secure location, but don't worry about that. I'm more concerned about how to insure them.*" *He paused, letting out a breath as if reminiscing, and continued,* "*As you can imagine, it's hard to insure these type of things.*"

I looked up, not understanding—this was the first time I'd heard about pieces of art and wondered if I was about to be let into another secret. I looked at my father and saw him smiling back, unburdened. What was I about to learn?

Jurgen probably now realized he did not want to learn anymore. He stood, repeating he would be in touch when he had updated the drafts, and leaned in to shake our hands. It was obvious he was keen to leave more quickly than he had entered. My father rose, gripped his hand, and said, "One more item for the signature copies. About starting clean, being careful. I have shortened my name to Mullen. I've used it for years on occasion. More common and untraceable. I even had my son Gunther's death certificate changed to Mullen just in case. Expunge everything. Make sure all the documents reflect that."

He'd never told me that about Gunther. More secrets. I suspect that room's oaken walls had sheltered many secrets, sordid secrets that made generations of partners like Jurgen rich. Something made me look at the wall's wooden knots, thinking the pockmarks were as twisted as the admissions cloistered within the aging panels. If I had not been brought up amidst the Stasi, I may have even been uncomfortable. But by the time I followed my father out, I was only thinking about Mullenboess's future riches and what other jewels Dieter had hidden. The former Dieter Mullenhauer that is.

***

Negev Desert, Israel — 1990

Beryl was dripping sweat somewhere between a small Bedouin town and Beer-Sheeva. She dreamed of water but was miles from the respite of jumping into the Dead Sea or the Mediterranean.

"Come on, you good-for-nothing *tironim*, you're behind!" her lieutenant barked.

Beryl was in basic training, the famed Israeli *tironut* recruit conversion of its youth from citizens to soldiers. Being targeted for the elite Mossad only made her training harder. She wiped the sandy sweat away from her forehead and picked up her shovel. Beryl's blisters were raw as she dug deeper into the baked soil. Her task was to dig a grave, then lie in it for cover. At least her earthen coffin would offer shade; perhaps that sick blessing was what her officer counted on while pushing his recruits to their limits.

"Yes, sir!" she answered, the muscles in her arms straining as she threw another shovelful of dirt to the side. Then, in a whisper hidden in the whistle of the breeze shifting from nearby dunes, "Bastard."

She had been digging for what must have been over an hour. People underestimate the volume of dirt to be moved for a six-foot-long by six-feet-deep hole. That was challenge enough before factoring in baked, hardened ground and merciless heat to the task. When Beryl finished, her body was stretched beyond exhaustion. Every muscle ached, and every inch of exposed skin without blisters chafed with a gritty mix of sweat and sand. She lowered herself into the grave, its cool shelter from the sun a mocking relief.

She didn't know how long she stayed down there. They could have buried her for all she cared. Just no more digging. How had people survived in this wasteland? The Bible referred to Abraham living there after being exiled from Egypt and even Moses scouting the area while searching for the promised land. "They clearly took the wrong fucking turn," she thought, spitting out dirt that caked around the side of her mouth.

"Private," the western word for a trainee or new recruit, "are you lazing about down there?"

Beryl stirred from her nap, not grasping the command.

"Private! Answer me! Get up."

"Yes, sir!" She pulled herself up, steadying her frame against the side wall, dirt crumbling as she vainly searched for a grip that did not exist. When standing, Beryl's head was still below ground level, proof that she had dug deep enough. She squinted, looking back up. The sun hid behind the lieutenant's head, casting a blanketing shadow over her.

"Get up here," he demanded.

An honorable soldier would have offered his hand, helping her climb out—but this was training, a morale-crushing test of fortitude. She placed her arms over the side and pushed up. With nothing to grasp onto, she had to leverage her way up, an awkward push-up infinitely more straining than a pull-up searing into her triceps. She dug at the side of the grave with her feet until she kicked a makeshift toehold and vaulted over the top. Beryl slowed her breathing and stood up, brushing the dirt off her uniform and standing to attention.

"Ready, lieutenant."

"Good, private. Now fill it up." He looked toward the dirt on the sides of the grave and, with a barely imperceptible smirk, walked away. It would take an exhausted person another hour or two to shovel the dirt back in and fill the hole. He telegraphed his bet she would complete it much faster. She rolled her eyes, knowing he enjoyed watching her lithe body shovel in a singsong rhythm, a model's gait wasted on the desolate pit.

Nobody doubted Beryl's drive and ability, which is why they kept pushing her even harder. That she knew. What she didn't know was orders had come down to complete her physical training in half the time as others, accelerating her move to a classified training course. She suspected the lieutenant wondered what mental hell his colleagues put special forces recruits through to match his brutal exercises; no matter, she resolved that whatever schedule he concocted to test her endurance would not break her spirit. Of course, Beryl had not been briefed on the timeline. For all she knew, she might be digging graves until winter.

The next morning, she was roused early from her bunk. After the orders were given, her resulting rustling woke her roommate. She shared her stark barracks with two other women recruits, all of whom bonded over the grueling routine. One of them was away on an exercise, and for the last week, it had just been Beryl and Merriam.

"What is it?" Merriam asked, sitting up on an elbow. "They can't be giving you any more shit. You came in first on the shooting range, and none of us have any idea how long we were digging in that heat."

"No, it's good news for once. I'm being transferred. No more grave digging."

"Wow. Daddy finally come through?"

"No way, he would never step in. We all have to prove ourselves."

"Well, if my *abba* were some higher-up, I'd make him get me the hell out of here."

"You're tougher than you think, Merriam."

"Well, I hope not so tough I scare off Jacob! I hear men can be intimidated once their little girls have come back from here."

"Hah!"

"What about your guy, Marco? Gonna find all that new muscle hot?"

"I could have whipped him before. Pretty boy future banker wouldn't hack it out here. But who could? Israel's another world. Always has been. Anyway, he's tough enough. And smart as hell."

"And hot," Merriam giggled. She had seen Beryl's picture with his arm around her, Marco's tousled black hair and movie-star smile making Merriam hot too.

Beryl gave her a mild punch on the arm, grinning. "Yeah. Plus, he knows what he's getting into with me. That counts for a lot."

"Good luck, girl. I'll miss you." Merriam stood up and hugged her.

"I'll miss you too. I hope you have my back out there one day." And with that, Beryl released her embrace, grabbed her gear, and stepped outside. She would miss Merriam but also knew she could not be sentimental with relationships in the military. She heaved her knapsack over her shoulder, Merriam's comments giving her pause as she stepped into a waiting military rover. Could Marco find her too tough? She pushed the thought away, not allowing the heat or girl talk to seed weakening doubts.

After traversing the desert, she was in another compound, this time closer to Masada. She marched into a bunkhouse, standing ramrod straight saluting another officer. Merriam was already a memory.

"Private, your progress appears outstanding," he began, looking over her file. "I suppose you're wondering why you're here."

"Where am I, sir? I haven't been given any orders or information."

"You'll speak when I ask, private. Is that clear?"

She nodded, not sure whether the question was a license to speak again. The new lieutenant allowed himself a slight grin. With a hidden sigh of relief, she realized it had been a trap. And she hadn't fallen for it, the nod the correct response. Rumor had it people thought she was destined for extraordinary things. His blank expression told her he was staring at an oddly redacted file, extremely unusual for someone at her level. She hid her smile as the question, "Who is Beryl Jaffe?" spread across his face. He looked up, staring back at her blue-green eyes, silently acknowledging that after her training, he wouldn't want to be pitted against her.

London and Scotland, The United Kingdom — 1992
Beryl and I were separated for just over two years. Her father wholeheartedly supported her studies at the Royal College of Art, recognizing the doors it would open. But Uzi was equally

focused on the fact school provides long breaks, which he choreographed to schedule Beryl's training. There was the initial six-month crash course when she enlisted in Israel's mandatory military *tironut* training following graduation. I was not privy to all the details; still, from what I gathered, her tour was advanced, allowing her to "graduate" within a year, additional service parsed out for special sessions over summer and other vacations.

People often question the merit of dual degrees, whether a JD-MBA, for example, is worth the extra time and money. Beryl's unique dual track, half public, pursuing studies at the RCA, and half covert, being drilled in Mossad special forces techniques, required a rare combination of intellect, physical skills, and emotional control. Beryl had proved her mettle in East Berlin, and whether or not the military was aware of her actions, she was a prized recruit. Her father knew it was his duty to hone an innate rational coolness that, if harnessed, could be wielded more dangerously than his namesake Uzi.

Not surprisingly, the Israeli military was circumspect about its training, and our communication at times was limited. While she was conducting mock raids and undergoing psychological stress tests, I was a carefree college lad at St. Andrews in Scotland, enjoying perhaps too much leeway. To me, physical separation was a state awkwardly suspended between commitment and an allowance to experiment. Unlike my Scottish-based philandering, Beryl did not have the freedom to cast about bars exploring what lay beyond our relationship. Maybe if I had focused on her packing a gun or digging a grave, my perceived permission to stray would have been castrated.

Regardless, no perfect accommodation existed when setting off to different universities, hours apart, and knowing it would be months between visits. We both dated yet stayed within each other's orbit. I suspect we lied to each other regarding our trysts. And then, suddenly, I realized I risked losing her. What an idiot I was. I finally mustered the courage to call and tell her I no longer wanted to date other people. I had not actually done anything wrong, but I still felt guilty. I needed to come clean. I could not rely on my broad Italian shoulders and manicured three-day stubble alone to win her back.

I picked up the phone. "Beryl, I don't want to continue like this."

"About time," she said, a bit coldly. "You know, Marco, it isn't that easy. Can't just say, hey, let's flip a switch."

"I know. What do you want me to do…to say? I'm on my hands and knees."

"Well, you've just done the first thing. Being honest. Keep that up."

"I promise. I'm all in."

"You better be. I need to be able to trust you—with my life. Not like a Mossad partner, but really not that different. There's real risk. And sacrifice. And I need real love. No faking it to get me in bed. We all choose our paths. You know I'm making this commitment too. If there's anyone in this world you know is serious and loyal, it's me. I'm asking you to choose."

"I have. I meant it. I'm all in."

Her tone softened. I continued to pledge whatever it took to make amends, and soon I saw a ray of hope in the Scottish fog. More than that, I pictured Beryl's hips swaying provocatively, a runway model's natural gait. Why the hell had I let her start to slip away? Was she so cavalier with her plans?

Born and raised within the Mossad's embrace, she dismissed frivolous temptations, controlling risks and manipulating destiny. It's not that she was calculating in a bitchy or untouchable way; rather, Beryl was earlier attuned to her role in life and how to balance that with her needs and wants than the rest of us. She could compartmentalize yearnings, rarely leaving herself unguarded. That control, however, relegated her to reckon with a certain quiet sadness that only she and other spies could understand. It was in that small chink of vulnerability where I lived, and which gave me my chance and purpose. We fell in love before she shut off, and with that, I could never be shut out. Whatever physical dalliances she allowed, the other men were mere moments, and the lifetime was, I prayed, reserved for a certain Italian banker from the shores of Lake Como.

After a bit more emotional pummeling, we began to laugh; and before hanging up, I knew I needed to leave Scotland. If I continued at St. Andrews, I would screw my way to a master's degree and, in the process, lose Beryl forever. The following weekend, I flew to London. By the end of my semester, with my fidelity pledged, I transferred from St. Andrews to the London School of Economics. Moving wasn't that difficult for me. Privilege had its advantages. Strings were pulled, and I was no moralist shunning the help.

***

Before I moved to London, though, I had quite a scare. Berlin was well in the rearview mirror, and I no longer fretted about an unannounced knock on the door from Scotland Yard or Interpol. On occasion, I wondered what happened to the brothers from the bar, Florian and Rolfe, and whether they might come looking for us. I reckoned that was highly unlikely, their goal to gain freedom now bequeathed to all Germans and tales from team Nazi best hidden. Dirk and I discussed the chances of their reporting that night to the police, but he assured me that if nothing had surfaced by now, we should feel safe.

Then, out of the blue, I received a terse message from the Canadian High Commission to come into their Edinburgh consulate as soon as possible. Unnerved, I discussed the mysterious request with Dirk and Beryl. We had no idea what it was about, and believing I had no other choice, I drove just over an hour to the consulate and soon found myself presenting my passport and the letter to an officer.

"Thank you, Mr. Bellagio. Can you please wait here a moment?"

"Of course."

After a few minutes, another officer, Deputy Assistant Something Seymour, arrived and took a long look at my passport. "Thank you for coming in, Mr. Bellagio. Can I ask you whether you ever travel under the name Dubois?"

"Um, not usually. It is my mother's name, which I use on occasion. Can I ask why you're asking?"

"We have a package that was forwarded from the German embassy asking whether we could find a Mr. Marco Dubois. Our records did not turn up anyone by that name, but in a cross-check, the name Marco Dubois Bellagio turned up. So again, I ask, do you ever travel under the name Marco Dubois?"

I don't recall exactly what I thought at that moment. I was no doubt paralyzed. There was also little I could say, an official from the High Commission holding my Italian passport and privy to my full name. "Now that you mention it, I did once travel to Germany and believe my visa may have been under Marco Dubois. I have a dual Canadian passport under my mother's name. But I'm sure you know that."

"Yes, we pulled up your Canadian passport," Officer Seymour nodded, probably glad I was not trying to hide anything. "These things can happen with multiple passports and citizenships. Could well explain things," he said, as he picked up a phone and spoke into it briefly. A few minutes later, another gentleman joined and handed Officer Seymour a package. In turn, he passed it to me. "I think this may be yours. Can you identify it?"

Puzzled, I unwrapped the bag, finding my duffle from that night in East Berlin. My pulse quickened, and I began to sweat. I remembered filling out that claim form crossing back over

Checkpoint Charlie, but it was difficult to fathom that my supposedly lost bag was being returned.

"Yes, this is mine. I can't believe it."

"Do you have any idea why this is now being sent from the German embassy?"

"None. I went with a couple of friends to a Bruce Springsteen concert in East Berlin, before the Wall came down, and lost the bag. I reported it stolen with a border guard and haven't thought about it since. Nothing valuable and never expected to hear about it again, let alone see it."

"Mind taking a look inside, see if there's anything unusual?"

I took a quick mental inventory of whether it might contain anything incriminating but could think of nothing. I rubbed my shaking hands together and said, "Sure," as I rifled through moldy belongings, still wondering what the hell was going on. "This is my stuff. I don't get it."

"It doesn't make any sense to us either. But the East Germans were sticklers for forms, and maybe it's nothing more than what you're saying. A claim form was filled out, and some bureaucrat found the bag in a lost and found and forwarded it. All they knew was the name and that you were a Canadian citizen."

"That's crazy. And why not send it to Canada? How did it end up in the UK?"

"The file notes it was tagged to go to Canada, but computer records had you registered as living here. So, a note was mailed to your address, and I guess the package was sent for holding until we heard from you."

"Unbelievable."

"Maybe so, but we tend to go with the simplest explanation, unless there's a reason to look further. In this case, the timing is strange, and a package marked with a stamp from East Germany is also odd, but beyond that, I don't see anything other than an old package tied to a claim form. If you don't have any more information, you're free to take the package. We looked up your background, Mr. Bellagio, and have no reason to suspect there's anything more to this."

"So, that's it?"

"Yes, please sign here to release the belongings. If you think of anything else, please keep us informed."

Officer Seymour handed me his card, and I walked out, my head spinning but my heart rate beginning to slow.

I returned home and dumped the contents out on my bed. I half thought about just throwing the bag in the trash, but I guess I was curious to look at the contents. Perhaps it would bring back memories, or I'd find some forgotten memento. Amidst the mess, I was dumbfounded to spot a clean envelope with my name formally printed on the front. With shaky hands, I managed to peel open the envelope. Inside was a one-page letter, bearing no address or signature. It simply read: "Dear Mr. Dubois, do not think you got away. We are always watching." I dropped the letter as if it bore leprosy.

Fuck! I immediately called Beryl and Dirk. Despite our chills, we decided once again to do nothing. Unless whoever sent this had a connection within the Canadian foreign office, there would be no direct link. If an authority was coming after us, surely it would have already happened.

"Whoever wrote this probably wanted to spook us," Beryl said. "They were frustrated, and this was the best they could do after failing to track us down. It wouldn't surprise me if this has been lying around for a couple of years."

"Still, it scares the shit out of me."

"That's what it's supposed to do. That's what they're good at. Were good at. Especially the Stasi. Keeping people off balance."

"So really, we just ignore it? Pretend nothing's happened?"

"Yes. Throw everything away and the memories with it. Last thing I want to see is your old dirty underwear."

Jesus.

***

Antwerp, Belgium—1993

I would propose before we graduated. Diamonds are traditional, but before shopping for a ring, I briefly traveled back to Holland, staying with my parents. I confided my plans, and while Beryl was neither Italian nor Swiss, my father was delighted. My mother was more reserved, though her blessings had little to do with liking Beryl, which she did. I suspect she would have preferred my betrothal to a beauty that came with a castle dowry, or at minimum a family vineyard. Financial mergers aside, my parents were citizens of the world and generally open and accepting of my romantic choices. The mixing of my French-Canadian and American mother, her lineage augmented by a grandmother from Budapest, with my Swiss-Italian father already made me a bit of a global mutt. With their blessings, I ventured south to Antwerp, Belgium, in search of a ring.

Antwerp was famed as one of the world's diamond trading hubs, replete with Jewish jewelers funneling cut gems between the ports of Rotterdam and Tel Aviv. I made the journey by train, disembarking at Antwerp's grand station then walking straight out into the city's bustle. A particular shop, Stein's Diamonds, had been recommended, which I found easily after a ten-minute walk. I pressed the buzzer, and a man came and unlocked the heavy iron bars guarding treasures tinier and more valuable than a box of Krugerrands.

As for our looted Krugerrands, I had begun investing the proceeds following the lessons of my investment class. After Berlin, we had agreed I would keep all the Krugerrands and find a way to convert and invest them—I being the up-and-coming banker. The three of us would share the profits then figure out what to do with them. I started with small bets and, following gains and growing confidence, took more significant and daring stakes. I had not yet told Dirk and Beryl of my success, but I would soon. For now, it remained a guarded secret, and I figured if I needed to borrow a bit off the top to bridge paying for an engagement ring, no one would be the wiser; I would pay the money back with interest before the wedding. To barter with the jeweler, I even exchanged some of my profits back into Krugerrands, thinking gold once again the best universal bargaining chip. Chips, I thought. What a horrid and symbolic circle. At least something good was coming of that evening that both branded and bonded us forever.

I told Mr. Stein I wanted an engagement ring and that my fiancé-to-be was Jewish. If she said yes, we would be married in Jerusalem. I had learned a smattering of Hebrew, which lent authenticity to my tale. Mr. Stein, a wiry, bespectacled man wearing a slightly faded vest, was initially distant but softened and beckoned me inside. He led me to a seat and spread a velvet cloth across the top of the glass case. Mr. Stein returned from exploring a drawer and pulled open the drawstring of a small leather pouch, gently shaking out a small fortune in diamonds onto the cloth. He took needle-nosed pliers, deftly pinched a stone, and held it up to the light on the table, nodding his head approvingly. I had no idea what I was doing, cast under his spell and at his financial mercy. I fingered the pouch of gold coins in my pocket.

After watching him pick up almost ten stones, holding them with the small pliers to spy the refraction of light coming through, and putting them down to peer even more closely with a magnifying eyepiece, I was no closer to a decision than when I first sat. I stood up a moment to stretch my legs and noticed a jewel case that had been to my back, holding different colored stones. I peered down and saw the most magnificent emerald. I asked why he had those, it being Antwerp and the store in the heart of the diamond district.

"We are jewelers, Mr. Bellagio. Diamonds are our trade, but gems are part of our soul."

"Where is it from?" I asked, curious and surprisingly interested.

"That one is from South America."

"You trade all over the world?"

"We are famous for cutting stones here in Antwerp not just trading. We have a network and buy uncut stones from mines around the world. South Africa, the Congo, Columbia."

"Some challenging locations, wouldn't you say?" as I thought about the history of Belgium kings exploiting their colonies and the scourge of apartheid. "You don't mind the politics involved?"

"We tend not to think of the present and focus on the sediments built thousands of years ago," he said, dodging the political debate.

I nodded and asked if he could bring the emerald to the table. It was the most magnificent stone I had ever seen. I was transfixed. It reminded me of folklore like the *Arabian Nights*. On the table, against the velvet cloth, it was a deep green, pure and regal. Held up to the light, it shimmered, and when twisted, I sensed a slight refraction of blue. Mr. Stein told me that revealed a flaw; a perfect four-carat emerald in this classic rectangular cut would be three times the price. Ha! What a fool to reveal that comparison. He must have thought my diversion with the emerald idle curiosity as he guided me back to the canvas of diamonds.

I indulged him briefly then turned back to the green gem. I stared at the emerald. With a flicker of blue when the light struck it just right, its translucent green was the mirror of Beryl's eyes. I found myself back in Holland's tulip fields, lying on a blanket, smitten with her green eyes as the reflection of the afternoon sun shot a hint of blue. She had eyes like the ocean, flowing green to blue like magic. "How much?" I asked. It cost me only half the

Krugerrands I was willing to spend. I bargained hard, knowing the value of gold, both in absolute terms and beyond the taxman's normal reach.

Beryl cried when I put the ring on her finger. "I know it's not traditional, but it kind of spoke to me." As I cradled her in my arms, I told her the story of how I fell in love with the emerald, like her. Gazing into the stone and her eyes, one and the same, transported me to the mystery and shimmering beauty of the ocean. I told her I wanted to marry her, and we could take a yacht out from Tel Aviv, alone in the Mediterranean, to test the emerald's quality. Would the ring or her eyes be a better match? They would both be perfect.

***

Jerusalem, Israel—1994

On September 27th we were in Jerusalem under a *chuppah*, a traditional Jewish canopy stretched over four poles, ready to say our vows. The ceremony was amidst an ancient olive grove, brown mountains beckoning the desert beyond, framing the horizon. Uzi walked Beryl down the aisle, her jet-black hair and suggestive model walk accentuating the modest white gown, a delicate, lacy train in her wake.

Shouts of "*Per cent'anni*" and "*Mazel tov*," Italian and Hebrew for a hundred years and good luck rang through the guests as we kissed. Two ancient tribes uniting. A minor miracle in the Middle East. For a moment, we were alone amongst the olives. Soon, we would be alone again in the middle of the Mediterranean testing the emerald's hue. With luck, that would be all either of us was wearing.

Our parents sat together. It was the first time Tony and Claire Bellagio and Uzi and Anna Jaffe shared a meal since sipping champagne in the grand garden hosting my graduation party. It was a long way from The Hague, the Mediterranean climate and dry heat wafting from the desert so different from the chilly North Sea. Most of The Hague's landmarks are manmade—palaces and monuments and boulevards lined with nations' flags. Here, the landmarks defined history itself. Tales, ancient and scarred, were indelibly imprinted into the mountains and valleys. Tony and Uzi were both titans of their fields—my father defending family wealth, and Uzi protecting the family of Israel.

The men paired easily, laughing and even comfortable enough to tell dirty jokes. Wedding nights provided easy fodder, and despite being the father of the bride, Uzi howled gustily, no pretense or shame. "We're all in this together," he would say. Beryl's dad was a remarkably open man, deeply intolerant of the type of prejudices and pride that too often led to fighting. His job bore witness to stupid squabbles justified by lineage claims. The expression "the enemy of my enemy is my friend" might be a political justification in the broader neighborhood, but he never failed to challenge the perverse logic.

Our mothers were a different story. I could already tell we were poised for a lifetime of cliché mother-in-law jokes and excuses for missing holidays. My mother, shunning her rural roots, had social climbed from a Manhattan bedroom community to the shores of Lake Como. She had edge and arrogance and perfect teeth. Always the best for her kids, be that clothes, schools or jobs. She accepted Beryl rather than embraced her. It helped that Beryl's looks could stun, her walk and hips impossible to emulate. My mother could picture green-eyed grandchildren, exotic little things mixing the elegance of Swiss crispness with the casual eroticism of the wild Mideast. She also suspected what Uzi managed, the machismo scent a thrilling secret to be preciously guarded or hinted at, depending on the crowd. Too bad she would never know half the truth, nor what Beryl and I had already escaped and how dependent on the Mossad I would soon become.

Uzi's wife, Anna, in contrast, was all warmth, little judgment, appreciate-the-moment spunk. She would have worn jeans with her smile to the wedding if it would not have offended the groom's folks. (My mother would have been appalled.) Under her simple cotton dress, she wore even simpler leather sandals, the kind one might have bought a couple thousand years ago on the other side of the valley. Her green eyes, which she so lovingly bequeathed to Beryl, beheld me as her new son. I grimaced, watching my mother tap Anna's arm, diverting her attention and likely whispering a wholly inappropriate question about Uzi's work. God help us. I actually looked up, this being the land of God and all—I was not particularly religious, but if there was a God, I would surely need his help now.

I made my way over to a table full of old ASH buddies. Dirk, Hamid, Bryan, Amanda, and Tracy all sat in the round, sharing a spectacular bottle of Galilean Shiraz. Who knew the local wine was so good? I guess Jesus's trick with water really worked. I wondered if the Bible delved into vintages. Did Jesus dabble in whites too? I mean, the whole blood of Christ thing required reds, but was there more complexity? There was a sermon on the mount and yet no mention of hillside varietals. I grew up with Chianti, and until that moment, never thought the great Italian vineyards might owe their roots to a distant miracle. A good Montepulciano Sangiovese is barreled along lanes where Dante strolled and conceived his famous *Inferno*. I began to wonder if my ancestors' wines had their origins in visions of hell, while the wines of Beryl's predecessors were literally blessed with the grace of God. Getting married paired with a magnum of Galilean Shiraz could make your mind spin. Enough with biblical diversions and allusions to heaven and hell—I yanked myself back to the moment. Pour me another glass, please, I thought. All I cared about right then was the alcohol content and that the wine was not hideously sweet.

Beryl had been imbibing herself, a necessary complement to schmoozing at a table of assorted relatives. Most focused on dissecting my very essence. Cheekbone structure, occupation, heritage, sperm count, and inseam were all fair game. I had shaken hands, hugged, kissed, and been virtually groped by the lot, most of whose names I could no longer remember. The two I did know, Beryl's sister Reena and her husband Ari, I liked with an ease of familiarity that was as comforting as it was surprising. Perhaps being an only child, I longed for that type of bonding. Reena, a pediatrician, and Ari, an ophthalmologist, lived with their two kids an hour from Tel Aviv in an ancient port town dating back to Roman times. We didn't have time to visit them this trip but pledged to return soon. I made a mental note I would have a big debt to pay as I watched them defending me at the infamous cousins' table.

Having escaped, Beryl whispered that Irma, one of her cousins, thought I had a cute ass—covertly squeezing my left buttocks to verify the analysis and then pulling me tight with her arms around my waist. I relaxed, indifferent to the stares, kissing her. Our friends could squirm or applaud. I didn't much care. At least we were providing more fodder for the cousins' table. Finally separating, her green eyes flashed that hint of blue, which caused a kind of kinetic mental chain reaction from her eyes to the ring and my loot of Krugerrands. I pulled free, beckoning Dirk to join me, taking the bottle of Shiraz and slinking to an isolated table.

"Better days," I began lifting my glass in a toast.

"No shit."

"Do you think about it much?" I asked, having seen him only a couple times since we escaped Berlin.

"I try not to, but it creeps back. Little things set me off. When I see a tram at dusk, turning a bend I can't see around. Anything having to do with Germany. I can't watch detective shows. Guns set me off."

"I know. I just had a flashback thinking about the Krugerrands. Sort of a link to Beryl's..." I hesitated, catching myself, preserving the secret of how I purchased the engagement ring. "Never mind. As you said, it's the little things. And then everything comes back, like a punch in the gut."

Dirk nodded, tilting his glass in a gesture asking for more wine. "Glad you're serving wine. Beer sometimes brings back memories too."

"I know this sounds a bit crazy, but as time goes by, I'm kind of proud of what we did. I mean, we took down some Nazis. These were evil people. Still living it up, unrepentant. That flag in the room. No shame, no denials. I could either wallow in guilt or convince myself we did the right thing."

"Sounds like you've seen a shrink."

"I wanted to. I just thought I could never open up despite doctor-patient confidentiality and all. Where's the line when you admit to finding yourself in a Nazi poker game and killing at least one person around the table? I've never said a word to anyone. I assume the same for you?"

"Of course. Never a word. I wanted to tell my dad, his ties to East Germany in the embassy and all. I would have liked to ask him something that confirmed we were in the clear, that no one was looking for us. Especially after that letter in your duffle. But I couldn't figure out how to do it without giving away too much. So, I once asked him if they ever found old Nazis, looked for cells, or whatever you call them. What did they do if they located someone on an old list? I figured if he knew what happened, that would be enough of a hint."

"What did he say?"

"Only that if they had a strong lead, they'd pursue it. But that a lot of time had passed, and people just wanted to get on with their lives. I'm not sure if I was being paranoid, but it seemed like he was waiting for me to say something. Like he knew why

I'd asked the question…Anyway, I chickened out and moved on to something else."

"I get it. I wanted to have a heart-to-heart with Uzi. He might be the only person I could ever trust about this, but never have. And yeah, it would be nice to know we're not on some wanted list…"

"What about Beryl? Did she talk to her dad? Wasn't that part of our plan when we were worried they might track us down?"

"I asked, but she won't tell me. Always changes the subject, tells me let it be."

"Maybe we should go see McCartney too."

"Funny."

"Hey, how's it going with investing the Krugerrands anyway? Now that you brought them up."

"Great. But give me a bit more time."

"Okay. As long as your investing is growing our little pot of gold. Any changes to the grand plan? Are we going to save the world like we talked about? Or at least buy a boat?"

I smiled. We joked if we struck it rich, we would all buy a yacht together. Dirk and I suggested all kinds of crazy man-sized toys, fantasizing over everything from dueling Ferraris to racing boats.

Beryl, of course, set us straight and plotted a nobler course. We had been in evil's lair and survived. Nazis were nothing to joke about. If we could turn their dirty gold into something good, we had an obligation to do that. We would donate the money to charity, maybe to a Holocaust memorial fund. I shouldn't make stupid bets with the money like I was playing poker at their table, staked with free gold. I had a serious responsibility and should honor it. Beryl implored us to treat the gold as if it came from melted jewelry and watches stolen from people loaded onto cattle cars and packed off to be incinerated or gassed. I was urged to ground my actions in honoring their memory. To act virtuously, I must distribute the proceeds as if it was a sacred trust, helping a generation whose parents and grandparents perished and could not pass down a proper inheritance.

We felt ashamed after her speech. The gold had been minted in South Africa and was not the melted product of hideous crimes, yet the symbolism struck home. We pledged a solemn oath, blood brothers and sister, to create a trust that helped the descendants of those butchered by Nazi crimes. The idea gave us a purpose and possibly salvation from our nightmares.

I took the goal seriously and started to build up a fund through stock trading. The Krugerrands provided serious seed money, and I maintained careful accounting. I even set up a charitable trust through a family lawyer. I swore him to secrecy. I trusted my attorney-client relationship no more than doctor-patient rules and chose to make up another story. Inventing covers was sadly a skill I had become adept at mastering. Maybe Beryl could bring me into the family business. I had a talent. I told the lawyer I had a friend from school who lost all their grandparents in the Holocaust, and a few friends joined together to grow a scholarship fund in their memory. The condition was that it be kept secret in case it didn't grow to be meaningful. We didn't want anyone to get their hopes up. *Follow Beryl's canon*, I told myself. *Stick close to the truth.*

"No boats, Dirk," I returned to the conversation. "Beryl would kill me. You too."

"And in her case, I guess we actually need to take that kind of threat seriously."

"Thanks for that. You're going to give me performance anxiety for my wedding night."

"Killer," he joked. "Seriously, how's the investing going?"

"I told you. Pretty well but give me more time. I want this to be big. Remember what we agreed."

"I know, ten years…What if you get divorced before then?"

"Shut up, Dirk. Come on, I need to get back to the reception. Guest of honor and all."

"Fine. And, Marco, really, good luck with the wedding night." Dirk smiled, raising his glass to me as I waved and stuck out my middle finger, walking back towards Beryl. I had much more anxiety about the growth of my Krugerrand fund.

And then Uzi pulled me aside, his expression serious. Shit. Had Beryl talked to him about East Berlin? I remember thinking, *What am I marrying into?*

CHAPTER 6

Germany and Switzerland—1994

The fall of the Berlin Wall, German reunification, Gunther's sudden death, and that fateful night a few years before shook my faith to its core. I had not experienced the war's collapse, but these events compressed into a few years felt like a similar upheaval. In my tenure with the Stasi, I managed to rise to the rank of lieutenant. My job was mundane, part of a group watching a neighborhood, enforcing rules, listening to suspected traitors, an occasional interrogation and beating. It allowed me to move about relatively freely and occasionally put real meat on the table. Most importantly, it taught me tradecraft I could use to our benefit in a naively trusting new world.

My second job was learning from my father and, while Gunther was alive, keeping shadow books for some of his clients. A former commandant might ask Gunther to keep office books for a new hardware store or cafe, working the shell game of shares for themselves, enough of a cut to keep Gunther fed and quiet, and the standard Stasi payoffs. Separately, I would meet with the same men, sometimes with just my father, and help keep the books tied to their Swiss or other mountain monarchy hidden accounts. My numbers and Gunther's were completely uncorrelated. The visible part of our accountings carefully documented a respectable life in East Germany, providing exhibits to substantiate happy (in truth, stifled) growing families with enough to get by and a little extra to scratch into the elite. The privilege of the elite, of course, was still comparatively meager — better bad food, better drab clothes, and the occasional simple luxury for the mistresses.

My dealings felt set amidst a fiction novel, tied to far off places I'd never been, riches I could not imagine, and secrets buried deep as a pirate's den. I often pictured Liechtenstein as a large valley filled with gold. But while the Wall held, I was forced to stay content with my dreams. Liechtenstein remained a mirage, and my father kept any knowledge of communications and how transactions were couriered in its shadows. I only dealt with the books. He would handle the transfers. Still, those transfers were limited; most dealings were ensuring that treasures were safe and well protected. One day, we and our band of Nazi clients would need all the records. Germans and Swiss and Liechtenstein bankers were sticklers for records and papers. A withdrawal after decades could raise eyebrows in the wrong circles, and my father insisted we prepare and have paper trails (well, some trails, not all) beyond reproach.

Our monotonous little projects were proceeding well until those series of shocks. First, that calamitous night when Frank Krueshof was shot dead and Uncle Karl and Papa ignominiously beaten. Seeing Florian and Rolfe nearly killed too, left gasping for breath through makeshift gags, had left my father seething. The plan for that evening, the scheme to help accelerate our goals and ease transport to the West, blew up unimaginably. In hindsight, we should have kept things simpler, never escalated with guns. At the time, though, we were obsessed with the difficulty of escaping and the opportunity to leverage a diplomat's son–the kid literally dropped in our lap. Papa argued we should shock, act boldly, that we may never get such a chance again. And he was right — we never did. It was such Cold War thinking. Bait the target with something irresistible like discovering Nazis then find a way to compromise them — except we never had the chance to frame them for shooting Reiner. I could have so easily doctored evidence to place the gun in that diplomat kid's hand. The one thing we never could have imagined was they would shoot one of us, let alone kill Frank.

After that fiasco, my father realized Rolfe and Florian could not carry out bigger plans alone. They were too young and raw. He never trusted Gunther to realize his long-delayed dreams but still needed him to play a part, hoping Florian and Rolfe would be the vanguard of the next stage. Just as we were recovering, the Wall came down, and not long afterwards Gunther died. My cover Stasi career was past the brink, my half-brother dead, my father aging, and my nephews not quite ready.

My father's continuing genius saw opportunity in crisis, just as he had in the war. I was elevated to number one son, put in charge of what Gunther could neither stomach nor imagine. Reunification proved a godsend for us, allowing my father and me to put that horrid night at the poker game and Gunther's heart attack behind us. Success favors the swift and the brave and the dirty, and we were perfectly positioned. My father had both the perspective and foresight to bridge history, reaching into forgotten nefarious pits for resources to seed the mouthpieces of the future.

Maybe it was the stifling oppression of the communist East, or a grasp of how the Nazis had disseminated propaganda, but he understood an explosion in media and communications was on the horizon. It was a new day, and people wanted to be uplifted and entertained, to connect, to forget the horrors of the war. A generation had literally been deprived of normalcy, and beyond wanting to embrace fantasies, people were craving choice and access. The world was on the cusp of new television channels, pay TV, video stores, and pocket-sized cell phones. For those like me raised behind the Iron Curtain, the notion of news and television beyond state-controlled media was a difficult concept to grasp. We didn't even have national networks. My father intuited the yearnings sooner than the rest and was particularly excited about mobile phones. I don't know how he had such insight. Again, my father was a genius.

After reunification, we could suddenly travel freely to the West. Leaving Germany for the first time, I went to Switzerland, fronting for some of my clients who remained reticent to travel, especially under actual family names. I visited those hallowed vaults in banks whose names few have ever heard of, housed in marble monoliths along boulevards near glittering mountain lakes. No matter whether Zurich, Geneva, Lugano, Zug, the procedures were the same. Names, numbers, papers, codes, quiet vaults; bespectacled bankers making careful notations in books locked in yet other vaults. This clique lorded over their secret accounts in genteel elegance, meticulous business mixed with slightly hushed tones, just enough questions, tiptoeing to whisper the right answers. I even visited Liechtenstein. I learned it was the second richest country in the world per capita, trailing only its sister pimple principality, Monaco. What Monaco flaunted in pomp, Liechtenstein hid in quiet banks and post office boxes. Liechtenstein was everything East Germany was not. I vowed to buy a chalet there and in Monaco one day, hedging my bets in the two principalities where some of the smartest in the dirty world stored the winnings of past bets and other more sinister schemes.

But first, my father and I needed to build our fortune, laundering past plunder into newly minted enterprises. His foresight of having me learn accounting proved providential. I sat with respected lawyers and bankers, including at Bauer & Hoffstein, setting up a web of companies and accounts. I could trade on the Frankfurt stock exchange, invest via Deutsche Bank, take loans at Credit Suisse. It was unimaginable and yet real. Only a few years after the Wall's fall, I partnered with a then small, and still largely private, venture capital firm to build a media and communications fund. We invested in emerging channels and in the new technologies enabling homes to receive bundles of television programs. By participating in different parts of the ecosystem, we were building libraries and infrastructure to fill a void left by stale newsreels and piecemeal access. While most people were focused on construction projects — which were obvious — and some on energy, the opportunities my father envisioned in building the backbone of an emerging communications landscape were dizzying. For someone schooled in eavesdropping with clunky bugs and reel-to-reel tapes, one could hardly imagine the notion of cellular networks. We soon started financing towers as quickly as they could be built.

In making deals and investing, we were not beholden to the mores of traditional business practices. A type of illicit freedom greased our success. My father's foresight proved invaluable, my Stasi roots making it child's play to place bribes and loosen tongues. I was surprised to learn how easily businessmen in the West were cowed by threats of physical violence. Negotiations took on a different tone when risks became truly personal and failing to acquiesce to contract demands courted beatings, compromising photos, kidnappings, or worse. Bankers and CEOs could be so squeamish!

My father and I kept Florian and Rolfe out of the high finances and ugly tactics, setting them on a different path to invest yet more of the profits. I remember the years following the Wall's fall for the freedom it brought all of us. The freedom to forget that poker night that almost ended it all, the freedom to reinvent ourselves in the West, the freedom to reach back into West Berlin for what was rightfully ours. I was so happy my father lived to help me steal this new beginning, his patience and genius rewarded!

Everything was back in motion.

1995 — London, England and Amsterdam, The Netherlands
After the wedding we moved to Notting Hill, a posh section of central London. Beryl accepted a job at Moultens & Barings, swapping out her desert khakis and gun for designer blouses and a new laptop. Moultens & Barings was an art appraisal consulting firm catering to high-end clients and galleries. It was an unusual choice for a star from the RCA where most vied to work at a renowned museum or one of the premier auction houses, like Christie's or Sotheby's.

Beryl, though, with her little Israeli side job, was not your typical graduate. She needed to keep a low profile while still gaining industry access. Moultens & Barings was perfect:

discreet, a bit mysterious, and yet very much in mainstream demand by those who mattered. And that mattering class counted museum curators, gallery owners, wealthy collectors, art aficionados, donors, insurance brokers, art lawyers, investment banks, and even some artists themselves. It catered to a cross-section that only a boutique independent could cultivate. As importantly for Beryl, Moultens acted as quiet advisors just outside the limelight.

With a coveted pass to the ecosystem's eclectic inner circle, she could cultivate contacts with the most intriguing collectors: those demanding anonymity. Nothing was akin to the mystery of the silent bidder, the buyer who might take a famous painting off the market to display privately in a secluded villa. Plenty of petty dictators, oil-rich princes, and criminal entrepreneurs coveted hushed bragging rights.

"This is so awesome. Seems like the perfect job," I said. "What's your title?"

"They keep it low key. Simply, analyst."

"That works. Unbelievable pay too! I can't really believe it. From what you told me, nobody gets hired there right out of school."

"It's pretty rare. But then again, not as many applicants. Everyone wants one of those Sotheby's positions. I'm more proud I got the job on my own. No strings from Abba. Nor from your dad or his pals."

"You deserve it. They're lucky to have you. And if they'd only known about the rest of your CV," I said, smiling.

"Enough. Where are you off to tomorrow? I can never keep it straight."

"Hong Kong. Be back on the weekend."

"I don't know how you go to Asia for three or four days. That's crazy to me."

"That's the SZG way," I falsely lamented, my employer being of such prestige that flaunting its acronym was sufficient reference, my tone hinting of macho badge-of-honor pride. I followed the diametrically opposite path in securing my job—I asked my father for help. I was neither embarrassed nor diminished in stature by brazenly trying to jump the queue. Why should I struggle for years and hope for a break so I could pat myself on the back? Well done, you did it on your own! I never craved such accolades or self-fulfillment. I was always confident; plus, I never understood that lot who preached the nobility of poverty or the dignity gained from hard-scrabble ladder climbing. Screw that! If I could jump to the top and avoid some of the paying-your-dues bullshit, I was rushing toward that door. Arrogant, privileged kid, luck of the sperm…For anyone wanting to hold me in disdain or judge me, I thought, *Get over it.*

I sat down with my father, or rather I should say my successful banker father who could grease my path. We evaluated options. Not options like should I start in the mailroom or as an assistant to an assistant. Instead, our talks began at whether I should seek a top entry position at a large bank or a boutique investment house. We also debated which financial center should launch my career. Should I stay in Europe, looking at banking hubs like London, Frankfurt, and Zurich, or should I consider Asian trading meccas, such as Hong Kong? Perhaps I should consider the other side of the pond and Wall Street?

Beryl brought me out of my smug musings. "The SZG way. Listen to yourself. You sound like one of those privileged ASH snobs. Born entitled, condescending to have to fly business class or something."

"Well, I am one of those ASH snobs, if you don't remember. And so are you!"

"ASH, yes, but I told you, I'm done putting up with that pretentious crap. Plus, doesn't exactly fit well with my Israeli sidebar and trying to keep a lower profile."

"Sorry. I know… It's just kind of cool to be jet-setting around the world."

"Well, don't get too carried away. Or I'll send you away."

Ouch. She was right, of course. Too easy growing up on the shores of Lake Como, attending a fancy prep school, and gliding into a high-paying job—a fair knocking down was needed to remind me of my privilege and not to take things for granted. Beryl was trying to pull me off that slippery asshole slope. She was the only one who would talk to me like that, and I've been forever grateful. I appreciated being that person who could pull strings and jump the queue. I was also that person who— genuinely—wanted to be thankful for that luck. Not so thankful, mind you, that I was striving for humble. Just not an asshole. One could only be so humble jockeying to become the richest man in the world. I wanted to fly into Davos, not walk around The Vatican.

I was invited to Davos for the first time that year. SZG always hosted a party for the movers and shakers. By then, I had settled in London, based in the City's skyscraper offices while frequently traveling to the Swiss Zurich Group's more understated lakeside headquarters. I rationalized it would provide good rounding, staying in Switzerland potentially making me appear too provincial. The real reason for London, of course, was the woman who just reduced me to an idiot. Still, looking at her right then, it was obvious I made a good choice. I was a lucky man. Needed to cut down on the asshole edge, though. Fast.

We finished our dinner, sitting in the garden of our townhouse. We lived in one of those circular enclosures built around a green, with a small garden out the back conservatory. Our little garden was like a pea in a pod, the back gate to the garden opening into a large communal garden. It was the perfect spot to retreat from work and self-recriminations, not to mention worrying that Beryl might be called up literally to hunt someone down. Just kidding. She was mostly on inactive duty, having completed her training. An emergency could come calling, but failing a war, she would remain a sleeper, developing her cover skills and proper career. I knew about most of it—at least I thought I did—and we pledged not to let the potential of her other calling interfere with our daily lives or our long-term plans. I believed her. Uzi seemed to lead a normal life, and in all our time at ASH, I never suspected the Jaffe's were anything other than another happy family with diplomatic plates. Uzi Jaffe—another reason I needed to improve my behavior. He was not the asshole-tolerating type.

***

As it turns out, I was pulled off my Asian project by an odd assignment that further entangled me with a member of the Jaffe family. Namely, my wife. A stunning burglary of a minor Van Gogh from a small museum back in the Netherlands occurred. My boss, Hugo Miles-Robson, pulled me into a conference room together with a few other confused associates. He was wearing his immutable pinstripe suit. In fact, his dress was so monotonous I imagined him donning pinstripe pajamas and underwear to avoid all choice.

"The Koningshaus Museum is a small jewel outside Amsterdam with a state-of-the-art alarm system. The thieves obviously knew what they were doing. The police say they were in and out in five minutes. It was the only piece taken, dust marks from the frame left along with picture wire on the wall. They knew what they were after."

"Hugo, what does a burglary of a painting have to do with us? Are we financing someone to buy the museum?" one of SZG's finest asked, clearly finding the police matter beneath our station.

"Silly question, William," Hugo cut him off. "That painting is worth millions, maybe tens of millions. Do you have any idea how many Van Gogh's exist in the world?"

"No," William sheepishly replied.

"And we are not buying the Koningshaus or financing someone to take it over. Though that would be a great project with a hefty commission. What we are doing is working with one of the biggest banks in Holland, which has a multi-billion-dollar insurance arm. Just like a loan, they syndicate their insurance coverage, and we are holding a part. If the Koningshaus comes to collect, we could have to raise over five million." Turning to William, "Which will come out of your bonus!"

I raised my hand then wondered too late if I should have ventured into the fray when Hugo nodded to me. "Sir, how do we know what it's really worth? Isn't it hard to pin a figure on rare objects like that?"

"Excellent point, Mr. Bellagio. We don't. And it is in our distinct interest that the value be as low as possible. We represent the inverse of an auction house in this matter. You lot of financial wizards are going to create the best model in the world to undervalue *Moonlit Fields*."

"*Moonlit Fields*?" I asked.

"The name of the painting. Most paintings by the great masters have names," Hugo said, opening a folder and handing us all color copies of the picture. Even I, an art novice, could recognize the bold manic strokes, the fractured field highlighted in a blue glow of the moon. I focused on the artist's signature in the bottom right corner and the caption below listing the work's title.

Everyone sat absorbing the challenge, some, including me, even pausing a beat to question the ethics of the pursuit. Apparently, a conspirator in the task, I asked the obvious, "Don't we need to bring in an expert who knows about art? Knows what museums pay for a painting like that? We don't have any background in something like this."

"Again, correct. I was just getting to that. Please sort out hiring a couple of experts for data points. I want the model by Monday. Marco, since you seem to know so much about art, take the lead."

He assigned me the task of coordinating the model and, I assumed, researching potential experts. He cast a "get it done fast, get it done right" glance at me and walked out of the conference room without another word. Shit. I actually needed my wife. I chastised myself for having been such an asshole preening over my business trips.

***

Before approaching Beryl, though, I decided to gather more background. I was apt to put my foot in my mouth without learning more about the heist and why the burglars may have taken that particular painting. Even though the police were investigating, I needed to become a detective myself. I had to visit the scene of the crime.

I booked a flight to Amsterdam's Schiphol airport, making arrangements to visit the Koninghaus Museum. Before leaving, I told Beryl, "I have a very interesting project I want to tell you about. I've got to take a quick trip to learn a little more first. Just for the day. Can we talk later? And sorry about my attitude last night. Really."

She nodded but didn't speak. I would be forgiven by the time I returned. Then I could enlist her aid in whatever this turned out to be.

I reviewed the police report during my short British Airways trip over the channel, banking over Brussels and arriving into Amsterdam's usual gray drizzle. It struck me that my departure and arrival destinations were bonded by North Sea borders, dreary weather, and a preponderance of blond hair, but not much else. The Brits and Dutch ought to be closer allies; guess the reserve of an island nation, for centuries cocksure of its preeminence, and independent frugal-minded traders, wary of empires and occupiers, were destined to forge closer economic than familial bonds. A microcosm of the grand European project. I resolved to lean on my Italian roots and play up discussions of pasta, a neutral intermediary seeking a bit of information. Everyone loves tortellini.

I hailed a taxi on the lower level, and we took off toward The Hague. Hugo's assertion that the museum was just outside Amsterdam was correct if you drew hour-wide concentric circles. In fact, I was headed between Amsterdam and The Hague, back toward school. Why did this assignment keep turning toward Beryl? If I kept on the road another few kilometers, I would pass ASH, able to wave from the motorway.

I was spared the pull of a reminiscing drive-by as the taxi turned away from the sea, looping toward the historic town of Leiden. A major university city that boasted traditional canals and windmills, Leiden was famous for Rembrandt's birth and the departure of American Pilgrims. The legendary voyage of the Mayflower and the history of Plymouth Rock included roots in Leiden where the Pilgrims first fled from England before later setting forth to the new land. I was quite early, and supposed if I had been interested, I could have visited the Pilgrim Museum.

Instead, I asked the taxi driver to drop me off a short distance away, deciding to amble through town en route. I crossed over the grand Morsweg canal, its near shore within view of the very spot where Rembrandt was born. With his family's original house gone, though, the less interesting replacement simply bore a plaque calling out the importance of what used to stand there. The interloping house now overlooked a small square, aptly named Rembrandtplaats. I crossed over a bridge spanning a slow current and centuries of onlookers, finding myself walking along the wide Rapenburg canal.

I entered a small cafe, my Italian veins craving a decent coffee. Soon I calmed, sipping an inadequate cappuccino and stuffing a dull bit of Dutch cheese into the belly of a hard roll before engulfing the mini sandwich. The patterned walls featured tulip drawings. I suppose the proprietors were trying to accentuate local charm for the smattering of tourists that strayed this far from the disappointing commemorative Rembrandt plaque. I paid, leaving no tip as befit the local custom.

I continued in the direction of Pieterskerk, its steeple guiding me. I could not help peering into living rooms and parlors, the tall windows of houses fronting the canal. The occupants traded the privilege of canal views for peering pedestrians, no buffer between their conversations and narrow sidewalks save for leaded glass. Many did not bother to dress appropriately for the inevitable encounters. I paused looking at one woman wearing only a bra and panties sitting in an armchair holding a morning coffee. She smiled, and I wondered if she planned her exhibition. Leiden's original red-light district, no longer operating to gawking tourists or actual customers, was long gone. Unlike failing to tip, I was unsure of the protocol when smiled upon by a non-whore sitting half-naked in a canal window. I suppose I should at least smile back, which induced a slight bow of the head before she returned her gaze to a magazine.

I wondered what she was thinking as I continued along the Rapenburg, spying mothers feeding kids and an old couple staring out disapprovingly from their table. Why was that woman, in fact all those people, fine letting me peer into their windows? Why not draw some blinds? That got me thinking, why does anyone do what they do? My mind drifted to the thieves' motivation in stealing the van Gogh. Was there something about that specific painting? Unable to connect the dots, I was shaken from my musings and voyeurism, the pattern of domestic life interrupted by a longer and more polished-looking building.

I looked up only to realize I stood beneath the street number I had been seeking. The Koningshaus Museum had narrow, high windows evenly spaced along its brick exterior, and proffered an elegant doorway leading into what appeared to be a grand inner courtyard. Otherwise, it was a nondescript building, wide by virtue of merging several canal houses with similar fronts. The inside architecture preserved much of the buildings' features, sporting a more open feel than its original occupants enjoyed. Inner walls had been punched through, connecting separate interiors via a maze of arches. The now-linked structures together formed a lattice of galleries considered to house one of the finest private collections of Dutch and modern art in the world.

I had vaguely heard of the museum from my ASH days, but back then I was hardly an art museum aficionado. I had not done much more than check the Rijksmuseum off the tourist-visit box. I never had the urge to go gallery wandering in Leiden and certainly did not expect to find myself visiting this local jewel wearing a suit and tie. I identified myself to the guard, grabbed a brochure, and was escorted to the director's office. I had to climb several flights of stairs and, on the second landing, followed the guard to the right, then down a half flight before climbing back up further. The stringing together of prior homes led to uneven floors, the second floor on one lining up a half-floor off the next. This disjunction was solved by a labyrinth of half floors and turns, which I supposed visitors might find quaint. I judged the design as somewhere between a sorry attempt at jerry-rigging an exercise route and an inside joke on those regulars forced to navigate dips and turns that remodeling failed to fix. Scaffolding should be dismantled not permanently reflected in a hodgepodge interior. Finally, mildly out of breath from the assault to the canal house's peak, I arrived at the museum director's office.

Mr. Hans de Vries shook my hand and pointed me to an old red leather chair, its cracks as worn as some edges of the 17th-century scenes hanging next to his desk. I looked up at a family dressed in black, silly white collars around the men's necks, black hats on everyone's heads, and hands gesticulating toward a carafe tipped to its side laying on a card table. The old Dutch masters flourished bringing the mundane to life. I turned away from the painting, not searching for its inner meaning. I had to give a nod of appreciation to the thieves and their taste. At least the work they stole gushed more vibrant brush strokes, declaring their brilliance through dashes of passion.

It was obvious why I needed the help of an art expert. It should be Beryl, not me, sitting with balding de Vries, so tall he must stoop to grasp my hand properly. I began the interrogation. From my informal art education living with Beryl, I knew to treat a masterpiece's loss with solemnity, especially if I wanted its caretaker to take me into his confidence.

"Thank you for seeing me on such short notice. First, let me say how sorry I am for your loss. I understand the theft of a great piece of art can stir similar emotions to death: grief, shock, denial."

"How right. I see you understand art, Mr. Bellagio."

More like emulating forgery, yet I let the comment sit, waiting respectfully as if at a wake. With an intake of breath, I dared to forge ahead, "Please call me Marco…I'm sorry, but I am only in Holland for the day, so, unfortunately, I have to turn to business. I hope you don't mind."

"Not at all. I'm still in shock. Whatever I can do to help. This is a catastrophe."

"I take it the Van Gogh was one of your most valuable works?"

"Beyond most. *Moonlit Fields* was our most prized possession. Irreplaceable."

"Of course. So why take it? I mean, how do you sell such a thing? Wouldn't any legitimate buyer know it was stolen?"

"Yes, I would assume so. Any buyer would check the provenance and discover that *Moonlit Fields* had been stolen from the Koningshaus collection."

Mr. de Vries gently eased into my trap, an unwitting conspirator helping formulate the basis of my undervaluation model. "So, hypothetically, if you were going to buy the painting at auction, let's say at Sotheby's, then the catalog would itemize its history. The auction house would market its uniqueness, how few Van Goghs ever come on the market. Perhaps they would list a comparable or even set a floor price for bidding."

"Yes, something like that."

"And the painting would fetch what the market could bear. For example, let's say this painting was worth twenty million dollars give or take."

"I would say give. I think it would go for more right now. Maybe even twenty million pounds."

"I understand. My question isn't what it would cost at auction, but rather about how the thieves would be in sort of a bind. They can't put it up for auction in London, can they? Won't they be forced to sell it for much less, maybe even as low as ten million?"

"Perhaps. I don't know. I've never tried to buy a stolen painting."

"Of course. I hope you don't think I was implying that you had. Or ever would. I'm just trying to understand the motive and how the thieves may try to sell the painting. If we can get into their heads, then maybe we have a better chance of recovering it."

"I see. I had not thought about it that way."

"So, you agree they will probably have to accept a bit of a discount then?"

"I suppose so, put that way," Mr. Hans de Vries confessed to me.

"Would you mind if I quoted you for my report? We're trying to capture all the possibilities. Bigger picture and all. We need to assemble a range of theories. Do whatever we can to help the authorities get it back."

"Yes, no problem. Happy to assist in any way that could lead to recovering our jewel."

"Would you mind taking me to the gallery where it was stolen?" With my argument's underpinning secured, I was eager to move on.

"Of course, follow me. It's down a few flights of stairs."

Of course, I thought, following Mr. de Vries left, then down, then right, then up, then down again. And then, there it was: a blank wall where picture wire and a faint outline of discolored fabric outlined where a picture had been hanging for years. I stared at the violated panel for a few minutes, again trying to get into the head of the burglars. However, the answer was simple. Millions. In whichever currency my report would denominate the theft and worth. I would keep the valuation in dollars, an easy benchmark rather than complicate estimates with conversions between pounds, guilders, francs, and whatever other denominations the thieves may be eyeing. It occurred to me that, just like my job would be made easier by sticking to a single currency, the thieves' job was simplified by converting a single painting. The most valuable one.

Having gained more insights than I had expected, I left the museum and soon found myself passing the window where I had seen the woman posing in her bra and panties. I was sure I was looking at the same house. Nobody appeared home, and I guessed she was probably fully dressed, possibly reflecting on her own insights from the morning. Maybe one of them was to close the shades, or a dirty admission she liked teasing the passersby. I wondered whether Mr. de Vries lived on the street and if I had also been peering into his house. I could have invented a whole story about walking in this neighborhood. Tuck that away for a day when I needed a convenient cover in Amsterdam. I walked on, soon finding a taxi along one of the main streets. Mothers and work-at-home women unsuspectingly sitting by their canal windows were now safe again from at least one gawker. But perhaps not from a visit by the police. My last thought before climbing into the cab was whether any of these people may have spied a thief scurrying along the canal with a painting-sized package under their arm. The taxi sped off back toward Schiphol Airport, and soon I was savoring a shortbread biscuit and glass of whiskey on another British Airlines channel hopper.

***

When I arrived home, I was ready to broach the topic with Beryl. Best to start with a bit of foreplay. "Did I tell you I was in the Netherlands today?"

"No, no idea. You just said something about an interesting project, and you'd be gone for the day. Why didn't you let me know?" she said in a tone that made me wonder if she was pretending. Mossad operatives have a way of knowing their husband's destinations, especially when leaving town. "Did you see your parents?"

"No, it was a short hop over. Just for the day and kind of last minute. I didn't even call them, so don't let on I was twenty minutes away. I'll never hear the end of it."

"What, tell them they missed a chance at time alone with you," she teased, throwing a piece of bow tie pasta at the wall to see if it would stick.

"You know, there are better ways to tell if the pasta is done."

"Not for me. See, perfect. Not sliding down the wall."

"You know we'll have to repaint that wall if we ever move."

"Here, can you open the wine? And try not to splatter any on a different wall." She turned her back to stir sauce into the cauldron of her al dente best.

I ignored her jibe and steered back to the Netherlands. "I almost called you. I was on the A44 and turned off in Leiden. I wanted to continue on to ASH. Not sure what I would have done but seemed so close I should at least drive by or something."

"Better you didn't. They'd probably have asked you to open your wallet. No grace period for collecting from graduates who go into banking."

I smiled. She was probably right, and fortuitously Leiden was an exit short of being solicited.

"Why Leiden?" she asked as I pulled the cork. No splatter, and, more importantly, no Brett smell.

"Crazy story, and by the end of it, it will involve you."

"What?"

"Not what you're thinking. Nothing to do with ASH. I'm involved with a project involving a museum."

"What?" she said again, now sounding like an echo. Enough teasing—I had better get on with the story.

"There was a theft at a small museum there. The Koningshaus. I assume you know it."

"Of course. I've been there a few times."

I should have realized. I doubt she lingered looking at women displaying their Hunkemöller lingerie en route. Maybe I should have stopped at Hunkemöller and bought something red and lacy for her. *Get your mind back on topic*, I mentally slapped myself. *And do not mention your little canal house peeping jaunt.* "A Van Gogh was stolen. *Moonlit Fields*, not among his best-known works, but still a major theft."

"My God! I've seen that painting. I haven't heard about the robbery. That's strange."

"Just happened, and I think they're trying to keep it out of the press for a while to give the police a chance to track down some leads."

"I don't understand. What do you have to do with any of this? Jealous of my second job, thinking of trying out for Scotland Yard? What else are you hiding from me?"

"No. Nothing like that. Although it would be fascinating to be on the inside of something at Scotland Yard. I'll keep that in mind," I played along. "Apparently, SZG is part of the syndicate, along with a bank, that insured the museum and could even be on the hook. I had no idea we were involved in that side of the business. But from what I'm learning, there's lots of money in insuring high-end paintings and museums. Just another type of financing, pooling risks, underwriting the policy. I need to start learning."

"I'd say so. You could throw me some business."

She'd given the perfect opening. "I was thinking that exact thing. This could be a real opportunity for both of us. In fact, I could use your help."

"That's nothing new. What this time?" She was smirking.

"I'm on a team putting together a valuation for the painting. We have to justify the insurance cover, and if there is a claim from the museum, there will inevitably be a dispute. Companies don't simply cough up millions of dollars without a fight. I could use your help with a valuation. I have the authority to engage Moultens, and we can do this formally."

Beryl stared at me, a flash of melancholy in her assessment. If she let on she suspected being set up, even if harmlessly, she hid it pretty well. "Hmm... very interesting. I've never been involved on that side of things. Insurance claims, I mean."

"Neither have I. Obviously."

"Are you suggesting I can set my price?" She took a sip of her wine.

I could not tell if the eye batting was an act, but the suggestion hit me, nonetheless. She had all the leverage, and more.

"Just don't screw me," I pleaded.

"Who exactly is doing the propositioning here?"

"Okay, you win. Seriously, I need your help. And this could be good for both of us. Really, who would have thought I could be throwing you work? And I get the sense Hugo is desperate. Full fees on this one. But I have to get some data points by the weekend. After that, who knows. This will give me an in to that side of the business. From the little I've seen so far, underwriting and syndicating this type of coverage is a multi-billion-dollar segment. And it all relies on valuations. Moultens has the perfect pedigree. We play this right, and you could be bringing in big fees."

"My God, you really are propositioning me. How could I resist!"

Beryl called her boss at home, and by morning, a fee had been agreed. A few more deals like this and Moultens could be poised for a name change to Moultens, Barings & Jaffe. Beryl, of course, had kept her name for professional use. She loathed the notion of Beryl Bellagio and the hideous prospect of being called BB.

We immediately set to work on the modeling, Beryl separately working up a valuation. I confided my goals to her, and while uncomfortable, she hailed from espionage circles. Manipulating a few facts here and there to curry advantage was not altogether foreign. Was personal advantage equal justification to state defense? Not a debate I wanted to weigh into presently. I needed my model done and tilted slightly off-axis. To death and discovery do us part.

***

Working together on the valuation of such an irreplaceable piece of art forged a strange bond. Beryl and I took the theft personally and kept abreast of even the smallest developments. But six months passed with no sign of the missing *Moonlit Fields*. The police had a few clues, one lead pointing to a ring in Eastern Europe that was shuffling the painting among ramshackle hideouts. Another rumor had the painting hanging in an office in Macao. Yet a different rumor, this one sourced by Mideast chatter but only passed along to me by Beryl as a Mossad tip, suggested the painting was aboard a floating palace accompanying a Saudi prince. Namely, the usual suspects.

There was one certainty: *Moonlit Fields* had not popped up on auction sites, whether legitimate or clandestine. I was surprised nobody had tried to fence the painting in underworld circles, which is where I had placed my bets. Maybe the notion of displaying the work in a trophy villa, boasting of being able to show it off, proof of being untouchable, was not farfetched. Being in the line of making money, that outcome at first seemed unfathomable. I guess billionaires, and ones with less than clean balance sheets, behave differently. How would I act? Assuming I was not pedaling in shady deals and had achieved my richest-man-in-the-world goal, would I think differently? Would I consider displaying a pilfered Picasso over the mantle? No way.

While the still-unsolved outcome was disheartening to Mr. de Vries and the Koningshaus, the heist proved profitable for the Bellagios and Jaffes. Beryl helped me spin my model, which won Hugo's approval. He was ecstatic. I effectively backed up a valuation of half the insurance claim, and we then indefinitely delayed any resolution through litigation.

I quickly learned there was nothing quite like the shell game of insurance litigation. First, there is the policy: what the buyers thought they were obtaining. A fool's errand for sure. Next, come the exclusions. These are finely crafted carve-outs ensuring that virtually nothing is covered. A web of cross-references and convoluted definitions ensures that actual coverage is shrouded in fog and solid arguments exist for denying claims. The definitions are almost a piece of artwork, deftly articulated with interlacing provisos of "notwithstanding," "for the avoidance of doubt," and occasional "including but not limiting to" thrown in for good measure. If one were able to put together the jigsaw and argue an interpretation, rest assured a rebuttal would be equally compelling. If someone succeeded in moving far enough through the gauntlet, then there would be the challenge of learning terms of art peculiar to insurance.

And finally, if they managed to come up for air and felt heroically confident they had pieced together a thread of logic, then all would be lost when they realized nothing so far mattered. Because all hundred-plus pages, which they had pulled out hair to digest, would be overruled by a lengthy and unintelligible set of schedules and appendices double or triple the length of the underlying rules of the game. Another group of attorneys would likely opine on the precedent or not of a particular schedule versus a prior clause versus a notwithstanding clause versus an exclusion nested in an exclusion to a schedule to a clause. Convoluted, to say the least, and yet by design.

God forbid anyone ruled on that labyrinth, then they would have to next wrestle with my valuation model. I might have argued it was infallible and not subject to interpretation; yet, even I knew better. And so did Beryl. And so did the bank and the insurance company and the Koningshaus museum and a set of experts hired by each to vet and contradict the other. Litigation could be a beautiful land of obfuscation and delay. To whoever had the deepest pockets to drag out the battle until the opponent folded often went the spoils.

Poor Mr. de Vries. Would it be salt in the wound if I advised I was compensated in full, with a massive bonus? Would it be further insult to injury if he learned that in addition to my bonus, my engagement of Beryl and Moultens landed her a massive bonus? No matter the result was as rigged as my jumping the queue to land the job at SZG and as indulgent as feeding at the trough of financial self-justification.

I didn't care. I was on my way. Beryl was on her way. I could happily and profitably move forward, indifferent to whether

Moonlit Fields or the heist's perpetrators were ever discovered. I could even boast that the incident led to other referrals, providing a pipeline of work to Beryl and Moultens. In fact, so much work that Beryl became the youngest partner ever in the firm's history. I, of course, kept collecting large bonuses and gliding up the ladder. I eventually moved on to focus on new specialties once Beryl had cemented the connections for herself. I thought little of art other than a mild interest for Beryl's sake. For me, it was always about the money, not the history or cultural relevance. That was a sacrilegious thought for an Italian to admit, hailing from a land boasting treasures from the Vatican to the Uffizi, Pompeii, and The Academy. I still found insurance to be exquisitely dull. I could not remain in that wasteland indefinitely.

I thought I was done with art and thefts and could forget the nuances and curator chit-chat. I was not, though, destined to forget. An unexpected twist was set to pull me back into the underbelly of provenances and auctions in the shadows.

CHAPTER 7

Munich, Germany—1997

I thought about moving to Liechtenstein, working from that mountain paradise. My father, though, was aging and wanted to spend his remaining years in Germany. He had suffered through the Nazi's defeat and then too many ignominious hibernation years groveling to the Stasi puppets. This was his time to emerge and grab what remained of his destiny, not to run and further hide. I still dreamed of buying my Liechtenstein or Monaco villa, overlooking a world-class ski slope or tucked into a switchback tilted above a royal Mediterranean harbor. For that, though, I needed to help my father fulfill the next phase of his comeback, which we would orchestrate from Germany.

We had moved around in search of new roots, but despite original plans, kept an apartment in Berlin as a kind of anchor. It had become time, though, for a total break, to leave the haunting memories of Berlin, that stifling city of my birth and prison to my dreams. Even though the Wall had fallen, and each day erased more division, the Wall remained an imaginary line. While the physical space became punctuated by remnant graffiti reminders, and lovers walked from the rebuilt bar at the Hotel Adlon to the Brandenburg gate unaware that they walked across a formerly impenetrable line, I could never forget the division. It lurked at the remains of Checkpoint Charlie and in the doorways of cafes and shops along the now trendy Unter den Linden. I especially struggled to pause at innocent intersections where before the same road dead-ended into the Wall. No number of cranes rising in Potsdamer Platz could change that history for me. The crisscross of U-Bahn and S-Bahn underground stops, now open to all, would connect partygoers of the next generation, yet always remind me of ghost stations past. I could not forget and would never forget. The same motto, taken up by Jews remembering the Holocaust sins planned right there, tugged at me in a less macabre and yet intensely personal way. I could not move forward when Berlin would always root me in the past.

My father and I moved permanently to Munich, that leafy Bavarian town that more than Berlin beat the heart of the Third Reich. My father felt at home there and had even spent much of the war in Munich. It held no memories of walls or Moscow-driven Stasi propaganda or even of shootings and embarrassments at the hands of foolhardy Western kids lured into a trap in the shadow of a rock concert. Instead, we found a new spring, groups of friends locking arms while holding liter steins of local weissbier spilling out of cafes, carefree bathers plunging into the Isar River. Fantastic museums, some miraculously spared by the war, beckoned tourists to view treasures of the less-troubled Teutonic past and German scientific achievement. Like Berlin, magnificent parks abounded, the largest the English Garden sprawling in the heart of the city. Perhaps wanting to flaunt the city's freedom, it became customary for nude sunbathers to show their wares. I watched, fascinated, but chose not to take part, my trunks always belted in place. Berlin was liberated, but in Munich, we found the perfect mix of uninhibited life and the grounding of Nazi history. Also, the suburbs housed a key source of my father's fortune. We were home.

My investments grew, my father seeding money that allowed us to take ever greater stakes in the small venture capital fund where we had become silent partners. After flipping a sizeable return in a media investment, we offered to buy out a lead investor for the equivalent of ten million dollars. It was a modest sum for a founder rooted in a sense of entitlement but still provided a nice retirement to a man who had risen from rabble and literally shot his way to the top. He wanted the *firm's legacy in the hands of loyal believers, the Nazi bond quietly paving fortunes into the future. We took over the firm and merged it into Mullenboess.*

Mullenboess Ventures grew exponentially in the 1990s. Most of our investments seemed unstoppable — remarkably, I seldom had to turn to blackmail. So what if a little threat of violence was occasionally necessary to jumpstart things? If I could put my past training to good use and turn things to our advantage, why hesitate? After all those years stuck behind the Wall, my father was loath to sit on the sidelines and wait while others seized this unprecedented moment. These were heady days of Internet and technology startups, where brilliant young scientists and entrepreneurs came to us penniless, begging us to fund their world-changing ideas. We focused on media and telecoms and soon diversified into biotech ventures. My father believed biotech was a key to the future, and soon the human genetic code would be mapped, unleashing boundless potential for developing new drugs. I tried to imagine the ramifications if the Nazis had mapped the genome first. If Hitler had the blueprints to our code, his plan for engineering the master race would have fostered breathtaking experiments. I believe my father harbored hopes for unleashing this potential. I found the idea fascinating and was naturally supportive. My passion at that time, though, lay in making money. I left reshaping mankind in a blond, blue-eyed fashion to more clever brethren.

As for media, the one dictum I absorbed from the hard East German years was the media's power to control the masses. The Muscovites at least got that right. Fast changes were enabling a new kind of reach. Cable TV and the Internet opened up an array of programming and communication, threatening the suffocating propaganda that brainwashed my youth. Surely, these new tools could be just as effectively deployed in a more subtle manner. Seduction would need to win over bludgeoning. Regardless of how new media lords snared watchers, we could sense new powers being unleashed and were confident control would lead to riches. And perhaps even some control ourselves.

I was now nearing fifty and labeled an Internet visionary. Funny characterization, given few of my investments were pure Internet. The wave of new technology, though, spilled over into fields as diverse as telephony and biotech alike, accelerating our growth and fueling crazy valuations. We gladly played within the bubble, eyeing dual strategies others could not fathom. Short-term gains and long-term control, even if sinister pursuits, shaped our choices. We had learned the lessons of the past, reaching for too much too soon, exposed on Russian fronts when patience and steady gains would have fulfilled our dreams. My accounting training's conservative roots persuaded us to manage our portfolio prudently, taking profits opportunistically, letting others shoulder the bigger risks. We watched and waited, the patience of methodical life behind the Wall giving us crash-saving perspective. We could afford to lurk, while those who had never experienced a great fall or scrounged for food recklessly bid up the value of software innards no more visible than the air we breathed. We were rich beyond imagination, yet we viewed ourselves as mere trustees, waiting to leverage that wealth for a grander purpose.

My father's greatest remaining concern was charting a path for my nephews, his grandchildren. Neither Florian nor Rolfe had the natural skills to succeed at Mullenboess. Sophie was arguably the ablest; however, aghast at our past, she had rebelled against the family and was cast out of the running early. There would be no compromising — to win, we needed to be the best and blindingly devoted. We could not dilute our skills to create a soft bed for my nearly brothers or deny our values for my almost sister. Something else would have to be found. Florian and Rolfe were both brave, bold to a fault, and could be charming. Unlike me, wary of straying too far from formalities, shackled by the stiff reserve of growing up behind the Wall, Florian and Rolfe had managed to straddle the Wall and were more daring. They could mingle and con in the open. I was better at plotting and executing in secure conference rooms. I was still leery of an eye watching me, peepholes everywhere, carrying out my routine in careful reserve. My nephews had grown up treating it more like a game, acting for the cameras while hiding their true nature.

I suggested that perhaps we employ Florian and Rolfe at one of our media companies. They could become producers, networking to bring us a new set of investors and marks. It was a good idea and would have worked. My father, as usual, had a better plan. He was a connoisseur of films and all the arts. His eyes widened, and I saw him relax, almost unburdened, as he saw a buried dream about to come true. As for Sophie, she wanted nothing from us. In turn, she was simply ignored.

Munich and Bonn, Germany—1997

Our push into the mobile phone market was a perfect example of how we took advantage of gutless competition and seized the future. It began on an ordinary evening, a winter's chill sending shivers that autumn was ending, with few weekends left to huddle and enjoy outdoor cafes. Papa and I had finished dinner with Florian and Rolfe, enjoying the gaiety of the biergarten. A waitress with lustrous blond curls dressed in Bavarian garb, her colorful blouse scooped to reveal barely restrained breasts, splashed down another round of traditional liter steins. My father eyed her and asked, "Would you have been serving those kind before?" looking with a scowl at a black family seated a couple tables away.

"Before?"

"During the War."

"I wasn't born then."

"Still. Would you have?"

"I don't know. I suppose," as she took away empty steins and turned away.

"Idiots. What has happened to this generation?" Dieter sipped his beer, looking down as if to spit before thinking better of sinking to the level of those ingrates. Then he looked over at another table, transfixed. A man had a new cellphone, a relative novelty. He was showing it to

his teenage son, opening it like a wallet. Dieter rose from the table and walked over to them.

Without introducing himself, he looked at the ruddy-faced man and simply inclined his head, beckoning with an entitled air. "May I?" and held out his hand. The man, a bit shocked, handed over the phone to Dieter. He took it in his palm and turned it over. The other man reached over and took it back, opening the flip phone and handing it back to Dieter.

"They call them flip phones. The newest thing."

Dieter opened and closed the phone, running his fingers over the tiny keyboard, examining the antenna and reading the manufacturer's branding and serial number etched into the back. "Danke," nodding his head, handing the phone back before walking over to Florian, Rolfe, and me. In under two minutes, Dieter intuited that flip phones would soon become necessities, a wireless umbilical cord few could do without. "Boys, this is going to be Mullenboess's next investment."

I was not one to question a direct order from my father but was surprised at the speed he moved. The next morning, he called me into his office and grilled me on the mobile market. Wireless phones were mentioned in the news, and we were following developments, but so many changes and opportunities materialized in the post-Wall Germany that cell phones were merely part of the noise. "You have not been looking! You are missing the big picture," he chided, demanding details and a plan within the week.

I set to researching and learned that the GSM standard had been introduced into Europe only a handful of years before. First trialed in Finland, the Finns were becoming leaders in the area, a new upstart Nokia making its mark on broader markets. In Germany, Mobile Deutschland had been launched only the year before. More amazingly, as the government was keen to shift from state-owned enterprises and shed its East German stigma, a zeal existed for privatization. The national telephone carrier, Deutsche Telcom, had been privatized within the previous few years and had just floated one of the largest IPOs in all of Europe. New types of phones, new carriers, new standards were popping up — a renaissance in telephony. I learned names I had never heard of before: Nokia, Motorola, Ericsson. It seemed the Scandinavians and Japanese were first to the game.

When I briefed my father, he perked up and asked me more about Mobile Deutschland. I added, "Mobile Deutschland has its current sales and distribution headquarters in Bonn."

Dieter's eyes danced, and I saw him smile. Broadly. A smile I had not seen in all the years in East Berlin. "Good. Make an appointment. We're going to Bonn. And book a suite at the Hotel Himmelgrun. It was one of my favorite places along the Rhine."

***

I researched the hotel and soon learned of its august and sordid history. An elegant building set sublimely along the river, the 150-year-old hotel had hosted a range of celebrities in the early 20th Century. The likes of Charlie Chaplin, Marlene Dietrich, Max Schmeling, and Kaiser Wilhlem II all graced its rooms. The tone turned much darker in the 1930s: Adolf Hitler apparently first stayed there long before seizing power and then frequented the hotel a rumored hundred times. In fact, he held important summits there, including with the Nazi high command. An important haunt, yet a less well-known retreat than his infamous Berchtesgaden. I found old photos of the hotel bedecked with Nazi banners, large swastikas waving where EU flags now flew. And of course, among its prior guests, was Obersturmbannfuhrer Dieter Mullenhauer. What kind of stars should tourist books give to such a hotel with ignominious guest pictures and reviews no longer displayed?

When we checked into the Himmelgrun, my father took me to a portrait hanging in the lobby of the former proprietor. "A childhood friend of the Fuhrer's," he said proudly. A next-generation member of the family owning the estate came to greet us, fawning over my father. "Herr Mullenhauer, what an honor to have you back," he said. "It has been a long time, no?"

"I was captive in East Berlin for many years. It was…unimaginable. So much is unimaginable."

"I know. We have many…former clients who come. But, you know, times have changed. We all have to change."

"Yes, sadly times have changed. Not the rest. You should be ashamed."

Rocking back and forth nervously, almost clicking his heels to attention, the toady heir manager offered, "May I show you to your suite? We have not kept the Fuhrer's suites…But I have a fine room nearby."

Dieter merely nodded, visually caressing the old portrait before following his bags toward the lift.

In the morning, we feasted on the grand breakfast buffet, seated at a prime corner table against tall windows overlooking the green landscape and flowing river. The tranquil grounds belied the history. The embroidered curtains and long row of double-high windows sweeping toward the current pulsed a yearning and melancholy grandeur. Dieter gazed out deep in thought. I could not grasp what he must be feeling, and for one of the few times in my life was grateful for my near innocence. I devoured my breakfast, taking extra bacon and sausage as a belly diversion.

Soon we were in a taxi to Mobile Deutschland and on arrival quickly ushered into a nondescript conference room. A pretty, young secretary offered us water, staring at my father as if she knew him. Of course, that was impossible, but my father was a striking man, and naturally questions arose about anyone his age, not to mention his lineage and demeanor. I had a chilling feeling looking at the woman, wondering whether my mother was pulled by that same spell. What aura had my father cast bedecked in his uniform at the height of his power?

Two middle-aged gentlemen, well-dressed in suits, came into the conference room. They introduced themselves and handed out business cards: Mattias Dietesmann and Helmut Burger, Managing Director and VP Sales for partnerships.

Dieter took control immediately. "Thank you for meeting. I've never been here but know Bad Godesberg and Bonn well. In fact, it's a pleasure to stay at one of my favorite hotels nearby, the Himmelgrun. I used to frequent the hotel and knew the owners — well back a few years before the Wall and all." The men stared at Dieter, that small introduction saying so much more. He was a Nazi. And obviously, an unrepentant one. They perceptively tensed, and I was sure my father noticed the effect.

"Yes, the Himmelgrun is quite a landmark," Mattias managed to reply. "So, what can we do for you, Mr. Mullenhauer? We understand Mullenboess is a new but quite impressive venture and that you are interested in some of our partners. And Mobile Deutschland of course."

"Mullen now — changed my name when we started the company. Fresh break after East Berlin. And, yes, Mullenboess has been remarkably successful. So many investing opportunities since reunification. We were fortunate to have deep pockets, and a ravenous appetite for new horizons has emerged with so many of us that were stuck in the East. You see, we waited for so long, for so many years. A lot of great wealth just waiting but unable to act. And, now…well, I see incredible potential with phones. I think this is just the beginning for Mobile Deutschland, and I want to own some of the distribution pipeline. I know you need to make deals with the new cell phone manufacturers."

"As I'm sure you know, we are already exploring or have relationships with a number of the top companies," Mattias said, visibly pulling back.

"No doubt. I am not here to deliver Nokia to you."

"I would think not," Helmut joined, the conversation already taking frosty overtones.

"However, there are other emerging players — Motorola, Ericsson, and others. I want the exclusive rights for distribution to the German market for Mobile Deutschland carriage. As you open stores, and people can afford to buy personal cell phones, you will eventually co-brand and carry many models. We can finance that growth."

"We agree. We think the market will grow quickly," Helmut said. "Especially with these new designs, flip-phones as we're calling them. We're making significant bets on the market. But I'm sorry, I don't see where Mullenboess fits in. We can easily reach out to Motorola, for example."

"Let me make you a proposal. One million Deutsche Marks for exclusive rights to Mobile Deutschland carriage for Ericsson and one additional manufacturer to be agreed. That's a lot of money. The market is still new, and you hardly have retail distribution. It needs to be built, and it will take a lot of advertising and time. Oh, and I suggest you accept," Dieter said, pausing for effect. "I don't want this to become unpleasant."

"Excuse me," Mattias said. "Are you threatening me? Us? This meeting was a courtesy, Mr. Mullenhauer. I'm sorry, Mullen. We arranged it because one of our bankers called, apparently after one of your associates contacted them. But that is all. We don't need your money or your assistance."

"Need can be an ambiguous word at times. But let's put that aside. We want this to go through, and so do some friends of ours. Friends who do not take rejection lightly. Friends who had friends at places like the Himmelgrun."

"Those days are long gone, thankfully," Helmut scoffed. "We don't need or want your kind."

Dieter looked over to me, and I opened my briefcase. He nodded, and I passed a report to him which he leafed through quickly then passed over to Mattias. Dieter said, "Here is our formal offer. You'll also note the family tree I have put together for both of you, and lovely photographs of your homes, children, wives. Things are so public nowadays. I was shocked to see those swastikas displayed in your yards. A bit much? Probably not the right image for your current jobs. Would hate for those to be shown to your bosses. Oh, and by the way, the local commandant is a loyal friend, son of one of our old cliques over at the Himmelgrun. So, I'd recommend this conversation stays between us.

But don't get too upset. Anger can lead to violence. Nobody wants that."

Mattias and Helmut looked at Dieter like he was a madman. How in god's name had he planted swastikas to adorn their lawns? And he even had them boxed in against approaching the authorities. Dieter, though, was totally relaxed, even smug. His blue eyes sparkled. Then in a sudden shift, he stared at the corporate functionaries with a ferocious intensity. This was no bluff. Dieter mouthed, "I will murder your children. All of them."

Without waiting for a reaction, Dieter stood up and exited the conference room. He never motioned for me to follow. I simply reacted and scurried after him, nodding to Mattias and Helmut in an effort to appear civil. I did not go too far, though; it was important for them to believe Dieter would follow through on his threats. I forced myself to shrug in an "that's the way it is" manner, disabusing them of any hope this could be ignored. I should not really have been surprised by my father's performance. The Nazis were always bullies, and my Stasi brethren were never fair or much for justifications. Take what you need or must. Victims were left debating risks with tricky odds and dire consequences. Winners and losers. Times had changed, but the essence of the game had not.

Within a month, Mullenboess had the exclusive German distribution rights for two of the key phone manufacturers distributing via Mobile Deutschland. Even though we hardly had a relationship with them, the Mobile Deutschland guys knew how to smooth those other waters. It was all about the incentives and how the message was delivered.

Zug, Switzerland—1999

I had been growing my pot of Krugerrands for ten years since fleeing East Berlin. Beryl, Dirk, and I made a pact that we would hold an annual meeting every year to discuss the returns, hoping we would have an epiphany and know what to do next. We scrapped the sports car lust of our early twenties and quickly came around to Beryl's insistence on acting benevolently. However, we remained stuck in high-minded dreams with too little money and too little time. After a few years, we became frustrated and vowed to approach our goals more seriously. We changed the venue from a bar to a dinner party and finally to an upscale restaurant. But 1999 would be different. I called a formal board meeting for our tenth year and summoned Dirk to our lake house in Zug.

Beryl and I were living in Zurich, Switzerland. The move was inevitable. On the cusp of turning thirty, it was time to take serious steps. I was a partner at SZG and was the manager of its Swiss operations. I was ridiculously young for such a post and was the envy of my peers, both within SZG and other upstarts within the broader banking community. I was atop the leading 30 under 30 bankers' chart, a coveted ranking on a widely known yet unpublished list. I had become co-head of our insurance finance group—thanks to Beryl's tutelage and a now highly honed skill of how to undercut the value of fine art when needed—and had most recently moved into managing valuations for private equity groups. It seemed there was an enormous market for private valuations.

My job was to figure out what a piece of property or art or whatever was worth. If it was to be used as collateral for a loan, it needed a valuation. The valuation could further be complicated by its liquidity. A painting could take longer to sell than a prime piece of real estate, for instance. It sounded boring but was quite useful for businesses considering mergers and acquisitions, banks making loans, insurance companies underwriting policies, and so on. Boring, but quite profitable stuff, especially coupled with a division setting complex ratios to benchmark values. Few understood the underlying math comprising a matrix that factored in the valuation and liquidity risks. Bottom line, the practice and methodology were ideally complementary to the wealth management and investment banking sides of SZG.

If people or businesses wanted to buy, borrow, loan, or just value something, we could handle the transaction. Following my valuation of *Moonlit Fields*, I started a habit of denominating transactions in dollars; it kept things simpler than always converting currencies and had the further ease of tracking common financial industry practices. Minimum deals were at least $5 million, which we called minnows, and a decent deal was tens of millions, which we referred to as fish. I was already a millionaire at age twenty-nine and had my sights on whales. In truth, I was worth a few million counting real estate (helped by my trust fund which kicked in at twenty-five). My problem—if fair to label it that way—was I lagged significantly behind my goal of a million dollars for every year. I would need to move fast to catch up. Guess I still had a bit of that asshole streak, which I needed to work on. I gave myself a pat on the back for at least being aware.

While work had been manic—and profitable—living in Zurich was an issue for Beryl. Zurich was not an art hub, and Moultens & Barings did not have a local office, that is until we moved. Beryl became the office. She commuted a couple times a week to their Basel office and, taking advantage of the location, schmoozed her way onto the board of Art Basel. Ms. Jaffe (she refused to take my name, which was fine with me) was the youngest board member of Art Basel and on their planning committee. I guess it was some consolation for the commute and exile from the daily London art scene.

I reflected on the path of our lives, sitting in the first-class compartment of the train speeding from Zurich to Zug. I liked to spend as many weekends there as possible. In the winter, uncrowded ski slopes were within an hour's drive, and in the summer, we retired to our small villa on Lake Zug, or Zugersee. We had a twenty-five-meter wooden pier, at the end of which I kept a small speedboat for tooling around the lake. Zug is a gem, the historic village nestled against the lake's shore quintessentially Swiss. The mountains beyond are scenic but not large enough to attract busloads of tourists seeking a Thomas Cook Switzerland experience—or those snooping from former East Germany. Uzi cautioned us to keep a low profile, and just in case someone chose to delve into our past adventures, I registered the property under the name of a trust. Paranoia aside, Beryl and I appreciated the privacy. What we forfeited from the grandeur of Lugano or pomp of Geneva, we gained from the relative lack of tourists. Who went to Zug?

Even people looking for a lake less crowded than what Zurich boasted tended to head toward Germany and enjoy the Bodensee. Zug was our secret, which I planned to keep. I certainly was not about to spread word that I could drive to Lucerne for lunch. Amazingly, the sleepy town had long boasted branches of all the major banks. Even more discreetly, Zug hosted legions of private banks and wealth management companies, the types of institutions whose clients had such vast resources that these select banks and firms could survive opening a branch to service a single client. For those who hid money in Swiss banks, even better to burrow that wealth in a rich town like Zug. The per capita income was a gazillion per year, which I hoped to increase.

As the train exited a tunnel and barreled into the sunlight, I turned to Beryl to discuss our upcoming board meeting. "Don't you think we should expand the board now?"

"Beyond Dirk and Jens?"

"Yes, you know how we always talked about bringing in Bryan and Hamid. They should have been there."

"But they weren't. I think it's too dangerous, raises too many questions."

"I know. It was just so hard when we had to lie to their faces. Remember we eventually broke down and told them I won all those Krugerrands in a poker game. Stupid. But at least they have no idea what really happened."

"It's still too easy to slip. That was stupid to say anything, and glad it stopped there. Training teaches keep a tight circle."

"Training?" I asked skeptically.

"Yes, training. And good fieldwork. And common sense. Why take the risk? Because it would be soul unburdening to talk about it with someone else? Because after all this time, you think we're free, statute of limitations expiring soon? Do you remember how we titled the deed to the lake house?"

"Come on."

"Wake me up when we arrive," Beryl dismissed the argument. "I never like this distance. Fifty minutes is too long to be nearby and too short to nap. Maybe we should have bought a place on Lake Como."

"Near my parents?"

"It was an example of distance. Only. Wake me up when we pull in."

***

Lucerne, Switzerland and Tenth Board Meeting—1999
Deciding at the last minute to splurge for the milestone of our tenth anniversary board meeting, we shifted locations and booked a suite at the Park Hotel on the shores of Lake Lucerne. The gold-braided wallpaper framed the floor-to-ceiling windows overlooking the lake. I could even spy a castle in the mountains beyond. Picture a perfect setting, and this was better. A waiter in tails brought us champagne, and we started the festivities with a toast.

Despite my suggestion, our club was limited to four, meaning just our lawyer and Dirk joining. Although I had set up the trust with my father's lawyer, I had ditched him for a discreet attorney known for handling Zug's quietest accounts. Jens was polite, intelligent, and forgettable looking. His strength lay in his ability to blend in and disappear. I had vetted him via two of the oldest banks in Zug and was confident his mouth was so sealed he could be medically certified as mute. Just in case, I paid him well and accidentally let ties to the Mossad slip. Carrot and stick, some call it.

We spoke to Dirk periodically for a check-in. Board meetings were supposed to be in person, and while we met once or twice by phone, all of us pledged to take the meetings seriously. We agreed to meet face-to-face on key anniversaries and when anything material arose.

Before the meeting, Beryl and I had drinks with Dirk and his new wife, Pavlina, in the hotel bar. Dirk told us how they had met when both studying at Charles University's law school in Prague, one of the oldest institutions in Europe. When Dirk had finished his law degree, coupled with an international relations master's, he begged his father to find him a local job. At the time, I filed it down as an odd choice. That was until I met Pavlina. Hard to beat the beauty of Prague—the town and the women. No doubt Dirk convinced his dad, Ambassador van Dijksen, to pull a string or two; a simple task for someone who had managed the GDR at the height of the Cold War. He probably had a lifetime of favors accruing with the dirt he otherwise pledged to keep secret. Securing Dirk a spot in the Dutch foreign service should have been a given once he was willing to pick up the phone.

"So, I was shocked when Dad phoned and told me he had landed me a consular position…in Budapest. Budapest! Can you believe it? The whole favor was supposed to be so we could be together in Prague."

"What went wrong?" I asked.

"I don't know. Maybe random. I'd been in Czechoslovakia, at Charles, when the Wall fell, and then lived through the whole domino effect. I was there during the separation, the formation of the Czech Republic and Slovakia. And I suppose I had insights into Germany too, given my dad's role and traveling there with him."

"If they only knew the truth and that you'd seen the dirty side of the East."

"Yeah, then I could name my ticket. Accidentally, I'm probably one of the few people with direct experience witnessing a reunification, having also been on the other side of the Wall, as well as a split. Anyway, I think the guys in the foreign service figured I had insights into Eastern Europe, and to them there's not much difference between Prague and Budapest. Snobs. And there was an opening."

"Well, it's not far, and I hear it's a nice place. What's the harm in living there a couple of years? Should be fun."

"What are you guys complaining about?" Beryl cut in. "Sounds like things are working out brilliantly for Pavlina." Turning to her, she said, "I heard you just got a great new job. Tell us about it."

"Yes," flashing her ice-blue eyes, she said, "Just started."

It was a good thing Beryl was now leading the conversation as I had trouble focusing in Pavlina's ambit. I doubted any man could resist her shock of blond hair and cartoon-character-high Slavic cheekbones. I knew her well yet still babbled when she looked me in the eye. And she was tall—not as tall as giant-height Dirk but still not far off from my eye level.

"Tell us about it. I'm sorry, I should have sent you something when you graduated from law school," Beryl said, either oblivious to the spell Pavlina was casting or coming to my rescue. Probably best not to ask for clarification.

"Oh, please. Buy me a drink when I survive my first year working with all these arrogant men!"

"Marco told me something about the firm and that you're the only woman in that office. Is that right?"

"Yes. It's a large American law firm, and they have expanded into Eastern Europe. It took a few years after the Wall came down for businesses to really believe, but now things are booming. Seems like there are growing opportunities everywhere, and they've just opened a new Budapest branch. I think the fact I speak seven languages got me the job. Budapest is going to be a bit of a hub for the region."

"Seven languages? Wow. I didn't realize that. I always heard Slavs were the best linguists," Beryl said, with a tinge of jealousy I rarely heard. "Fluently?"

"Well, yes, I guess so," Pavlina said, not flaunting her prowess.

"When we went to your wedding, I knew Dirk had met his match. But now I see he's outmatched!"

Pavlina lifted her glass in a toast to girl-talk victory. "And from what I've seen, you've bested Marco! To us!"

Shit. That was all I needed, Beryl becoming chums with Pavlina and talking about Dirk and me behind our backs. Then I had a true flash of panic as I saw Beryl cozying up and giggling with the Slavic goddess. Beryl wanted to recruit her! What man could resist her wiles? Certainly not me. Seven languages, diplomatic spouse cover. Almost too good to be true. If Beryl was not already pandering and plotting to recruit her as a Mossad compatriot, the thought could not be far from maturing.

Had I inadvertently opened the door when cavorting with Beryl at their wedding last year in Karlovy Vary? Pavlina's parents owned one of the world-famous spas and treated us to Bohemia's best. Heavy drinking, steam rooms filled with naked blond bodies, romantic medieval town with arched promenades—*we should return to the hot springs for a future board meeting*, I thought. Could I write off the decadence of lingering in a co-ed spa on my tax returns? Good thing I moved on to business before my mind wandered further.

I motioned that we move to the conference room, Pavlina politely excusing herself, not being a member of the fund's inner circle. I wondered if Beryl would support keeping it that way or if she might think bringing her closer could bear compromising fruit. I decided to keep my distance from both of them. I grabbed Dirk's arm, not-so-gently steering him out of the bar to a private room overlooking the lake. It was time to start the board meeting.

I began, "Dirk, I have some great news. I have managed to turn our little fund into $35 million. I'm also confident I can spin this into over $50 million within a couple more years."

"My God! That's a multiple of when we last met. Are you kidding?"

"Have you ever known me to kid about money?"

"Lots of other things, but never that. Amazing. How'd you manage that type of return?"

"We'll get to that. Some smart moves, some luck, some connections. A bit of the usual stuff...," I said, trying to appear modest in front of Beryl and knowing I was simply better than most at investing. I did not emphasize that I piggybacked many of these investments on my SZG trades, nor confessed I may have had some tips on the direction winds were blowing from time to time.

"Wow," Dirk said quietly through his breath. "I think this is big enough we should finally give it a name."

"A name?"

"Yes, a name. We always refer to it as our little German account. But now that we have real money and should be ready to start talking about what to do with it, I think we should have a proper name."

"Like what?" Beryl asked, skeptical and slightly mocking. "Jungleland Fund, Springsteen Partners? Berliner Heister?"

"Funny. I was thinking more along the lines of a reference to Krugerrands. But, more subtle."

"Sounds like you already have a suggestion."

"I do. How about Krumarkt Fund? Combines Krugerrands and a nod to the German Deutsche Mark and even sounds a little Dutch. Come on, let's enjoy this a little."

Clearly, Dirk had thought about this a lot. Beryl looked over at me. "Sounds good to me. I don't care—I think we have bigger priorities."

"I don't care either," I concurred. "It's only among us. As long as the name doesn't tip off anyone. Maybe we should at least make it partners. How about Krumarkt Partners Fund?"

Nods all around.

We invited Jens to join us, and after an hour of reviewing the books, he left, and the three of us sat down for lunch. Pavlina was back in her suite making some business calls and would join us for dinner. Despite fully trusting Jens, the delicate nature of our newly named Krumarkt Partners Fund's roots was for the triumvirate's ears only. Who knew where conversations could turn, and we relished a bit of privacy.

We kept to our pledge to found a trust for Holocaust survivors. With our initial pot of gold already spinning threads into so much money, we could genuinely make a difference. Despite the temptation to start allocating gifts, I argued for patience. If I could keep doubling money every five years, we could reach well over $100 million by our twentieth anniversary. I even set the gaudy target of eventually surpassing $500 million. We should think about enough money to create a recognized global trust, akin to a university endowment fund. The charitable trust should endure for generations. We would earn our redemption, and Beryl's vision could come to fruition.

Self-congratulations mixes brilliantly with carpaccio and crème brûlée. We toasted and slapped virtual pats on the back for the better part of an hour before Dirk brought up a shocking subject.

"Hey, Beryl, I got wind of something the other day I thought might interest you. We have a meeting of the East European group every month to compare notes. Hungary, Czech Republic, Slovenia, Slovakia, Romania, Albania, Croatia, and Germany. I know, Germany doesn't really fit, but given the history with the East, there are still a lot of rogue groups. It will take a generation for certain parts of the old East Germany to catch up. Anyway, most of their economies are behind, and there are a lot of criminal gangs that work across the region. You'd be amazed. Marco, do you remember when your Mercedes was stolen in London?"

"Of course."

"Did they ever find it?"

"No. The police said it was probably long gone."

"Well, I'll bet it was driven somewhere in Eastern Europe. These gangs strip down the parts. Everything is sold and used. By the time it's done, it's like a fish stripped down to its skeleton. Usually, once a car is stolen, it's gone within thirty-six hours, stripped within seventy-two. Almost impossible to trace."

Interrupting, Beryl asked, "And you thought this would interest me? Why?"

"I'm getting to it."

"You diplomats love to talk, don't you?" She smiled, digging back into dessert.

"Okay, I'll cut to the chase. In our last meeting, we were talking about some of these gangs and how they were diversifying and becoming more sophisticated. We've always been concerned about drugs, cars, and especially human trafficking. Then one of my colleagues started talking about art."

This got Beryl's attention and mine too. We both put down our spoons and listened more carefully.

"Seems there's a big market in fencing stolen art. Some of these gangs hide the pieces and then work as middlemen shipping them to buyers all over the world. Mideast and Asia are becoming bigger buyers. Proof of making it in the world or something. I don't really get it."

I thought back to the van Gogh and how that helped accelerate my career—and Beryl's. I wondered if there could be a connection, if the thieves had driven the painting from the Koningshaus to Croatia or Albania, stashed it in a farmhouse, and sold it to a rich tycoon in Hong Kong. The police had focused on where it might have ended up, not a network of go-betweens. It could be possible.

"Did we ever tell you about this project we worked on years ago involving a stolen van Gogh? I was assigned to one of our insurance divisions. I hired Beryl and Moultons because my boss at the time needed a valuation."

"Of course. I remember it well because you were able to throw Beryl that work. And then it turned out to be the gift that kept giving."

Beryl gave me a nasty look, not keen on the suggestion of having been thrown work rather than deserving it. I quickly continued the conversation, diverting from the affront. "Not quite how I would characterize things," making apologetic eye contact with the person I hoped would remain my wife, then continued, "Do you think it's possible that painting was taken to Eastern Europe? Then maybe sold from there?"

"Sure, it's possible. I don't know if they were into this sort of thing a few years ago. But if it happened today, that's one of the first places you'd want to look."

"Hmm," I mumbled. "Interesting. You know, they never recovered that painting. *Moonlit Fields* it was called." I thought of poor Mr. de Vries and wondered if the litigation was still ongoing. Probably. Those cases could drag on forever. No worry of mine, though; I had long since spent my bonus.

"That is interesting." Beryl now joined, slight forgiven. "I've heard rumors of gangs fencing art. Luckily, not many of the museums I've consulted for have lost a major piece. It's been a while since I was brought into one of those investigations."

"Well, the next part of the story is more interesting. My colleague got a tip that one of these networks was fencing stolen art, but the pieces were not taken from a museum. It seems a few pieces surfacing haven't been on the market for decades. Pieces that disappeared as long ago as World War II. They think some of these old pieces could even be art stolen by the Nazis. And now somebody is offering them for sale."

"Jesus." There it was. Old habits die hard.

"What?" Beryl said. "Are you saying someone discovered or hid pieces of art for fifty years and is now selling them on the black market?"

"That's exactly what I'm saying."

"And what makes you think they're tied to the war or even stolen Nazi art?"

"I don't. That's just the rumor we picked up. Maybe the bad guys were a bit squeamish in trafficking the stuff, so they started chatting."

Beryl spent the next several minutes grilling Dirk on the details. I wasn't sure if she was fascinated, interested because of her art training, or disturbed by this theory. More likely, her Mossad tentacles were roused. Nazi trails resurfacing years later had a way of kicking the agency into motion. The Nuremberg trials, conducted by the allies after World War II and convicting many notorious Third Reich leaders, had become a piece of history. As the three of us knew too well, however, there were hundreds, maybe thousands, of other Nazi officials and officers who had slipped away. Maybe there was a link. Maybe not. By the end of lunch, it became clear my wife wanted to figure out what was happening, and Dirk agreed to introduce her to the team leading the trafficking investigations. It seemed current efforts in recruiting Pavlina would need to be deferred in favor of more interesting prospects.

***

Well, maybe not. Beryl knew a great find when she saw one and, like any well-trained operative, seized the moment. The speed was the inverse of litigation, Pavlina onboard before I filed my expense account from my latest Hong Kong jaunt. I didn't know more about the recruitment or whether Pavlina went to Israel for any kind of training but guessed my lack of knowledge was exactly how it was meant to be. I would not have been surprised to learn that Beryl soon took advantage of my next time jetting away at thirty thousand feet to fly Pavlina to London for the day to hatch her latest plot.

***

London, England — 1999

"Pavlina, you look wonderful," Beryl hugged her as they sat in a conference room in Mayfair, the London headquarters of Moulton & Barings. "How's the law firm?"

"Fine — and gives me good cover to pop over here. I arranged a meeting this afternoon over in the city."

"Perfect. I may need you to come back a bit more often. There's something in Soho I want to talk to you about."

"Really? Couldn't you have just given me a ring? You don't mean going over to Soho now?"

"No, nothing today. And this is too sensitive for a call. By the way, this room's secure. I told the firm, with the value of paintings we handle, we could be a target. What if someone penetrated our files, our valuations? They thought I was crazy at first, but I managed to scare them. Then I had our friends in Tel Aviv bug the place. We sweep it weekly."

"My God, Beryl."

"Well, what did you think you were getting into? You've now gone through your crash course in Israel."

"I know, I know. It's just all surreal. Never thought I'd be an agent for the Israeli government. And I've never been on an assignment, you know."

"I know. And that's why you're here. I've got something for you."

Pavlina tugged inadvertently at her sweater. She was still a novice, unable to cloak her emotions with Beryl's ease. Beryl noticed but did not chide her. The seven- language-speaking beauty needed to gain confidence. It would come.

"I'm going to set up an off-the-books arm of Moultens. We're 100% up and up, trusted by the elite. But we're valuers, appraisers, consultants. We don't sell anything. What I'm going to do is set up a subsidiary in Soho, known to only a few select people, that can help broker or source pieces for extremely high-end clientele for private transactions. You want to buy a Picasso that doesn't pass through auction, or someone wants to quietly unload a piece for a few million. That type of thing."

"Does that really happen?"

"Yeah, unusual, and most of the time it's on the black market, but there's nothing wrong with it in theory. Think of it like million-dollar garage sales."

"I wish! Will Moultens actually handle this?"

"Technically yes, but in reality, no. This is fully a Mossad op. Because I'm in charge of some of the admin here, I can sign papers, and we have lots of legal entities. I'm sure you're used to that. I may even have you look them over."

Pavlina chuckled. "No problem. I've never seen any shady books in Eastern Europe. Remember, exposing all that corruption and networks stretching to the Mideast is how you hooked me."

Beryl gave Pavlina a warm smile, ignoring the history. Recruiting agents was not something she liked to reflect upon;

theirs was a dangerous business and recruiting involved no less perfect information than the field. "So, I create a subsidiary, have it do something innocuous, maybe say we need to hold pending insurance settlements in a separate entity. Then we use that company to explore our little garage sales. And I'm making you the president."

"Thanks for the promotion, I think."

"Well, it's not really you. We need an alias. Here's the cover," Beryl said, sliding over a file including a passport, driver's license, and several other papers. "I'll need you to sign where the tabs are marked. You'll have to practice a signature."

"Ingrid Greggory?"

"Have a better name?"

"No, I guess it's fine. I just never pictured myself an Ingrid. And what will I do?"

"For now, nothing, but I suspect you'll be able to speak to any European buyers in their native languages, plus pass for a public-school-educated Brit. And with your looks and charm, they won't dig too deep if meeting you in person."

"A bit sexist, isn't it?"

"Tis the game, isn't it?"

Pavlina lifted her Perrier bottle in a mock toast. The two women could easily have been models yet had chosen to leverage their considerable assets in different ways.

"So, what's this Soho dealership called?"

"The simpler, the better. SohoMasters."

"I like it."

"I hope our new clients will too." Beryl smiled, happy with her new recruit. "Oh, and we may have Ingrid's first intriguing assignment. Ever been to the Emirates?"

CHAPTER 8

Munich, Germany—1999

When my half-brother Gunther died, my father had asked me to take responsibility for watching over Florian and Rolfe. He was not averse to my keeping an eye on Sophie, but we both recognized she craved distance more than help. At Mullenboess, he left me in charge of investments, which were continuing to flourish. Mullenboess, though, was only part of the plan. My father wanted to diversify and had hinted at an incredible secret back when we set up the company: he owned an extensive art collection.

That disclosure of owning valuable paintings disturbed me at first, for I had thought I was fully in his confidence. Since then, I had only heard about his collection in passing. In retrospect, I should not have been surprised, for my tentacles were raised when we visited the Alte Pinakothek and he wandered off with Uncle Karl after the Wall's fall. My Stasi instincts had kicked in, but there were puzzle pieces missing that I would need to wait for him to reveal. My only other clue was that my father had given each of Florian and Rolfe a masterpiece, instructing them not to talk about the works publicly. If a visitor ever inquired, they were only to mention the paintings were family heirlooms entrusted to this generation before passing with their histories to the next. When I pushed for more details, he merely told me this was a prized secret, offhandedly repeating that his wife, Ute, had inherited a collection from her parents before she died in the war. She encouraged my father to become a collector, his position as an officer giving him privileged access — to the victor go the spoils. I felt he was not entirely forthcoming, perhaps embarrassed that he had not given me, the bastard son and no relation to Ute, a painting too. Instead, and honestly much to my preference, he had made me a partner in Mullenboess.

I might never know the whole truth and suspected much of his description may have been a lie. Was the deceit to protect me or something else? Was I being paranoid, jealous of the bond between his only wife and their legitimate son and grandsons? It remained an awkward subject, and I learned not to ask more about the provenance. For years, all he divulged was that the paintings he sold to seed Mullenboess Ventures were but a small part of the collection and that before the Wall fell, he had sold a painting or two on the black market. Those sales, I learned, had been the source of a vault full of Krugerrands.

The reason my father brought up the collection after all those years was that he wanted me to help Florian and Rolfe set up a gallery. He would give them a few paintings for the showroom, providing instant credibility. I was to source other works, adding depth. It seemed it would be problematic to display the whole of my father's collection in the gallery. Several of my father's paintings were of museum quality, and it might dilute values and even raise suspicion to have too many of them in one place.

His goal was for Florian and Rolfe to establish themselves in the fine arts world. They were natural salesmen, charismatic pitchmen, who would enjoy the museum and auction circuit. Once they built the business and began networking, we would then find partners to facilitate quieter sales. My father was not in a hurry. I sensed, though, there was more to the plan, a hidden purpose. Until then, content in my role growing Mullenboess, I dutifully accepted my father's scheme to help his grandchildren launch a business where their talents appeared better suited. It was not in my nature to contradict his plans *for these nephews cum stepbrothers of mine. My role was to help shepherd the furtive movement of paintings. Harkening back to my Stasi training, I could help educate my nephews in ways to cultivate buyers who wished to peruse the private side of collections. My father was only interested in wealthy buyers, the kind who would want to keep their purchases anonymous, the select group who needed to brag and deal with only one another. There were also lessons to be applied in how to document transactions and transfer large sums of money — quiet transfers to discreet accounts I had set up with my new partners in Liechtenstein and Monaco. Before these sales, though, Florian and Rolfe must be patient — learn the business, gain credibility, become known in the right circles.*

***

Tel Aviv and Caesarea, Israel — 2000

Unlike the CIA, often referred to as "the agency," or British intelligence whose arms MI5 & MI6 went by their directorate names and numbers, the Mossad didn't have a universal nickname. Perhaps that was because Mossad was already an abbreviation, the State of Israel's Institute for Intelligence and Special Operations' Hebrew name being *HaMossad leModi'in uleTafkidim Meyuḥadim.* As depicted in movies and spy novels alike, the Mossad, like most businesses in Israel, practiced rather informal office decorum.

I could picture Uzi reclining in a chair, wearing jeans and a polo shirt, smoking a strong narrow-rolled cigarette. Others may have remarked he looked relaxed, but I always bristled with near x-ray vision when with him, sensing the ready tension coiling beneath his surface. Perhaps he let his guard down around family, or maybe I imagined things that were not there. No, he was Mossad, and the man who cultivated a professorial air was quietly and perpetually processing every element in his orbit.

From Beryl's description of meeting with her dad, I felt I was sitting in the Mossad's headquarters, hanging on every word of conversations I would only later be formally read into. In an ode to normalcy, Uzi's office overflowed with family photographs, an occasional still of him with a prime minister or ambassador mixed in haphazardly. He kept pictures of his three daughters on his desk, along with one including his wife Anna smiling serenely. In private, Uzi loved to talk about his family, but as I learned from Beryl, being part of the Jaffe clan was complicated.

Reena was the oldest, happily married with two kids and living with her husband in Caesarea. They were both doctors— Ari an ophthalmologist and Reena a pediatrician. They chose careers that rarely summoned them to the hospital for emergencies. Israel and the Jewish people had enough of those. Having grown up in a Mossad family, Reena wanted a quieter life, far from plotting and intrigue. Uzi never spoke of details— operationally, he could not—but the three girls felt his anxiety, a telepathic bond that can only link with another family member. Sometimes he would be gone for a week, returning with a sad, glassy stare. They could only imagine what he had done or seen. Reena never wanted to and instead imagined her father was a battlefield medic, called for heroic duty, and shattered coming home after watching firsthand the horrors of war. In truth, her dreamworld was not too far from reality. Uzi was too often witnessing the effects of shrapnel.

Maybe it was her fantasies born of denial that led Reena to become a doctor. She had always wanted to help people and loved children. Israel was only bearing its second generation of natives, and she wanted to help care for and usher in its third and many more. Caesarea was a seaside town on the way to Haifa from Tel Aviv, an American-style windy suburb dotted with tiled roofs and manicured lawns. Parts of the neighborhood looked transplanted from Orange County, California. Fruit trees dotted the land with the ocean nearby. From the right angle, driving up a gated driveway, it was hard to see the difference. The fact that King Herod had built the port and tourists could visit a near perfectly preserved Roman amphitheater served to distinguish this was no Newport Beach. And Reena was far from an Orange County housewife. Raising kids and being a doctor left little time for backstabbing prettier neighbors.

Beryl later told me that Uzi admitted to losing track of time staring at the photos of his three girls while waiting for her to arrive. There was something about their upcoming meeting with his boss that was particularly unnerving. Likely, he could not get thoughts of Germany and East Berlin out of his head.

***

Reena was excited. Tonight would be a family reunion, baby sister Beryl in town. Too bad Marco was not coming, Reena thought—business again in another far off place. What was it with so many men today? They were always on a plane, too exhausted with jetlag to help with the kids when home. Reena smiled contentedly at the small radius of life she staked out. She was lucky to have Ari persistently nearby.

They would be going to a concert tonight at the Roman amphitheater, some famous Russian violinist whose name she could not remember. The Romans knew how to build. Two thousand years old, and the crowd still entered through original arches and sat in tiered rows. Stadium seating before it was in vogue. In the distance, the Mediterranean waves gently washed to the shore, just far enough away not to spoil the acoustics from the array of modern speakers. Most brought their own cushions rather than courting a literal pain in the ass by sitting on the ancient stone for two hours. The archaeologists objected to the crowds, complaining that they were jeopardizing ongoing discoveries. The mayor shot back that if they had not dug it up in the last two thousand years, good luck; moreover, a weekly concert only allowing people into the area where tourists visited daily added little wear and tear. The amphitheater was built for productions, for Christ's sake. Perhaps Jesus even visited and approved of the acoustics and vista beyond to the sea. If that was not enough, then revenues from the gate, funding their sloth-speed trowel picking, should shut them up. For Christ's sake!

That night's performance should be magical, a warm evening under the stars, the haunting reach of the violin echoing between the stones and sea. It would be perfect—except for missing Hannah. Their middle sister had died a few years before in a skirmish on the Lebanese border. All Israeli women served in the military. No exceptions for daughters of Mossad operatives. In truth, they were usually more eager to enlist. Reena missed her every day, as did Beryl. Hannah was the strawberry blond beauty, the only one of the three without raven black hair. She had wanted to go into the military for a career, fiercely patriotic and keen to devote her life to protecting the state. She never made it past basic duty, her draft service after high school.

At least she didn't leave kids, Reena thought, looking at her little girl, fearing Hannah's career could have given birth to orphans. It was a horrible thought. Growing up surrounded by enemies and with a father in the Mossad left Reena deeply scarred. Paranoid fears of death plagued her. Living by the sea, helping mothers with their kids, was her escape. She did not understand how baby Beryl was so untouched and had gone into the family business. Perhaps it was the years in the Netherlands. Reena had already graduated and never lived in The Hague, experiencing carefree European life.

***

While Reena thought about Hannah and what could have been, Beryl was driving with her mom Anna from Caesarea to Tel Aviv. They were going shopping—a bit of rare girl time—then having lunch before Beryl had a meeting with Uzi in the afternoon.

"How's Marco," Anna asked casually, interested as a mother but not prying. At least not immediately.

"He's great. He's doing amazingly well at work."

"Always work with the two of you."

"We're in the prime of building our careers. And, honestly, Marco's years ahead of where he predicted he'd be."

"I know. I'm very proud of both of you…But, you're not worried about his being away so much? I mean traveling all over the world."

"Well, I'm away a lot too."

"But you're not a rich Italian stud alone for days on a different continent."

"Come on, Mom. You don't think guys are hitting on me? I'm not a bad catch either. You've got to trust us. Marco's not having affairs. He'd be too scared! You do know Dad's line of business?"

"All right. Sorry I implied anything. I just imagined women all over him. So, tell me more about your job, why you're here visiting. Ever going to tell me what you really do? I know you're not meeting your father at work to catch up and have a coffee."

"Mom, you know I can't talk about that. And I'm a partner at Moultens & Barings. I have one of the most prestigious jobs in the entire art world. That's pretty full-time. Do you think I have much time for anything else, to get involved with Dad's adventures? When I'm in town, they ask me about some things…It isn't always the good guys that can afford a Picasso. Oil money buys a lot of trophies, and they want to keep a close eye around the Gulf. And on occasion, I hear things. That's all," she said, hoping the half-truths would suffice. She hated lying to her mother.

"Okay, no more grilling. I'm very proud whenever I read about Art Basel."

Beryl smiled, no sin in being proud of her accomplishments no matter what local texts — like the Bible — may preach. "Where should we go?"

"That's up to you. You're the visitor."

"How about something more exotic, not the fancy shops."

"My specialty."

"I know."

"Let's go to the old port by Jaffa. We can park near the beach, or closer to the clock tower, and walk around. We could go to the flea market, find some boutiques."

"Perfect. I'd love to buy some scarves. I love all that Moroccan stuff you wear."

Beryl admired her mother's taste and sense of style, such as taking a simple cotton blouse and accenting it with an Arabic mosaic scarf. Anna glided past shops in a way that made boutique-window mannequins want to turn, exuding casual elegance, absent the pretense of Swiss or London couture. Beryl was always conscious of blending in. Being part of the art world, she was expected to display a measure of sophistication yet was careful not to be the trendsetter. Perhaps that was her Mossad family background — observe and disappear in the crowd. Balancing these imperatives was challenging, especially as a woman. Men had it much easier. Her dad's standard jeans and a sweater or blazer allowed him to wander inconspicuously through most circles. People were not judging his shoes or jewelry. Nor were potential clients apt to study the stitching on his jacket a little too closely, peering to confirm whether the coat was indeed from an overpriced designer's latest collection or merely a knock-off.

When they arrived, Beryl linked her arm with her mother's, that easy sway of her walk mirrored in her mother's gait. They detoured up the hill into the old town, the fortress ramparts beaten by centuries of sandals. Tel Aviv's famous beaches stretched to the horizon below them to the north. The city's high rises and international hotels, lining the strip, loomed as a reminder of the modern state, steel and glass triumphs over desert warfare. Tel Aviv always leaned toward the future. They paused for a coffee, sitting next to a lemon tree, listing to the hive of languages. Beryl rested her head on her mother's shoulder, closing her eyes briefly. She inhaled the sea air and smells of lamb and coriander wafting from a nearby shawarma stand. Eventually, they moved, subconsciously keeping track of the time.

Mother and daughter, gabbing and silent, paced by genetically linked biorhythms, continued their arms-linked meandering. They eventually came to the flea market. Mixed stalls of clothes, leather goods, and gadgets crowded together in haphazard spacing came alive. It was impossible to predict from stand to stand whether they would be pulled in by a friendly tug or sometimes given the evil eye. Jaffa, predominantly an Arabic neighborhood, was frequented by all. In the flea market alone, one felt the warmth and suspicion of modern Israel ebbing and flowing, like the shawls blowing from the wind testing the makeshift racks. Beryl bought a rust-painted scarf, immediately tying it about her neck and covering her hair. The small accessory transformed her appearance entirely. She was now a young woman of indeterminate background, draped in cultural ambiguity. She clung to her mother, walking back to the car, adrift from responsibility.

***

Unfortunately, wedged between regressive womb snuggling and an ethereal concert next to her sister in the ancient amphitheater of Caesarea was the real reason for Beryl's trip. They needed to hurry for her to make it to Uzi's offices. While informal in appearance, the Mossad nevertheless tended to be a punctual group.

A half-hour later, Beryl, new scarf folded neatly in her purse, sat in a conference room with her father and three other men. She had met David and Moshe before, veterans of the office. Both men were somewhat nondescript, fortunate characteristics — or rather lack thereof — for their roles. Beryl barely remembered Moshe, though smiled seeing David Wolfe, a man she privately thought of as "the scientist" given his unruly hair and tendency to drift off into thought. In contrast, Noah, the third man, bore the vivid marks of war pulling and pushing all over his face. A veritable exhibition map of military service, his right charcoal-black glass eye never moved, an unnerving feature next to his brown left eye and the crooked scar pointing to an elfish-reconstructed right ear. Whether his survivor-encrusted face had anything to do with it, Noah seemed to be in charge and was introduced with some title inferring jurisdiction over enemy financial crimes investigations. After introductions, Uzi nudged them toward the danger.

"Beryl, tell us what you know."

"Honestly, not that much, but I have concerns. That's why I wanted to come and talk to you in person. You all know my background."

"Yes, you've been quite helpful," Noah said. "That tip from Pavlina on one of the Saudi Prince's spending sprees was very interesting. He wasn't on our radar before. It seems he may be funding some unpleasant folks when he isn't decorating his yachts with French impressionists. Guess SohoMasters and sending Pavlina to meet him at that party in Dubai is proving worth the investment." Noah paused, a genuinely warm smile encouraging her to continue with today's nuggets. "What do you have for us?"

"We may have stumbled upon a group suspected of fencing stolen art. But not your typical pieces. Artwork that hasn't been seen since World War II. Artwork stolen by Nazis. Honestly, we had heard rumors of such things but didn't know if they were real. Being roundabout in the business of off-the-book sales, and hearing rumors, was part of the reason we set up SohoMasters in the first place. I just never imagined hearing something like this."

Uzi had been briefed in advance and watched his colleagues' eyes, at least Noah's good eye. They were all veterans and had seen their share of plots and missions, yet they could not hide their piqued interest. Noah and Moshe visibly shifted in their seats.

"There's more," she continued. "I have suspicions that some of the activity is being orchestrated by family members of those Nazis. Pieces that have been hidden in their family for years." She paused, letting the implications linger.

"You're suggesting that pieces of art, hidden for nearly fifty years, are now being sold by the sons and daughters of former Nazis? And that these pieces were stolen from Jews in the war?" Moshe asked.

"That's exactly what I'm suggesting. And not just sons and daughters, maybe also granddaughters and grandsons. Maybe even loving ones."

"What are you saying? That they're Nazi sympathizers? Neo-Nazis?"

"I don't know. They could just be taking advantage of an opportunity. Not unlike finding valuables in a bubbie's attic. If you discovered a bunch of old masters' paintings in a garage and realized they were authentic, what would you do?"

"I'd find an appraiser and then figure out how to sell them. Then I'd buy that villa I always wanted with a small vineyard overlooking the mountains and lake in Galilee," Moshe said, trying to lighten the mood.

Beryl ignored his comment. "And if you knew they were your parent's and they were Nazi's? And you were suspicious of how they came to acquire these masterpieces?"

"Or worse," David said. "What if you were well aware and it was now time to cash in? Can you imagine having millions of dollars of art in a basement just sitting there? Maybe whoever stole it was not willing to part with it, or whoever found them was waiting for their parents to die. Enough time has gone by for the risk to diminish. Who would know? Who would suspect?"

"But then," Noah said, "I would argue go to an appraiser, sell them on the market. Old works come up all the time."

David shook his head. "Not old stolen works. Works that may have been forcibly sold for nothing or stolen from Jews. Beryl, I assume anything of value has its provenance researched thoroughly?"

"Absolutely. If the painting is by a famous artist, then it can be traced. If a painting was owned by a prominent family or was in the hands of a known dealer or had been in a museum, there may be records. After the war, people filed claims, and the allies kept records. All imperfect but more information exists than you might suspect. Children who remember paintings from their house growing up—their childhood memories and anger and loss drive them to search for some form of restitution. Others may be motivated by plain greed, knowing they should have inherited millions of dollars. Lots of people have registered claims. Reasons can be all over the place. For some, it makes them feel better, grasping to hold someone accountable, any type of recognition. It's like declaring this was real, this was mine, these Nazi bastards stole this painting from us, and nobody should forget that..." She stopped, shaking her head and looking around the room to make sure her speech was resonating. "Another pointer to remind us of the crimes, to not forget, to try to right some of the unspeakable wrongs. And what do claimants have to lose? Emotionally, it helps some of them cope, to talk about what happened in a less direct way through the art or other losses—the homes they were kicked out of. For a child who lost their parents, maybe their whole family, a claim could lead to tracking a lost painting. Yes, it's rare, but it does happen. Finding the painting or even piecing together a bit of lost history can bring some closure." She paused again, realizing she had lost herself a bit, immersed in the tragedy. "Just putting a painting that may have that emotional baggage up for sale could be pretty risky."

Sighing, still resisting the hypothesis, but moved by the prospect of holding the perpetrators accountable, Noah took out a handkerchief and wiped his forehead, suddenly realizing he was perspiring. The air conditioning at the Mossad headquarters never worked well. The director famously used it sparingly, arguing they should never stay too comfortable. Soldiers and agents were sweating out in the field. Beryl saw the concern etched in Noah's face and sensed his skepticism was wilting. Indeed, he was willing to consider the unimaginable thread and said, "Could they really be talking about paintings wrestled from Jews, harbored by offspring living normal lives? Could masterpieces be in the hands of not-so-innocent community members, mothers and fathers going about their professions, nurturing their sons' and daughters' lives in blissful denial, the fairy tale all resting upon a rotten foundation?" He thought to the next generation, bad seeds born of evil seeds. Noah asked, "Would you do it? Would you put a painting like that up for sale?"

"I'm not the daughter of a Nazi trying to sell art. Nor am I wondering if my father bought it with a gun."

"But you don't think it's a crazy theory?"

"Of course not, or I wouldn't be here. I think it may be very real."

"My God," Moshe mumbled. "This is unbelievable."

"It could be worse than unbelievable," Noah said. "Don't ever doubt the past coming back to haunt us. Sadly, it's the lot of the Jewish people. It's why many of us here at this table joined the service. To protect the unspeakable from ever happening again and find and punish the perpetrators of the past. We don't know how deep this could be or where it may lead."

"What are you implying?"

"Well, if this is all about money, why wait so long? Maybe there's been some of this trickling out for a while, and we just didn't notice. But now there's enough out in the open, and it's noticeable. What if it's part of a larger plan? What if their Nazi ideology never died, and this is a way to fund neo-Nazis?"

"You always manage to point out the worst," Uzi said. "Thanks again, Noah."

"My pleasure. I'm too old to worry about finger-pointing. Our job is to consider all the possibilities."

"And it may lead nowhere," David added. "Listen to you guys. It's like the lore of lost treasure, of finding a clue where the arc of the covenant is buried. This is the real world we're talking about. Not *Indiana Jones*. Sure, I don't have any doubt old art with a sordid past comes on the market. I don't have any doubt that the Nazis stole paintings from relatives of people we probably know. Paintings that should be hanging in museums. Museums here in Tel Aviv. I have no doubt that some people sell paintings they suspect were illegally obtained in the war. But let's not be paranoid. Let's not go down the slippery slope of a band of Nazi's kids suddenly marketing paintings fifty years after the war because their grandpa happened to die and left a Rembrandt over the mantle, or they found paintings cleaning out their Nazi grandpa's garage and decided to top off their retirement accounts. Come on. I don't believe it. Save me the conspiracy theories."

"Are you willing to take the risk?" Noah asked, his tone accusing.

"What risk? This isn't like someone is hurling another rocket toward us over the border and hoping our Iron Shield missiles can intercept it."

"No, this is a moral issue. This goes to the heart of Israel. Honoring our ancestors. Honoring the commitment this state was founded on. And if you're wrong and my cockamamie theories are right, we could prevent descendants of the men who sent your parents to die in the gas chambers from profiting. We could stop them from reaping a windfall by selling paintings stolen from our friends' relatives who lost their possessions and dignity then lost their lives. Shall I go on? Are you willing to risk that? Are you willing to lose again?"

David slumped in his chair, deflated, and Uzi put a hand on his shoulder. Before Noah could go on, Moshe interrupted. "Beryl, can you give us a few minutes? This is getting a little personal... No need for you to be involved any more than you are."

"Okay. But I'm already involved. I can't exactly forget what I already know. And suspect."

"I know. Thank you." The quartet excused her.

Beryl, truthfully, was happy to leave, her theories laid bare at the table. Her grandparents and countless other family members had perished in the Holocaust. The fight was as personal for her as for many of the men in that room. She was a brave woman, exposed through her job and family to more secrets and graves than anyone should witness, but she was not a robot. Maintaining humanity, acknowledging fragility was necessary. Retaining and focusing those emotions played a crucial part in the Mossad's training. She strode to the women's room, quickly catching a glance of her moist face in the mirror before opening a stall. For five minutes, she thought of her orphaned mother, the grandparents she never met, a grandfather who had been a tailor crafting the finest suits. All of them perished in concentration camps, heads shaved, bodies ravaged by hunger, flesh and memories incinerated because of a perfect mix of monstrous propaganda, cowardice, and lust for power.

It was all so unreal—distant black and white images that could not possibly be true yet proven by the raw authenticity of fact. It was just happenstance she attended ASH in the Netherlands, that oasis of tranquility for the diplomatic and business elites, set amidst leafy woods by the North Sea's dunes. The neighborhood provided little shelter a half-century earlier, no more refuge than Anne Frank and others found forty-five minutes north along Amsterdam's canals. There had been no more safety in quiet three and four floor skinny houses along narrower canals in Leiden, Delft, Goude, and Haarlem. The rot and complicity stank everywhere.

Beryl had toured the Anne Frank House, the unremarkable house and now neighboring museum set along the otherwise beautiful Prinsengracht canal in the very heart of Amsterdam. The old-world Pulitzer Hotel, originally built when the grandson of the famed Joseph Pulitzer, the namesake of the Pulitzer Prize, bought several grand canal houses and strung them together to create a five-star boutique hotel, was just a five-minute stroll down the canal. The Pulitzer Amsterdam sported a glass conservatory, tranquil courtyard in the middle garden, and rooms with crown molding, gold leaf, and beams harkening back to the city's golden age more than four hundred years past. There was perhaps no more charming hotel in the city, some might say in all of Europe, with bedroom windows overlooking the quiet sidewalk and boats meandering through the canal.

Many of those tour boats would call out to their guests, repeating the announcement in multiple languages, to be ready as on the right they would soon be passing the house where Anne Frank lived. The house that was not off the beaten track but square in the center of the city, alongside one of its two or three grandest canals, a fifteen or twenty-minute walk from virtually anywhere you wanted to be in the city. The normal, though on the affluent side of things, house, where today and yesterday one could easily stroll to the famous parks and churches and museums; a house from which it was even possible to walk to the Rijksmuseum or the van Gogh Museum where non-stolen van Goghs, not managed by poor Mr. de Vries, safely hung. The same house where behind a wooden bookcase, a bookcase able to hinge open to the side revealing a hidden door, lay a concealed steep staircase up to an attic. Upstairs held small bedrooms where the young Anne Frank had lived with her family, jotting for eternity her adolescent yearnings and unfathomable fears of discovery. This very typical house, on a beautiful canal, down from a stunning five-star hotel, shivering in the very heart of the city. If that were real, anything could be real.

Beryl's mind wandered back from Amsterdam to Tel Aviv, jarring back to the reality that she sat head in hands in a bathroom stall in Mossad headquarters. Perhaps it was an appropriate place to be drawn back to the horrible memories of the Holocaust. Maybe that was why the building she squat in existed—to ensure people like her did not forget, to prevent unspeakable atrocities from happening again, to thwart the sons and daughters of Nazi murderers and thieves from profiting and comfortably taking a junior suite at the Pulitzer Hotel.

Beryl washed her face and put on the scarf she had bought with her mom earlier in Jaffa. It brightened her mood. Her mother had overcome the horrors of her roots. She led a happy life, a carefree spirit who cared not for the dust on her sandals. Beryl's father was a hero, a man devoted to protecting the country. She thought his job description should be more of a motto. Perhaps something of a superhero creed: seeking out rot festering in men born into and descended from hatred, making the world a safer place. Alas, his title was analyst, now special advisor. She was proud to be home.

Her mind briefly drifted back to thinking of her sister Hannah, taken so young. Coming back to Israel always seemed to dredge up mixed feelings, memories of loss casting a pall over the happiest of reunions. She could do nothing to rewind time and prevent Hannah's death. The prospect of recovering stolen art and taking action to avenge haunting images of the war was another story. Maybe focusing on achieving something good would help her find more peace with Hannah's passing. She didn't know, but it was at least a calming thought. Yes, Hannah would have been fully supportive of taking down these bastards, she nodded to herself. She would be acting for all the lost souls of Israel, kindred spirits deserving of restitution. So many victims in such a short span of time. Beryl hoped her father, and David, Moshe, and Noah, would back her quest.

The rest of the conversation she missed resembled a family squabble. In the end, the Jaffe family's logic prevailed. Too much was at stake to ignore the possibility. They should at least sponsor an investigation, allocate enough resources to understand if there was rot lurking in plain sight they had simply overlooked. Noah came away shaken enough at the slippery slope probabilities he decided to brief the prime minister. This could be politically explosive if any of it happened to be true.

***

Beryl called Marco later that afternoon. "Sorry, hon, I'm going to be in Israel longer than expected."

"Something wrong? Are your folks okay?"

"No, everybody's fine. It's business. I'm looking forward to going to a concert with Reena and Mom tonight. We're hearing a famous violinist at the old Roman amphitheater. I've never seen a concert there. Can you believe it? I'm pretty excited."

"Okay, you had me worried."

"Yeah, I just had some meetings Dad arranged that took longer than expected. I have a couple follow-up meetings, and a few people who should be involved are out of town and won't be back before the weekend."

"So, the usual."

"A bit. Guess princes buying Monet's is a hotter topic than I expected. Nothing to worry about. Should we rendezvous in Zug on Saturday?"

"Zugesee or Red Sea, your choice, I can fly there. You don't sound too good."

"No, no, I'm fine. Really. I'll meet you in Zug."

I thought what a shame we were so often apart, punctuating itineraries by bringing each other up to speed on breakfast buffets, if not the full scope of our business. Despite Beryl's attempt to sound upbeat at seeing her family, I sensed a loneliness in her voice, an almost haunting tone, and wondered what had happened in Israel. It would be a while before I learned the details. Quelling my usual snarky impulses, I wished we were together spending a routine evening watching the sunset over the Zugersee. Leave it to Beryl to expose my heart.

***

Beryl's mind was distracted during the concert. Seated between Reena and her mom, she was momentarily transported by the violin's soulful and haunting tone. The violinist's bow drew out a high note so cleanly it floated up past her then drifted in the wind out toward the sea. She felt the warmth of her sister swaying against her, Reena's lean frame just enough to kiss against her side. It was almost enough to escape. For a moment, she put aside the hard stone beneath her and the absence of her missing sibling, Hannah, who should have completed the sister sandwich. She even shut out the meeting with Noah, David, Moshe, and Uzi, and the problems lurking, the fear of missiles hurtling from aggrieved neighboring militias.

Life in Caesarea was complicated. Life was complicated. Beryl knew her life was going to become even more complicated. Her mind drifted out to sea following the note. Suddenly, she had a vision of a team of Israeli naval seals lurking beneath the ocean, out beyond the columns of the Biblical-aged amphitheater by the calm Mediterranean. They were listening to the notes too, ready to surge onshore to apprehend someone in the audience.

Her vision, of course, was not true. The fact that such a concept could be real was her problem. Caught between visions and dreams. No longer relaxed, her eyes scanned the crowd as her sister continued to sway. Reena, still rocking, eyes closed, brushing against a taut body, managed to block out her sister's alertness to the crowd and ever-present dangers. It was better to be a pediatrician mom, worrying about ear infections and drying the kid's clothes after a water balloon fight.

Reena had asked Beryl whether she and Marco were going to have kids. Beryl answered her truthfully — yes, eventually. It just wasn't yet a good time. The planning of an agent — could you really pick the time? Wait too long, and it was too long. Beryl knew that, deflecting the answer. She was just passing thirty. There would be plenty of time. She hoped. Would she enjoy living in Caesarea with her family, raising funds to help the amphitheater's restoration, and planning picnics? Or did she picture a brood in idyllic Switzerland, growing up along this lake or that, ponytailed girls hurtling on water skis and boys playing tennis, dreaming of Wimbledon? She would take them to museums and teach them about art. They could spend their summers at the lakes and other holidays in the Holy Land. She and her hypothetical kids could have it all. Those were the dreams conjured up by the wailing violin, the scent of her mother leaning in, her warm and dead sisters, the fear of next-generation hormones growing stale.

The afternoon at Mossad headquarters had brought Beryl back to a different reality. She was no longer the art evaluator extraordinaire, partner at world prestigious Moultens & Barings, married to a hunky Italian now worth more than they could count, living between a Zurich apartment overlooking the lake and mountains and a getaway to a more perfectly picturesque villa on the edge of Zug's own lake. She had been brought back into the fold of the Israeli secret intelligence agency, the most feared and successful secret service in the world. Somehow, she was in the familiar embrace of an agency fabled for capturing Nazi war criminals hiding in Argentina and bringing them back to face justice; the agency that hunted down the murderers of Israeli athletes at the Munich Olympics and, once captured, applied a different form of justice; the agency that had masterminded an escape of thousands of Ethiopian Jews, spiriting them from another slaughter and safely to Israel. And those were just highlights. These and other fodder for Hollywood reenactments were frequently packaged like a marketing brochure for the public, and certain politicians, who dared to curb budgets and specific operations. Beryl could almost hear Marco whispering, Jesus Christ.

***

The next morning, while workers were picking up litter strewn from the evening's concert, Beryl drove herself back down the coast into Tel Aviv. Soon, she was back at Mossad headquarters in the same room, at the same table, facing the same men. Noah, David, and Moshe sat on one side, Beryl and her father across.

Noah began. "I have good news. We've approved devoting significant resources to investigate. This will have support at the highest levels. If there are people selling art stolen from Jews in the Holocaust, art that was in Nazi hands and that is now being sold on the black market — maybe even to benefit Nazi families —

then we need to know. And we need to stop it, get those paintings back, and try to return them to their families. If we cannot locate the rightful owners or their heirs, we'll make donations to museums."

"That's fantastic," Beryl said.

"I'm glad you approve. Thank you for bringing this to our attention. But first steps first."

"Meaning?"

"Right now, from what you outlined, this is all conjecture. You talked about rings in Eastern Europe, information you had, theories. Right now, this is all a theory. A worst-case fear of sorts, correct?" Noah asked.

"Yes. As I told you, I've spoken to the people at the task force Dirk put me in touch with, and the suspicions seem credible. I've seen the notes, talked to the team. But they're not going to devote resources to chase this down. Most of their mandate is stopping drug trafficking. Some stolen paintings and trying to sort out decades of chains-of-title isn't in their mandate. Interesting stuff, but nobody's going to risk their jobs. To them, it could be another false lead, worse, just another conspiracy theory. The chatter, though, they picked up is real. Otherwise, I wouldn't have come here, wasted your time. But yes, still ultimately a theory until we link an actual sale."

Noah nodded. "Okay, so first step is we form a team and investigate. Let's see if there is any truth to this. If yes, we'll have more than enough to do. Until then, it's a small team, and we keep this among the people in this room. David and I will be point. I'll keep Moshe apprised, but otherwise, he won't be directly involved. Anyone added I need to approve. Directly. For now, I will be your primary contact for the mission."

"Understood."

"Oh, and one caveat. Uzi, you can't be involved. Normal protocol since we need to keep Beryl in the game. We need her for entry into the art world."

"As I assumed," Uzi said. The Mossad had a firm rule of separating family members. Uzi could be briefed, but he would not be a member of the core team running the mission.

"Next," Noah continued, "I suppose we ought to give this little project a name. Any ideas?"

Beryl thought back to the fated burglary at the Koningshaus that had brought Marco's and her careers into a twisted helix, breathing a bizarre kind of new life into their relationship. That van Gogh had never been recovered. Maybe spinning the name of *Moonlit Fields* for this project would sprinkle good karma, and the picture would be found. "How about Operation Moonlight?" she offered. "Long story, it reminds me of a painting that was once stolen in Amsterdam, and Marco and I worked together on a valuation for the insurance company. The painting was called *Moonlit Fields*, so nothing too close."

"Works for me," David said as Moshe also nodded in consent.

"Then Operation Moonlight it is," Noah said, ready to move on to more important elements. "Beryl, how do you propose we start? Anyone else you suggest essential to the team we need to think about?"

"I'm not sure. I've brought you all I have right now. I think with Pavlina and SoHoMasters we're in good shape if we can find some links."

David jumped in, "Follow the money. We at least have a strong suspicion of a ring or syndicate fencing stolen art. Beryl, you said when you talked to people at the task force, they had concrete leads on a couple transactions. We ought to be able to start there, trace it to the source. Whoever is making most of the money either owns the stolen pieces or knows who does."

"Sounds like a good place to start," Noah said. "David, why don't you head up that angle? One of your specialties anyway."

"And maybe he can work with Marco," Beryl suggested. "You're not going to find anyone more connected in banking circles, and he can snoop in some of those not so easy to ask places."

"You sure you want to involve him?" Uzi asked, concerned about this becoming too much of a family affair. Marco was fair game because he was not Mossad, but the line was thin.

"Very limited. Need to know elements—and if possible, I'll try to keep the Mossad out of it, or at least downplay that link. Because we worked together on peeling back the whole art insurance market, he's heard about some of the uglier sides of the business too. He won't need much to get up to speed. I can trust him and tell him I need some help tracking down an Eastern European ring that's fencing stolen art. He was at the same meeting when I first heard about this, so there's only so much I can hide. I'll say we're worried museums and others buying pieces don't realize what they're getting into, and the stuff will be uninsurable. I won't bring up the Nazi angle, and if he remembers, I'll downplay that, telling him that's just one of the possible theories, though farfetched." She shrugged. "Whether he'll believe me…I don't know. Let's not dwell on that wrinkle. I'll focus on the need for help back tracing the finances to see if we can help the police figure out who's behind it. I'll tell him I have a deal through Moultens and the police that if we break the ring, I get to sell the art. One hundred percent of the commissions. Zero cost basis and millions of upside. He can buy that new boat he keeps talking about. He'll be eating out of my hand."

The men looked at her, a bit stunned until Noah said, "I don't want to ask about the rest of your marriage. I have enough trouble dealing with Sara and manipulating dinner. I'll tell her I had brisket for lunch so I can get out of her meatloaf again for dinner."

Even Uzi laughed. "I've had her meatloaf. It's not that bad."

"I never invited you for three-day-old leftovers."

"And for that, I thank you!"

"Okay, enough. Fine, bring in Marco, but try to keep it vague. Work with David to prompt the questions. Tell him you're tracking a Mideastern buyer that these guys may be selling to, so we offered to help. Mutual interests and all." Noah paused to scribble something on a piece of paper and slid it to Beryl. "How to contact me. Memorize the phone and email, then burn that please."

Beryl read the information and asked for her dad's lighter. She burned the paper in front of them, borrowing Noah's ashtray for a more dramatic effect. Holding their attention, she then said, "By the way, what I described before, I want to make that part of our deal. I want the commission on anything we recover and can't find the rightful owners, and for whatever reason, we…I mean you, then decide to sell. You'll have to give it to someone, might as well be me."

Uzi squirmed a bit, never liking to mix personal gain with state business. At the same time, he beamed inwardly, proud of his daughter's chutzpah. She had brought this mess to them and was taking a risk becoming further involved—even offering Marco's assistance. What were they going to say? She had manipulated them flawlessly. And why shouldn't they have an upside? There was no conflict of interest, all the pieces out in the open. When he saw Noah lean over and whisper to her, and Beryl smile in return, he knew a bargain was struck.

In less than two hours, Beryl was back in Caesarea playing with her niece and nephew, throwing water balloons in Reena's backyard. Within forty-eight hours, she was back in Switzerland and in another day on the too-long-for-commuting train to her house in Zug. She would break the news to Marco over dinner, softening him up with an expensive Montepulciano Sangiovese. She would accent a dress with lapis lazuli earrings and her favorite green jade necklace. Coquettishly turning her head to the side, maybe playing with the necklace in her cleavage, then touching her earrings while tossing her hair back, she would have his full attention. The green and blue would catch the colors of her eyes, that piercing green with a flash of ocean blue, and Marco would be putty. Men were so easy, she thought. Unfortunately, working with Noah would be more of a challenge.

***

Zurich, Switzerland — 1999

I was surprised when Beryl brought me into Operation Moonlight. She recounted the background information, and remembering the previous conversation with Dirk, I was certain she was downplaying the most lurid tangents, such as implying the Nazi connection was merely a red herring. I think it was her meek attempt at plausible deniability. Perhaps she was trying to protect me. No matter. I was willingly hypnotized by her jade necklace, dangling with its tip pointing between her breasts like a bawdy tattoo, her eyes sparkling and catching a hint of blue reflecting her earrings. I agreed right away, abandoning my customary attention to due diligence. I accepted the premise about an art ring in Eastern Europe fencing stolen paintings and the police agreeing to give her any recovered loot to sell, millions in commissions if we could locate the bad guys. I thought back to my stolen Mercedes. Maybe Dirk's tale was indeed genuine, and we could even take advantage. It should be easy for me to help trace some of the money if we could find clues leading where to start. As I said, she had me by the necklace. I never stood a chance when it came to Beryl.

***

It took months for Noah and David to perform the initial legwork, filtering the chatter passed along by Beryl. Even more time would pass before we uncovered decent leads. Frustrated by the slow pace, David suggested that my local language skills plus familiarity with certain arcane banking practices might accelerate the hunt. To ensure I understood proper protocols, and perhaps with a hunch that sitting together would foster trust, David joined me in Switzerland. I was initially fearful of the babysitting. However, his intuition was spot on, and we learned a shocking amount from each other. I suspect it was the first time either of us had confided dark trade secrets to a colleague so openly.

The thing about money trails is that, on the one hand, they never lie. On the other hand, they are challenging to piece together because people — at least smart people and those who want to hide something — rarely use their own names on accounts. I can hardly imagine AllianzCredit Bank asking, "Mr. Marco Bellagio, hand over your passport and sign your name, please." That tack was so, for lack of a better word, common. For those like me with at least eight digits to their bank accounts, procedures were handled differently.

People in that category never open an account themselves. Again, too ordinary. Their lawyer or accountant, who has a power-of-attorney to handle such pedestrian matters, opens the account. Then that same attorney or accountant uses their power-of-attorney to transfer items between trust accounts and private limited companies, the beneficial owners of which are themselves the trustees of the trust accounts. Preferably, these are not natural persons, meaning real individuals, but rather the trustees are corporations. Ultimately, beneficiary ownership flows through to Mr. or Mrs. Nine digits, but getting there requires jumping through countless hoops, covering a handful of countries, several trusts, and more lawyers, accountants, and banking institutions than they ever want to acknowledge.

Sadly, my account sleuthing skills were not doing much to help the search, our efforts uncovering little after another few months. David had returned to Israel, and we spoke regularly.

Occasionally, he would fly over for a few days, and it was just after one of those trips that we caught a break. A thin lead following rumors from Dirk's original Eastern European task force caused us to target a handful of suspicious transactions involving pieces of art. At first, we had been drawn to a brokerage firm, but after some digging, it seemed a dead end. However, David counseled we keep following the money, and just on the edge of giving up, I decided to retrace a few of my earlier steps.

On this second pass, with keener eyes than when I started, I caught the scent. And that whiff of suspicion ominously pointed to Germany. I had an aversion to German finances ever since seeing Springsteen. A murder or two had that effect on me, especially those with a Nazi tinge. And I was the lucky one. I was only thinking about one or two bodies. Beryl was haunted by six million.

The further I dug, the more I was convinced I was on the right track. Moreover, I had met my match. The accounting was brilliant, with a yin and yang pulse of devious moves, combined with hiding in the open. I sensed an underlying core of conservatism and pedantic care. Whoever lurked behind this had a deep understanding of how to manage ledgers and shuffle numbers. The scheme also had a sinister flamboyance, as if to toy with anyone coming near, suggesting old money arrogance. I wanted to meet whoever concocted this marvel of financial obfuscation.

Then, finally, I found a small mistake that unlocked the trail to decoding the carefully orchestrated secrets. One of the trusts had listed a physical address which had to be corrected. Maybe someone moved. I'm not sure. What mattered was that innocuously chronicled between two false leads hid a promising address. It was in Germany, and I called David Wolfe, asking him to come over immediately so we could better discuss the breadcrumb. Reading the trust's name and address, he agreed.

Our analysis of that little chain persuaded Noah to sanction a covert team to survey the house and learn everything they could about the inhabitants—and hopefully the owners. It took them a while to greenlight breaking in, but it was worth it. What came back shocked us to the core.

CHAPTER 9

Munich, Germany — 2000

With my father's guidance, it was easy to help Florian and Rolfe establish high-end galleries in Berlin and Munich. My father was not concerned with the names and locations so long as I oversaw the venture and approved. Once my father had changed his name and altered Gunther's in death, succeeding generations bore the inconspicuous Mullen label. I easily settled on incorporating Mullen Antiques. I believed the simpler, the better. I insisted we also trade in rare vases and occasional antique Christian icons. My Stasi background counseled we should remain circumspect in our actions. Why risk highlighting paintings hung as a lure for other paintings hidden from public view? A rare impressionist gem would stand out less amidst a cross reputed to be from the Czar's collection. I would task Rolfe and Florian with mastering some Russian, Egyptian, and Chinese history.

Everything was proceeding well, the pillars of Mullenboess maturing, my nephews' business launching, my father's designs finally in sight. Except...I sensed my father growing restless. The new millennium had turned, but to former Nazi faithful there was more to an epoch than merely a number. The Nazis had been heavily reliant on symbolism. Hitler notoriously obsessed with finding artifacts that would bolster the Nazi's claims and underpin the mystique of their ordained rule. The Third Reich itself was conjured up as a successor to the glory of the first Holy Roman Empire. Given the design of the Third Reich to be a thousand-year reign, my father felt a deep hollowness. Instead of Berlin as the new capital of the world, heir to the Byzantine throne of Constantinople, the new millennium was co-opted by a hodgepodge of capitals and countries escaping not just the shadow of Germany but also the former Soviet Union.

To Dieter Mullenhauer, all the so-called progress the world reveled in after the Wall's fall was sacrilegious. Worse, any hopes of reviving the past within his lifetime were fading. He was now in his eighties and had only so much time left. It didn't surprise me that one day he asked me to call Jurgen Kranz at Bauer & Hoffstein to update his will. He told me it had something to do with the new galleries. It would be a while before I understood what he meant.

Munich, Germany — 2001

Noah sent Aaron, whose last name shall never be revealed, for the stakeout. Aaron was a legendary undercover operative who had been in terrorist backyards in Syria and Lebanon and the Middle East-dominated neighborhoods of Brussels and Marseille. With olive-skinned features, four-day stubble, and a slightly hawkish nose, Aaron seamlessly blended into the streets. This assignment in one of Munich's wealthiest neighborhoods was perhaps the easiest of his career. Aaron's biggest challenge was not being able to walk down the street inhaling a doner kebab. The district was all high-end cafes with no takeout in sight.

Bogenhausen, a former village now within greater Munich, was dotted with churches and villas. The house Aaron was watching looked like a mini castle. A circular driveway that began at a high sand-colored stucco wall cut a swath through a park-like lawn. The center of the house rose three floors in an ordered pattern, symmetrical columns shrinking in numbers with each level. Tall rectangular windows flanked the central peak, fronted by a narrow balcony. A turret capped the outer right wall, the Bavarian flag fluttering from the top.

Aaron waited until the Mercedes E-Class left and no further signs of life stirred. It was mid-morning, and the sun streamed through the windows. With binoculars, he could scan much of the first two floors. He had timed when the cleaners and gardeners worked over the previous few days and felt confident the house would be silent until the afternoon. If he was wrong, he knew how to be quiet. After walking around the wall's perimeter, he identified a back gate for a later getaway. Grabbing a tree branch, he casually hoisted himself up and swung over the front wall, landing softly on the park's grass. Still moist from morning dew, it captured his footprints. They would soon disappear along with any trace of his trespassing.

Picking the lock, he eased the door open and quickly scanned for an alarm pad, surprised not to find one. Probably few burglaries occurred in that neighborhood, and he guessed the owner must be overly reliant on the high walls and gate. Downstairs, through the living room, he spied a set of French doors. Moving swiftly, he came to the doors and saw they led to a study. A large oak desk sat between paneled walls. Grand bookcases framed the rest of the room, their shelves neatly packed with photos, bound volumes, and various personal trophies. He froze staring at what he thought must be an old master painting on one wall. Aaron was not an art expert, but he swore it reminded him of a famous Flemish or Dutch painter. Even without being an authority, he was confident the other wall held what could be a Picasso. If those telltales were not enough, the small Nazi flag and swastika bookends confirmed he was in the thief's lair.

Aaron took out a camera and shot several pictures, stuffing the camera back in his knapsack as he moved behind the desk. The drawers were not locked, and he quickly found letters, bills, and other notes identifying the owner. He pulled the camera back out and grabbed random papers with letterhead. About to move on, a stack of bundled papers bearing the same last name, but a different address, caught his attention. The other address was in Schwabing, another upscale area in Munich. Did the owner have another house nearby, or a partner, possibly a relative also involved? He set a number of the papers on the desk, shot more pictures, and added one of the documents with the other address to the sheets he was taking. There was no need to search the house further — time to go.

He quietly closed the desk drawers and shut the French doors behind him, making his way to a side door leading to the back garden. Even though all remained still, better not to retrace steps and risk being seen scaling the wall onto the street. He made his way to the back gate and circumnavigated the woods to his car, parked where he left it a couple of blocks away. As he expected, it was the most straightforward job he had undertaken in years. Why was his heart pounding like a hammer? He couldn't get the image of the Nazi flag out of his head. He hoped his hands had not been shaking and the pictures blurred.

Before filing his report, Aaron decided to venture over to Schwabing. He crossed past the English Garden, and not far from Leopoldstrasse quickly found the address across from an entrance to the grand park. The townhouse appeared modest next to the virtual castle he had just left. Sensing he was on the right track and not wanting to waste more time with surveillance, Aaron trusted his instincts. After a half-hour strolling the neighborhood and keeping an eye on the house, he felt reasonably comfortable nobody was home. Again, he found himself scaling a wall, this time reversing course and entering from the rear. A small set of stairs led him to a kitchen back door; he could easily look inside and see all was dark. Fortunately, like the other house, no pets were complicating his unannounced visit.

Quickly opening the door and pausing to confirm no chirps from an alarm were sounding, Aaron of no last name softly stepped through the downstairs rooms. He climbed the first set of stairs before finding an office, this one more modestly decorated. Another masterful oil painting hung on the wall, this work displaying fleshy women in a garden. He took out his camera again, not realizing he stared at an original Rubens. He next turned the camera onto the desk, capturing the small Nazi flags on each front corner as if the desk were masquerading as a military vehicle. Right place again, he thought, his stomach churning in the presence of — whatever the hell this was.

Fifteen minutes later, he was done. He had seen enough. Aaron felt nauseated, worse than any feeling he had from canvassing back alleys in Syria or other hellholes pickpocketed in the Mossad's service. Noah had forewarned him there was a bizarre chance of involvement by Nazi sympathizers — yet his briefing had simply focused on finding the owners' names, something about a suspected group of art thieves. It had seemed an odd job, especially for someone of his talents. Now he wondered whether the photos would shock Noah or if he had known all along. Fuck these people.

He made his way back out the same way he had entered and briskly walked to a U-Bahn stop a ten-minute walk away. That afternoon, he caught a flight to Frankfurt and transferred to a regular El Al flight to Tel Aviv. With his precious camera and papers from the now discarded knapsack safely tucked in his carry-on luggage, Aaron of no last name closed his eyes. He hoped he would never return to Germany.

***

Back in Tel Aviv, Noah read the classified report compiled by Aaron and slid it over to David. The photographs sickened him. Some of the images were unimaginable at any time, let alone over fifty years after the war. He wondered what Beryl would think. David stared at the names, wondering who these men were.

Classified. Director's Eyes Only

First subject: Florian Mullen. Residence, Bogenhausen, Munich. Managing Director, Mullen Antiques, GmbH. Born, 1965, Age 37

Second subject: Rolfe Mullen. Residence, Schwabing, Munich. Managing Director, Mullen Antiques, GmbH. Born 1967, Age 35

Suspect that the two men are brothers. Whether a Nazi past or sympathizers, unknown. Recommend further investigation. See attached detailed report.

***

Israel — 2002

This time I accompanied Beryl to Israel. I was gobsmacked when she told me about Aaron's report. Our little clue, which turned up that single address hidden within the layers of numbers and shell companies, had led to the discovery of Florian and Rolfe Mullen. The matter had become so sensitive that we were soon aboard a Swiss Air flight to Tel Aviv to confirm whether our past and present had become sickeningly linked.

Despite needing me, the growing profile of the case made it harder to circumvent rules limiting family members from working together on a mission. There was little choice but to continue my involvement under the guise of my not being Mossad. Already tiptoeing around that line, Uzi told us there would be no exceptions permitting me to enter Mossad's headquarters. In fact, I would be subject to extra scrutiny for being married to an agent. Certain policies were sacrosanct, and privacy and security concerns remained paramount.

David and Noah therefore arranged to meet us in Jerusalem. Beryl insisted we stay the weekend to visit Reena and her family. Business priorities, though, had Uzi speeding along the highway, passing the Tel Aviv exits, and driving us toward the holiest of cities. The ride would be about an hour and a half, and we planned to stay overnight. It was feasible to make it to Caesarea; however, we were assured of a stressful afternoon and decided to book a hotel, bags in the trunk.

I assumed plenty of safe-houses and offices existed, yet David and Noah must have wanted a temporary location, nothing I could point to and reveal under torture, I supposed. Guess a country used to tribal bickering for millennia knew better than to trust extended family. Maybe I was being paranoid or needed to concoct an excuse why I was not brought more closely into the fold. They advised our destination was the Hebrew University of Jerusalem, or HUJ, as it was often better known.

I took some solace in finally being admitted to part of Beryl's inner circle with her father. On the drive, Uzi told me he had reported our little incident after the Springsteen concert in East Berlin to his boss at the time—who had been none other than Noah Berenbaum. Uzi had verbally briefed him, then submitted a redacted and classified summary which was securely buried in the files. For a long time, I had wondered if Beryl had indeed spoken to her father. It was not exactly the type of wedding gift I had dreamed about when Uzi pulled me to the side the weekend of the ceremony and told me Beryl had talked to him. Not to worry, he said, they had cleaned up the files after the Wall fell. And, keep the conversation between us.

"Beryl was right to tell me, you know," Uzi said.

"She's been a pro. You know, she never confirmed whether she talked to you. I can only imagine what you thought."

Uzi did not bite. "As I said, it was a good thing I knew. Today's meeting is already a bit awkward. If I hadn't briefed Noah back then, this would have become an inquisition."

"We had nothing to be ashamed of or hide. Our actions were thoroughly justified."

"I agree, but you were also reckless."

"Yes, but I could also argue what we did was good. Maybe even heroic when you think about who they were. What did Noah think?"

"Doesn't matter. I made it clear to him the event was traumatic. I didn't want Beryl to have to relive the ordeal. And we both agreed there was not much to pursue. Germany was teeming with ex-Nazis, and without more than names that could have been altered, there was not much to investigate. Exposing what the two of you did, encountered, was best left alone."

I looked at Beryl, who uncharacteristically kept her head down, listening silently. I wasn't sure what troubled her more—her earlier failure to acknowledge the discussion with her dad or the rekindling of the memories of that awful evening. I hoped not the former. Beryl had done what we all agreed, in a manner least likely to compromise us in the future. Back then, I was certainly not part of Uzi and Noah's inner circle. Poised to walk into an awkward meeting, my standing was still compartmentalized. Jesus, this was a tough group. I was relieved we were meeting at HUJ, not in Mossad's headquarters. I fantasized about sneaking away, maybe auditing a class on ethics or psychology. Shit.

Soon, we arrived on the outskirts of Jerusalem, winding our way to the top of Mount Scopus. The famous university sat amidst what had become known as the West Bank, its sprawling campus looking down over the ancient city. The glittering gold Dome of the Rock rising from the heart of the Al-Aqsa Mosque stood out as we stopped to take in the view.

Uzi recounted some of the campus history, and I was surprised to learn that Albert Einstein had taught here and that amazingly both he and Sigmund Freud once joined Israel's first president, Chaim Weizmann, on the university's board of governors. I felt stupid not knowing any of this distinguished history. Uzi continued the story, proudly listing a litany of Nobel Prize winners and lecturers from the world's who's who. I would have to gift one hell of an endowment to make an impression, not that any such notion interrupted Uzi's tour. Too bad I had not thought about that before—I could have escaped my future grilling by taking refuge in my own wing.

After winding through olive and cedar trees, the scented landscape serenely perched amidst so many competing interests, we parked and walked to a building near the law school. Its entrance was not marked, and Uzi offered no further explanation. A guard at the door nodded to him and eyed me carefully as Beryl and I followed. I wondered if the youngster knew his guest shared a name with his weapon. Probably not, though the thought made me smile. In a moment, we passed another guard, and I found myself in a simple conference room. A blackboard on the far wall was washed clean, and at the table awaited Noah Berenbaum and David Wolfe.

They immediately stood, greeting Uzi first, then Beryl. David broke away, clasping my shoulder and warmly shaking my hand before he formally introduced me to Noah. We had spoken on the phone but never met in person. Beryl had warned me about Noah's ugly scars, elfin ear, and mismatched brown eye and black glass eye. I was ready, though still drawn to Noah's facial battle map. I averted my stare and looked back to David, remembering how Beryl had first described him as looking like a scientist lost in thought experiments, his hair unruly as if anxious about the results. At that moment, I really didn't care what he looked like. I was just happy to see a friendly face.

"Welcome, please sit down," Noah said. "Thank you for coming all this way. I know you appreciate the sensitive nature of the matter."

We all nodded, the reasoning obvious. David then spoke and thanked me personally for my efforts that had uncovered the address. We had already become close, so it was only for Noah's benefit that he highlighted how their financial forensics team was more used to burrowing into suspected terrorist accounts. My approach was somewhat novel for them. They were ready for the next leg of investigation, hopefully linking the suspects with stolen paintings.

Noah then turned to the uncomfortable subject of Beryl and my extracurricular adventure in East Berlin. I listened stoically, wondering just how much Beryl, and in turn Uzi, had passed along; regardless, I trusted they had faithfully reported events and the story itself would not be new to me. They omitted much of the detail, and I wondered if they were offering the courtesy of merely presenting a synopsis. I opted to keep quiet, already self-consciously trying to avoid looking into Noah's glass eye. The less staring now, and the less said about that evening, the better. I assumed they knew everything, and if they wanted more detail would press Beryl later. Noah thankfully moved on, opening a file and handing us a couple of photographs.

"Are these the men you met?" he asked.

I studied the two photos carefully and found my head nodding yes before I spoke. "They look different, but yes, that's them. I remember that weird white streak in Florian's hair. That's how I could tell them apart." *Shit,* I thought, *so much for burying the past.*

"I agree," Beryl said, moving the pictures back and forth as if different angles or light might change her judgment. "That's Florian and Rolfe. They're brothers, or at least that's what they told us. Seem to have gained a bit of weight, and they look much more serious. Professional. They were just a couple of kids when we met them."

Uzi reached for the pictures, searing the images into his head before handing them back to Noah. "So, it's what we suspected. I guess what we feared."

"I'm not even quite sure what we feared," Noah said. "Right now, we don't know much. From your encounter several years ago, we believe these guys are the grandchildren of a Nazi officer. They also grew up around a bunch of other ex-Nazis who were living in East Berlin. They are the principals in a company called Mullen Antiques, which deals in pricey art and antiques. Not exclusively paintings, but they certainly move high-end art, including items selling in the gallery for over a hundred thousand euros. What we want to know is what's in the back room."

"And how it got there," David added. "Beryl, any thoughts?"

"I'm still digesting all of this. How can these be the same guys that we met that night? It seems impossible."

"That whole night seemed impossible," I said. "We knew they were probably stuck in East Berlin. They knew their grandfather had been a Nazi, but whether they were close to him and setting us up… I don't know. The grandfather seemed comparatively rich. Even so, I assume they weren't able to bribe their way out. But they had to do something once the Wall came down. Not a stretch that they might have thought about fencing art—these guys were always con men. They set us up, marked us as complete fools."

"And they could have a source of goods from their old Nazi network. Who knows what was in Grandpa's basement," Beryl said.

"That sounds like a bad joke from a horror film," David tried to break the tension.

Ignoring his colleague, Noah continued the questioning. "Do you remember seeing any artwork in the house that evening?"

"Not in particular. That's not what sticks out. I remember a Nazi flag in the corner," I said.

"Neither do I. I probably would have remembered a Rembrandt over the table," Beryl said, slightly annoyed. "I did know a bit about art, even back then."

"Doesn't mean anything," David said. "It was East Berlin, after all. If they had access to something like that, it was probably hidden. Definitely would have drawn attention, and that wasn't the type of thing you did there."

"I agree," Noah added. "Which means we move to phase two. We assume these guys are linked, and worst case, they are moving art for old Nazi pals. Maybe even family. The grandfather could still be alive. Doesn't really matter. Once we grab them, we'll find the source."

"Grab?" I half-choked out, not able to catch myself. Damn, I needed to be more careful in the midst of a Mossad what-do-you-recall session.

"An expression. We're not going to drop into Munich, tie them up and bring them back here. At least not yet." Noah paused, and I wondered if he was toying with me. He continued, "I want to catch them in the act, see how they're operating. They may lead us to others. People tend not to share secrets easily that have been hidden for fifty years. And for all we know, these two are not the masterminds here. I want the grandparents, if they're still alive, not these kids."

David listened and mumbled it was because of the Nazis he had never met his grandparents, had never even seen them in pictures. There was nothing left. One day, when we had been poring over the ledgers looking for clues, he had opened up about his motivations. He did not live for vengeance and had joined the Mossad out of a duty to protect Israel against an ever-expanding array of terrorist groups and neighbors that wished her harm. It had never crossed his mind that he would hunt Nazis. That seemed the stuff of folklore. Simon Wiesenthal still hunted some down, but there had not been a high-profile case in years. Sometimes the past is best left buried. As he reluctantly bowed his head, I knew he was acknowledging that, once again, Israel did not have that luxury. Every day, it confronted the truth and wrestled with the contradictions, quagmires, and inspirations bequeathed to the next generation. Hunting down Nazi spawn was not his quest, yet it appeared to be his destiny.

David spoke up, "I want the grandparents too. For the sake of my grandparents. For all of them."

The meeting ended with Noah, like the last meeting with Beryl, advising he would be the lead and they would form a team for this next phase. It was okay to read me in fully. At that point, there was nothing to hide. It was up to me whether I wanted to participate. I said yes. This time it had nothing to do with sleeping with Beryl. It seemed like there were multi-generational scores to settle around the table. Beryl and I were excused and walked to the university's cafe for a coffee, leaving Uzi behind with Noah and David.

When Uzi joined us later, he looked ashen. We decided to abandon our plans, canceling the hotel room, and drove back mostly in silence to Caesarea. The three of us played good soldiers for the weekend. Uzi and Anna hosted a traditional Friday evening dinner ushering in the Sabbath. I dug into the fresh challah, dates, and blintzes with the zeal of downing my preferred bruschetta and olives. I tried to forget about the horror of seeing Florian's and Rolfe's photos by drinking heavily. Thank God Uzi stocked vodka and didn't rely solely on sweet Sabbath wine.

Beryl spent time with Reena, playing with her kids, and I joked with her husband, Ari. He being a local ophthalmologist and me being—well, me—the two of us shared little in common beyond being part of the extended Jaffe clan. I killed time asking about advances in Lasik technology and whether he had any good tips for investing in the underlying medical technology.

My idle question later led to an introduction to a brilliant engineer and high-tech start-up located near Haifa. Apparently, they had devised a quantum leap in calibrating the machines, improving efficiency, and reducing risks having something to do with folding back a flap which I did not understand. I made millions and became closer with Ari.

Before leaving, we agreed on an itinerary with Uzi and planned to return in a few weeks. He suspected Noah and David would not need too much time to dig up the past. Israel was full of good archaeologists.

CHAPTER 10

Munich, Germany — 2002

August 14, 2002 was a tragic day, and I found it difficult to speak. My father had a sudden heart attack and died. My beloved father. Florian and Rolfe's grandfather. With his passing, perhaps I was free to share some of his secrets. On Wednesday, we would read his will, and Florian and Rolfe would learn unpleasant details from his past. I wondered if he would be loyal to me, whether my fealty would be acknowledged and rewarded. I was, after all, a bastard son, easier to deny. Easy to disinherit. My father would not do that—I was quite sure. With Gunther's passing, I remained the only son he had, even if half what he may have wanted. I was still his blood, his direct descendant. My mother, Astrid, was a good Nazi. A blond-haired, blue-eyed believer, she was probably too young at the time to question. I could picture her as a naïve and pretty blossoming woman, working as a clerk in the office, flattered by a senior officer's attention. These types of affairs happened in the best of times. Privileges and power merely boosted the seduction in the worst of them.

Now they were both gone, and for the first time in a while, I reflected on the passing of my gentle mother who cared for me and died in her fifties of cancer. The wretched medical care in East Berlin did not bother with older women who could no longer bear children nor any middle-aged man or woman with debilitating conditions that could be expensive to cure. To be in such condition and maturity was to be sentenced back to the Middle Ages when considering life expectancy. I thought of her breathing. The rhythm of the rise and fall of her breath echoed the rise and fall of the Reich, expectant and life-giving, anxious and spitting; another breath, sucking in hope with a new child nurtured behind the Wall, a final breath not strong enough to blow down the walls of isolation and loneliness.

I did not know how much my father tried to help. By that time, they had drifted apart. After my father's wife Ute died in the war, I might have hoped the loss would bring him closer to my mother, his once lover. That dream, however, was not the result. I did not know why. I certainly could not ask him when he lay dead in a casket, awaiting burial. I took solace in knowing he still looked after me. He groomed me for the future, to carry on his dreams, to watch over his imperfect grandchildren. I wondered if when he gazed upon me, did he ever see my mother, did he wonder about traveling with her in the West, enjoying the spoils of Mullenboess' gains? What was it all for? What duty did I still owe? What would he ask of me? My father taught me so much, but he failed to prepare me for the day he died. Yet, in my heart, I knew that was asking the impossible. He was a father, an officer, a genius. Of all things, he was certainly no saint.

Entering the old church, I looked around to see a reasonable crowd assembled, close family clustering toward the front. I shook hands with Florian and Rolfe. Even in these times of grief, my relationship with them was somewhat formal. I was therefore surprised when Florian, grasping my hand, pulled me toward him and hugged me as if I was his father. In many ways, I was. I had always been there, closer to his age, closer to his father Gunther, more caring perhaps than his other relatives. Rolfe and I next embraced, both of us crying. The old man meant everything to us.

I spied Sophie, my niece, Florian and Rolfe's baby sister, sitting alone in a pew. She had been estranged from the family for years — a bit like Gunther's wife, Daniela. Daniela was scarred by the family history and bitter about her plight behind the Wall. When Gunther died, she simply slipped away from our lives. Good riddance. I did not need another sucking on my father's inheritance, let alone an ungrateful half-relative who preferred to deny her lineage rather than embrace its glory. I didn't think I had seen Sophie in at least five years. I heard she had moved north, was living in Hamburg with her husband. I went over to her, and she stood. I told her I was sorry about her grandfather, and she thanked me, returning the gesture of a brief hug.

After the funeral, we met back at Florian's mansion. I retreated to his study, also joined by Rolfe and Sophie, closing the French doors. We sat before the stately oak desk, the paneled walls and bookcases lined with bound volumes pressing in on us. The Nazi flag and swastika bookends failed to stir any emotion, merely reminders of Papa's past. To our sides hung a cubist gem and a jolly Frans Hals portrait, among the gifts to the boys from their beloved grandfather. At least, I had always thought of them as gifts, my exclusion making me foolishly wrestle with feeling inferior. I had therefore been surprised, and a bit ashamed, to learn after starting Mullen Antiques that Papa had not ceded title of the paintings on display. They were merely on loan, collateral to be used only in an emergency, a promise of grander times ahead and security against days perhaps less secure. It was still hard to leave life in East Berlin entirely behind.

My father's lawyer, Jurgen, had entrusted the will to me, and I moved behind the desk and prepared to read it aloud. I hoped my voice held firm. I opened the folder and read:

To my beloved Family,
I leave you two letters. There is also a third, but I will come to that shortly.

First, my will, which is short and to the point. I hope you will be pleased and carry out my wishes. The second letter explains some of the background to my assets. Once you read this, please destroy it. It will do none of you any good. The danger is obvious.

Will of Dieter Mullen
Born Dieter Mullenhauer 1917, Landshut Germany

First, I leave 100% of my stock and all assets of Mullenboess Ventures and all affiliated entities to Werner Boesseneker, my adopted son.

Second, I entrust and leave 100% of my art and artwork equally to my grandchildren Florian Mullen, Rolfe Mullen, and Sophie Dietzheim; provided they sell not less than two-thirds of the collection within the next five years and the balance – save for keeping two pieces each, if they desire – within the following five years, the proceeds to be used as set forth in the third letter. I appoint Werner as trustee to help manage and oversee the sale of those paintings and administer the funds received as set forth in the third letter. I expect the sale of the paintings will exceed one hundred million dollars and that each of my grandchildren will still be left with at least ten million dollars. If not, I instruct Werner as trustee to ensure that each of Florian, Rolfe, and Sophie be given a minimum of $10 million from the proceeds, with the balance remaining to be used as set forth in the third letter. Of course, all this can be done in Euros, or however Werner sees fit. Despite my distaste of the Americans, I am not blind to the worth of their currency and that auction houses often prefer dollars. I have left instructions about the third letter with a bank, as my trustee, the letter to be kept sealed until the first two thirds of the paintings have been sold. Werner has been provided further details.

Third, I leave the rest of my property and assets to be shared in the following proportion: 50% to Werner Boesseneker and the other 50% to be shared equally between my grandsons Florian Mullen and Rolfe Mullen. Sadly, I leave nothing to my daughter-in-law Daniela, who has chosen to abandon her family.

Signed and duly witnessed,

Dieter Mullenhauer (and acknowledged for the additional name sometimes used Dieter Mullen in respect of any property titled under such assumed name)
March 5, 2000

I took a deep breath and looked around. I had what I wanted, what I had been promised, what I was owed. Florian, Rolfe, and Sophie looked a bit shocked. I was not sure if it was disappointment or joy, likely a mix of both. Their grandfather was both loving and distant to them, and no doubt there was reasonable fear he would leave them nothing. He did not hide his Nazi roots, and the generation following the next generation grew up with a tangled web of shame, love, confusion, and greed.

Sophie was the liberal, no Nazi lover, and kept her distance once leaving for university. I kept my eyes closely on her, worried she could reveal the contents of the next letter. I decided she should not be privy to it. Take her ten million, be silent, be gone forever. I did not want to share knowledge she would have to forget. Best never to know. To be honest, I was quite surprised that Dieter had left anything to Sophie. Perhaps there was more of a connection than I realized, or he was being diplomatic to prevent a family squabble. No matter, I didn't want her involved more than necessary and assumed she was equally surprised by his generosity—even if she was granted less than her brothers. She had to understand isolating herself from Papa and his beliefs would have consequences. Hopefully, she would realize her good fortune and take her prize without further contest or snooping. Rolfe and Florian, despite their limits, at least could be trusted. They were bonded to my father's ideals and would not betray their true German heritage. The brothers were likely disappointed the vast majority of the fortune was bequeathed to me. And yet, they knew I was a son, of their father's generation, and that I had no heirs. They were still rich—very rich— and if they treated their dear uncle with respect, then the balance of the fortune may still become theirs. The plotting and scheming could wait.

The pot's distribution was just equitable enough to prolong a tentative family partnership.

I asked Sophie if she could excuse us. The next letter was marked for the attention of Florian, Rolfe, and Werner only. That was a lie, but she suspected nothing, already profiting better than anticipated. She gave me a brief hug and kiss on the cheek, pausing to give Florian a hollow, surrendering stare before leaving through the leaded glass French doors and making her way out.

I then turned to Rolfe and Florian and began. "There is a third letter, as stated. I do not have it. All I know is that it contains the instructions for dealing with the proceeds of the sale of the art. I am to maintain all the proceeds in a trust account, and once I provide proof to the trustee that the paintings have been sold, together with a proper certified accounting of the proceeds, they will release the letter. The trustee is a bank in Liechtenstein. I will give you the name and contact information to reach the trustee so you can confirm this for yourselves. Please tell the same to Sophie. Just say in a moment of grief, I forgot to give her the name and number."

Florian asked, "Uncle Werner, you have no idea what that letter says? What the instructions are?"

"No, I'm sorry. But let me get to the second letter, and maybe that will help."

"I don't understand. This is all very mysterious and strange."

"True, but not out of character with your grandfather, don't you agree? He led quite a remarkable life and had to be very careful with his information almost his whole life. I don't find it that strange that he is being just as careful in death."

"I suppose put that way. Still, I would have hoped…"

Rolfe interrupted, "Is this why he staked us in the gallery, wanted us to learn the art world? So one day we could help him sell off a hoard of paintings? Where did all of this come from anyway?"

"I think that's… too extreme. Yes, it's plausible he was scheming the whole time, knowing he ultimately wanted to sell the paintings. But does that matter? I know he genuinely thought the gallery work would

be interesting, help you see the world. And I know he thought you would be good at it. Better suited to cocktail parties and marketing than sitting with me and poring over numbers at Mullenboess. All of that is true as far as I know. As for the rest, I don't know. He obviously… he didn't want to discuss most of this with you, or any of us—or we wouldn't all find out this way." I hesitated, beaten down by the day. "I can tell you about the history of the collection, though. That was the subject of the second letter."

"Then let's get on with it. What does the second letter say?" Rolfe said. "Enough secrets."

"I'm afraid the second letter has been destroyed." I paused, checking my nephews' expressions. I continued before they could challenge my words. "He started to write it, but then destroyed whatever he started. I'm not sure when exactly. We now know he made his will, or revised it, a couple of years ago. Maybe he drafted the letter then or planned to do it and then found it too risky to commit to paper. So, he told me the story, what he had meant to include in the letter."

"When did he do this?!" Rolfe blurted. "How do we know you didn't destroy the letter, that what you are going to tell us is the truth?"

I scowled and chided my impudent nephew, "Rolfe, you'll just have to trust me. The letter has no bearing on what we each inherit and does not change the will. Let me first tell you what it meant to say, and then you can decide. I have nothing to hide. He told me this story a couple of months ago, fearing he could fail any day."

"Go ahead," urged Florian, Rolfe suspicious but nodding his head for me to proceed.

I continued. "You already know about his wartime past, his role as Obersturmbannfuhrer in the Nazi army. He was a loyal soldier and did things that in today's world, not in the height of the war, some may consider unspeakable. Back then, they were necessary, even honorable. Dieter Mullenhauer, Papa, served proudly in the Third Reich and believed in the Fuhrer and his goals until the end.

"*Back in the war, one of his assignments was to protect the Alte Pinakothek, right here in Munich. He was also in charge of cataloging works and paintings in the museum and pieces being moved there. Eventually, everything was going to be transferred to a grand new museum being built by Albert Speer in Berlin. Until then, he was in charge of logging and storing the paintings and other works. The city was coming under attack, and everyone feared the museum could be destroyed. Papa was given new orders to move all the paintings from the museum and hide them in a safe place.*

"*Papa's unit had constructed a bunker nearby, built into the side of a small hill, where they would hide and store all the artwork. He told several of the men loyal to him that certain paintings were reserved for the Fuhrer's private collection, and they needed to create a separate storage area in the bunker. I guess he concocted a lie because he feared someone might steal them, and it was his sacred duty to protect these pieces. They did not doubt his story, and they built a separate, secret room in the bunker. Ultimately, hundreds of pieces were hidden there. It was a giant storage room. When they were done, Papa shut the steel door and sealed it like a tomb. They even covered up the door so it appeared to be the end of a tunnel. He marked it to return later. He worried that the men who had built it, and in particular the last of them that moved the artwork inside and helped seal it, might betray the secret. All those men perished. I never learned how, and I did not feel comfortable asking for details. I assume he killed them or arranged for them to be killed.*"

I stopped for a moment, letting the tale of the burned second letter take root. I had heard the story once, and this would be the only time I repeated it. I continued, "After the war, my father, your grandfather, told no one of the buried treasure. The Alte Pinakothek was severely bombed, much of it destroyed. Men who had helped move paintings from the museum to the bunker returned, moving the stored treasures to another facility and eventually back into the grand museum. Of course, I mean paintings saved in the main bunker not Papa's secret room. It was considered a triumph that so many of the works were preserved.

"During that time, Papa was stranded in East Berlin and could not confirm what had happened. From limited reports, he knew that paintings had been found and returned to the museum. He had no idea whether his secret storeroom had been discovered. It was only after the fall of the Berlin Wall that he was able to return to Munich. He was cautious, returning with two of the only men he would trust, Uncle Karl and Thomas Mainz. You remember Thomas, his old friend from East Berlin who was there that fateful night after the Bruce Springsteen concert. Thomas, Papa, and Karl had to rent a small backhoe and dig into the mountain. Amazingly, they found the original tunnel to the bunker and its false turn and end. Under a spotlight, my father, your opa, found his old markings, MD, his initials placed backwards, scratched into stones.

"It took a few months to figure out a plan to dig into the opening and arrange to take the paintings away without being detected. I will save the story for another day. What's important is that everything was there. Nothing had been touched. The concrete-lined room held. A few cracks and minor damage in one corner, but virtually all the paintings were just as they had been left. The experts at the museum had already wrapped them for storage; if they had only known they were packing for half a century.

"Papa arranged to sell a couple of paintings from time to time. Those first sales even gave us the seed money to start Mullenboess Ventures. He had already shortened his name to Mullen, making sure your father's name was also changed in any records, needing to hide his past. As I'm sure you know, you were born a Mullenhauer. The remaining art is safely secure in a warehouse — and I have the codes. I am now the only living person who has seen these paintings since they were hidden during the height of World War II. Uncle Karl saw them too, before he died. Maybe Thomas did as well. Honestly, I don't know. Tomorrow, the two of you will be the next. At some point, I suppose we will also show Sophie if she is interested. But she can never hear this *story or know how these paintings came to be in our warehouse. That's one reason my father, your grandfather, destroyed the second letter he had drafted and simply told me about its contents. I would suggest that we try and keep her away and just give Sophie her share of the money. I doubt she will want to know more.*

"That's all. I guess we now follow the will's instructions. We sell two-thirds of the paintings — we will need to look at the inventory and make decisions — and then we will learn what the third letter says, what the rest of his plans are... He never shared the next stage with me. The third letter."

"So, he's still controlling us from beyond the grave," Florian spoke almost to himself.

"Yes, I suppose. Did you really expect anything else?"

We talked for a few more minutes and agreed to tour the warehouse the next day. Florian and Rolfe did not want to wait. I asked if I should call Sophie, and they said no. For now, she did not need to know. We would delay her tour until, and if ever, she brought up the source of the paintings. Hopefully, it would never arise. We agreed to meet back at Florian's the following morning.

Jerusalem, Israel — 2002

Beryl and I were recalled to Israel. It had taken the Mossad much longer than we expected, but I suppose given the stakes they wanted to be thorough. At least, finally, I could stay overnight in the hotel we had canceled after our meeting at HUJ. I didn't know why David and Noah chose Jerusalem for the rendezvous a second time. It was inconvenient vis-à-vis Tel Aviv, and perhaps it making no sense was precisely the reason. I would never understand Mossad as an outsider; exactly as they meant it to be. Noah picked us up at the hotel, and we drove outside the city, up the hillside past the Mount of Olives, arriving again at the university. Same process, same tough-looking young guards at the doors, a different nondescript conference room.

Noah chaired the get-together as before. Already exchanging pleasantries in the car en route, he moved straight to business. "We've learned quite a bit so far. David, why don't you run us through it."

"Happy to. We have analyzed Mullen Antiques, which appears to be a legitimate business. No obvious ties to other entities, owned by Florian and Rolfe Mullen. Looks like they recently opened a second branch in Berlin." David looked around before continuing, knowing that the whole subject made us anxious. "They moved to Munich sometime after the Wall fell. Records are not clear, but seems they lived in Berlin for a time and moved after reunification. A lot of people in the former East wanted to move. Just not that many could afford it. Someone must have helped them. You don't just move from East Berlin and open a high-end gallery in Munich."

"I'm betting it was their grandfather," Beryl said. "Or him and some of his Nazi pals. I doubt we took all their Krugerrands. They had resources."

"Krugerrands?"

"Just an expression…I assume we tried to get back any hidden gold from people like this," she passed the blunder off, a bit awkwardly.

I held my breath, watching David's puzzled expression, and dared not look at Uzi. Could we remain poker faced enough to keep a secret from the Mossad elite? I wondered whether Beryl had tipped her dad about this too. He would probably condone what we were doing. But even so—shit.

Fortunately, Noah cut in, bringing the conversation back around. "Until we have a better idea, that's our working theory, that they were backed by their circle from East Berlin." He looked around before continuing. "What's interesting is that the Munich gallery launched with some flair. All of a sudden, they were on the market and were offering pieces you don't find every day. Seems they wanted to show they were players. We also learned from Beryl's research that they started establishing themselves in the art community."

"Yeah, neither Pavlina or I had ever heard of them. They're still pretty small," Beryl said, moving past her gaffe like a pro. "But when I called around, people I trust said they knew them. Met at an event or two, had enquired about some sales. I was told that despite the gallery, they were discreet. My contacts liked that and thought they could be a good source for moving prized pieces. Basically, they were making it onto insiders' shortlists."

"That's consistent with what we've discovered," David said. "We are detecting a material uptick in activity. It's like selling bootlegged alcohol or drugs. There is a spike in chatter around deliveries. Recently, there has been a big spike. More than when you came to us with that first hunch. Admittedly, we've also tried to seed a bit of the talk. No reason to wait when you can prime the pump."

"I'm not following," I said.

"When you traced that original flow of funds to Germany, it was real money, but not much volume. Now we're seeing a big push to sell pieces."

"How do you know?"

"Because we set up a couple of teams to reach out. We're using SohoMasters in London and have set up a similar front in Paris. Places where Florian and Rolfe are less likely to have contacts but major centers for the art world. I've brought in Pavlina, and under her alias, she's approached Mullen Antiques asking if they might be able to help acquire art for clients that were looking to buy pieces that were not on the market—quiet transactions. I had her drop hints that SoHoMasters heard Mullen Antiques might have access to inventory. Growing fast and making the insider lists would lead to these types of inquiries. We have to assume that's exactly what they wanted.

Dropping some bait in the market, and we came to fish. They just don't realize we're dangling our own lures."

"Sounds complicated, figuring out all this deception."

"Our specialty." David smiled.

"Okay, so they have inventory they're trying to move," I said, not a spy and trying to make sense of the riddles. "Let's say I was a buyer. I go to my dealer in SoHo, tell them I want to buy a Mondrian but want a good deal. Maybe something that isn't on the market. They go out and shake the trees and find people like Florian and Rolfe that have access. But that's it. They find the painting. I buy it through my dealer, end of story."

"Yes, and that's how we plan to take them down," Noah cut in.

"Why the Eastern Europe ring then and stolen paintings? I don't get how that fits in."

"Maybe it doesn't," David said. "I was wondering that myself. Why need them? Except these guys seem new to the business, sort of appearing overnight. They may be able to build connections with high-end buyers, like you, hypothetically. But they also needed to learn how to move this stuff. It's ugly business. Otherwise, you just put it up for auction legitimately and go to Sotheby's. Except the big houses will scour the provenances, hire people like Moultens & Barings to vet the history. Their necks and reputations are on the line. They can't auction a painting that sells for a million euros, only to have the buyer come back in a year claiming they've learned the piece was stolen. So maybe they do a dry run, try to find some middlemen they can blame if it goes sour. Or maybe they have a lot to move and are developing different pipelines. That's what I might do, just like a real business. Diversify your distribution lines, don't rely on just one path."

"Jesus, David," I said. "You think they're that sophisticated, setting up a whole network like that?"

"Think about it. You saw the paper trails. They have high-end stuff, and we're seeing the makings of ramping up the supply chain, moving more works. And there's a lot of money at stake. Millions, tens of millions... God only knows how much if we're right, and they're just getting started. Wouldn't you cover your tracks, set up a full shadow business, be smart?"

"In theory. I don't think like that."

"Yes, you do, Marco." He shook his head. "You think exactly like that. Just in the world you deal with, the legitimate world. You probably get some inside information here and there, set up accounts, cover your tracks. I'm not implying anything. I'm sure you're an honest man. Just that lines can sometimes become blurry. Can't un-hear what someone may have hinted to you. And why take unnecessary risks? You set up corporations, structure trusts, make sure you hedge your bets and risks. You structure cut-outs just like the bad guys do."

I shifted uncomfortably as he continued, "The difference is what you're doing is fully legal, done in the name of prudence. That's why when you watch all these crime shows, you wonder, 'Boy, that guy was so smart, why did he go to all that trouble? Why not just be legit? He could have been successful.' And you know why not?"

"Why?"

"Because at the core of what he was doing was something rotten. The source of the funds, the source of something, there was something to hide. Everything else is legit, but it's all just a big fucking cover-up. And I think that's what we're seeing here. These guys look all fancy and legit on the surface, but it's all just a cover-up because they're selling stolen paintings."

Noah interrupted. "I think the Eastern European ties are a red herring. Maybe they sold to someone who then fenced it in another sale there. Or not what they are focusing on, maybe a way to sell some additional inventory, and we just got lucky.

And that's how we found them. Never dismiss luck and forget straight lines."

"Hell of a theory," I said. I looked across the table, jolted back into the reality that I was talking with the Mossad. What good could come of my questioning their theories? What was I even doing there? Then I also remembered the money. I especially remembered the money after the insinuations about my trading tactics and my entire profession's ethics. Hints of truth or not, I should not have been the one attacked! Why should I have risked my life for nothing? Of course, my wife, noble goals, all of that. True, but after what I had been through, was there any harm in a little personal upside for risking my life? It would not change anything about the bigger mission.

Beryl had sweetened the pot with the prospect of making millions from the recovered art. They had agreed to give Moultens the deal, and Beryl could keep the commissions. If they were going to use me to impugn my integrity, then I could play hardball too. I continued, "When we started this, there was also a promise that the stolen works from this ring would be given to Moultens. You know, whatever works are recovered, where no one can find the owners. Beryl would get the commissions. But now you're saying there isn't even an Eastern European ring?"

Beryl gave me the stink eye, embarrassed that I would even consider bringing the notion of profiting into the mix, given the stakes and what we had now uncovered. I was a bit befuddled. Hadn't she started this, proposed that benefit? I was willing to take on the Mossad (stupidly, no doubt), but not Beryl. I was reconciled to caving, but Noah surprisingly came to my rescue.

"No, as I said, I don't think there is a material Eastern European ring. Anyway, that's not who we're after now. But I will keep my word. We involved you, and there was a deal. Any recovered artwork will be managed and sold through Moultens and Beryl. That's not our expertise. If we manage to recover anything, first we try to find the owners and make restitution. That's what's important."

"I agree." I was sincere in my tone and sincere in truth. I hoped I was rehabilitating myself with Beryl. I was not a heartless asshole. What we were uncovering was sick. If our hunches were correct, I wanted the paintings returned to their owners as much as anyone in the room.

"But if we can't figure out the provenances, or find the owners or their heirs," Noah said, "then we need to sort out what to do with the rest. That we turn over to Beryl. None of us have focused on what happens then. If there are commissions from pieces sold at market, they're yours to keep. That was our agreement."

"Thank you. I hope you don't think I'm—we're—trying to take advantage."

"No, I don't. You wouldn't be here, sitting in this conference room in Jerusalem if that was your motivation."

Beryl looked relieved. Foot out of mouth—at least temporarily. Maybe she would be easy on me after her Krugerrand slip. Score even. "So, what next?" I relished changing the subject back to the hunt.

"Follow leads, test the theories. Good detective work. That's what we do. There's only one way to know."

"What's that?"

"Question Florian and Rolfe or catch them in the act."

"And how exactly do you propose to do that?"

"Well," Noah answered, "we need to run a sting where we can get close to them, confirm our suspicions are accurate. Kind of a dry run, see what they give up. This is all going to take some time." He paused, his exaggerated exhale signaling this was not going to be wrapped up overnight and that this type of operation needed to be carefully planned. "Then after they've been set up, we come back and take them down. Once they realize what's happened, we'll have all the leverage."

"You still didn't really answer my question about how."

"We have an idea or two." Noah's good eye had a mischievous twinkle.

***

About an hour later, Beryl, Uzi, and I arrived at the King David Hotel in Jerusalem proper. Beryl and I had a suite, outfitted with tall arched windows and ornate drapes pulled to the side, offering a vista over palm trees to the sandstone-colored wall of the old city. It was magnificent and surreal. Crusaders and other zealots had fought over this very spot for the last two thousand years. I bet one of the Knights Templar would have loved my room; little plumbing or room service offered during those days of intrigue and slaughter. We decided to take a walk and called Uzi to join us.

It was a short stroll to Jaffa Gate, one of the main entry points to the ancient walled city. The scene felt like the moment before a movie set is called to action. From one direction came a line of Greek Orthodox priests in somber black regalia, the lead man carrying a large silver cross, the glint off the icon reflecting the gray in his scraggly beard. From another direction marched a group of orthodox Jews, this particular sect wearing oversized black hats, the men's knotted hair dangling beneath their ears in what I could only describe as mini-male frontal pigtails. As they shuffled near, my eyes were drawn to a group of teenagers in shorts, t-shirts, and backpacks talking to a middle-aged couple unabashedly sporting fanny packs. The husband accentuated his outfit with a camera slung over one shoulder and a guidebook grasped in the other hand. He turned to watch a man in a long flowing robe barely avoid being bowled over by the Orthodox scrum, pushing through with an air of proprietorship. Amidst this near crash of humanity, weaving out of each other's way, were would-be tour guides calling out options in at least five languages. I wanted to call freeze or action, but these were not actors sporting costumes on a soundstage. I stood literally at the crossroads of the world.

Beryl looped her arm in mine as she had done in so many other cities and nudged me forward, walking through the ancient gate and down the famed stone paths. I took out my guidebook, Uzi begrudgingly traipsing behind, and told Beryl I wanted to follow part of the stations of the cross. I wondered whether Jesus walked on this very cobblestone and whether this was truly the spot when the heft of the cross was too much to bear, and he fell to a knee before being helped along. The weight and majesty of history was omnipresent. Soon we strolled beside vibrant markets selling tacky souvenirs alongside more appropriate mementos. I easily passed on snow globes featuring the wall, along with crosses of all shapes and sizes. I considered if I should bring something back to my mother from the Holy Land and began to peruse the stalls more discerningly.

I felt a chill thinking about the meeting we had just left and the probability that much of the vibrancy I now witnessed was the result of so many Jews surviving the war and being determined to build again. Fortunately, the sorrowed path of wandering thoughts was diverted by stumbling into ancient historical markers. I found myself in front of the Church of the Holy Sepulchre, perhaps the most sacred spot in Christendom, even more so than the Vatican. The church had been built around the spot where Jesus was said to be crucified. I entered and went to the catacombs, descending a staircase illuminated by candles and scrawled not with graffiti but the scratched markings of crusaders who succeeded in their pilgrimage. I decided to light a candle. I would tell my mother, who would be more touched than receiving an apron displaying a wall and gate.

We stopped by a cafe, and Uzi took out a cigarette. He lit up proudly, marking his spot like a dog peeing after having looked down at men smoking hookahs in the Arab quarter. I would have been happy to linger in the other quarter, taking a drag on a water pipe, inhaling the spices from the nearby stalls. Not the time. I needed to focus, not drift, knowing Uzi's nonchalant stance belied his inner scheming. I considered whether I was about to plot revenge against men whose grandfather's mission was to erase the possibility of what buzzed around me. Bruce ought to have written a song or two about this—not sure why his songs were coming to me now. Maybe there was something about being by another wall.

Sitting down at a table, confident we were alone, the chatter of passersby making our conversation unintelligible to straining ears, Beryl returned to Noah's challenge. "I think we could use Hamid. He would be perfect. It's not like you or I can approach them. We need someone else. Perfect pedigree and he speaks the right language."

"Hamid?" Uzi asked incredulously.

"Yes, Abba, you remember him, don't you? He was one of our friends from ASH. He was supposed to go to Springsteen with us in East Berlin. Except he was unlucky and got stopped at the checkpoint, along with Bryan. That's how it ended up being just the three of us. You know, Marco, Dirk, and me."

"You mean the lucky one," he said.

"Yes. Better put."

"Why him? Why not one of our people?"

"Because he has the ideal profile. And we can trust him."

"You could be onto something," I mused. "His background is unrelated but could be a great cover. He grew up a Shell brat and spent time in the Emirates. Both Dubai and Abu Dhabi. But what makes him an interesting candidate is that after his father got him a job at Shell, he next moved to work for Deutsche Bank, I think in Frankfurt, trading energy futures. Meaning, he speaks fluent German which could come in useful. Anyway, after a time, he wanted to open his own place, and I helped him with some funding to get started."

"And," Beryl cut in, "Hamid's made a fortune. He now runs one of the biggest hedge funds trading energy futures. He's partners with Marco in a bunch of businesses—they own the new FC Zug football club together, and he's part-owner of one of those English clubs. I forget which one. He plays in exactly the crowd that would buy art. We could set it up that he is fronting for someone in the Mideast, or he could be interested himself."

"You really trust him, one hundred percent?" Uzi pushed.

"Absolutely," I said. "He's my partner. I don't hop into bed with just anyone." I gave Beryl a little kick under the table. Should have known better; a sharper kick spiked back. Jesus, that hurt. It took all my self-control not to squeal. Plus, that was not the appropriate place to be invoking Jesus' name without due reverence.

"Your expression doesn't exactly convey confidence," Uzi said.

"Sorry, I think it was something I ate back at the last stall," my pained expression at least authentic. "All of a sudden, I have this sharp pain… in my stomach. Can you excuse me? I'm going to find the loo," I fibbed, focused on grimacing out of Uzi's view, hoping I could walk it off.

"Don't worry, Abba," I heard Beryl say, apparently not concerned about Uzi's scrutiny as she watched me limp off. I paused behind a large palm at the front of the adjacent restaurant to hear how her conversation played out. She continued, "I can vouch for Hamid. Trust us. And I have another idea that may help with our backstory. Mind if I take a trip to Dubai?"

"Dubai?"

"Do you remember we sent Pavlina there under her SohoMasters cover? She met that gallery owner that led us to the Saudi prince."

"Yes, but I'm not sure I like where this is going."

"Connect the dots, Abba."

"That's why I said I wasn't sure I liked where this was going. And if we're going to enlist Hamid, we need to come up with a backstory. I don't want him knowing this is a Mossad op. At least not yet."

CHAPTER 11

Munich, Germany — 2002

The day after my father's funeral, I drove Florian and Rolfe to Flugplatz Schleißheim, an old airfield on the northern outskirts of Munich. The seldom-used field was in the town of Oberschleißheim, not far from Schleissheim Palace, former home to Bavarian rulers. The ornate palace complex, including sculptured gardens, was a popular tourist destination. We would not be visiting today. Instead, we drove ten minutes away to a bleak field, stopping in front of a former hanger on the edge of the airfield. My father had bought the building years ago, shoring up the ceiling and installing modern alarms and cameras. He also added heating and air conditioning, together with humidity filters and controls, monitoring the inside to ensure proper conditions for storing the art. He assumed some damage was done from all those years in the bunker. However, the works, sealed for decades in the concrete vault in the middle of the hill, were in remarkably good shape. Some of the most valuable paintings created in the last several hundred years, whether by luck or perfect planning, had been shielded from internal and outside elements for more than a generation.

Nobody ever came near this warehouse, and neither people nor cars were visible as we walked around the perimeter. I punched in the numbers on the modern electronic keypad, walked in, and turned on the lights. The building was a shell, empty except for rows of crates lining the floor. My father had arranged the paintings by century and painted color-coded lines on the floor. Artifacts were arranged from the 1600s through the 1900s in four neat aisles.

"My God," Florian said, looking at the nearly 1,000 square meters of loot. "This is amazing. Werner, did you help build any of this?"

"Not me. Dieter and Uncle Karl, I think, helped to arrange and store everything. I helped with the camera surveillance system — but at the time, I didn't realize what it was for. Glad my Stasi training came in useful for something."

"Ha!" roared Rolfe.

"And how much of this is from the old museum? You know, pieces that would have been archived, so it may be hard to sell. People may claim it's been stolen and should be returned to the museum," Florian asked.

"I wondered that myself and talked about it with Papa. He didn't think too much should be compromised — however you want to call it. He estimated a third or more could be traced to the museum, maybe less, but almost certainly less than half. You see, he was responsible for acquiring many of these pieces and kept a second list — a kind of shadow list. Anything that may have come from unclean sources not registered in official records. The odds are even better given the destruction of records and passage of time. One of our jobs has to be comparing the inventory here to remaining museum records. Then we can cross-reference and be careful about those pieces. I was even thinking that, perhaps, if it's a small percentage, maybe we donate it back."

"Wouldn't that expose us?"

"Not if we're clever. I was even thinking it could help your business, the new gallery. You could claim when your grandfather died, he left certain property to you in his will. When you went through the house, you found an old storeroom packed with paintings. He had told stories of being part of a unit responsible for protecting paintings from the museum when bombing started. In the rush, he had moved some artifacts to the house before part of it was destroyed. But he didn't realize that when they moved some of the items, several pieces were *stored below ground in a bunker with a door cut into the foundation. When you were given the key and searched the house, you found this trapdoor which was rusted shut. You were stunned to find a small underground bunker. The people who moved items there must have forgotten about it, were probably killed. He never sold them, never hung them. You could present him as a hero, rescuing the art. Have a wing named after him or you, and direct people to the gallery. It could be fantastic publicity."*

"Werner, you're truly a nasty one," Rolfe said, shaking his head. "I can see why Opa trusted you. I could never come up with a story like that. Completely believable!"

"Interesting idea, Uncle Werner," Florian said, pondering the dizzy balance of greed, guilt, and discovery. "Let's see. First, we need to go over the inventory and do that check you described against the museum."

"It shouldn't be too hard. I have a complete inventory of the artwork here, and I have started assembling whatever official museum records I have been able to piece together. I think with more research, we could figure out what matches. I suggest the two of you take that on. On the way back, we can stop at my flat, and I'll give you the lists."

"Perfect," Florian said. "But you said only thirty percent, and not more than half. I'm confused where the rest came from? I heard a story about Grandma Ute being a collector. And now you're talking about a shadow list?

"Ah, well, maybe his wife did have a few paintings. But when he told me the story, there were some more hints…more came to light."

"That sounds…a bit mysterious. There shouldn't be anything to hide anymore, after all this time," Rolfe said. "It's ours now. We have a right to know. Was it stolen? Did he buy it? From your story, clearly, it was not for Hitler's private collection."

"No, it was not for the Fuhrer. Whether it was bought or stolen, I guess depends on your perspective."

"I'm not following," Florian said, the brothers' expressions puzzled.

"*I guess I have to spell it out for you. Yes? We have just driven north from the city. What is just a few kilometers west of here? I doubt you visit often. One of the camps. Dachau. Most of this stuff,*" as I spread my arms wide to gesture to the expanse of the warehouse, "*was owned by Jews. My father, your grandfather, was able to negotiate extremely favorable prices. And in some cases, I suspect the works were well, you might say, abandoned. Do you think a mid-ranking officer could simply acquire a collection worth millions?*"

I let the question hang in the air. We were almost close enough that smoke from Dachau's chimneys could have blown over this way decades ago. Those ashes, carried in the wind, bore a much greater stench than the waft of manure from a neighboring field. I added, lest Rolfe and Florian think I had gone soft, "I think Papa found this warehouse almost poetically situated. A reminder of our goals, of not being defeated without achieving some purpose."

"*My God,*" *was all Florian could muster at first. "Did Opa visit Dachau? I mean, go there back in the war. He didn't work there, did he?*"

"*No, I don't think he ever worked there. That wasn't his job. He would have said something. I don't think he could have hidden that from me. Whether he went, I am not sure. Maybe, probably even. I think it is certainly possible. It was close by. I'm certain he knew what was going on. He was part of the assembly line – the Jews were rounded up, stripped of possessions, sometimes forced to sell valuables. He took and stored some of the paintings while at one point assigned to help safeguard key museums. I doubt many paintings on his private list ever hung in the* **Alte Pinakothek***; museums tend to display only a fraction of their collections and it would have been easy to hide works among archives. I'm sure he also collected other valuables like jewelry he could trade or sell. The Jews went one way on the train; he went the other. He once told me he sometimes saw the trains depart. He didn't have to worry about the owners bothering him about what happened to their paintings. He wouldn't see them again. Whether he visited Dachau, had a question about an item of inventory, wanted to confirm a date or* *artist, I don't know. My guess is maybe at some point, even if it was just curiosity, he went to see for himself."*

"My God," was all Florian managed to say again.

I ushered them back outside, the dung-tinged smell from nearby pastures a breath of fresh air compared to the imagined scent of ashes and charred bodies looming over the crates.

"Now you know why I thought it better if we kept this secret from Sophie."

Dubai, UAE — 2003

There were no flights from Israel to Dubai. Israelis were not welcome, at least officially. Beryl took a circuitous route that started with a purported holiday in Greece, then a skip over to Turkey, and finally a flight to the United Arab Emirates. When she landed in Dubai, she covered her face with the scarf she had bought with her mother in the Jaffa market and hailed a taxi. She had booked a suite at the Jumeirah Towers, just near Jumeirah beach.

As Beryl looked over the Persian Gulf, she could only marvel at where fate had brought her. Covered head-to-toe and wearing oversized sunglasses, she felt relatively safe and took a short stroll along a seaside sidewalk. Cranes were everywhere, high-rises blooming from the sand, funded by endless resources flowing underground and carried away in supertankers. Pavlina, traveling as Ingrid Greggory, had attended a party on a superyacht hosted by a minor prince and an art broker. Onboard, she had been unabashedly shown a gallery of masterpieces, including a Mondrian, hung in a lounge that SohoMasters had used to bait the invite. Thank God Pavlina had managed to dump a heavy sedative into the lecherous dealer's drink before he pawed her further. By the time he woke up in one of the staterooms, she was long gone.

Beryl continued down the walk, anxious to orient herself, keen to appear calm later when approaching her target. Although she was used to walking amidst a cross-section of cultures, the mix of ethnicities in Jerusalem often dizzying, she could not help but feel a stranger on those Arabian shores. Before leaving, she recalled her lesson with Noah.

"Remember, you can tell a person's status by their dress," he lectured.

"What do you mean, exactly?"

"The Emirates are a rigidly segmented society. The majority of people in the UAE, and in particular Dubai, are foreigners. Most of the workers are Asian—from India and Pakistan. They may wear anything, normal pants and shirts. Then there are Westerners. You've spent enough time living in Holland to be able to identify them. They'll dress like you're used to, but next to the Asian workers, they'll probably appear a bit more upscale, like they've been shopping at the Gap—polo shirts, cotton blouses, sunglasses, and Nike caps, not loose-fitting long sleeves. Country clubbish, or however you want to label it. But it's the Emiratis that stand out. The men will wear their traditional robes and headdresses, or keffiyehs as they are known. The keffiyeh may be white or red and white, almost always held onto the head by a simple black agal—a black cord keeping the keffiyeh in place. The women are often more discreet, usually wearing a headscarf and clothes covering their full body. Natives are sometimes harder to spot then the men. Anyway, don't get offended if an Emirati cuts in front of you. They have priority. Always."

"Priority?"

"As I said, it's a segmented society. The people are generally diplomatic, but if you're waiting in line at a restaurant, for example, the Emirates can just cut to the front. It's their country, even if they're a fraction of the population. Everyone else is merely a permitted guest. Strict pecking order. Emirates first, sister Mideastern visitors and Westerners second, and the Asian workers at the bottom. Separate and not equal."

"Almost like a caste system."

"Except with only one local caste, where oil riches entitle everyone to sit at the top. Well, not actually one caste. There's the royal family of course. Princes and anyone related to the royal family sit at the very top."

Beryl heard Noah's tutoring in her head as three Emirati men passed her on the sidewalk, and she stepped to the side. They were laughing lightly and barely acknowledged her as they strode forward into the restaurant. All were wearing long white robes, sandals, and headdresses in a traditional white, black, and red checkerboard pattern. The men's robes, covering them from neck to feet, had a costume feel to mere interlopers, and she briefly imagined herself on a theater set where a director would soon call for a wardrobe change. The mundane scene was routine locally, though, and she had to overcome her inclination to stare. The robes were striking, even to someone used to Jerusalem garb.

She decided to follow the men into the restaurant. It would be a relief to escape the scorching sun. Inside the doors, she had the feeling she could have been in any Western hotel or upscale lounge. Shiny floors, polished marble, sleek lines. She noticed the men brushing past to the front and quickly being seated by a fawning waiter. Biding her time, she was eventually escorted to a table without a sea view. That was fine. She could survey the patrons better from the corner. Mossad training kicked in like a reflex even when only looking for a snack. The UAE was infamously dry, so she opted for a shrimp cocktail and fruit juice rather than a virgin this or that drink. Beryl drained the cool juice too quickly, not realizing how parched she had become from just a short walk in the brutal heat. No wonder everyone covered their heads.

By the time she paid with her black American Express, under her cover Laila Alisime, her heart rate was calm, and she had morphed into a local expat. If the next taxi driver pushed for conversation, she would smoothly lapse into a boring discussion. Beryl mentally rehearsed a speech about how she lived in a yonder tower, replete with opulent soaking tub, gleaming white marble, and floor-to-ceiling windows with blackout shades overlooking the Gulf. Of course, she would add how she was looking to move to something more six-star.

Fortunately, her actual driver viewed it beneath him to converse with a Western woman, and Beryl was able to prepare for her mission until she stepped out of the taxi in front of what was supposed to be a seven-star hotel. Same sweeping marble, obligatory fountain, but an extra star to accompany an extra digit on the bill. Confidently striding to the concierge desk and asking directions, in moments she was riding up a glass elevator and entering the Al-Nuria Gallery. She had a meeting with an art dealer Pavlina had been introduced to on some prince's yacht.

"May I help you?" a young woman asked.

"Yes, I have an appointment with Mr. Al-Katabi?"

"And your name?"

"Laila Alisime, from SohoMasters in London."

"Ah yes, Mr. Al- Katabi has been expecting you. Please follow me."

Beryl walked through a modern gallery with an abstract by Juan Miro highlighted in the middle. Probably worth at least four million, she thought, as she strutted into a conference room filled with a large black onyx table flanked by gold-trimmed chairs.

"Ms. Alisime, so kind of you to come visit. Please, please sit down. I am Saeed Al-Katabi. Please call me Saeed," he welcomed her, dressed in a silk suit with a dark blue patterned tie. Beryl knew he was not an Emirati but had wondered whether he still may try to pass himself off with a royal hue. Fortunately, he did not fit the description of the creep Pavlina had drugged. Beryl relaxed but made a mental note to be wary of any especially solicitous associates of Saeed.

"Thank you, Saeed. Your gallery is spectacular. The gallery's reputation precedes it, but the accounts do not do it justice."

"You're very kind. But it is what our clientele expects, as I'm sure you know," a hint of suspicion in his voice. "So, Ms. Alisime, what can I help you with? I hear that you can often assist with acquiring special pieces. Is that the way to phrase it?"

"Yes, and I understand we may even be friendly competitors for the tastes of your local yachting set. My colleague Ingrid was a recent guest on the yacht of a minor Saudi prince that was visiting here not too long ago."

"Of course, I remember the party. Hosted by another dealer who was kind enough to invite me. A little gauche for my taste, but the yacht's collection was quite impressive. And your colleague was quite charming. But honestly, I did not expect to hear from you when I gave her my card. As you said, I believe we are friendly competitors."

"Well, sometimes, competitors can also help each other out...Maybe even be partners. I suspect you can relate to very picky and demanding clients and that sometimes it can be challenging to obtain precisely what they are looking for. Even when money is not of much importance." Beryl paused, confirming she had Al-Katabi's full attention. "You see, I am trying to find a Rousseau or ideally a minor Matisse. And uncharacteristically, I'd like to acquire it publicly, not in a hush-hush sale. It's a long story, but in this instance, I'd even like it to be known that it was purchased in the Gulf. If we can find a way to work together, I was hoping you'd be able to announce the purchase in your catalog."

Al-Katabi looked perplexed, and Beryl debated whether she had stretched her tale too far. The publicity was all important, yet it was also uncustomary in these circles. She looked at him, wondering how to persuade him, yet unable to provide details. Beryl continued, trying to sound offhanded, "As I said, it's a long story—settling a bet. I'm sure some of your clients have made you play silly games from time to time."

Al-Katabi sat back, stroking his manicured beard, clearly wondering how he was being played. The indulged, uber-rich princes often made absurd requests. Nothing like having unlimited money and inventing challenges to fill your time. "And if I helped you?"

"If you could find me such a painting, I would purchase it through your gallery. And, of course, at a very fair price."

"That's all?"

"That's all."

"I don't think I understand."

"There's nothing to understand, Mr. Al-Katabi. Excuse me…Saeed. I'm just a buyer looking to buy an expensive painting."

"And you don't care where it comes from?"

"Not at all. As long as it's real, and as long as I can buy it from your gallery. Oh, and soon. I'm in a bit of a hurry."

Beryl had done her homework and could read Al-Katabi like a book. He had no idea what Beryl was up to, but he was used to odd demands from eccentric buyers. He was also loath to ignore SohoMasters and make a needless enemy. Moreover, he was looking at a way to expand his market and earn some of the easiest money he had ever made. Despite their wealth, these damn princes could be cheap, expecting people to offer bargains for the privilege of their business. Worse, after presumptuous haggling, too often they cloistered their new bragging rights inside palaces where hardly anyone ever saw them.

"I believe I may be able to help," he said, giving her a supercilious smile. "Perhaps you can come back tomorrow afternoon? And if I'm able to find something to your liking, can

I ask you to join me for dinner? I will have my assistant arrange an evening out in the desert."

Beryl had heard about the opulent custom of banquets in the desert, replete with tents and carpets. If this would-be sheik wanted to show off, she would gladly oblige to cement the relationship. Plus, now that she knew the gallery's layout, coming back would provide the perfect opportunity to plant a few bugs if needed. A tiny one concealed under this table would be a fine start. Hopefully, though, she would conclude her business quickly, and there would be no need for eavesdropping.

Like some who could conjure a megawatt smile, Beryl had a preternatural ability to make the green in her eyes sparkle, a twinkling lure. Al-Katabi sat nearly hypnotized, Beryl's eyes standing out with her scarf shrouding all but her face, as she accepted, "I would love to, Saeed. I hope you'll find a painting that rescues me."

"I think you need not worry, Ms. Alisime. I look forward to seeing you tomorrow."

***

London, UK and Zurich, Switzerland — 2003

Hamid was game to join our adventure, and we were keen for a bit of redemption. Oddly, I harbored mixed feelings, tinged with some guilt that Hamid was stopped from crossing over the Wall with us, while at the same time grateful that his inability to pass safeguarded him from walking into a Nazi trap. I elected not to tell him about our encounter with Florian and Rolfe in Berlin, sticking to the facts of the sting at hand. Hamid was one of the few who had a good inkling about Beryl's double life but had the tact never to confront us directly with his suspicions. To sow plausible deniability, and more importantly to heed Uzi's directive, we advised him we were working with an Interpol investigative unit, mentioning further in passing that given the delicacy of the operation, Beryl would be enlisting some Israeli help. With an eyebrow raised, Hamid graciously accepted there were elements best left quiet. I assured him he would mostly have to play himself.

In essence, I was sticking to the playbook of leaning close to the truth. Beryl would research the type of paintings Mullen Antiques would likely possess, and Hamid would feign interest as a keen collector. Noah and David would arrange acquiring another painting or two for Hamid that would form the base of his collection. Completing the backstory, they would also doctor the provenance of these works to bolster his image as a collector. The more intricate part of the con would be convincing Mullen Antiques why Hamid wanted to buy art on the edge of the black market. Noah and David's team were also inventing that backstory. The Mossad, as usual, was ahead of me, already orchestrating purchases through a dealer in Dubai—thanks to Laila, alias my wife.

It took a bit of time, but ultimately Hamid became an accredited collector of Henri Matisse. Beryl gave him a crash course in the artist's background, explaining that Matisse, during one period, became enamored with harem scenes. He painted abstract sex fantasies such as placing Western women in North African garb; others featured reflections of conquered peoples. Matisse's abstract visions, expressed in vaguely erotic pictures, with props from Muslim countries and hints of harem conquests, could provide the right—albeit warped—undertone. Plus, Matisse painted in the early 20th century, and it was not inconceivable new collectors imported his works from France to Germany. While the Germans shunned degenerate art, Matisse had become famous, and it would be the perfect type of painting to wrestle from a Jewish home and yet not find itself above a Nazi mantle. They would set the bait, looking for one of his series of odalisques—French for a concubine in a harem. This was not the sort of painting an energy trader would tout on the open market, especially not one looking for a discreet bargain. The trap was nearly set.

***

Munich, Germany — 2004

Florian asked his brother, Rolfe, "Have you heard about this new soccer club, FC Zug?"

"Yes. You mean the one with that Mideast money behind it?"

"I don't think it's Mideast money, not some sheik. One of the owners has an Arabic name, Hamid something. He's also part owner of Crystal Palace in England. Putting a lot of money into the club."

"I wouldn't want Arab money coming into Munich, into German football clubs."

Aghast, Florian said, "Fully agree. I don't understand why the British are not banning them. I mean, allowing fucking Arabs to buy into their clubs?"

"We're still the only ones to count on any type of racial purity. The Brits have been letting half those towel heads buy up London property. Why are you bringing this up, anyway?" Rolfe asked.

"I was asked to set up a meeting at the gallery. Apparently, this guy behind FC Zug is spending money on more than football. A collector."

"Maybe we'll see if we can peddle him a forgery."

"Ha! That would be something. But we have enough stock to get rid of. And he's rich enough I'm sure he has good experts that would check the authenticity."

Florian was disgusted at the prospect of dealing with those types of people. He was a proud Aryan, properly descended from the best Nazi stock. Uncle Werner had insisted, though, that he cultivate whoever would pay premiums. They could not always choose their buyers; if distasteful, then try to relish taking advantage of them.

Rolfe continued probing, "Do you know what he wants. How did you meet him?"

"I didn't. I received a call from a broker in London. Remember that woman we met at the museum party in Frankfurt last month, who was so impressed we had a Rembrandt drawing in the gallery?"

"Yes, yes, I do. She was stunning. I even remember her name, Ingrid. What about her?"

"That's the one. She said she acted for a client and was looking for a couple of specific paintings. She was putting feelers out, said that's how they did it. She had taken my card and remembered I had told her to call. I'd noted in passing we had access on occasion to private collections. Appears she remembered my mentioning having access to quite a range, including some 20th-century paintings that had fallen into the wrong hands over time. I think I said something vague like that."

"Well, that's what we were doing, throwing bait in the water. So how did you answer?"

"I told her we may be able to help, but we didn't work in the dark. If we were going to take risks, I needed to know who she acted for. She was reluctant to give me a name and said she had to ask her boss. I guess she was just the eye candy."

"A shame. I could have seen asking her out."

"And why not? What's the problem?"

"I'm not going to waste my time with an assistant. If I just want a fuck, I can have Werner arrange someone."

"Fair enough. Anyway, where was I? Yes, she got her boss Simon on the phone, and we went back and forth until I think he accepted I wouldn't budge. He finally divulged they worked for Hamid Khan. The name was familiar, but I couldn't place it. I called up Werner, and it didn't take his team much digging. He confirmed the guy just invested heavily in FC Zug, has ties to

Crystal Palace and runs an energy hedge fund. Simon also mentioned that Kahn had recently bought a couple paintings through a broker in Dubai, but he didn't trust them and was looking to diversify. Werner's diligence guys got hold of a catalog out of Dubai that backs that up. Seems to be the real thing."

"And what's he looking for?"

"A Matisse."

"I think we have a couple of those, don't we?"

"Indeed, we do!"

"Didn't Werner say Opa hated those pieces? All the degenerate works."

"Yes. He only loved the neoclassical landscapes, the Dutch masters. But he wasn't stupid. Maybe he saw they were becoming valuable."

"Have you talked price?"

"No, I told him I'd get back to him this week with what we have. Then he wants to come and visit in person."

"What will you do, move them from the warehouse to the gallery?"

"Of course."

"I'd like to come. This should be fun."

***

Hamid's broker and Pavlina's (as Ingrid) fake boss at SohoMasters, Simon Middleborough, was, in fact, Jonathan Stein, a London-based Mossad asset. Mr. Middleborough, sporting an Etonian tie and claiming to hail from the Royal Borough of Kensington and Chelsea, dutifully arrived in Munich. David and Noah were not keen about the cost of a suite at the Bayerischer Hof yet acknowledged that the posh hotel was both the most marbled and appropriate place for a representative of Mr. Hamid Khan to stay. The gold leaf alone bespoke old-world elegance and new-world pretense. More importantly, unlike many European hotels with cramped lobbies, the grand sweep of the famed landmark's interior allowed back-up watchers to loiter in comfortable lounge chairs, a copy of Der Spiegel in hand, without attracting notice.

After lunch, Simon casually strolled ten minutes to Mullen Antiques, not surprisingly finding himself the only customer. Florian and Rolfe proved a perfect likeness of their surveillance photographs, and his initial impression was they were quite charming. If this was a front, they played the part to perfection.

"It's a shame Mr. Khan wasn't able to make it in person," Florian lamented. "We were so looking forward to meeting him. We're big football fans. Of course, Bayern Munich supporters."

"I would expect nothing less," Simon said, making sure to accentuate his crisp upper-crust accent. "I'm also sorry Ingrid was not feeling well and had to cancel," not betraying that Noah and David were wary of the brothers and deemed it prudent to limit exposure to the unknown and less attractive Mr. Middleborough. Keeping his demeanor all business, Simon was soon led to a private side gallery, with nothing but two original Matisse's hanging against black curtains. He played his role perfectly, caressing the treasures with his eyes. "They're quite magnificent."

"Yes, indeed. And hard to find today," Florian said, not-so-subtly bidding up the value.

Both paintings featured single women. One reclined naked on a sofa, her body, outlined with heavy shading, somewhat out of proportion but still alluring. The other woman was dressed in a prominent hat and sat next to a table with a pitcher and bowl of fruit.

Florian continued, "I was not sure from our conversation which composition might appeal more to Mr. Khan. Whether he would prefer something a bit more daring, in line with the great artist's revolutionary style, or rather might like, how shall I say it, a more conservative piece."

Simon thought it over, tempted to tell Florian that Mr. Khan was no prude and surely would prefer the bluish hewed naked woman, the more classic Matisse of the two offered. Knowing that this purchase was merely a pretext to setting up a direct meeting where they would lure the brothers with a request for a piece from Matisse's harem series, the choice was quite clear. "My own taste leans conservative, and if it was my money, I would buy this one on the right with the lady wearing the stylish hat. However, Mr. Khan is a connoisseur of Matisse's more abstract works, and I am sure he would prefer this lovely woman, so supinely stretched out on the left. May I ask a question before we discuss price?"

"Of course."

"How did you come to acquire these? We'll, of course, need a full provenance, but perhaps you can tell me the important bits now."

Florian and Rolfe had expected this question, and Rolfe launched into his prepared lie. Crafting a fake provenance was much easier than forging a masterpiece. "It's really quite simple. We bought it from a collection in Berlin. After the Wall came down, a lot of art came onto the market. Before then, people were reluctant to sell heirlooms unless they were paid in hard currency — which was scarce. When everything opened up, all of a sudden people could get cash. And they were desperate to start new lives. The opportunities were amazing. Our family invested in two sizeable collections, and that gave us connections to others."

Simon's radar was on alert, listening for clues pointing to the true source of the art. "Very interesting. But how did you afford a collection of museum-quality works, even at discounts? I accept there were opportunities. Even so, paintings like these, the collections, could not have been cheap."

"No, quite right, but not nearly as expensive as now. Remember, they were unusual times, and once the Wall came down, people were eager to move on. We were fortunate to have cash—my grandfather helped us. He was an art lover and was quite generous helping us launch our business. I'm not embarrassed to admit we took advantage of the opportunity."

"Rather roguish, it sounds." Jonathan, rather Simon, began to haggle, "All the same, I don't have an issue with your making a fair profit as long as I'm not fleeced. I trust you'll remember what you bought them for and also consider that my client may make more purchases if he's happy with this painting. And, surely, there will be a—let's say—proper discount if you cannot provide the provenance from before that purchase. Do you have paperwork from when you bought those collections? Things were, obviously, quite messy in Berlin for a while."

"Of course, though acquisitions from that area and time can be complicated… I would not claim everything is airtight. Which is why we are speaking, yes? We specialize in discreet transactions like this. With works that, let's say, may not be best suited for public auction." Florian tried to hint at what could not be directly spoken, rescuing Rolfe from the line of attack.

Simon's cheeks rose in a faint smile, a willing if far from transparent conspirator. "I understand, Mr. Mullen. Under the circumstances, I am prepared to overlook certain ambiguities in the provenance—assuming, of course, these paintings are authentic. It would be more troubling if they had a more sordid past. I don't mean to imply anything about you. I hope you understand it is a natural concern that pieces can have a taint to them when sold outside of auction. In the most extreme cases, speculation of theft can even arise."

Florian bristled, making a show of being offended. The veiled accusation, however, was both fair and expected. "I take no offense, Mr. Middleborough. These are natural concerns with pieces this valuable, and I have to warn you expensive. I doubt someone of Mr. Khan's stature would invest in art where something as damning as theft could be suspected. Rest assured we legitimately purchased these from the owners in Germany. I'm sure we have the old handwritten receipts, but I can't promise we were given earlier documents from the sellers. Records from that period, as I mentioned, can be less than perfect. But these are real Matisse's, acquired in Berlin, of that there should be no question. We have a reputation to protect...Our buyers trust us," Florian emphasized, knowing they could easily forge paperwork. Uncle Werner's Stasi training would come in handy.

"Thank you. Whatever you can find would be helpful."

"Of course. Shall we discuss price, assuming all else can be put in order?"

"Yes, let's get down to it."

Half an hour later, Jonathan Stein, aka Simon Middleborough, left the company of brothers Florian and Rolfe Mullen and began walking back toward the Bayerischer Hof. The price for one painting was nine hundred fifty thousand euros, almost a bargain. He wondered whether Hamid Khan might keep it as a souvenir of the escapade. If not, surely the painting would look lovely in an art museum in Tel Aviv. Perhaps that would allow the purchase to be allocated from another budget. He was glad David and Noah had the task of briefing the director on the cost of buying the Matisse from Mullen Antiques. Not his problem, and more importantly he had successfully laid the groundwork for another meeting—a meeting where they would abduct these bastards and learn the truth behind this stolen lot. And even more critically, he now had a vital piece of information. The grandfather was involved. The Nazi grandfather! My God, he thought, walking on the same cobblestones where Hitler himself had walked a half-century before. Perhaps our worst fears are valid, he mused. *My God. My God.*

CHAPTER 12

Munich, Germany — 2004

When my father and I helped my nephews, my near stepbrothers, set up Mullen Antiques, we had every expectation they would quickly gain connections in the art world. At the time, they had no idea what my father would bequeath and demand in his will and that he stored such a rich trove of paintings nearby. Nor did they have any inkling they would be pressed into service helping to launder so many of the paintings — and that my father's will would accelerate the timeline. My father, a genius in so many ways, had been patiently waiting. He nearly lived to see the fruition of his scheme and realized the timing was close. He did not live to see the inquiry from Hamid Khan, which somehow did not sit right with me. Just a feeling.

I never fully trusted Florian and Rolfe to vet their potential buyers properly. I gave them latitude, though with a clear caveat to alert me if there was a hint of anything out of the ordinary. Most of the time, it did not matter. But when a famous person appeared, someone playing in the billionaire circuit, someone who could claim to be my equal, asking for a quiet meeting, that was the type of instance I expected to be flagged.

Mr. Simon Middleborough's meeting request surfaced to my attention, and I had my staff look into him. He appeared legitimate: Eaton schooling, art masters, longtime assistant to Mr. Hamid Khan.

Of course, all those things could be fabricated, which I suspected was the case with several elements. At the time, though, there was nothing particularly untoward, and our diligence on Kahn confirmed he was a collector. There had even been a recent purchase of a Matisse out of Dubai. I approved Florian and Rolfe going ahead and meeting him. It was only later I would discover what was behind this slippery ploy to purchase Matisse masterpieces. I should have known better and trusted my instincts.

Munich, Germany—2004

It was a few months before Florian received another phone call from Simon Middleborough. "So sorry, I've been meaning to get back in touch. But working with Mr. Kahn, you know, there's always something urgent. Anyway, do accept my apologies, and I'm pleased to tell you that Mr. Khan was delighted with the painting. So happy, we'd like to inquire about an additional purchase."

"That's wonderful news. We're always thrilled when our clients are happy. Sounds like you made the right choice between the two paintings."

"Indeed. Having seen his reaction, the other painting would have been a mistake. The nude was perfect, and he'd be interested in another from one of his other themes."

"Themes? I'm not sure I understand."

"My apologies, I mean series. Do you happen to have anything from the artist's series of odalisques? That would be a perfect complement." Simon, rather Jonathan, had researched Matisse in-depth and learned about the Western women harem paintings. Noah and David delegated the details, and Jonathan was sure inquiring whether Mullen Antiques happened to have one of these was the ideal follow-up inquiry.

More an opportunist than an art lover, Florian did not know; however, he promisingly advised, "Let me check. I'll get back to you as quickly as I can, hopefully with good news." What a surprise it had been to hear back from Mr. Middleborough—and at such a time! They were beginning to feel the time pressure of unloading much of the art, the threshold from Opa's will— moving so many paintings was challenging, and they could not afford to wait until near the deadline to ramp up sales. Why the pressure? What was that third letter all about? No matter, Florian and Rolfe were pushing their network and had a couple other sales pending. Perhaps they might convince Mr. Hamid Khan to acquire a few works. He could certainly afford it. They would consider offering a discount for buying in bulk. If they could woo him to visit in person, Florian was confident he could sweeten the pot.

As luck would have it, they had another Matisse, and it fit the request. The work depicted a young Turkish woman, likely a concubine to an Ottoman sultan, lazily reclining in a blue and green hammock. She gazed out as if the viewer of the painting had just interrupted her. The dark-haired woman, certainly no virgin, was wrapped in a sarong-style white cloth from the waist down. The rest of her was fully exposed, her arms crossed over her head in an elbowed pillow, her bare and unnaturally large breast thrust up invitingly. It was perfect.

Florian called Mr. Middleborough back and suggested that Mr. Khan come in person. He and his brother would also like to show him some other special pieces. They were reluctant to part with this particular painting as it was a favorite of his grandfather's, and they hoped to keep it in the family. He knew that Mr. Middleborough would suspect this a fib, yet one had to play the games. Perhaps if Mr. Khan were there, Florian hinted, he could consider multiple pieces and persuade them to part with the heirloom. Mr. Simon Middleborough, aka Jonathan Stein and sometimes Mossad special agent, played his role equally well. Mr. Khan was an extraordinarily busy man and left art matters to him, his trusted broker, to vet and acquire. Did Mr.

Mullen want him to lose his position? Was he supposed to suggest that he could not acquire what Mr. Khan's pocketbook desired without Mr. Khan appearing in person?

After a period of ridiculous puffery, both men tired of the fake jousting. Mr. Middleborough relented, assured that Mr. Mullen would proffer a substantial discount. There was also the possibility of a small lost Matisse sketch that could potentially be parted with as a thank you commission, a small token of appreciation for Mr. Middleborough to cherish personally should Mr. Khan purchase more than the odalisque tart. Mr. Middleborough promised to come back to Florian with a proposed date and time should he overcome Mr. Khan's reluctance and coax him to fly to Munich. Both men hung up, overjoyed. Their respective traps were set, each oblivious to the other's scheming. Such results, though, were not unusual in the world of peddling stolen art.

***

A few weeks later, I received a phone call from Jonathan Stein confirming the team was on the ground. Jonathan traveling as Simon Middleborough, together with Aaron of no last name, and Pavlina as Ingrid Greggory, accompanied Hamid Khan on a commercial Lufthansa flight to Munich. Noah Berenbaum and David Wolfe decided that leaving Pavlina behind a second time might arouse suspicion. On the positive side, she could serve as a translator if any documents needed to be reviewed, Jonathan not speaking fluent German. Hamid may have ordinarily taken a private jet, but Noah and David, taking every detail into account, worried it could compromise Hamid's negotiating posture. Florian and Rolfe could track his arrival, and a private jet would likely increase the price charged. Credibility required limits to fiscal restraint, however, and they were greeted by two drivers and taken in sleek BMW 7-series to the Bayerischer Hof. Jonathan, Hamid, and Pavlina departed, while Noah, David, and Aaron stayed hidden behind the tinted glass as their driver sped off.

Beryl and I had already checked into the hotel the day before, and we were out playing tourist. For precaution, in case Florian and Rolfe were staking out the hotel, we wore hats and glasses when walking through the lobby to the elevators to alter our appearance. Uzi Jaffe always preached caution, and when on other than routine business, I often engaged a bodyguard and traveled under Beryl's name, Jaffe. While it remained unlikely we would be recognized after so many years, especially when not being searched for (I hoped!), extra vigilance was warranted knowing the Mullens could be watching. Uzi had also arrived but was staying at a Mossad safe house only a fifteen-minute walk north from Rolfe's townhouse in Schwabing. Soon, David, Noah, and Aaron pulled up outside to join him. The team would be making preparations for an interesting interrogation.

There would be no more direct communication among the team until the meeting took place. Uzi had stocked the house and earlier let Beryl know everyone would stay in for a quiet meal and go to bed early. Tomorrow would be a busy day. Back at the hotel, Beryl and I in one room, Hamid, Jonathan, and Pavlina in others, all purposely in different wings, we respectively ordered room service. For extra precaution, I asked the waiter to leave our tray outside; we would fetch the meal in a few minutes, presently indisposed. Beryl even added a small giggle. I checked through the peephole to make sure he followed my instruction and saw the waiter smile. I guessed he was wondering what Beryl looked like, used to overhearing romantic interludes. If he had stayed, he would have been sorely disappointed. The evening was sadly all business, reviewing details of the next day for the umpteenth time.

In the morning, as prearranged, Hamid, Simon, and Pavlina met in the breakfast room, partaking in the grand buffet. They then went back to their rooms, freshening up and retrieving their briefcases before meeting again in the lobby. Jonathan, transforming into Simon, dressed in a classic Savile Row double-breasted gray suit. In contrast, Pavlina, morphing into Ingrid, sported a hip-hugging dark green dress with too revealing a neckline, all designed to keep eyes off Jonathan. Their driver was already waiting, and within a few minutes, they would be entering Mullen Antiques. It was a relatively short walk from the hotel yet being driven was more in character. Hamid would have rather walked off the Bavarian breakfast.

The plan was relatively simple. They would proceed with negotiating for the painting, haggling hard enough to be perceived as genuine. Hamid would make one request before concluding the price—he would agree right then and make an immediate twenty percent deposit if they would join him for a drink to celebrate. He would reserve a private room at the Bayerischer Hof—he would insist. They had already reserved a room at six o'clock, a small conference room with one side door for serving. Aaron would enter to serve, and then he and Jonathan would quickly incapacitate Florian and Rolfe while Pavlina signaled the rest of the team. The serving door was just down the hallway from a fire exit where their driver would be waiting, the car running. Beryl and I would seal off the hallway once Aaron entered, ensuring no one saw them taking the brothers out and dumping them in the car. The team would spirit them away to the safe house where Noah, David, and Uzi all waited. The entire takedown and extraction would take five minutes or less. The brothers should be blindsided, celebrating their sale, offering no resistance. It was a simple, straightforward plan. Those were always the best.

***

Jonathan Stein, now playing the part of Simon Middleborough, and Pavlina van Dijksen, masquerading as his assistant Ingrid Greggory, accompanied Hamid Khan. The group strode confidently from their car to enter Mullen Antiques, Simon leading the way.

"Florian, Rolfe, good to see you again," Simon said, offering his hand. "I think you remember my associate, Ingrid." He nodded to her as she moved in for double cheek greetings. Rolfe, in particular, hugged back a bit too closely. "And may I introduce you to Hamid Khan."

"Welcome," Florian said, brushing aside the Ingrid bait and moving to shake Hamid's hand.

"Pleasure." Hamid smiled. "I love the Matisse Simon chose from your collection. Looking forward to seeing this new one."

Once Rolfe reluctantly turned from Ingrid, shaking hands and engaging in compulsory chitchat, they beckoned the trio to follow them into the same private gallery where Simon had viewed the prior Matisse. Absorbing his role, Simon was looking forward to seeing what was in store for them today, and nodded to Hamid that it was safe to follow. When they entered, the lights were dimmed for dramatic effect, and on the far side, a drape covered a painting resting on an easel.

"Please come in and wait a moment," Florian said.

He moved to the far side of the room and reached behind the easel while Rolfe shuffled to the side, granting Hamid the honor of standing in front for the flourish of the reveal. Jonathan, Hamid, and Pavlina were caught completely off guard when Florian lifted the drape in a dramatic gesture with his left hand and stood pointing a gun at them with his right. Even the Mossad can be surprised.

Jonathan, an experienced operative, whispered to Hamid to stand still. Pavlina tensed, her training kicking in, but scared and facing her first test at gunpoint in the real world. Hamid needed no encouragement to keep his mouth shut. He was terrified. Rolfe now stepped out of the shadows to the side and addressed the captives.

"Mr. Middleborough, I have some questions about your role here and what you've heard about us in London circles. Perhaps you and your associate will be good enough to tell us more in a moment. But, Mr. Khan, we are quite well acquainted with you. We have studied your holdings. And by the way, neither of us think much of FC Zug's chances in the Swiss league," he snickered. "If you cooperate, we will let you go free. It's not actually any of you that we are interested in."

"What are you talking about?" Jonathan interrupted.

"We are interested in Marco Bellagio," Rolfe said, shocking his no-longer guests.

"What?" Hamid blurted as Pavlina's eyes went wide, baffled by the mention of Marco and wondering if they knew about Beryl too. If they did, that would lead directly to SohoMasters and mean her cover could be blown.

"Your partner in FC Zug," Florian said. "You see, we happen to be acquainted with him. It's been a long time, and we would very much like to catch up. And you're going to help us get into his finances. Meet your new partners."

Hamid had no idea why they would want to talk to Marco or how they believed holding him at gunpoint could help them extort money. Was it some type of crazy mafia shakedown? He stood, perplexed by the proposition and frozen in shock, staring at Florian holding the gun.

Jonathan Stein, however, had been fully briefed by the Mossad team—including about Marco and Beryl's prior encounter with the brothers and their Nazi kin in East Berlin. That information had been highly classified, sequestered as need to know. This mission, back in Germany, meeting the Mullens, had been specifically cleared as need to know as well. Jonathan had to act fast and calculated they had no idea of his nor Pavlina's true identities. As far as Florian Mullen was concerned, he was pointing a gun at Simon Middleborough, an art broker from London who should be scared shitless. He continued to act the part, hoping Hamid would speak again. Fortunately, he did not have to wait long and slowly moved his hands behind his back, appearing supplicant.

"Marco?" Hamid almost mumbled, "I don't understand."

With Florian's attention on Hamid, Jonathan pulled the hidden gun nestled in the small of his back. In one fluid motion, he brought it forward and fired twice. The first bullet knocked the gun out of Florian's hand, severing a finger. The second one blast into Florian's chest, about five centimeters to the side of his heart. He wanted the bastard to live for questioning. Florian screamed and tumbled down, his disfigured hand reaching for his chest, blood everywhere.

Not waiting for him to hit the ground, Jonathan turned and held the gun at Rolfe's head. "Get on the ground. Now!"

Rolfe had moved toward his brother, stunned and naturally reacting to help him. Now he froze, kneeling first, then lying flat on the ground. Jonathan kept the gun trained on him, yelling at him to hurry, put his arms behind his back and lace his fingers together. It was happening so fast Rolfe could not process the actions, merely following the orders.

"Hold this, keep it on him," Jonathan instructed Pavlina, handing her the gun and keeping an eye on Florian, now writhing on the ground. Once Pavlina took the weapon, Jonathan raced to the side of the easel and ripped off some picture wire. He took the metal cord and tied Rolfe's hands, not minding that it was so tight the cord cut into his skin causing Rolfe to bleed mildly.

Jonathan next moved over to Florian and checked the chest wound. He should live. Jonathan's shot was perfect and tunneled straight through. He looked around and, not finding anything appropriate, tore off his shirt and undershirt. With a swift motion, he ripped his own t-shirt, tearing a piece into a makeshift cotton rag. When coming through the gallery, he had seen a wet bar and ran over, dowsing the strip in whisky. He quickly returned and plugged the hole in Florian's chest. Florian screamed, cursing him in German, before Jonathan struck him in the jaw and knocked him out. Jonathan refocused on the wound, motioning Hamid over and telling him to hold the cloth tight until the bleeding seemed stanched.

"Ingrid, call David and tell him to get a medical team ready and be on standby to evacuate," Jonathan said.

As he was cradling Florian and wrapping his bleeding hand, Aaron burst into the room. He had been watching the gallery from outside, but the sound of gunshots brought him inside, on alert. He had paused, not knowing who was shooting and from where. Aaron had no choice but to tread carefully, despite fearing he may be losing critical seconds if his comrades were under attack. When he made it into the room, he quickly surveyed the scene and assessed the mangled situation. Aaron was already on the phone to Noah talking in rapid fire Hebrew, obviating the need for Pavlina to call for help by the time Jonathan looked up.

"What the fuck happened?" Aaron finally asked when he hung up from Noah.

"This asshole pulled a gun on us. Somehow put together that Hamid was partners with Marco. Went to shit from there. I shot him. Brother Rolfe over there isn't hurt. Well, not yet." He moved over and gave him a wicked kick in the ribs. As Rolfe screamed in pain, Jonathan doubled his jaw punching pleasure and knocked the other Mullen out. Jonathan grabbed a handkerchief from Rolfe's pocket, furiously rubbed off blood spots freckling his chest, then pulled his shirt back on. Presentable enough.

"Shit," Aaron exclaimed. "Car's already outside. I'll take this piece of shit. You take the other, let's go. Hamid, Ingrid," being careful to still use cover names, "when we get outside, try to distract anyone nearby so we can get them into the car. The less seen, the better."

As if they had practiced this meticulously, Aaron and Jonathan each took a Mullen brother, slung the groggy bodies over their shoulders, and marched toward the front door. Hamid followed, speechless, and Pavlina trailed, checking to make sure they didn't leave anything important behind. In the chaos, she almost forgot to hide Jonathan's gun away in her purse. Outside, the driver had pulled onto the sidewalk, blocking anyone from walking past. As they emerged, Pavlina looked in both directions and noticed a woman appearing to be shopping with her mother. They were walking towards her but a good thirty yards away. She sprinted toward them and pointed behind over their shoulders, causing them to turn their heads. It was enough of a diversion; by the time they looked back, Aaron and Jonathan, with their driver's help, had stuffed the Nazi spawn into the back seat. Jonathan squeezed inside, and Aaron climbed into the front passenger seat. They were already pulling away as Hamid and Pavlina came back toward them on the sidewalk. Aaron called out, "Go back to the hotel, and go to your rooms, and stay there. We'll call. Go. Now!"

Within fifteen minutes, Hamid and Pavlina were back at the Bayerischer Hof, and Jonathan and Aaron were pulling up to the safe house. They pulled the car to a side entrance on an alley used to take out the trash and store bicycles. David opened the door and walked to the front of the driveway, screening for passersby. While he stood lookout, Jonathan and Aaron dragged the brothers into the house, depositing them on the floor of a lower ground bedroom. The windows were screened with blackout curtains, and Jonathan turned on a nearby stereo. Aaron kept watch as Jonathan went upstairs, changing his blood-spattered shirt and washing the evidence of the shooting off his face and hands. A full shower would have to wait.

When he came downstairs, a woman he had not seen before was tending to Florian's wounds. Noah whispered that her name was Elena, and they had her on call for emergencies; no need to know more details. Elena was working quickly, taking Florian's pulse, listening to his breathing, concerned the bullet may have punctured a lung. She enlisted Jonathan's assistance as they propped him into a sitting position in a chair, and she inserted an IV, adjusting its drip. After half an hour, Florian had a proper bandage on his chest with his hand wrapped tightly in gauze. What an hour before had been a manicured hand holding a gun was now a wrapped mitt, a soft beige boxing glove without fingers.

"He'll live, and I don't see evidence of any major internal bleeding. He's lucky. I'll need to get an x-ray for more, but I don't think he'll need surgery, at least not immediately," she said.

Noah replied, "Thank you, doctor. Hopefully, you won't need to operate. Do you think we can talk to him for a few minutes before you move him for the other tests?"

"Yes, he should be stable. But I ought to stay nearby. His condition could change quickly."

"Why don't you go upstairs and grab a coffee or something. We'll shout if he deteriorates."

Elena nodded and left the room. She was highly experienced in these matters, and they had used this safehouse once before for emergency surgery. A master bathroom functioned as a mini-operating theater, and a small bedroom was equipped with x-ray equipment. It was equivalent to a mini field hospital, and they could address most urgent concerns. There had been no plans for operating today; Elena was not even on standby. Her emergency beeper sounded just before she was about to take a jog. She had dropped everything and arrived at the house within two minutes of Jonathan and Aaron hauling the wounded men into the house.

By this time, Rolfe had stirred and was snarling. Once in the house, they exchanged the rough picture wire for professional flex cuffs. His arms were now also bound to a chair, and they had put a pillowcase over his face.

No reason to delay, Noah and David thought, and pulled off his hood. Rolfe nearly threw up when his first vision was of Florian slumped in another chair. He struggled to process the blood staining the bandage on Florian's chest, his brother's arm now a wrapped club, mottled bruising from his cheek to chest making him look like a broken jigsaw puzzle knit together with flesh. "What the hell did you do to him?"

"I shot him." Jonathan now stepped forward. "Don't you remember? He was pointing a gun at me, after all."

"Who are you?" Rolfe snapped, clearly in shock. "Where's Ingrid? What is going on?"

"Forget about Ingrid. She's back at the hotel. I'm Simon Middleborough, don't you remember? I'm buying a Matisse from you. You were even kindly going to give me a little drawing for free as a thank you gesture."

"Is this a burglary? You're doing this to get the painting?"

"No. I was defending myself when you guys held us up at gunpoint. Now, we're the ones who would like to know what the hell is going on! How do you know Marco Bellagio, and what do you want with us, with him? Why did you pull a gun on me?" Jonathan paused and walked over behind Florian, bending down so that his head was right above Florian's bruised face, his head hanging down toward the arm stuck with an IV. "By the way, your brother Florian is in desperate shape. Cooperate with us, answer our questions, and we'll get him to a hospital, and he'll live. Don't and, well, he probably won't make it. Then we'll really start on you. Your choice. And I don't play by the rules."

"Who are you, really?" Rolfe said, his voice cracking, tears running down his face. His head hurt like hell. He'd been knocked out and probably had a concussion. His wrists ached, the ties having cut deeply, the raw skin now irritated and stinging. However badly he hurt, his pain was inconsequential next to Florian's suffering. His brother's skin was grayish, his breathing shallow. He didn't know if they were bluffing, but he had seen his brother shot point-blank in the chest, and it was likely he was clinging to life and needed help fast.

Rolfe looked back at Simon. "Who are these other guys?" eyeing Noah and David. Ever cautious, Noah wore tinted glasses and a cap, disguising his easily identifiable battle-marks. Neither of them had talked in Rolfe's presence. Aaron with no last name had slipped out of the room, preferring to remain invisible, listening from the doorway.

"They're friends of mine. Let's leave it at that. I brought in some bodyguards in case you tried to swindle us. Million-dollar paintings under the table can be a dirty business. We were not taking chances," Jonathan lied, his story plausible. He was keen not to reveal his true identity. So far, nothing concrete undermined their story that he was Simon Middleborough and this was all about an art deal with Mr. Hamid Khan gone wrong. Well, there was the fact he was packing a gun, but perhaps doubling as security might also be plausible deep in the art underworld.

Jonathan continued, "It's you, not me, that needs to answer some questions. And I'd do it fast," eyeing Florian, reminding Rolfe the clock was ticking for his brother. "Now, why did you turn a gun on Mr. Khan and ask about Marco Bellagio? No bullshit. What the fuck is this all about? It doesn't sound like selling a Matisse to me."

Rolfe's head was throbbing, and he was not prepared for the pain or the interrogation. He started talking, not having a better plan. He could have simply stayed silent, but he was neither brave nor the type to endure self-sacrifice. The fact was that even in East Germany he had been among the privileged lot, and since then had dived headfirst into the indulgences of the decadent West. His best hope was giving them what they wanted and somehow getting away alive. He thought back to the poker game in East Berlin when Frank Krueshof had been shot and they had been beaten, nearly left to die—much like tonight. That evening had left him more scarred and timid than emboldened. How could it be happening again?

"What do you want to know?" he said, succumbing.

"How do you know Marco Bellagio?"

"It's a long story. I once met him in East Berlin when Florian and I were just kids. There was a horrible mix-up at a poker game. My grandfather was there. Marco shot some people. My family has wanted to find him ever since. His girlfriend too."

At least the asshole was coming clean, Jonathan thought. Best to guide him. He didn't care about culpability back in Berlin. Not part of the mission. He wanted to know about the grandfather and the art.

"Okay. So, you thought you would hold Mr. Khan hostage or something and trade him for Marco? Long-term revenge in the making or something like that?"

"Something like that. We were going to use him to set up Bellagio. We had a plan to take both of them down, get their money first. It was a shock to us to discover him, a rich banker. When we met, he was just a cocky kid who killed our friend."

"I'm sure there's another side to that story. Mr. Kahn told me that his partner, Mr. Bellagio, once got mixed up with some Nazis in East Germany. I'm guessing that your friends were involved in the shooting and also your grandfather, the one you told me helped you start Mullen Antiques. Am I on the right path?" Jonathan paused.

Rolfe had not been expecting this linkage, but perhaps it was not entirely impossible since they had introduced Marco into the puzzle. Kahn and Bellagio were close partners; an encounter with Nazis in Berlin might have come up privately. A lot of time had passed.

Jonathan suddenly punched Florian in the gut—not too hard, just enough to cause him to cough reflexively, triggering blood to trickle out of the loosened chest wound.

"Stop!" Rolfe implored. "I'll tell you what you want."

"Tell me about your family, about the source of the Matisse."

"My grandfather died recently. He left Florian and me his art collection in his will. He'd given us a couple of paintings before and helped us start the gallery—wanted us to go into the business. That's the truth. What I told you before."

"And where did he get the art? Was it stolen?"

"I don't know. He never talked to us about the details. We were stunned when he died and we found this warehouse full of paintings left to us."

"I don't believe you," Jonathan said flatly and moved to punch Florian again.

"No, no. Stop. They're from the war. He got them in the war and hid them. When he was dying, he thought it was time to sell them, set us up."

"You mean the war here in Germany? He was a Nazi? A Nazi officer?"

"Yes."

"And the paintings. Stolen? Taken from museums? Stolen from Jews?"

"Yes."

"Which ones?"

"All of it, probably. I don't know." Rolfe was now crying, head in his hands.

After a few more questions, and prying the location of the warehouse from him, Noah and David quietly left the room. Noah moved upstairs and placed a secure call to Tel Aviv. David called the Bayerischer Hof and summoned us to the safe house.

***

I knew something had gone terribly wrong. Beryl and I were waiting for Hamid, Pavlina, and Jonathan to return so we could set up the snatch in the conference room as planned. Except, Pavlina had rung our room and left an emergency abort coded message: be prepared to run. Not much later, David told us to pack up and get over to the safe house. What the hell was going on?

Beryl and I stuffed anything valuable in our carry-ons and rushed downstairs. On my way through the lobby, a bell boy saw us heading for the exit and ran over to us. He was calling my name. How did he know who I was?

"Mr. Bellagio. Mr. Marco Bellagio?"

"Yes, sorry, I'm in a hurry."

"There is an important message for you. The manager told me to give you this."

"What?"

The bellboy did not speak further, simply handing me an envelope. I took the fancy stationery, gold embossed with the hotel image and address, and dashed out the door with Beryl. The doorman blew a whistle for a taxi, and I walked around to the far side, letting the doorman open the car door for Beryl. As soon as I sat down, I opened the letter. I was pissed they thought I would leave without paying the bill and had the audacity to chase me down in the lobby.

The enclosure was not a bill; neither was it any message from the hotel. It was a curt note addressed to me:

To: Mr. Marco Bellagio

I know what happened at the Mullen Antiques gallery this afternoon. If any harm comes to Florian or Rolfe Mullen, I will hunt you down. I also know about your past. E. Berlin. Do not doubt my intentions.

Wait for another message at the hotel concierge desk at 9:00 pm this evening.

What the fuck? I showed Beryl the letter. Of course, being a Mossad agent, she had been suspicious when the bellboy chased us down. The possibility he was handing me our bill never crossed her mind. Our minds were of similar thinking now, though. She echoed, "What the hell?" turning the letter around in her hands.

CHAPTER 13

Munich, Germany — 2004

I left that note for Marco Bellagio at the Bayerischer Hof. My father, rest his soul, had asked me to look after my inept nephews. Florian and Rolfe truly failed at this simplest of tasks. And I am the one that tracked down and recognized Mr. Bellagio. And then Beryl Jaffe. I knew Hamid Kahn was staying at the hotel, so it was not much of a leap to track them down as guests once I smelled the purchase was a con. Maybe I should go back a few steps.

The purchase of the first Matisse was straightforward. If there had been nothing more, then Florian would not have been shot and abducted. When Mr. Middleborough came calling for a second time, however, I became suspicious and decided we should undertake another background check. In fact, I would do it myself. I had a tingling sense we had missed something, and after years in the Stasi employ, my feelings are well-honed. I could sense trouble others did not see. I could unmask the best of liars. I investigated whether Mr. Khan was on the board of any art museums or societies, if he was on the private lists of the major auction houses, if anything in his background or family's background suggested significant art collecting. There would ordinarily be several boxes checked for someone of his wealth, yet I came up with little beyond a handful of recent purchases orchestrated by Simon Middleborough. I began to dig deeper. I read about his businesses, about how he became wealthy. I focused on where he spent his wealth: not on art. Instead, he invested in football clubs and other sports. He was a director of a club in the English Premier League. That was where he focused his time, where he socialized, the access bought by his millions.

I wanted to grasp what motivated him, why he spent time on frivolous sports. And then, there it was. FC Zug, a minor football team. Honestly, who cared? Why bother when he already controlled a UK team, the biggest market for football in the world? I saw the clipping and realized I had seen that face before. Smiling next to Hamid Khan was Marco Bellagio, partner in SZG, banker, and FC Zug co-owner. That face was seared into my memory.

You see, I had not been there that fated night in East Berlin. Yet I heard. The house was wired, and one of my colleagues shared the raw tapes. I listened to Uncle Karl pretend to sacrifice Reiner, professionally grazing him with a bullet to put fear into the weak Westerners and set the stage for framing them. I heard Marco shoot and kill Frank Krueshof. I listened to my father scream in pain. I heard them tie gags around Florian and Rolfe's mouths and kick them until I could no longer hear their screams. Later, I learned there were some still photographs too, though thankfully only in black and white; it was enough I could picture red blood stains everywhere.

That night clearly did not go as planned. We had encouraged the boys to look for strangers, and that concert was the perfect opportunity. East Berlin was swarming with young, naïve kids partying for a few days. That had never happened before. We lived in desperate times. Those of us who had a little bit of money still struggled. You never knew when food would be scarce. Even working for the Stasi provided little protection. We would rat each other out for a morsel. If an apartment with better heating was at stake, I wouldn't have hesitated to sell out a relative.

We were all looking for people to swindle, to exploit. Maybe we would rob them. But we were searching for a bigger opportunity. A pipeline to the West, to smuggle in goods, was our dream. When

Florian and Rolfe discovered that kid Dirk was a diplomat's boy, it was too good to be true. They lured the stupid kids to that poker game. We all had a role to play, made them think we were fighting, staged some drama. If we could compromise them, we could own them. I would commission the tapes, our standard weapon of blackmail. None of us thought it out well. We were improvising until everything went to hell.

After listening to the tapes carefully, and questioning Florian and Rolfe for every detail from the time they met in the cafe before the concert until they arrived at my father's game, I could easily follow the Westerners' trail. I found the guest house they stayed at by the lake. I talked to the elderly owners, Martin and Christina. I discovered their passport numbers in the logbook. All visitors had visas, and the three of them came in together; one thing we excelled at back then was paperwork. Eventually, I had my hands on their visa applications, and with those files, I had their pictures. Perhaps mug shots only, but finally I knew what they looked like. What he looked like.

I memorized their faces because one day I wanted revenge: for not taking the boys to the West, for upsetting our plans, for killing Frank. When I saw his face again, smiling next to Hamid Khan, I thought it must be a mistake because the name did not fit. For years I had been on the lookout for Marco Dubois. In fact, I had found the border patrol's report for his lost luggage, located his bag at the guest house, and sent the bag to the Canadian Embassy with a note to Mr. Dubois tucked inside. If I could not find him, maybe his bag would, and the note would make him squirm. I had nothing to lose, and we were trained to unnerve our prey. It simply never occurred to me he had changed his name or traveled under a false passport — or that he had a passport under his mother's name. He was just a kid going to a concert. Guess I wasn't really cut out for the Stasi, or I would have dug deeper, figured that out before. Now it didn't matter because, no doubt, this was the same guy.

With his real name, I first considered tracking Marco Bellagio down in Switzerland. My research revealed I would need careful planning. He seemed to employ security. Photographs at events suggested he often traveled with a bodyguard. Surprisingly, I never found a picture with his wife. They were obviously very careful. Could he be worried about being discovered, or were his precautions routine trappings of being part of the jet-set? Regardless, I worried how difficult it might be to deal with the Swiss. The Swiss police tended to be partial to local bankers. I decided to take my chances on German soil, to use Hamid Khan to exact my toll on his partner. I wanted to ruin Marco Bellagio first, to hollow him out from the inside, before I left him to rot in a gutter. I had waited a long time and could plot my vengeance. I would start by coercing Hamid — I had learned the barrel of a gun could be a great motivator. Once I broke him, I would burrow into their businesses. Then, when I exacted financial ruin, I would move in for the kill.

I should have learned my lesson with Florian and Rolfe before. I should have acted immediately, not plotted a painful downfall, and simply enacted my revenge. Biblical. An eye for an eye. But no, I trusted my nephews and savored my thoughts of a slow torture. So often in the Stasi, we numbed ourselves watching others suffer, the gradual process of compromise perfected. Methodical moves. My training itself had compromised me. And now, as a result, I found myself for the second time needing to clean up their mess. Thank God my father did not have to suffer through their failures a second time. He entrusted me to watch over them. I needed to deal with my misjudgment.

Munich, Germany — 2004

We showed the letter to Noah, David, and Uzi, desperately seeking counsel. Beryl and I were convinced the note came from someone who had been at the poker game that evening. Our past was finally coming back to haunt us. They agreed.

Uzi was the first to speak. "It has to be one of their friends, someone who was there that night."

"But how did they piece it together, figure out it was us?" I asked.

"That's not really that difficult," Noah answered. "It was our mistake to use Hamid. He's your partner. There are pictures of the two of you together. He's a high-profile person. That's why we used him. We thought he was the perfect bait. And he was. It worked. They fell for it, and we were one step away. Somehow, they put two and two together."

"I agree," said David. "Maybe it was a coincidence or just bad luck. Maybe they looked into Hamid's background, decided to do some research. Doesn't matter. He must have found a picture of you together, or some article linking you. And then it all came back. Just like it did for you when you saw the pictures of Florian and Rolfe."

"It makes sense. I can't think of a better explanation," Uzi said. "You said 'he.' It could also be a woman. Maybe they told their wife, girlfriend, daughter.... We don't know anything, except that whoever it is, they made the connection. It's possible. But that would mean they've been looking for years, which I don't think is likely...Why now all of a sudden? Had to be a picture, something connected with Hamid...I was always worried about this sort of thing. That's why I asked you to beef up your security, just in case. And why we've always been careful to keep any photos of Marco and Beryl out of the press."

"Stupid of us," Noah spat bitterly. "We should have anticipated they could link the two of you."

"Let's not waste time beating ourselves up. We'll have plenty of time to evaluate that later." David tried to slow the tide of second-guessing. "We never thought they would look further into Hamid. That was part of the calculation. He was high-profile, his money and interest in collecting would be taken for granted. Shit...Forget about it. We don't have much time. We need to figure out a plan to deal with this. Quickly."

"Do you think my cover is blown?" Beryl asked. "I mean, if they looked into Marco...Could they have connected me to SohoMasters? And Pavlina?"

"I don't think so," Noah said. "They didn't say anything about her at the gallery. If they knew, why hide that? They were gloating. And probably more compelling, Rolfe never said anything when he broke down. If he'd known about Ingrid being Pavlina, I doubt he would have held back. No way."

"Well, let's be extra careful. We can't be sure," Beryl said. "If they found Marco, we have to expect they would look into his family."

"Jesus," I muttered, not sure which worry to fixate on, ping-ponging back to the note. "I assume we go back to the hotel and wait for the message as instructed?" I asked, a bystander in my own hunt. I was not sure what my role had become—prey and fugitive both came to mind.

Uzi, worried about Beryl, and I hoped his son-in-law too, said, "Yes. I don't see a choice. At least it's a public place. Nothing will happen there. And they don't know Aaron—at least let's hope not. We'll place him in the lobby with you and tell him to disguise his appearance just in case. I'll have coffee at a table across the room, maybe sitting with David."

"And what about me?" Beryl asked. "We have to assume if they know about Marco, they at least know I'm his wife. I think I should go with him."

"Too dangerous. Why increase our risk of exposure?" Uzi said.

"Marco's not trained, and odds are they know about me—not about SohoMasters or the Mossad, but at least about our being married. This is controlling our risk. I'm going."

Noah and Uzi looked at each other, knowing they would not win this argument. No good options existed.

Noah nodded, "Okay, I get the logic. I just don't like it." Already focusing on tactics, he continued, "Whether you go or not, we need to sort out three other elements. We have to think through what happens when you get the message. For now, I agree Aaron should be on the spot. Uzi, probably you too. Let's assume even if they connect Beryl, you're not compromised. We don't know how many watchers they may have, and we need eyes. We can't bring in more people on this short notice. That's enough inside — we need to spread out to be able to tail wherever they tell you to go. Let's keep Pavlina out of it in case Beryl's right. They've seen her a couple times, so let's not tempt the connection. Same with Jonathan. We can have him stay back with Pavlina and keep an eye on the brothers. I think David and I should wait in a car in case they instruct you to take a taxi or have a car waiting for you. We'll be ready to follow. But we also need to think about Florian and Rolfe. And the art."

"What do you mean?"

"Whoever this is, that may be what he wants too, and that's our leverage. Remember, the paintings are worth tens of millions. I think we should move the art. Immediately. Take it back to Israel. They never mentioned that in the note. We can claim we don't know anything about it, don't have it. They won't believe us, of course, but they also don't know that Florian and Rolfe cracked. They won't even know it's missing. I doubt that's their priority right now."

"Maybe," Uzi said, pondering the plan. "I suppose we have nothing to lose, and it takes one of the pieces off the table. We still have the brothers."

And me, I thought. Best to keep my mouth shut. Lovely being a pawn.

"Exactly. So, we move the art and wait to see what they want. If we deliver the brothers, we've met the demand. Does anyone have a better plan?" Noah looked around, seeing a lot of worried yet blank faces. "Good. Uzi, you work on staking out the Bayerischer Hof. David and I will think about routes around the hotel. Marco and Beryl, put your heads together and think about who this could be. You're the only ones that met these guys. Think it through, and then interrogate Rolfe again. See if you can get something out of him. Jonathan and Aaron, get working on confirming the warehouse location and moving the art. I'll make a call to the office and arrange a cargo plane and a local team. Oh, and Marco, just tell Hamid to stay put. No need to expose him to any more risks. We all meet back here in three hours. Hurry."

Jesus Christ. There I went again. I needed to think of better panic words than Christ and shit. Seems like I ought to have a wider go-to range for panic swearing.

***

By 8:30 that evening, we had as much in place as we could muster. Our further interrogation of Rolfe came up empty. We had decided not to mention the note. Too many games were being played, and we were wary of sharing information. Neither Beryl nor I could remember much about the other men that evening.

"I don't remember anyone clearly other than Florian, Rolfe, and their grandfather," I confessed. "I barely remember the guy they shot in the leg and dragged off. It all happened so fast."

"What about the guy you shot?"

"Well, yeah. Of course. I'll never forget him. Frank. But I don't think a dead man left us that note."

"Fair enough…There was also that uncle. Karl, they called him," the name had stuck with both of us. "But same thing. Rolfe said he died a while ago too. Makes me sick that these guys peacefully lived out their lives. Anyway, dead-end leads without their coughing up more information."

We finally gave up, unable to remember much more, devoid of further clues. If Rolfe and Florian had told the truth, and their grandfather was dead, then our list of surviving Nazis from that night was short. At least we thought they were all Nazi officers. Maybe that was a flawed assumption. Thinking of them as party faithful, mass murderers, though, made it easier. That was how

I had always justified shooting Frank, assuming those geezers were all old ranking Nazis. No reason to change opinions, especially when our other working assumptions were proving correct. We had been right about the art. Shit! It was probably all true.

Beryl and I sat quietly, reflecting on what might happen in less than an hour. I thought they would give us instructions to meet somewhere else, just like in a movie. Shit! I still could not come up with a better word. We waited in our room, the gold gilding and flowery drapes teasing us to enjoy the hotel's elegance. I stared at my watch constantly, checking the time every few minutes, failing to slow or speed the second hand, until finally heading down to reception just shy of nine o'clock.

While our attempt to narrow down the author of the note had proven futile, the rest of our team was moving ahead with professional focus. The most impressive part of the day's edition of Operation Moonlight was the removal of the art. Jonathan and Aaron managed to locate the warehouse then rendezvous with a local team thrust into urgent action. Two freight trucks pulled up to the warehouse, and an assembly line loaded the crates. Within two hours, the warehouse was virtually empty.

When I heard about the efficiency, I made a bad pun in my head: these guys should moonlight as professional movers. God, what an idiot. It was not the time to allow my mind to wander its typical sarcastic path. How did these Mossad guys maintain their focus and cool? I would never be one of them. Was it a slight to my manhood that the closest I would come was marrying one? There my mind went again.

Thankfully, the movers left the warehouse and drove the loaded trucks to the airport without incident. From what I was told, bypassing security was also not a problem. Ever since the infamous Munich Olympics and murder of Israeli athletes in 1972, the Mossad had the local police's full cooperation. Guilt and horror for once worked to our benefit. The trucks entered via a side gate, passing with a wave from the guard, no inspection of the contents. They proceeded to the cargo area of the tarmac where an unmarked Israeli cargo plane waited. After lowering the cargo entry door, the movers hauled the paintings for the second time in a few hours. Aided this time by Israeli soldiers who would escort the loot, the unloading and loading were completed with military precision. By the time the clock struck nine o'clock, the plane was taking off, heading south toward the Mediterranean. Its final flight plan, unfiled of course, would take it safely to a military airstrip outside Tel Aviv. The hoard of stolen treasure would finally be home — of sorts.

***

Just after nine o'clock, Beryl and I approached the concierge desk. The same bellboy who had delivered the last note approached us, advising a gentleman was waiting for us at a table in the corner of the bar. That was not what I was expecting. How could whoever this was meet us there, with no notice? Maybe that was precisely the point. Fortunately, I was not in charge of planning, and the Mossad team had been prepared for all options, Aaron already positioned as backup in the lobby.

We walked to the bar, and seated alone in the corner was a middle-aged man. He had shocking blond hair, parted so neatly his scalp betrayed not a hint of age-revealing roots. When he turned toward me, his milky blue eyes danced, distracting from the slight sag in his cheeks, a sign that despite the handsome glint he had turned past his prime. Werner Bosseneker (though I did not yet know his name) was a stunning specimen who could have been a movie star had not the weight of the years in East Germany weathered and saddened his face. I scanned the room and did not recognize anyone else. It was impossible to believe he was there alone. Certainly, we were not. Soon, Aaron followed us, avoiding eye contact, before moving around the corner to a more discreet distance. For extra precaution, Aaron wore a sweater and fake glasses, changing his appearance to a casual observer. Werner nodded to us, and we made our way over to his table. Beryl and I reluctantly sat down, no one offering their hand in greeting.

"I suppose you want to know my name, Mr. Bellagio and Ms. Jaffe," Werner began, immediately putting us on the defensive.

"Among other things," Beryl answered, naturally taking the lead. She did not even flinch at the confirmation of her being compromised. It had been too much to hope that this guy did not know about Beryl.

"My name is Werner. I am not inclined to offer my surname presently," his tone as formal as his grammar. "I am an old friend of Florian and Rolfe's family. I thought I could intercede on their behalf."

"Intercede? That's an interesting word for threaten."

"Let's not sling accusations, shall we?"

"How do you know who we are? And how do you know about what happened at Mullen Antiques?"

"Surprising, Ms. Jaffe. I thought you would lead asking how I knew about the events back in East Berlin."

"That too," I added. "Why don't you cut the bullshit and tell us who you are and what's going on here."

"Patience, Mr. Bellagio. All will be clear. Let me first start with recent events. It should not surprise you to learn there are cameras in a gallery like Mullen Antiques. I was alerted to Mr. Khan's visit and was watching. I thought the meeting might become interesting. Watching is something I've practiced my whole life. You see, I also lived in Berlin and was trained to watch there."

My body tensed. I knew he was telling the truth. His tone was so sinister, I could imagine him as if in a newsreel, sitting in a room with a tape recorder or camera, calmly watching. Werner epitomized the dispassionate arrogance of Stasi watchers, waiting for someone to slip and in the privacy of their living room betray the state. Only this was personal—and potentially worse. I did not know how to respond, and suspected Beryl felt the same. We both continued to listen.

"So, I know what happened in the gallery from the video cameras. And the two of you? When Simon Middleborough and Ms. Greggory first approached the gallery and bought the Matisse on behalf of Hamid Khan, I was not suspicious. He was the type of buyer we seek. But when Mr. Middleborough called a second time and was looking for a more specific work, I was alerted. This can be a precarious business, moving art with, let's just say, a less-than-ideal provenance. Florian and Rolfe have instructions to let me know of any unusual transactions or requests. From there, it was quite simple. I had my colleagues conduct standard research on Mr. Khan. When I reviewed the file, there was a report on business associates, which naturally included Mr. Bellagio."

Werner paused, turning directly toward me, his blue eyes piercing as if igniting a blue light laser, confirming what we had already deduced. "When I saw a picture of you with Hamid Khan, I recognized you immediately. I couldn't believe it, could not put the picture down. Could it really be the man from East Berlin that night? At first, I refused to believe it, the coincidence unfathomable. But I could not deny the truth. And something tells me, Mr. Bellagio and Ms. Jaffe, that the same goes for you. Are you telling me this is a coincidence, that you just happened to be helping your friend buy a Matisse from Florian and Rolfe? Surely you recognized them from that evening."

Ever cool, Beryl was not prepared to cede any ground. "I don't know what you're talking about…Mister…Werner? You seem to know enough about us. It seems only fair that you give us your full name."

"Why don't you just call me Mr. Berlin. I think that is apropos. Mr. Werner Berlin."

"Not very amusing, but okay, Mr. Berlin. I accept the gallery had cameras, and you saw what happened. You must have also seen that Florian pulled a gun on Hamid Khan, and he and Mr. Middleborough defended themselves. What I don't understand is why Florian pulled a gun on them? Why involve us? Can you explain any of this?"

"That should be obvious too, shouldn't it? We wanted to get to the two of you. For East Berlin. For killing one of us, for running away. What confounds me is how an energy trader, an art broker, and his assistant were able to defend themselves, and who that other man was that came to their rescue? I suppose you are going to plead ignorance about that too?"

"There's just so much that neither of us seems to understand," I cut in. "Perplexing, isn't it? You telling us some tale about East Berlin, even though neither of us was ever in East Berlin. You do recall a Wall, correct? A Wall that kept people like us out, a Wall that was virtually impenetrable to cross. And as for the gallery, Hamid told us he was coming to buy a painting, and he wanted to show it off to Beryl. She happens to be in the art business, in fact, quite a famous appraiser. We thought it would be fun to visit Munich, maybe see some museums tomorrow."

Werner's voice rose. "Enough of this mock debate, this one-upmanship of denials is leading nowhere. We could continue this silly game for a while, but I don't have the time. Let me put it to you more directly. I expect you to release Florian and Rolfe Mullen. I will be back here at 10:00 tomorrow morning. Bring them here, and then leave. I will have someone help collect them. If you do that, I will keep quiet about what happened in East Berlin, as I have done for all these years. If I don't see them here in the morning, then I will share this file with the newspapers. Oh, and perhaps Interpol as well. I think they will both be quite interested."

Following the threat, Werner reached down into his briefcase. I tensed briefly, fearful he might draw a gun, but then realized the absurdity of that in the middle of the modestly crowded bar adjacent to the main lobby. Instead, Werner slid us a thin file. "Perhaps this will refresh your memory of East Berlin."

Beryl took it and flipped through, seeing black and white grainy photographs of us some fifteen years earlier. There we were in the room, bodies on the floor, blood around, the calamity frozen in still life. My greatest fear realized. Shit! I wanted to kill Werner on the spot. I knew Beryl was capable, but this was not the place. I felt Beryl's hand gently on my thigh, trying to calm me.

She said, "Interesting reading. But photos can be doctored. I hear that was one of the Stasi's specialties. I am beginning to wonder about your background."

"Does my background really matter, Ms. Jaffe? What's that expression? A picture can paint a thousand words. Surely a phrase you know as an art lover." He let the verbal dagger linger.

"Let's say we did know where Florian and Rolfe were, and we were able to help bring them here tomorrow. What assurance would we have that you wouldn't hand a copy of these over anyway?"

"Ah, a fair point. In some ways, you don't. But if you were actually in East Berlin, and these are real pictures, then you know that Florian and Rolfe's family have a past they prefer to keep quiet. Some people still tend to have a rather dim view of Nazis. If I exposed this file, then their whole family is exposed, the gallery falls into disrepute, their name and that of their relatives slandered. I don't see the incentive in that."

"And what if we were to expose them anyway?" I asked.

"Exactly how? You would incriminate yourself to expose a couple of old Nazis? I don't think so. You both seem to have quite a comfortable life. Why upset all that? Besides, do you think I have given you everything in that file? I am not stupid enough to hand over everything. Certainly not the tapes."

"Tapes?"

"Yes, tapes. You see, in the east, there were always people watching, listening. In fact, I was one of them. In a moment, I am going to get up and leave. I expect you to stay here for five minutes. I have colleagues in here watching, and I will be alerted immediately if you get up. I would expect if you are smart—and I take that to be the case—that you have associates here too. Perhaps even those people you claim not to know who rescued Mr. Khan." Werner made an exaggerated gesture of looking around; fortunately, Aaron had disguised himself well, and if Werner had identified him when entering, he hid his knowledge well.

"How do I know you're not bluffing? You may hand that file over anyway just to ruin me," I said.

"As I said, I could. And I would warn you not to test me. If I have to sacrifice Florian and Rolfe, at least I will have the satisfaction of finally seeing justice for East Berlin. Believe me, I have thought about it—and I had intriguing plans for your confessions before your friends managed to upset those plans at the gallery…An unfortunate turn of events, at least for me… Going public is very tempting. Still, we both seem to have past secrets we would prefer to keep. I was very close to Florian and Rolfe's grandfather and promised to watch over the boys. They have had a difficult enough life—which today's adventure has not improved. I don't have any desire to make it worse. But we all have our limits. My offer of a détente remains. I expect on reflection, however imperfect, you will see it the same way. I would advise you set them free here tomorrow. Goodbye, Mr. Bellagio, Ms. Jaffe. Or, should I also say, Mr. Dubios? By the way, did you ever get your luggage back with my little card? Oh, and please keep the file."

Werner Berlin, as I knew him, stood up and strode out of the hotel. I motioned with my hand toward Aaron to stay put, let him go. I quickly placed a phone call to Noah, alerting him to what Werner looked like, asking him to try and follow him. Unfortunately, Werner had anticipated this, not surprising for a former Stasi spook. When Noah later pulled the hotel's security footage, we saw that when Werner left, he doubled back along a side hall. In fact, the same hall we had intended to use in our failed plan to lure Florian and Rolfe back to the hotel and nab them. Werner exited the side door we had identified and strode into a car which quickly pulled away, unfollowed.

After waiting in front of the hotel, Noah and David eventually realized Werner had evaded us. They came inside and joined Uzi, Aaron, Beryl, and me in the small conference room by the hall. Uzi had bound downstairs when being signaled that we were meeting in the bar but remained at a distance until Werner had stood up and left. The debriefing was somber. Beryl and I averted our eyes when Uzi flipped through the file. Not exactly the impression you want to make on your father-in-law—even one who works for the Mossad and already knew. As Werner had amplified, a picture can paint a thousand words. Shit.

Uzi broke the ice. "He never asked about the art, the warehouse?"

"No, it never came up," Beryl said.

"At least that's one good thing. It's possible he doesn't realize that's our angle. We need to pray he doesn't discover it's been cleaned out before the morning. And you don't remember meeting him before. No idea who this Werner Berlin really is?"

"No. I'm sure he wasn't there that night," I answered. "But for all we know, he could have been watching or listening. Clearly, they had the house bugged and outfitted with remote cameras. Those pictures are real. Too real."

David joined, "Probably was with the Stasi. It would fit."

Noah added, "But it doesn't matter. We need to look forward not back right now. He's had this information all along and hasn't used it. The Stasi is long gone, and the police probably won't be interested in a fifteen-year-old case behind the Wall."

"But they didn't have us before," Beryl said. "They may have had the files, but they had no idea who we were. Hadn't put anything together. Until now."

"Which makes it very effective blackmail material," Uzi acknowledged. "But I agree with Noah. It's quite unlikely the German police would pick this up. And if we had to bury it, I'm sure a word explaining that a group of ex-Nazi officers pulled a gun on you would convince them to keep it quiet."

"But our reputations. Even if we get off, it's not like a statute of limitations is what I want to use to clear my name," I said, panicky.

"I didn't say we want this to get out. It would be a disaster. I was just thinking through options — worst-case scenario, we can keep you out of jail, have it go away."

"Wonderful," I said sarcastically. "Finally get to play an Italian mobster. A little bribe and I get to walk free."

"Marco," Beryl snapped, embarrassing me on the spot. My selfishness shone through, and it was not the time for wisecracks about being a wiseguy.

"Sorry, I'm just…can't believe any of this. What are we going to do?"

Noah said, "We're going to do exactly what this Werner Berlin asked. We bring Florian and Rolfe here tomorrow and hand them over. Maybe we can get more information out of them before then, maybe not. We try to follow Werner, or whoever picks them up. We keep an eye to see if there's a link to other Nazis, and if so, we go after them. Likelihood is probably not; they're probably all dead. And we have the art. Remember, that's what we were after anyway, to find the art and bring these guys down. The grandfather's dead. We have stopped Mullen

Antiques, and hopefully, we can find the paintings' rightful owners. What happened in Berlin…well, we can't do anything about that. Hopefully, it stays quiet. We have to wait and see. We're both holding cards the other doesn't want played. He was right about that."

Everyone let Noah's analysis sink in. I looked down at the file, glancing at Beryl, but she was lost in her thoughts. Like me, she was likely wondering how after all these years, that night surfaced. Deep down, we were both always afraid that night would rise up to confront us. Was it possible to forget killing a man? Was it possible to forget meeting a group of Nazi officers — actual Nazis! — in the present? This stuff was for history books not live confrontation in the new millennium. The surreal nature of everything was too much to absorb. In reality, it was virtually impossible to bury the truth. And the truth was in that file sitting in front of us.

"I don't feel comfortable handing them over and letting Werner get away," I finally said. "This has been hanging over us for years. And now, we'll never be able to relax if he's out there. And once he discovers the art's gone, he's not going to be happy."

Noah countered, "I understand. But we've all done things we want to forget. You find a way to bury it and move on."

"Yeah, but I'm not Mossad. I didn't ask for this."

"Shit happens. And when you married Beryl, you married into the Mossad. You had to know you could become involved."

Uzi shot Noah a seething look, letting a bit of his restrained nervous energy pulse openly. That was unfair. "Families are always off limits, Noah. You know that."

"Sorry. You're right," he said, acknowledging he had crossed a line. Nazis had a way of making him ignore protocol. His body language sagged until he recovered enough to climb out of his verbal foxhole. "Look. This happened before they were married. Cannot be undone. We can only help hide the past, and I still think this is the best strategy. I'd love to get Werner too. We all want that bastard. We'll try to follow him and catch him. You have to come to terms with the reality, though, that we may never see him again. He stayed hidden for years. I'd now say with ninety-nine percent certainty he's ex Stasi. If he doesn't want us to find him, we probably won't. Let's take the victory we have. Does anyone have a better idea?"

Well, I did. Kill him. But that was not going to achieve a thumbs-up around the table. Noah was right. We probably would never see him again. And if we failed to hand over Florian and Rolfe, then it was lose-lose. He would probably let them rot, reconciled to their exposure as a price for ours too. Who knew what other skeletons this guy had. I was sure a lot. A chill came over me. Old Nazis. He was there, a friend of the family. That meant a friend of the grandfather, maybe even related. This guy was rotten to the core. It was like a bad joke — what do you get when you mix a Nazi with a Stasi agent? At best, nothing good; at worst, I didn't want to find out.

Noah was probably correct — cut our losses or take our victories, whichever spin provided more comfort. I saw no other realistic choice. I nodded my head, mumbling, "Okay," looking over to Beryl and Uzi. I would support what they said. I was beaten down — this lemming was not capitulating as a ploy for marital relations or rehabilitation. I was whipped in every sense of the word. Shit.

Beryl asked, "Abba, do you agree? It sickens me to let him go. It's wrong. Hideous. Think of what these guys must have done. But we may never find him again, and I can't let these pictures out there either." Looking despondently at Noah, a defeat in her eyes I don't remember seeing before, she continued, "No, I don't have a better idea."

She wiped tears from her eyes, and I slid over and put my arm around her. Uzi did not say anything, eventually raising his eyes toward Noah, head still cast down, and nodded slightly.

Uzi was cutting his losses. I think only Noah took it as chalking up a small victory.

"Well," Noah said, "at least he didn't seem to know about Beryl's cover and involvement with SohoMasters. Or about Pavlina. He seems to only know her as Ingrid Greggory. Some consolation."

"Wonderful. We all get to keep our fake names," Beryl said, ending the conversation.

***

Florian and Rolfe were still our hostages, or prisoners, for lack of a better description. They were certainly not guests. They were also our only leverage against Werner until we released them. While Beryl and I went back to our room, Noah and David headed back to the safe house. Florian was now alert and stable—at least awake enough to be interrogated, according to David. I was spared witnessing that next interrogation. From how it was described to me, it was ugly. David and Noah were angry and likely out for a measure of vengeance. In the brothers, they saw the face of the grandfather, Nazi evil incarnate, the murderers of David's family. They were seeking retribution for the sins of the grandfather, and maybe grandmother and father too. The indignity of the brothers compromising Beryl, one of their own, merely added to their rage. Still, they needed to walk a line, fulfilling our pledge to deliver the two at the hotel the next day, able to walk, not beaten to a pulp. They would need to be clever in their interrogation and, given Florian's fragile condition, could not push him much further. Torture would be too good for the two conspirators, yet the Mossad crew were not animals. Despite whatever blows they might fantasize meting out, they were ultimately professionals and would adhere to tightly scripted rules. They would not stoop to the level of these Nazi spawn scum.

I don't know all the intricacies of what happened in that room. Beryl told me they considered bringing in Pavlina, wondering if softening them up might work. The leaders, though, were not in a patient mood, and I inferred they decided it was time to play tough. My mind imagined Aaron of no last name beating them, tearing fingernails, even severing a finger or limb. In truth, I was probably not told the goriest details, which was fine with me. I just wanted the nightmare to go away, the whole damn affair to disappear. I tried to forget, hoping to erase the memory as simply as dragging and dropping it into trash on a desktop screen and clicking empty. If only actual memories could be wiped as easily as digitally stored pictures.

Putting aside the means, though, the fruit of the team's labor was quite helpful. Ultimately, they learned names and information about associates in the art underworld. Rolfe divulged other family friends that used the nefarious services of their gallery. David, Noah, and Uzi felt hopeful they might have grabbed hold of the beginning of a ball of yarn, which properly pulled could untangle a knot of more hidden Nazi art.

Aaron and I believe Jonathan (still acting as Simon) also interrogated Florian and Rolfe as to Werner's identity. The brothers, though, knew better than to disclose anything about the gentleman going by the alias Werner Berlin. Death would be better than rescue and having revealed personal identifying details about him. All they would divulge is they called him Uncle Werner, an affectionate term, and he had been a lifelong friend of the family. David and Noah were inclined to believe them, especially after what they had suffered along with Aaron's extracurricular encouragement. Nevertheless, one reason for the beating and interrogation was to sow disinformation.

"Florian," David said, Aaron holding Florian's head up, so he was forced to look at him in the glare of the halogen lamp. "I'm obviously disappointed you're not telling me anything useful about your so-called Uncle Werner. But never mind. We already know all about him. I just wanted to hear it from you. From your lips."

"How, what?" Florian mumbled, disoriented, still critically weak from the gunshot wound. Whatever additional message Aaron had pummeled out had left him on the edge—delivering him tomorrow to Werner would be more than challenging.

"Did you think we could simply find Mullen Antiques, know about your past, know it was the two of you in East Berlin? To set this whole thing up with Hamid Khan and not know about your uncle. We know he and your grandfather helped set this whole thing up, staked you in the gallery. We know about the Nazi past. About East Berlin. And all about your Uncle Werner."

Continuing to speak, now addressing both Rolfe and Florian, "We are going to release you tomorrow. In exchange for your lives, we have three demands. First, you never mention anything about meeting us—ever, to anyone. Second, you close Mullen Antiques and continue cooperating. The names you provided, others that are dealing in stolen art from the war, better bear out. And last, tell your Uncle Werner that we know all about him and where to find him. He thought he was safe hiding in plain sight. Not true. If he dares to release the files from East Berlin, we will expose him and come after him. We will never forget he is out there, and he will never be safe. I swear this on my life and the lives of those murdered by your grandfather. Don't fuck with us. Today will seem mild. You don't want us to go there. Deliver that message."

With that, Aaron slapped Florian, who, in his weakened condition, snapped back out of consciousness. Rolfe looked up, crying, shivering, stripped down, and begging for them to stop. Noah nodded and gestured for David to follow as they left the room and moved upstairs.

***

"Do you think it will work?" Noah asked.

"I had to try. They don't know what we know, and Werner has to be worried. If he thinks we have information on him, it may persuade him to keep silent. A bit of insurance on not releasing the files."

"But won't he think if we know, we'll go after him anyway?"

"Of course. Do you feel bad he may always be looking over his shoulder?"

"It's almost like you enjoy this, David."

"Never. But this time, maybe just a little." He allowed himself a half-smile for the first time that day.

***

At ten o'clock the next morning, Noah, Jonathan, and David brought Florian and Rolfe to the Bayerischer Hof. The brothers were cleaned up and bandaged. Elena, the Mossad doctor, and her team had performed nothing short of a miracle. Aided by years of grisly experience on the front lines of mini-wars and far-too-routine car bombings, the team had become among the best in the world at stitching bystanders and victims back together. Rarely, though, had they been forced to overcome the challenge of stabilizing a man shot point-blank so he could stand within a day—a combination of luck and a morphine cocktail.

Florian was unsteady but by leaning on Rolfe was able to shuffle forward. The staff and those wandering the lobby looked shocked at the two well-dressed men who appeared like they had just emerged from an all-night drinking binge that ended in a bar brawl. As he was already known from the meeting—and apparently camera—at the Mullen Antiques shop, Jonathan escorted them. Noah wore tinted glasses plus a pasted-on mustache, taking care to hide his face, often looking down and cocking his head to the side with his hand covering his deformed ear. Aaron and Uzi, having already been in the hotel lobby the day before, stayed away so as not to cause further suspicion. They had no idea who Werner had watching, and the same people popping up in the exact place without explanation was a potential complication to be avoided.

After the four men sat down together in the lounge, the same bell boy that had delivered the earlier note to Marco appeared at their side; apparently, he had been given a description of the brothers. The messenger asked which one of them was Rolfe. When Rolfe nodded, he handed him a note, which Rolfe read quickly before folding it in his pocket. Willing himself to stand up, he then helped Florian stagger to his feet. He looked at Jonathan, who he still only knew as Simon Middleborough, and told him it was time for them to go. Noah had earlier made the tough decision not to invest much hope in following them. Werner was a pro and would have them chasing their tails. Also, with Beryl and I now compromised, they needed to step back for a while. Operation Moonlight had recovered the art and thwarted whatever plans the Mullens had, which would have to suffice for the time being. Aaron and one other operative would try to track them back to Werner but were ordered to abandon the chase if they were spotted or determined the effort futile. Sadly, that was exactly what happened.

After they left, Jonathan called our room, and I rushed to the bar with Beryl. I stopped on my way and asked the concierge to call Hamid's room and ask him to join us in a few minutes. I had talked to Uzi and convinced him we owed it to Hamid to fill him in on some of the background. He already knew we were involved in a sting to recover stolen art. I would have to tell him more. At that point, there seemed little harm letting him know

Florian and Rolfe were suspected of peddling art collected, rather stolen, by their grandfather in World War II. As unbelievable as it sounded, we were busting a ring that had been laundering masterpieces stolen by the Nazis and hidden for more than a half century.

I would also tell him that, incredibly, this all tied back to people we had met years ago in East Berlin. The trip he had mercifully aborted. We would drop that we had an inkling—it all sounded so implausible—but when Moultens & Barings came across paintings being sold on the black market with rumors of Nazi theft, we were reminded of stories overheard years before. Sometimes the truth is indeed stranger than fiction, and Hamid would believe me. The past couple days had been so shocking, he'd have no reason to doubt the explanation.

I would, of course, leave out the goriest elements, including my killing someone in Berlin. There would also be no mention of the Mossad's involvement nor Beryl's double identity. I could only ask him to believe so much, and I was not authorized to divulge more. For now, I hoped he would accept that the Mossad crew were part of an Interpol art investigative unit. If he pushed for more, I would have to reiterate that Beryl had included a couple of her Israeli counterparts, asking her father for help, given she needed a team she could trust absolutely. Maybe Hamid would put it all together. Maybe I would break down and quietly admit more—but not that day.

Ah, I made one other confession of sorts. Full disclosure tends to be not quite so full when dealing with personal cover-ups and Nazis.

"Hamid, do you remember those Krugerrands I brought back from East Berlin?"

"Yes, the ones you won at an all-night poker game. I remember you bragging about it, but you were so shitfaced when telling me, you said you couldn't remember much else from that night. You were lucky to get back across the Wall."

"Well, there's a little more to it than that. We actually won that money from Florian and Rolfe. That's where we know them from. And their grandfather was there—a Nazi officer who apparently was the guy behind all this stolen art."

"Holy shit."

"Yeah. Anyway, Beryl, Dirk, and I made a pact. The money we won. It was in our minds blood money. Nazi money. We wanted to do something good with it. We vowed to invest it and use the money to help victims, set up a fund, maybe an endowment if it grew enough. And over time, it has. We have a board meeting every few years to assess where we are. I'd like you to join that board. After what we put you through, I thought maybe if you saw some good coming out of all this... I don't know. For us, it's been a bit cathartic. It's obviously a secret. Nobody can ever know the truth behind the fund."

"I'm not exactly sure I want to be reminded of these guys. But yeah, with the three of you...and to turn this crap to some good. Yes. I'm in."

"We've named it the Krumarkt Partners Fund. I'll let you know when we schedule our next board meeting. Amazingly it'll be the fifteenth. After this week, we have a lot to discuss."

CHAPTER 14

Liechtenstein and Germany — 2004

I could no longer fully hide, though I was doing my best to stay incognito. Marco Bellagio, Beryl Jaffe, and their merry band still had no idea who I was. Simply Werner Berlin to them, a family friend of the Mullens of soon to be bankrupt Mullen Antiques.

Perhaps they would trace the change of family names from Mullenhauer to Mullen, and through diligent sleuthing, eventually identify Florian and Rolfe's grandfather, my father, Dieter Mullenhauer. Yet, I, Werner Boesseneker, did not exist in any public documents. Hiding was something the Stasi taught me well. Even as Mullenboess Ventures grew, I was careful to hide all ownership and stock interests via impenetrable trusts and shells in my beloved Liechtenstein. Of course, it might be possible eventually to track me down. Despite my desire to skulk as a ghost, one cannot easily disappear. If they found my father's real name, if they linked him to Mullenboess Ventures, if they dug deep and found someone named Werner involved on one of its supervisory boards, and if they then made the leap from that first name to me…it was possible.

Perhaps I should have used an alias for my first name, but at the time it seemed harmless and the likelihood of discovery remote. I even relished keeping my name to taunt them, teasing close while in truth providing no meaningful lead. I could now see the slope from hubris to danger; a paper trail could be deeply buried but not absolutely hidden. Still, I was not too worried and took comfort that any linkage was incomprehensively attenuated, obfuscated through techniques learned by the masters of gray. Ah, my East German roots finally valuable. The unforeseen benefits of a bastard's name. I would keep my name and my alias. Who were they to make me change! Let them sniff a bit and wail with frustration.

I would be lying, though, if I claimed not to be worried. This turn of events was a disaster. There was now a scent and a motive to follow the scent. The bloodhounds would not leave after just reaching the edge of the woods without picking up more clues. Florian and Rolfe, of course, conveyed the hollow threat that their captors claimed to know who I was and where to find me. Did they take me for such an amateur? Did they think I would genuinely be frightened? I took the idle threat as a ploy by men unskilled at this game, men hoping the very notion could convince me to keep the file still hidden. What is that phrase politicians use to keep nuclear arsenals at bay? Mutual non-deterrence or something like that. I conceded, at least, that we, too, had a similar détente. It would not serve me well to be exposed, and I was dedicated to preserving my father's memory, his name, and achievements. That much, I agreed.

And these novices should at least be smart enough to realize it would not serve them well to dredge up their inglorious past. The intrigue of murders in a foreign country, unreported no less, and fleeing to another jurisdiction, should make them pause if not wholly abandon any boundless pursuits. The fact that Marco Bellagio and Hamid Khan were high profile and wealthy augured for further discretion. The downside in disclosure was beyond steep — probably life-ruining. What could possibly be the upside? Some moral cleansing, an unburdening of the soul? Please. I was far too pragmatic for such moralizing and expected people who had pulled off and hidden their past to share a similar perspective. Could you imagine an ethical cleansing earned by exposing a bit of ethnic cleansing? Ha! I would sooner see pigs fly.

And yet...I could not rest easy, the far strands of my identity exposed. I would bury myself back in the shadows, back in the East Berlin practices so ingrained I could snap back to them as a reflex. I would not be found, exposed to a downfall of unimaginable scale. Let them take that stupid risk if they wanted to waste efforts excavating. I would burrow underground. My father hibernated for years, finally awaking with his art trove. I was patient and could afford to wait. I was no longer in such a hurry. I could outwait the impatience of their relative youth. I already had my upside and would neither cede nor jeopardize my position — even if I had to sacrifice Florian and Rolfe.

I remained loyal to my father, but he was now gone. I would fulfill his wishes and hope to open the third letter. But how could I meet the conditions to open the third letter without the art? I had to find a way. And should I have felt obligated to provide Rolfe and Florian a third chance? Three is the charm, some say; three was also the limit. Surely, they must have confessed the location of our warehouse — it had been emptied! They left me with an impossible dilemma and tempted me to break my promise to that insolent banker and his pretty wife. What was my limit?

The Hague, The Netherlands and Fifteenth Board Meeting— 2004

We had more to talk about than usual. There were now four board members. Beyond Beryl, myself, and Dirk van Dijksen, Hamid Khan had joined us, nearly bringing the whole band back together. Dirk has asked if Pavlina could sit in, but we decided to keep her out for now. One Mossad member was enough. We also talked about asking Bryan Anderson, our old ASH pal left behind at Checkpoint Charlie, to join. There was significant temptation, a closing of the circle of sorts. However, Bryan knew nothing of what had happened on the Wall's far side that day; further, he remained oblivious about recent events that allowed the past to haunt the present. I argued we had left him behind back then, and cruel or not, we should continue that course. I reckoned the reasoning was apropos to marriage vows in reverse. Rather than for richer or poorer, until death do us part, we were bound to keep ourselves for richer or poorer, apart until death. My soliloquy over, and despite the shared guilt around the table, everyone agreed. Pavlina and Bryan would remain excluded.

On the agenda, we had three official items and one unofficial. The official matters of business were (1) the status of the recovered art, (2) the establishment of two new museum collections, and (3) a financial update on the fund. The other matter was unofficial; for that, we would excuse Hamid and Jens. I had almost forgotten about Jens, my dull lawyer, his silence rendering him nearly invisible. Had it not been for his note-taking, I would not remember him being there at all.

I had chosen the venerable Mauritshuis for our meeting, returning to The Hague symbolic given all that had transpired. We were due a bit of a reunion. The museum, converted from a former count's residence, sat adjacent to the Dutch parliament. Looking across a small lake alongside the government's seat, the semi-moat separating ministries from the grand consulates and banks surrounding the noble brick buildings, visitors could marvel at the juxtaposition of old and new. In the foreground loomed the massive parliament, itself part of a Golden Age castle structure, replete with gold leaf and rows of flags. The Prime Minister's office occupied a hexagonal turret-shaped extension, not many paces from the legislative body and the old museum. From certain museum galleries, you could almost peer down into the prime minister's office perched on the lake's edge—at least for those who knew where to look. Of course, I was one of those people.

Before the meeting, I strolled the far side of the lake, marveling at how the new high-rises and the twists of modern architecture beyond managed to blend centuries of achievement and aspirations into a single vista. Though I had not considered it before, the symbolism of looking back and looking forward was a perfect pretext for our meeting. It now struck me hard, making me wonder if perhaps I had subliminally made the link. Back near ASH and my high school roots, the benevolence of my privilege shone in full glory. Rather than a cocky senior, the son of a wealthy Italian banker, I was now myself a rich banker. Rich enough that I had booked a private conference room in one of the most famous art museums in the world. All I had to do was follow a grand staircase, open a secret door hidden in the matched wallpaper—just around the corner from Vermeer's famous *Girl With A Pearl Earring* and a roomful of Rembrandts—and show the guard my ID. I was then quietly ushered into a gold gilt, 17th century themed conference room with a frescoed ceiling. The museum personnel were even kind enough to leave the Wi-Fi code on the table together with an assortment of biscuits. Once the others joined me, I started the meeting. "Beryl, can you give us a report on the art?"

"Not much beyond what we discussed, but, Hamid, I assume it would be helpful for you if I recapped?"

"Yes, absolutely."

"Okay. First, all the art from the warehouse made it safely to Israel. A museum team has been quietly cataloging everything for the last several months. The good news is we can identify most of the paintings—meaning who the artist is. Additionally, in several cases, we can also determine the provenance. Namely, if the painting was from a museum, in a well-known collection, or otherwise documented. That's the good news. The bad news is that for more than seventy-five percent, maybe even as high as eighty-five or ninety percent, we cannot trace the owners. That's going to make restitution very difficult."

Dirk broke in, "So you're saying that for maybe one out of ten paintings, you may be able to return them to the owners or their heirs if you can figure that out? Two in ten if you're lucky?"

"Exactly. To be honest, if we return one out of ten to families who had them stolen, that would be a pretty good result. You have to remember these have been missing for over sixty years. And, essentially, all the original owners are…no longer alive. If we pushed that number up to two out of ten, it would be a miracle."

"And are you going to publicize it? You know, put out a notice with a hotline. Allowing anyone who thinks that one of the paintings was stolen from a relative in the Holocaust to apply?"

"Yes, we're setting that up and planning to go live in a few weeks. The biggest problem is fraud. We expect an avalanche of people claiming rights. Most of the pieces are very valuable, worth hundreds of thousands at minimum, and many in the multi-millions."

Hamid said, "I can see that. It's got to be virtually impossible to prove a chain of ownership. A painting hung in a house in Frankfurt or Munich, people remember it, but there are no papers proving anything. The owners were someone's grandparents or even great grandparents. They're most likely all dead. Probably no death records. In the worst case, the Nazis forced them from their home, herded them onto trains, and they perished in a concentration camp. No records of the people, no records of the house, no records of the art. How the hell do you prove anything? Even if they're telling the truth."

Beryl said, "That's what I was saying. Almost impossible. And sadly, we expect to be dealing with a lot of dubious claims. It won't surprise us if most of the inquiries turn out to be erroneous or fraudulent. Basically, we're about to be punished for trying to do the right thing. What's the saying, no good deed goes unpunished? And we need to set standards to authenticate the claims. We want to be fair. It's another tragedy. Many people will have legitimate claims but will not have enough proof. I've set up an advisory board through Moultons & Barings. We'll have global art experts set standards, set minimum proof guidelines, and require a certain sign-off of an approved committee to release a painting. This will take years."

"Christ," I jumped in. "Can't do the right thing, it seems. Can you imagine finally finding a long-lost heirloom stolen by the Nazis, and now you could be accused of scamming, trying to defend yourself. Insult to injury."

"You have a better idea? I think we still try to do the right thing."

"No, I was just...of course we should try and do the right thing. I was just, maybe, stating the obvious. It's depressing."

Everyone nodded, capitulating to the sad reality. Tragedies have a long tail. I realized the biggest tragedies had consequences spiraling through decades.

"What about the rest?" Dirk asked, trying to change the subject, everyone frustrated. "Surely there must be some with a clear provenance, but no place to return them. Or others where nobody makes a claim or you're pretty sure the claims aren't valid."

"That's a bit more upbeat," Beryl said. "We have decided to sell about one-third. The proceeds will be distributed between a memorial fund and a fund to help two galleries supplement their new collections. Those collections will be seeded by remaining paintings and will be housed in dedicated wings. In at least one of the collections, there will be accompanying educational displays when you enter, describing the horrors of the war, the Nazi looting, and the fate of so many art pieces. For the other…well, I'll get to that in a minute. We have some interesting plans."

"Where are the galleries?" Dirk interrupted.

"One is in Israel and will be cross-marketed as a cultural heritage collection. We're in discussions with Yad Vashem, the Holocaust Museum, as to how we can cooperate. The Israeli collection will be the one with a detailed educational display.

The other will be right here in the Netherlands. We decided not to take them back to Germany—just didn't feel right. It's easy to pop over here and keep an eye on things, and Amsterdam has several of the world's most famous art museums—which brings me to my next topic. Purchasing a building to house the art."

"What?" I said, not having discussed this before. I felt a Mossad angle I was not privy to surfacing.

"It was actually Noah and David's idea," she sheepishly revealed.

I should have known, clearly not having been read into some scheme. More Mossad games. I also realized Beryl felt comfortable mentioning their involvement, as both Dirk and Hamid had now been briefed on the broader mission to recover the Nazi art. Hamid remained blind, though, to the more sordid background.

"Really," I said sarcastically. The glare my wife shot me in return confirmed there would be no reenactment of our marriage consummation tonight. I would be lucky to escape bruising. This was when there could be a downside to marrying a spy.

"We believe what we uncovered is not an isolated event. It's the tip of the iceberg for other black market art sales. It's big business. We also suspect there are others trying to launder pieces stolen from Jews in the war." She paused, looking around. "So, our idea is we use these pieces to start a new museum, but don't highlight where they came from. This gallery will not include the educational piece at the front. Instead, we'll claim we acquired the bulk of the collection from a private collector who harbored the pictures in East Berlin until the Wall came down. If we make it elegant enough, a big enough splash, we are putting out a notice that we're willing to buy paintings with questionable provenances. Believe me, the bad guys will notice. People in the Florian and Rolfe set will be thrilled. The only people we'll piss off are the Eastern European rings. If you can sell to a reputable museum rather than at a discount to shady guys in Albania and Bulgaria, we'll siphon off the business. It's a win-win-win. Hurt the criminal rings, display the paintings again to the world, and hopefully take down some more bad guys, helping to further populate the gallery. It's a virtuous circle! I was initially worried we could take a minor reputational hit if people start accusing us of displaying stolen pieces. But Noah assured me that by working with the cover of Moultens and some quiet whispering, the authorities will understand we're setting up a sting not flaunting stolen pieces. We just need to be very careful, not act too often, and make sure to silence whoever we catch so word doesn't get out — pretty delicate act to keep the plan going."

"Wow," Dirk said. "That's genius. And devious. How'd they come up with this?"

"Deceptions in deceptions, all for the greater good. Part of their job. Our job." Beryl smiled, proud of her new venture. Technically, we were still sticking with the Interpol cover story; however, it was wearing thin, and I marveled at my partners' tact. Then, looking at me, batting her eyes, "Sorry, honey, the guys made me promise to surprise everyone together."

I knew better than to utter another word. I could only dig a deeper hole for myself. Smiling broadly, I rapped approval gently on the table, in a "way-to-go" tap, tap, tap. Of course, though, I wanted to know how much further the little Mossad group had taken this under my nose. "So," I asked, "do you have a location picked out yet?"

"We do. And it's right nearby," Beryl gushed, given license to divulge the last tidbit.

It dawned on me why Beryl had so enthusiastically endorsed the location for this meeting. I had been suckered into believing it was sentimental, coming back with me in the shadow of ASH. Role reversals? Male emasculated? I preferred terms like snookered or blindsided or naïve. Perhaps it would be simpler to repeat what I already knew: I married a Mossad agent. Shit! Well, she was gorgeous, I was still married, and we certainly had an exciting life. Fifty percent score? Mossad secrets and all, Beryl had to know I would not like being sidelined. I wondered how much Uzi knew—probably all. They had made up their mind about this little scheme, and would consulting me really matter? Shit.

David and Noah had sanctioned buying an old canal house that had been a minor palace, or at least residence of someone tied to royal blood. Lots of those mansions could be purchased for the right price. It was a double house, four stories high, located only a ten-minute walk from where we currently sat! My ego was taking a bashing. Beryl informed us she had arranged a private tour, and we were set to walk over, have some lunch, and then come back to finish our board meeting. Claps all around— except from me. "What an awesome surprise," I insincerely said.

Set back along the elegant tree-lined Lange Voorhout, facing a grand park that coincidently housed a weekend flea market where people sometimes bought old paintings, sat a new home for the restitution-deprived loot. I walked up a few marble stairs and was handed a glass of champagne by a Mossad toady who had obviously been in on this little surprise. Another guy without a name stood casually, smiling at me as he asked if I would care for a canape. I should have been happy—for Beryl, for Noah and David, for the pictures to have such a glorious new home and purpose to boot. But back in the shadow of high school adolescence, pettiness was hard to shake. I walked up the grand staircase and was stunned to find none other than David, Noah, and Uzi waiting.

"Marco, welcome," Uzi beamed, mildly gloating he had managed to keep the surprise.

Shit. Again. I was a bit overwhelmed. It was good to see all of them, and I gave Uzi a big hug. He proudly led me into the gallery where he spread his arms wide. They had not just purchased the building; they'd fully outfitted it already. Masterpieces and mere jewels were interspersed, one wing housing old master's drawings and paintings. I recognized Rubens' style in one giant mural of two pink, fleshy women sprawled on a divan, laughing about another secret kept from me. Taking it too personally? I drew back to the moment, ushered into a gallery with a range of impressionists and more modern art. I saw a Gaugin and a Picasso. Beryl had created a mini-Louvre. Most of the art was from less famous painters, yet I was assured they were well known. The price for each piece mounted against the black walls—an ode to the ashes of their owners—would cost more than anyone outside circles like mine and Hamid's could ever afford. Poor Mr. de Vries and his missing van Gogh *Moonlit Fields*. Who would visit the Koningshuas with this new jewel nearby? Equally pitiably, he would remain blind to the irony that Operation Moonlight plus my under-valuation had dealt him a one-two blow.

"Is all this from Mullen Antiques? The warehouse?" I reflected on both the scope and horror.

Uzi answered, "Some of it. Not all. We kept most of those paintings in Tel Aviv when we got them out, had to do a lot of arguing to convince people to send anything back to Europe. But we ended up finding several more. When we interrogated Florian and Rolfe, we squeezed a few more bits of information. Some of their sources. Thieves tend to know other thieves—a remarkable thing. I had assumed at the time they were lying, but not the case. I guess we really had them scared. We were able to track down others selling stolen pieces, one of them a similar old Nazi family that had managed to keep eleven highly valuable paintings hidden all these years."

"Wow. That's amazing. I assume, like with the Mullen's plunder, you tried to track down relatives of the original owners. Any luck?"

"Unfortunately, no," he said, hanging his head. "We'll keep trying." Pausing and almost hypnotically continuing, "We'll never stop trying to bring them home. These are all just on loan as far as I'm concerned."

I raised my glass. Beryl had not meant to hurt me. They all wanted this to be a surprise. This museum represented a crowning achievement, our takedown of Mullen Antiques, a key to an even bigger victory. What Uzi and his team had accomplished was remarkable. Beyond the brilliance of what they had carried off, the restoration and remembrance, was that this collection would now help bring down more bad guys. Perhaps it would even help ensnare others with sinister links to the worst evil of the last millennia. It was audacious. I had not been looking for the bigger picture. Maybe I was not cut out for the Mossad.

"So, how do you plan to do it? I mean, use all this to catch others?" I asked Uzi.

"Oh, I'll leave that scheming to Noah and Beryl. I'm getting too old for this. Let me enjoy my victory lap."

***

We returned to the Mauritshuis after lunch, imbibed and reinvigorated. The new museum, to be coined Berlinerhaus, was our purpose manifest in broad daylight. Having tackled our first two agenda items, we turned to the Krumarkt Partners Fund and what we could add to the cause. I had already briefed Hamid on our lofty goals once we built a sufficient endowment.

My investment of the fund had been spectacularly successful. I had spun our initial pot of gold into $35 million at the last meeting and had now more than doubled that sum. I had come into the meeting proud but was now surprisingly melancholy.

"Guys, I came here today excited that we now had $75 million built up. That's truly amazing. But after just touring the

Berlinerhaus, seeing what Beryl has done," I paused, looking at her, this time utterly sincere, "I feel like there is so much more we could do."

"I agree," Hamid joined. "After what I've seen, I want to help. I'm going to match your funds."

"What?" Beryl was jolted. "You mean you're going to contribute $75 million?"

"Yes, that's exactly what I said."

Wow, but on the other hand… that put me in an awkward position. My wife, whom I love, and with whom I had just made amends a minute ago, could look at me like a cheapskate. High School, ASH—peer pressure! But now some with serious financial consequences. Well, the fund's seed money came from a poker game. Might as well go all in.

"Hamid, that's, well, unbelievable. And you know what, I can't match that, but what if Beryl and I were to pledge $50 million, bringing our total to $200 million today? With that kind of base, plus contributions if some of the Mullen's pieces are sold, then we're talking really serious money. And, add in that Uzi told me they'll treat any surplus paintings from this Berlinerhaus scheme, ones that don't go into the gallery, the same way. A share of proceeds, after Moultens' commissions, will go into the fund. I don't think it's overly ambitious to set a target of $1 billion by the twenty-fifth meeting, if not sooner. What do you think?" Pausing and turning to Beryl, "Of course, only if Beryl agrees. She knows where my heart is, but I can't exactly give away that type of money without checking." I was all in. But being married to a beautiful Mossad agent, I knew that's what it took.

"We're in." Beryl took my hand then threw her arms around me. She was all in, too. At that moment, I felt like the luckiest man in the world. Moments and thoughts like this were crucial. They helped keep memories in abeyance of having a Stasi file with photos of killing someone hanging around your neck.

***

Seeing the Israeli team at the museum rekindled a gnawing question, and I desperately wanted to pull them aside for a serious chat. However, I decided to invite them for dinner and park my business for a few hours. I did not want to ruin the moment; plus, my discussion was for Beryl, Uzi, and the rest of his Mossad pals alone. I considered involving Dirk and Hamid, but there had been enough danger in our pasts for a lifetime. If I could avoid embroiling them in any further drama, I vowed to try my best. The meeting ended and Hamid headed to the airport while Dirk took a train home to Amsterdam and Pavlina. I thought about him trying to contort his giraffe frame into a standard train seat. Well, returning home to the Slavic goddess would be a good salve for pending muscle cramps. They had managed to move from Budapest, Pavlina now a junior partner in her law firm and engineering a transfer of offices. She spoke Dutch, of course, just one of her seven languages; check that, eight, alias Ingrid Greggory now also spoke fluent Hebrew.

Noah, David, Uzi, Beryl and I went to a restaurant in Scheveningen. While Scheveningen is technically a suburb of The Hague, locals consider it a separate town. The beachside residents reluctantly share their boardwalk with the rest of the country on sunny summer days when throngs of beachgoers descend. The natives love their sun but are equally content on a clear windswept day when they can gaze to the Hook of Holland south and almost to Amsterdam's edge in the north. I had booked a famous fish restaurant, salivating for a piece of Dover sole, washed down perhaps with a good French white wine. I reserved a private dining area, hoping for good weather. Like the rest of the day, I was rewarded, the evening mild enough they set a table outside, placing us out of earshot from the riffraff and beneath necessary warming lamps. We inhaled the salt air, the Israelis shivering against the North Sea and wishing they were instead dining on Mediterranean sea bass along the more benign beachfront of Tel Aviv. Next time, perhaps. They had to suffer through a good meal overseas on occasion to catch the bad guys.

I broached my dreaded subject. "Any news of tracking down Werner?"

"Not yet," Noah answered. "Not surprisingly, there is no Werner Berlin, which we assumed all along was an alias. Frankly, we don't even know if Werner is his real first name. Could be anything. The only lead we have is Florian and Rolfe, and the name Mullen is quite common. There is nothing in their corporate books about other investors, and as far as we can tell, their father checks out. His name was Gunther Mullen. We could try variations, but it's a bit of a wild goose chase. And probably more so trying to figure out who the grandfather was with such a common name."

David pledged, "But we're still working on it. We won't give up."

"Thanks," I said. "Sort of what I was expecting. Of course, hoping for more. Did you ever get anything else out of Florian and Rolfe?" I asked, the tone of the question innocuous for inquiring about information dredged from a beating.

"Not much beyond that evening." David failed to take the bait. "They coughed up a couple of those other names that we tracked down. That's what led to recovering a number of the paintings in the new Berlinerhaus exhibition. Anyway, we have people still watching them. They both returned to their homes in Munich and have basically stayed put. I guess that's not surprising. Where else are they going to go? If they left, they'd have to hide out somewhere permanently, and that's not so easy."

"And Werner," I said. "What's your theory on where he is or what he'll do?"

Noah took this question. "To be honest, we have no idea where he's living—can only make some educated guesses. As you know, we weren't able to follow Florian and Rolfe back to him after cutting them loose at the Bayerischer Hof. So, our working theory is that he's in Europe and probably Germany. That's where he grew up and will be most comfortable. He must have a lifetime of contacts there, and most importantly, that's where people will be whom he trusts. Hard to grow up under the Stasi regime and fit in lots of places. He's probably always been secretive, and it will be hard to develop a new circle. He'll stick with the people he's known for years. It's possible he could be in another German-speaking area, like Zurich, but our analysts are betting on Germany. And I agree."

"Makes sense, I suppose. Now to my paranoia. Hope you don't mind. Do you think he'll stay put? We won't hear from him again?"

"That's the million-dollar question, right? Our biggest problem is he knows who you and Beryl are, and we don't know much about him. Look, first, it's a good sign that he's gone quiet. No contact, no release of information. Then, the next question is, what's his incentive? He has everything to blackmail you, but what does he have to gain at this point? Money is probably the only thing. And our guess is he has plenty. If they had all that art, there was probably more. Look at the pattern. They had a stash of Krugerrands in East Berlin, a place starved for hard currency, and could afford to throw coins on a poker table for fun. That implies there was plenty of money to go around. Add the warehouse of art to that, and these guys were rolling in it. Our analysts bet that if they had that much art just sitting collecting dust for years, there must be other money hidden. And that is talking about years ago, before the Wall came down. If they had that type of wealth stored up and have been smart investing it, no telling how rich he is. This guy is smart and not averse to cheating, so my guess is he's fucking loaded. That tends to lead to the conclusion that if he doesn't need the money, then there's no reason to fuck with you."

"Other than to fuck with me. With us. Because of what happened years ago."

"Well, yes, there's that. And that's what keeps us worried. But we think the risk is not that great. He already has Florian and Rolfe freed, and their grandfather, whoever he was, is dead. What's his motivation? Got to be limited. If he comes after you at this point, it would be out of spite, personal revenge. That could be. As you said, he may just want to fuck with you. But if he comes after you, he also risks surfacing again, exposing himself, and sullying the family name further. We would not stay quiet about the Mullen family… And this is a guy who has lived in the shadows his whole life. We think he'll stay there. We hope he stays there. But as David said, we're not giving up trying to hunt him down. The Nazi connection is good enough reason by itself."

Glad to know my well-being was so high on the priority list. I guessed I had to console myself that hunting a potential Nazi collaborator, or at least some guy whose name we did not know, who sheltered former Nazis and helped launder their money, would be to my benefit. Shit. How did I get there?

"That's it? We just wash our hands and live our lives? You're asking us to look over our shoulders the rest of our lives? We let this guy get away, and God knows how many others are out there like him," Beryl said.

"You, better than anyone, know we are realists," Noah chided. "We won't give up, but we also need to accept the facts. Unless he tips his hand again, we probably won't find him. He was raised in the shadows. He knows how to be forgotten. But we do have another idea we'd like to discuss."

I was nervous when a Mossad officer teased. It was not quite like *The Godfather* and being made an offer you could not refuse; however, it was difficult to ignore when the Mossad proffered a suggestion. That happened to be especially true when you were married to a spy and your father-in-law, a Mossad lifer himself, was cutting off a fish's head next to you. Oh, and it was his boss with a glass eye and grisly scar pointing to a freakishly reconstructed ear that was dangling the bait.

I wanted to mouth, "What the fuck?" to Beryl, scared this was turning into a recruitment dinner, but managed to keep my eyes down and mouth closed as Noah continued. "Going through the books of Mullen Antiques, David's team found a thread to a couple of Swiss banks. We're tracking that down and suspect there's dirty money there. Even though we didn't get anything directly out of Florian or Rolfe, when we asked Rolfe about where the money was going, and asked if he knew about any Swiss accounts, he looked at us like we'd scored a hit. We've always been suspicious of private banks—even some of the bigger ones—willingly cooperating with the Nazis and allowing them to maintain accounts. They plundered the whole fucking continent, and that money is hidden somewhere. This is the best lead we've had in years."

"What about the secrecy laws?" I asked. "You do know I come from a banking family, a banking family that considers Swiss bank privacy to be the eleventh commandment."

"We Israelis believe the eleventh commandment is we shall never forget."

"Are you asking me to help you penetrate a Swiss bank?"

"Who better?"

Jesus Christ.

CHAPTER 15

Liechtenstein — 2008

I kept my word — so far. Despite wanting vengeance, I was ever pragmatic, making sure my nephews stayed out of trouble and I stayed out of sight. For several years following the shakedown at Mullen Antiques and my rescuing of Florian and Rolfe, I retreated to my chalet in Liechtenstein. Nobody ever went to Liechtenstein. It was a spot so small on the map that nary a pin could fit to mark the valley and mountain. My chalet, to be honest, was more of a refurbished modern castle, unapproachable save for a winding driveway. Nobody bothered coming there, and for further sanctuary, I paid a private security firm to ensure no snoopers came past the bottom gate. I also donated generously, through a trust, of course, to one of the prince's favorite charities. So long as those wire transfers cleared and I paid my taxes, I was sheltered by the royal moat.

I also felt protected in my alpine haven wedged between Austria and Switzerland, one a soulmate to the Third Reich that nurtured the Fuhrer and the other the center of the hidden accounts I did not keep in the vaults of Vaduz. Vaduz was that Gucci and bank-lined corridor of a downtown that passed for our capital. My German tongue, regal accounts, and Teutonic features allowed me to blend in seamlessly. If it would not call attention to myself, I could have easily declared myself Count Werner Boesseneker, and passersby would bow. I admit I might have enjoyed the groveling. Such deference would be a nice antidote to the memories of my East German servitude. I wondered what my father would think of my becoming a count. I doubt he would have liked it, but he might have also found a bit of irony and pleasure. Perhaps I could still consider that next step up when more time passed, and I was freed of my Mossad pests. For a few more hushed millions, I expected the prince might comply.

Yes, I had a good idea regarding my pursuers' true loyalty. Florian and Rolfe had heard some of the gang speaking Hebrew when they thought the two had been knocked out cold. That clue and some digging into Beryl Jaffe's travels put me on the trail. The Mossad were quite clever, and I was not able to verify their involvement with absolute certainty. Nonetheless, the circumstantial facts were overwhelming. An Israeli passport, frequent travels to and from Israel, a father who worked for the Israeli government — probably Mossad as well. I revisited the tapes and reconstructed those events, remembering that Beryl kicked away the gun and disarmed Uncle Karl. That was the action of a trained operative, someone schooled in self-defense and more, not your routine high school kid. The more I focused, the more I became convinced it was their hand in my almost downfall. I had stupidly focused on Marco Bellagio, and yet my real nemesis appeared to be his wife.

Looking back, it all made sense. Those Jews had a difficult time forgetting their past and tended only to look upon the flaws of my father and his compatriots. They viewed hunting down my kind a duty, and I didn't take their motivation lightly. If I could find them, they could one day find me. I needed to remain vigilant, and thus I lingered in my castle and delayed pursuing the acquisition of a befitting title. My time was filled with maintaining Mullenboess Ventures and tidying up some family affairs.

The fact was I could fund my castle, donate to the principality, and do whatever I wanted because my wealth had become extraordinary. My father's vision proved providential, and our media and telecom investments multiplied as we leveraged our portfolio along the insider-

tip-laden path of technology upgrades. It was so easy to move from videos to DVDs, and flip phones to smart phones. Of course, Mullenboess was diversified, and our entire portfolio was the envy of money managers tethered to more scrupulous methods. Because of that success, I was able to salvage a promise my father made, a promise that was jeopardized by the calamity in Munich that forced me into hiding.

Before we discovered that our warehouse had been breached soon after Florian and Rolfe were freed, I had been confident that our operation in Flugplatz Schleißheim was secure. Because the theft occurred within a day of their abduction, it did not take a detective to deduce what happened. I was furious. My father's prized collection! Kept for over sixty years! Hidden from all, a bridge from his glorious past to our visions for the future upended! And by Jews — can you imagine? I am glad my father did not live to see this catastrophe. What made the theft worse was that it could not be undone. I knew it was impossible to recover the art, and the irreplaceable nature of what had been taken was the very reason it was always so special. To think that some pieces hung in a gallery in Tel Aviv was too much to bear.

I wanted to expose Marco Bellagio and Beryl Jaffe immediately, dropping off a copy of the file to the local Berlin police. And yet, for the very reason I had hesitated before, I resisted. Ever the realist, I was forced to seethe and wait. It was horrible enough to see my father's legacy tainted, and I could not risk further damage to the family. Any release and surely Florian and Rolfe would be ruthlessly slandered, and ultimately my father's name publicly besmirched. Equally troubling, it would have opened international floodgates into tracking me down. I loved my chalet, and Interpol alerts could become inconveniences when visiting my Swiss accounts or traveling to Berlin and Munich for Mullenboess meetings.

Worse still, the deadline for selling the art and paying my niece and nephew their share of the proceeds loomed. My father had set his plan in motion, and the trust was very clear about payment timing. As trustee, I had to give Florian, Rolfe, and Sophie a minimum of $10 million each from the proceeds. The expected sales price should have *been a multiple of that, maybe ten times, leaving them these crumbs. The dispensation of the rest of the profits was presumably tied to the mysterious third letter. That the proceeds were zero was unimaginable.*

I wondered what was worse: finding we had failed my father and his master plan, to be revealed in the third letter, or failing to provide for his grandchildren per his specific bequest. Neither failure was acceptable. I would fund the $30 million for my niece and nephews from my own pocket, an act not of personal benevolence (especially paying Sophie — the thought!), but of honoring my father's wishes. I, however, was not privy to the contents of the third letter and dreaded what it might demand. Would failing to sell the art in some manner compromise those plans? I was nearing sixty years old and not as strong as before. I shivered at the thought of failing him when it mattered most.

***

Switzerland — 2009

I should have been content, my life nearly perfect. I was mega-rich, happily married, and living between Zurich and my lake house in Zug. I had also become a father, Beryl giving birth to boy and girl twins the previous year. We had been through enough drama for a lifetime and decided to wait no longer: carpe diem. An appropriate Latin phrase from my Roman ancestors. Despite my mixed genes, I felt Italian at heart. I supposed that would even please my mother, the vestiges of her American and Canadian roots hidden from the next generation. I wondered what she would have thought, knowing it was her family name and my Canadian passport that had unwittingly sheltered me. I would hold that secret, allowing my parents, our parents, to revel in the joy of becoming grandparents.

I had two stresses, though, weighing me down. The first was mundane, the type of family squabble and conundrum faced by everyone marrying for love — yet outside of their faith. We would have to settle how to raise Mateo and Aliza: Jewish or Catholic. Each of our family's religious bonds had been untainted for generations, suggesting some fictional purity that was both anachronistic and grounding. There was no simple resolution, and the spats it would cause with our parents downstream were arguments to put off for as long as possible. I agreed to a circumcision for Mateo, it now the recommended course for boys by doctors. Whether we would be parading the children around a communion or bar mitzvah beneath the Wailing Wall would be a fight delayed. I suspected the Mossad had a playbook for that one. I would be approached sooner or later. I was also reconciled to relenting. Candidly, I was a modernist, tied more to my money than ritual. I was also married to a beautiful, green-eyed with a speck of blue Mossad spy, whose stride brought runway models to tears. Who would people bet on? As usual, I was fucked if I wanted to continue to get fucked.

My biggest concern, though, lay with my past and whether Werner would reveal our secrets. Too frequently, I would pause with a slight chill, wondering where he was and what he might be plotting. Despite David and Noah's persistent efforts, years later we were no closer to identifying or locating him. The Mossad was correct to predict his Stasi skills would serve him well in disappearing.

At least the Mossad left me alone for a few years while the children were infants. Perhaps they realized how much we had been through and decided we needed a hiatus. However, they also knew that I remained haunted by thoughts of Werner, and by tugging at my conscience—especially now being a parent—they could enlist me in their next adventure. Noah and David could be brutally clever. They knew it would take nothing less than soul-crushing guilt to betray my heritage and help them penetrate Swiss banks. No doubt they grasped that my becoming a father, my kids one day to learn the fate of their great grandparents, added a second immutable layer of leverage. When Beryl resurrected the plea first floated by Noah, I tried to resist. Some chance. By that point, I was so compromised I probably would have acceded to my own bris. Caught between my kids and Uzi's pals, I capitulated.

The best lead David's financial forensic team unearthed from Mullen Antiques led to a private bank in Lugano, Switzerland. They even found a reference to an account with a number sequence indicating it was decades old. The Mossad team was convinced it had a Nazi link and with luck tied back to the family. Because the account was so old, I learned that for a while the Mossad did not feel pressure to act, biding their time for the right political moment to strike. The objectives of Operation Moonlight had been met, and this was perceived as an entirely different play. Tel Aviv was content to wait. Moreover, penetrating a Swiss bank was far from a trivial matter. Failure would create years of blowback. I was not privy to what changed. Perhaps it was simply the passage of time and fear that the generation who first opened these accounts was about to disappear. Whatever the justification, there was a surge of momentum, and I was reluctantly recruited as a pawn in their latest gambit.

***

Almost mockingly, like everything I touched related to the horrid Mullen clan, the targeted bank was along a Swiss lake, a short drive from Lake Como and my namesake town of Bellagio. How could I ever admit this to my father? There were certain lines a Swiss banker would never cross, this being one. It was as strict as the legendary Mafia omerta, breaking the code of honor and a sin deserving of death. And yet, there I was, about to walk into Banco Inter Credit Rafael, better known as Banco ICR.

I took the train from Zurich, arriving at Lugano's station, set on the hillside's upper terraces above the lake. I scanned the vista, the amoeba-shaped waters shimmering and the distant mountains framing the landscape much like my native Como. I took the cable car down into the center of town, disembarking into a maze of marbled streets and overpriced shops. I was early and sat down for an espresso at an outdoor cafe, gazing past the wide plaza and across the lake, watching cars traverse the banks over a low bridge seeming to float atop the calm water. Noah wanted me to bring Aaron to the meeting, but I assured him it was best I try alone. There was always time for muscle later if needed.

Banco ICR was not my primary bank, but I was always keen to spread my funds. As luck, or rather bad luck, would have it, I even maintained a relatively small account tied to the Krumarkt Partners Fund there. It was the perfect place for quiet money. My account, though, was in Zug not Lugano, and the bankers at this branch were mere acquaintances—handshakes at cocktail parties and charity events type of familiarity. No matter, they knew me and would be appropriately fawning. Marco Bellagio, son of Anthony Bellagio, bothering to come in person to Banco ICR's Lugano haven was not a daily event. If I played this right, in three decades, little Mateo could feel a similar rush. I left a generous tip and walked five minutes down a routine street. At the next corner, I found the unpretentious granite and steel building. Banco ICR's name was modestly set into a plaque, smaller than the building's number, the nameplate a confirmation not an invitation to enter. I pressed the buzzer, looked up at the camera, and acknowledged the welcome by an obsequious young clerk who rushed to open the door. I soon found myself waiting in a tasteful conference room without a lake view. Real money knows where to spend and not to spend.

Striding in, Bernhard Alfonso, his gluttonous belly arcing through the pinstripes of his suit rather than yielding to the designer's plotted straight lines, greeted me. "Marco, wonderful to see you again. I was surprised to see the appointment. I don't think you've ever visited us here, is that correct?"

"I'm afraid so. Now I've made amends, hopefully." I forced a smile.

"No need for that. I'm just happy to host you. What can I do for you? I wasn't given any instructions. I could have had whatever you needed prepared."

"Thank you. It's a delicate matter, which is why I thought it would be better to discuss in person."

"Seems to be our specialty." Bernhard nodded, inhaling the scent of fees.

"I'll get right to the point. I need to trace this account number," I said, handing him a several-digit code.

"Is this yours?" Bernhard asked skeptically, the prior notion of fees turning in a perilous direction. From the sequence, he could immediately identify this was a very old account.

"No. And what I am about to tell you never leaves this room. I need your help, and I expect you'll be reluctant to cooperate, but it has to be done."

Bernhard visibly stiffened, not used to being threatened. His greatest anxiety likely came from overly ambitious bets at the golf club and whether his wife might suspect he was sleeping with their new clerk. He was, of course, but that was hardly the point. He was certainly not accustomed to being challenged under his roof or at Banco ICR.

I continued, "I believe this account is linked to a former Nazi, or possibly a relative, who has been concealing money here for a long, long time. I am trying to find him—or it could be a woman, but let's assume for the time being it's a man—and want you to send a message that there is an irregularity with his account, and you need to speak."

"What?" Bernhard nearly spat, visibly losing his composure. "A Nazi account? Are you serious? And you want me to contact this person? We don't keep that kind of company. Maybe forty or fifty years ago, it was possible, but not now. And even if that were true, contacting a customer like you're suggesting…that would be against all our policies…I can't do this."

"Bernhard, sadly, I can confirm it is true. This is an old Nazi account. And I don't think those are the types of customers you want in the twenty-first century. It could be equally damning for it to be exposed. I don't think you would want that type of scandal."

"Marco, are you threatening me? I would think you of all people would understand the protocols of banks like ours."

I had decided my strategy in advance, believing the only hope of both succeeding with the bank and preserving my credibility was to bond with Mr. Alfonso. I would feign being blackmailed myself—again, sticking close to the truth being the best of strategies when concocting a tale. "Look, I am taking you into my confidence, and this discussion can never leave these walls. I think you know my wife, Beryl, is Israeli and works at Moultens & Barings. She's quite a famous art appraiser."

"Yes, of course, I know about your wife," Bernard conceded warily, clearly baffled where this conversation was heading. Certainly not in the direction of fees.

"She became involved with an art sting where a stash of old master paintings stolen by the Nazis was uncovered. She tried to return the paintings to their rightful owners, but for most, when she couldn't track them down, she didn't know what to do. So, she sold them at auction and kept the commissions."

"What's the problem? That sounds like a good outcome. Messy but respectable."

"Except the Mossad got wind of it. They are threatening to expose her—arguing she knew what she was doing and twisting the facts to imply she was somehow complicit in covering up the past and then profiting. They don't take fencing Nazi art lightly. Like they don't take Nazi bank accounts lightly. And now they've come to me — and threatened me! If I don't help them find the root of this account, they've threatened to expose me as a Nazi collaborator and ruin me. I couldn't believe it! Of course, none of this is true, but I have no doubt they can make up some backstory that would bury me. They have enough on Beryl to create a plausible inference, and that's all it would take. This is how they operate. If they get wind of a lead to track down a Nazi or their ill-gotten gains, they'll do anything to succeed. Contorting the facts. Even blackmail. Even framing me."

I let out a heavy breath, my posture and demeanor begging for sympathy. I was quite pleased with my act. It was so good I half believed myself. That was dangerous. I was no pathological liar but being able to deceive oneself into believing in a fake reality is at best the beginning of the slippery slope; at worst, and honed, this can be the culmination of the art.

Bernhard said, "Jesus Christ," and I was glad I was not the only one so uncreative in cursing. I hoped the kinship was a positive sign.

"And they know you're here?" Bernhard eventually asked, putting two and two together.

"I'm afraid so. Believe me, I didn't want to involve you, involve the bank. My God, I have some of my own secrets buried here. This is the last thing I would ever want to do. You must know that." I was getting quite good at this. I felt I nearly had him snared.

Bernhard was now sweating, almost unconsciously pacing the conference room, wishing the conversation was simply a bad dream. He unbuttoned his jacket, any pretense of corseting his gut the least of his concerns. I let him sweat, stewing on the information, letting it sink in that this was not a bad dream. My very presence, my unprecedented personal presence, was breathing confirmation that this problem would not easily disappear and that he was now intimately implicated.

"I have no doubt they will resort to violence if I don't cooperate. I hope I'm protected. I mean, Beryl is an Israeli. I assume they would never touch her." I let the thought linger. I wanted to telegraph that despite being in serious danger, I had a marital layer of protection—Mr. Bernhard Alfonso was not so lucky. The Mossad would not hesitate to squeeze him or his bank to trace and recover Nazi loot. Worse still, he likely knew all too well the secrets hidden in his numbered accounts and dusty safe deposit boxes. Odds were his grandfather had willingly helped shelter Nazi theft. Much of what he had inherited was the product of corrupt collaboration. I suspected Bernhard had always tried to push those thoughts away. It had not been his complicity. And yet, there he was, staring at one of his most famous clients, the sins of the father coming crashing down on him.

"I don't know what to say," Bernhard lamented. "I can't betray my clients. Without that, there is no bank, no Banco ICR. My family has worked here for generations."

"Bernhard, that is sadly why you're in this predicament. And unless we cooperate and help clean up this shit from generations ago, there will be no bank." It was not like me to swear, and what I said and how I said it shook him to the core. His frightened, somewhat hollow look back at me told me I had won. "You have no choice. I have no choice. Now let me tell you what you need to do."

For the next fifteen minutes, I described how he needed to set the trap and reach out to this mystery account's owner. He would need to blame it on an IT conversion, claiming the bank in its analog-to-digital conversion flagged a mismatch on this number. Unfortunately, given the nature of these accounts, it had to be done in person. Wired confirmations were too—traceable. The old code's structure would no longer work because the new system only took certain strings and required letters, numbers, and a symbol for security. He needed to explain that the account had been private and secure for over fifty years, and unfortunately, this was necessary for it to continue that way.

Hopefully, after the owner came in and reset the code, no one need tinker with it for another century. He could come into any branch in Switzerland; and if it were too great a burden, being such an old customer, the bank would come to him. The bank just needed a personal signature next to the new code. It would take only a few minutes, but the meeting could not be avoided. When Bernhard questioned what would happen if the owner refused, I told him to advise the client the bank would be forced to close the account. Maybe he should add the closing would also trigger a commission charge. That should get his attention.

Bernhard was horrified—even after the first glimmer of some fees. In an hour, he had gone from the exultation of welcoming one of his most distinguished clients to possibly reaching out to an ex-Nazi and conspiring with the Mossad. Maybe Bernhard would be lucky and have a stroke before having to communicate the message. I could see anguish written all over his face, probably wondering if he had enough money saved to just walk away. It would be a foolish plan, though; they knew who he was, and he could not simply walk away. He was already entrapped, secretly recruited! I could almost hear him thinking, how did this happen?

***

It was a stroke of sheer luck that the account belonged to Werner Bosseneker, even though the Mossad was yet to learn his full name. Noah and David had hoped the account would trace back to a family member, but they never dared believe it would lead straight to Werner. Perhaps the account was so old the owner never thought to change it. How could it be discovered? They would have been further amazed to learn it had been set up at the height of the war in 1943.

"Has he made contact yet?" Noah asked Marco, talking on a secure line.

"Yes, but there are a couple of problems."

"Tell me."

"Bernhard cooperated just as you thought. I still can't believe it. And remember our deal if this works out."

"Yes, we'll honor our commitment, just like we did with Beryl when we recovered the art. Same here," he pledged.

"Good. Well, Bernhard sent his request to the only address they had on file. No phone number. Just a post office box in Berlin. There was no reply, so he sent a reminder and just received a phone call. That's why I wanted to talk to you."

"Who called? Do we know who we're dealing with?"

"Yes and no."

"What do you mean?"

"The caller—it was a man—had done his research. He knew details about ICR and Bernhard Alfonso and had clearly checked him out before phoning. As for whether it was actually the account holder calling, Bernhard told me he'd been able to verify that it was at the beginning. I'm not sure how. He didn't tell me. Maybe there was some verbal account identifier too, or he could quote the date the account was opened. I didn't push. Assumed it was a step too far for Bernard to divulge. Whatever it was, both people believed the other was authentic. The caller asked if he could give a new number over the phone, arguing this was quite unorthodox. Bernhard obviously refused and said they would need to meet. He repeated the options that he could come into one of the branches, or Bernhard could arrange for someone to go to him. He even volunteered to come personally."

"You really got to him, good job," Noah said. "So, come on, what's the punch line?"

"The caller refused to give his name, but he said he was in Berlin, and it would be better if Bernhard came there. He would have to think about the location. When Bernhard asked if he could at least give him a name, the man paused. And then he said, 'You can call me Mr. Berlin.'"

When Alfonso said he would appreciate his full name, especially if he was to travel to meet him, he said "Werner Berlin."

"Holy shit."

"That's what I said. We've got him. Can you believe it! We've got him!"

We shortly hung up the phone, Noah pledging to come back to me after consulting the team about next steps. They would need to put together a plan for Berlin. God, I hoped that would not involve me, but by this point I knew better. The last thing I wanted was another Nazi encounter in Berlin.

CHAPTER 16

Liechtenstein — 2009

I was, of course, suspicious being contacted out of the blue by Banco ICR. None of my other banks had ever contacted me that way. However, the protocol was all in place. We had maintained the safe deposit box as a contact for all these years in case of an administrative nuisance like this. Could it be legitimate?

This was a different world, and Banco ICR was our oldest account. This account dated back to the beginning, far before East Berlin. Before I had been born. The account had been set up at the height of my father's power, even before he hid the art in the secret vault he built during the bombings. I wondered how the young officer Dieter Mullenhauer set up a Swiss account from Germany back in 1943. It could not have been easy. Had he been able to travel there? Did someone help him set it up? I would never know the answer, hidden even from me, his last surviving son.

But perhaps genius had its limits. Could he have anticipated at the height of the war, more than sixty-five years ago, that we would now be in the digital age? This was long before cellular phones and computers. There was no notion of digital. The beauty of the bank codes was just that — a simple string of numbers and letters committed to memory. Nobody could have seen that far into the future, to imagine not just computers but a complete digital shift. Authentication protocols, security — nonsense! The old system and codes had worked for almost seventy years. Through everything!

On the surface, the request made sense and was entirely rational. Yet part of me could not believe it. This was precisely the type of play I would have made at the Stasi. The thought even occurred to me it might be the Mossad. Unlikely, and ingenious, but I had to consider the possibility. I would agree to meet Mr. Alfonso in Berlin — but on my terms, and I would be watching. I had always been good at watching and listening.

Berlin, Germany — 2009

Werner Berlin, the putative owner of an account identified by a string of numbers and letters, who also appeared to own a safe deposit box in Berlin, agreed to meet Bernhard Alfonso, scion of the family behind the nearly century-old bank Banco ICR, in Berlin. The location was the refurbished Hotel Adlon Kempinski, literally at the threshold of the Brandenburg Gate. My whole life felt like a circle closing. Beryl and I, together with Uzi, Noah, David, and the rest of the extended team were anxious. This could be the breaking of the dam. In one stroke, the Mossad could crack the impenetrable Swiss banking system, capture Nazi collaborator Werner Berlin, and possibly recover an incalculable trove of hidden Nazi money. Noah had alerted the prime minister of the operation. For once, I simply kept my mouth shut.

The first significant decision would be whether anyone accompanied Bernhard Alfonso to the hotel. It was a given we would have watchers there. Aaron would be in place, as would David, together with a couple others. We debated whether I should join Bernhard, the sight of me stunning Werner. However, we all deemed that risky, a move to rub it in the asshole's face rather than tactically savvy. Everyone ultimately agreed Bernhard should be alone with the team stationed nearby.

Beryl and I took a suite in the hotel, Noah booking it under false names and passports. We would take no chances. I was bursting with nervous energy and asked Beryl to make love. She told me I was crazy; we were on assignment and needed to go to sleep early. Failing to persuade her that the endeavors were hardly mutually exclusive, I was lucky not to be relegated to the couch in the living room. Little victories, I supposed. Hopefully, we would have the motherlode tomorrow.

We set the meeting for 11:00 a.m., a table reserved in the corner of the lobby. Beryl and I would stay out of sight until Werner Berlin arrived. If he saw us, he would be spooked and likely run; worse, the lobby could become a shooting gallery. The plan was for Aaron to call us once Werner had joined Bernhard Alfonso. We were the only ones who had met Werner up close, and without any photographs, we needed our presence to identify him—especially if he was disguised. Aaron moved to a seat in the lobby, taking out a newspaper and making sure he had a good, but not obvious, sightline to the table across the floor. He called our room at 10:45 and then my cell phone, testing both connections. The Mossad was thorough. So far, I gave them an A on planning. Actually, I should downgrade that to a C. No one had managed to take a picture of Werner during our prior rendezvous, the fact Werner had cleverly surprised us not cutting it as an excuse.

According to Aaron, at 11:00, a man looked around the lobby and asked the concierge if he could point out a reserved table. The concierge nodded and walked him over to where Bernhard Alfonso anxiously awaited. Alfonso stiffened as his client walked over to the table. The gentleman had slightly graying hair and was finely dressed in a blue blazer and handkerchief neatly folded in his breast pocket. His cologne reached Alfonso before his hand as the two men shook formally.

"Mr. Berlin, Mr. Werner Berlin, I assume," Alfonso probed. "Thank you for coming."

"Yes, Mr. Alfonso, I recognize you from your pictures. I had my assistant check into you. I hope you don't mind. This whole meeting is a little irregular."

"I understand," Alfonso said, relaxing a bit. This Mr. Berlin did not outwardly appear very threatening and certainly was not old enough to have been a member of the Nazi party in 1943. Alfonso later told me he thought maybe he was the son. The notion had sent a chill through his body, and he took a sip of the Perrier he had ordered to calm his breathing.

While the two began talking, Aaron lazily took out his mobile phone and rung me. Beryl and I dashed out of the room and hit the elevator in less than twenty seconds. In well under two minutes, we were at the edge of the lobby. I could see Bernhard Alfonso clearly, deep in conversation with his client. There was just one problem. The man at the table across from him was clearly not Werner Berlin. I had never seen this gentleman before. I whispered to Beryl, and she shook her head. She had no idea who he was either.

We quickly strode out of view, peering around in case Werner Berlin was indeed in the lobby and had sent whoever this was as an advance man. It would not be out of character for him to take such a precaution. I dialed Noah first and relayed the message that this was not Werner Berlin. I also signaled Aaron. Unfortunately, there was no way to notify Bernhard, short of walking up to the table. I had given him a description, hoping Werner would show up, but suspected Bernhard was not sure if this man of the right age and height was indeed the same person. I waited, dumbfounded about what to do. We had talked about this possibility but had ranked it as unlikely. I downgraded our planning to a D. My phone rang back, and it was Noah.

"We don't have a choice. Whoever this is, we need to grab him. Hopefully, he'll lead us to the real guy."

"You don't want to let them finish and follow him?"

"No, if he was this careful, he'll cover his tracks. For all we know, he was paid a hundred euros to take the meeting and leave a new code. He may have no idea who Werner is, may never have met him. Remember, we're dealing with an ex-Stasi officer. He'd know how to use a cut-out."

"Shit," I murmured into the phone. "How do we know this isn't the real guy with the account at Banco ICR?"

"You want to bet there just happened to be a second guy out there, linked in some way to Mullen Antiques, calling himself Werner Berlin?"

"I know. Stupid. What's the plan?"

"Go back to your suite. We'll handle this. I'll be in touch soon," and with those crisp instructions, Noah severed the connection. Shortly, we were back in our room. Beryl and I had been away less than fifteen minutes and had managed to achieve nothing. I suppose that was not fair. We figured out we had been double-crossed at our own game. Jesus Christ. This spy stuff was hard.

***

Beryl and I received a knock on our door well after lunch. We had ordered room service late, not wanting to go out, and thought it was the busboy finally coming around to retrieve our cart. I looked through the peephole and was surprised to see Noah and David. Good thing Noah had not pressed his glass eye to the frame, or it would have given me a heart attack. I opened the door, and they strode inside, taking a seat on the couch. I was now doubly glad it had not become my bed last night.

"I'm afraid it's as we feared," Noah said, his tone frustrated. "This guy, this faux Werner Berlin who came this morning…as soon as you left, we grabbed him and brought him to a room we'd set up at a small hotel around the corner. Both of us were there, plus Aaron. We worked him over pretty good."

Beryl and I exchanged glances, wanting to ask more. Somehow, I managed to keep my mouth shut, waiting for Noah to continue. We were, after all, much keener to learn what this messenger said than the methods used to coax information.

"After a few minutes, he admitted he was not Werner Berlin. Werner Berlin was the man who sent him. This guy works as a waiter at a restaurant in Berlin and took the job for some extra money. His name is Stephan Schultz. We already ran him through the system. He checks out, works at a biergarten not far from boulevard Under den Linden, no priors. We're keeping him a couple days, sweat him out a bit. We'll do a thorough check on his bank accounts, make sure nothing was wired that we can trace. Same with his phone. But my gut is we won't find anything. Whoever this Werner Berlin is did exactly what we feared—found some stooge that looked a bit like him to go in his place and deliver the new account number."

"Are you saying it's a complete dead end?" Beryl asked, her tone more despondent than hopeful.

"Basically, yes," David said. "I agree with Noah. This guy Werner is smart and must have sniffed out that this could have been a con. Even if he thought it was real, no reason to take a chance and show his face."

"Shit." I was back to my eloquent responses. "What do we do now?"

Noah answered, "I don't think much. We'll see if we can get anything else out of this Stephan Shultz, but if not, we have to let him go. We haven't told him who we are. We needed to make up something plausible and advised we were from a special investigative branch of financial fraud. We told him there had been reports bankers were scamming customers by trying to make them change account numbers and then charging exorbitant change fees. A bullshit story, but no way for him to verify anything. Plus, he's so scared about being implicated in a bank fraud, he'll keep his mouth shut."

"Nice touch," I said, earning me a withering stare from Beryl. She did not take any of this lightly, and honestly, neither did I. The jokes were helping me from going over the deep end. I wondered whether anything positive came from the fiasco, pondering what would happen to the accounts.

"What about Bernhard and the account? There must still be something we can do there. Some further lead," I said.

"That's the only good thing," David said. "We're going to have a little talk with Bernhard. The money from that account, we'll have him transfer it to us."

"And our deal?" I asked.

"Yes," Noah answered. "I promised we would live up to our pledge. We'll transfer 100% of the money to you to put into your Krumarkt Partners Fund. We know you're about to start making the first grants, and so long as it's going to help Holocaust survivors, it seems more than fitting. We want to get this money back to heirs, but this would be even harder to trace than art. Better to work through a private fund to try and funnel it back."

"Thank you," Beryl added. "You know we will treat it well…solemnly. On our lives," she pledged, touching her heart.

"Do you need me to talk to him again?" I asked. I had been the go-between with Banco ICR so far, the only person to broach the Nazi dirt with Bernhard Alfonso. If I needed to have a second conversation, I was more than willing — even if it was completely against my banker's code of ethics. The scales had tipped for me thinking of the dirty money, how the bank profited and grew on the backs of Jewish corpses rotting just the other side of the Alps. I looked at David and thought about his grandparents. Jesus Christ.

Noah replied, "Marco, I think you've done enough on this one. We promised you we'd help keep your reputation intact.

Bernhard already thinks the Mossad is blackmailing you, so we'll see that through. Let's just have you introduce him to David. David will play his part, making it clear he has been pressuring you. Then you leave, and David will take over. Make him see the error of his ways, so to speak. I don't think we'll have too much trouble having him turn over that account. And David can be quite persuasive. We'll squeeze him for others…other leads."

"You're going to make him an informant?"

"Why not? We have him scared shitless. We could probably take down his bank. We have one dirty account out in the open. I don't get the sense he's going to stand on principles. From the research our team's done, seems like this guy basically inherited his job, like most of these private bankers, been in the family for years. He hasn't done anything wrong, but in his heart, he knows the truth. He knows what's buried in his vaults, the blind-eyes turned by fathers and grandfathers and uncles for years. Same for him. How deeply do you think he wants to look into the background of their oldest clients? Those accounts are like kryptonite. Built the bank, helped pay for his fancy house overlooking the lake, but the less he knows the better. We never forget what happened, and we'll tell him neither should he. Cooperate, and he can keep living his life like nothing ever happened. So, they lose millions in accounts. That's the price. Very simple negotiation. Take it or lose it."

"How many do you think there are?"

"Other dirty accounts, you mean?"

"Yes."

"Impossible to tell. But our guess is a lot. Maybe twenty or so, but personally, I suspect more. Let me ask you. How legitimate do you think any current account is that was opened by a foreigner between the late 1930s and the end of the war, say 1945? What odds would you place on those?"

"Not great. They're not all dirty, but not great."

"Our point exactly," David said.

"And you think Werner Berlin, or whoever he is, will be okay with his account just going poof?"

"Okay, no. But what's he going to do? Make a claim? No different than the art. He'll have to accept it and move on. Pound sand."

"And you don't think this will provoke him, push him to release those files on us?" Beryl asked.

"Probably not," Noah said. "We've thought about that. But the motives, the incentives don't change. We think he will treat it as a bit of a game. Remember, he is ex-Stasi. This is now cat and mouse. He's on the run, and there will be setbacks, but to him, he's still winning. He's in the wind, and we don't know who he is or where he is. The next move may even be from him, baiting us this time."

"Jesus Christ," I said. There it was again. "Is this ever going to end?"

"In some ways, it did in 1945. In other ways, it never will," Noah somberly said, looking at David. The sense of loss we all felt was profound. "What we're all doing here, this is a tiny price we're paying. At least we have them on the run. We're taking back long-lost treasures and stolen money." Noah paused and looked at us, stopping to point to each one in turn. "Every one of you should be proud. You are doing a mitzvah. The State of Israel thanks and blesses every one of you."

For once, I was speechless. I looked over at Beryl, and tears were running down her cheeks. At the sight, listening to Noah, the weight of it all crashed over me.

***

Although we failed to nab Werner—his full name then still a mystery to me—we could at least revel in our success prying funds from Bernhard Alfonso and Banco ICR. I should have known better, though, expecting the Mossad to bask in their victory similarly. Intertwined with politics, every success or loss simply brought a new calculation. It was only a matter of weeks before Uzi approached me with a proposition. The scheme that we had used could be deployed against any bank. We had pressured Banco ICR because we had ferreted out a real account. The lie was in luring out the account's owner to confess the money's origin sins. Noah, however, urged repeating the ruse with multiple banks. Why not bluff that we uncovered another account?

After our success and staring into the abyss of where the Banco ICR money had come from, I was a more willing participant. Noah's speech, thanking me on behalf of the state, hailing the righteousness of our actions, cut through my sarcastic defenses and left me emotionally raw. I thought of Beryl crying, tears for relatives she never knew murdered along with David's grandparents. It began to dawn on me that Noah had delivered a kind of benediction, and that the Mossad viewed my help, our actions, as not only righting wrongs but imbued with grace. I began to rationalize, banker codes be damned, and yet, deep down I continued to wrestle with my predicament, knowing I needed to find a better middle ground.

I was not actually handing over accounts or breaking secrecy rules. I was coercing bankers, who had their cushy lives handed to them without sacrifice or moral searching, to close decades-old accounts torn from the ghettos of Nazi Germany. This was not dirty money stolen in shakedowns, drug running, or political embezzlement. I would leave that battle to others. This money was tainted with the indiscriminate discarding of good human souls, the rot of ethnic cleansing, the ashes of my wife's relatives blackening concentration camp ovens. These accounts rose from barbarism and hid evil. I could find no justification why the lucky few bankers of the next generations should profit from the sins of the past. A bit hypocritical? Not necessarily, and for the moment I put aside the risk of any personal familial reckoning. In my heart, I did not believe my father was complicit.

At Noah's behest, Uzi shocked me by lobbying to bring in Pavlina to help with the ruse. Yes, Pavlina, Beryl's prized recruit and Dirk's wife, was apparently joining our ensemble. "Marco, I don't want you taking all these meetings alone. It's a given that everyone you meet will feel uncomfortable. Reluctant."

"I agree. I had to put on my best performance with Alfonso."

"Well, I have a suggestion. Take Pavlina with you. She'll soften the tone. No offense, but any banker's eyes will be on her not you."

"What? I agree all those bankers will be drooling over her. But so what? Bringing anyone else along is risky. These meetings are sensitive enough. Won't they be uncomfortable confessing with two of us there? It's my relationships that will get us in the door. We don't need some honey pot."

"That's not where I'm going. At least…well, hear me out. Sometimes two voices can be stronger than one. She can claim to be from the Mossad—and never mind it happens to be true, which we'll of course deny. Anyway, it will be so outrageous, this gorgeous woman there as your assistant. She'll say something to you in two or three languages, including Hebrew—which by the way, she's picked up brilliantly. They'll be completely caught off guard. You can claim that you were blackmailed, the Mossad had pictures of the two of you together and threatened to show them to Beryl."

"Are you kidding? You're going there?"

"Worse, actually. If they refuse, and you have to persuade them, Pavlina can tell whoever you're convincing we have the best digital experts and have photos of Pavlina with them. We'll set them up. Have Pavlina bump into them somewhere, a bar, a coffee shop. She will drop something, maybe a lipstick, and they'll pick it up. When they hand it to her, she'll thank them with a hug or kiss. And we'll be there to take a photo. Then the alterations can begin. Maybe they'll even remember the encounter, and the fact they met her before will throw them off balance and make them believe it. With the photos, we can manipulate it to include a shot with the two of them, but she's taken her top off. Here, take a look," as Uzi slid me a doctored photo of Pavlina and Bernhard Alfonso. Shit!

"My God, Uzi."

"Hey, hopefully, you never need to use them, and this is just Plan B. Marco, remember the big picture, what we're trying to do. Why."

"I get the endgame. It's…just the tactics."

"Well, I didn't think either of us would prefer using photos of Beryl."

I knew he was joking, but he had me momentarily until breaking out in a chuckle. Or would he have used his own daughter if necessary? Jesus. The possibility drew me back to thinking about my parents, what my father would think, and how I had pulled off the con. In reality, I was not willing to pick a bank randomly then fabricate an account. Of course, it could be done that way. However, I was still a banker by heart. This was my family, even my heritage. I would not wantonly sabotage the code nor my family's reputation. I thought about my father and what he had built. He had not achieved my level of mega-wealth; yet, if it had not been for his name, reputation, introductions, and loving help allowing me to jump queue after queue, I would not be where I was. No, I would not play Russian Roulette with my banker comrades and partners.

And then a solution, the perfect solution, dawned on me. I had a way to target a list and protect my dignity. It would be another secret I must harbor. That was my real challenge, not whether we leveraged Pavlina to suggest some sordid tryst.

"Fine, Uzi. Just tell Pavlina to keep her panties on."

***

I received a flattering and odd invitation out of the blue. I've kept the only copy of it on my desk for years:

European Shoah Institution Annual Gala

Honoring Marco Bellagio & The Krumarkt Partners Fund

Black Tie

March 19, 2012 Grand Hotel Amsterdam

RSVP to honorgala2012@nbdw.nl

I remember immediately calling David Wolfe. "Hi, David, I got the invitation."

"How did you know it was me?"

"The RSVP email address. Dead giveaway. Thought you guys were better at disguise. Though putting Noah's initials first was generous of you."

"This was one we didn't want to hide. In fact, we're quite proud to have it out in the open. What you've done is extraordinary. And last month in Jerusalem. Wow."

A few weeks before, Beryl, Hamid and I had arranged two private ceremonies in Israel. The first was opening a Krumarkt Partners Fund wing at the museum which housed the paintings we had spirited away from the Mullen's warehouse. The wing was devoted to history, and interactive displays replete with videos and testimonials added morbid context to the vibrant art. The second event was organized by Friends of Yad Vashem, the

Israeli Holocaust Museum. We met with seventy survivors of death camps, roughly one for every year since the infamous ovens started incinerating souls. I expected the moment to be haunting, to shrink from old men and women hollowed out from a life of trauma. After all, in looking at options to start funneling proceeds from our fund we were forced to confront the past, a past that crowded my thoughts with images of emaciated bodies and lifeless stares. Instead, I found those living links to the unimaginable, vibrant and inspirational. A conversation with a nearly 90-year-old woman named Ruth, bearing an Auschwitz tattoo, branded a symbiotic wrinkle onto my memory.

"How are you not bitter?" I asked.

"I am bitter. But I also survived. It was a gift to lead a normal life. I wasn't going to have them take that too. If you look around, you'll see some of the most driven people you'll ever meet. Relentless at building a future. Desperate for living. Committed to memorializing the truth. Skilled at walling off incomprehensible sorrow and somehow permitting moments of joy."

"I can't imagine. I really don't know what to say," truly lost for words, humbled in her, in the gathering's, presence. "I'm sorry and I'm glad," was all I could sputter. Ruth nodded her head as her lips edged up in the hint of a smile. "Thank you. I don't want anyone to try and get inside my head, to try and imagine what it was like. That's a recipe for going crazy. Maybe even suicide. But not everyone has been able to move on." She looked around at the table and said, "Most of us here are the success stories. Maybe not success…I'm not sure of the right word. I don't like the label survivors either. It implies we're somehow lucky or skilled. Truth is we just survived. Somehow. Certainly not God's will. Faith is something I definitely lost in the camps. Camp, another inappropriate word. Maybe prison, or hell. There are a lot of us, okay, I'll say survivors, who are haunted and still cannot cope. But at least we're here, and as I said, I've lived a full life. My heart breaks for the missing, the dead, the next generation who never knew…will never know their parents, grandparents…So thank you for helping them."

As part of the evening, we had announced millions in grants for victims and their families. The Krumarkt Partners Fund was mature enough that it was past time to start using some of the funds. The interest alone was millions per year, and we could still grow the base while beginning to make good on our founding pledge. We started to pay medical bills, set up special psychiatric outreach programs, and established grants to pay college and graduate school fees. A great deal of attention had been focused on the actual victims—and rightly so—but there was only so much that could be done for them past the turn of the new millennium. They had either moved on like Ruth or retreated into a darkness unlikely to be penetrated. The next generation, though, was also deeply traumatized and we could help to put them on a better path—counseling, easing the burden of educational costs, underwriting legal fees to pursue restitution claims, even providing housing for those who wanted to care for their aging relatives. It was a long and noble list. And it was theoretical no more. One of Ruth's daughters became among the first to take advantage of counseling, and her niece sought Beryl's advice about pursuing a claim to a piece of looted art.

David interrupted my thoughts: "Marco, are you listening? What you did, talking and listening to every one of those survivors. It couldn't have been easy looking so many in the eye. Reliving the past, unfiltered."

"Unfiltered thanks are easy," I said. "How many times do you get to look someone in the eye you've helped? To really see."

"In the Mossad, not often enough. But those times are the ones you cherish."

"So let me just have those moments. Those personal, unfiltered ones. I don't need this award, to stand in front of a ballroom and be lauded."

"Are you sure? When I put the screws to Bernhard Alfonso, I convinced him to underwrite the event. Probably a conversation we should filter."

I laughed. In fact, I relaxed into a full guffaw. "Yes, I'm sure. But thank you, David."

"Okay. The invitation was just a draft. Only RSVP so far was Noah's."

"Funny."

"I don't mean to be funny. Are you sure about this? Would be a great honor, a wonderful evening. More than well deserved."

"I'm sure. I didn't get it at first, caught up in building the fund, how big it could become. Now I understand what Beryl was always trying to say. Help when no one could help before. Christ, David, we're doing good in the sense of the word that is so meaningful most could never appreciate it."

"In Hebrew, we call it a *mizvah*. A good deed. A selfless act of empathy and kindness."

The Mossad remained a step ahead of me. Again. I thanked David—again—and told him to convey my sincere appreciation to Noah. I remember closing my eyes and picturing Ruth and her extended family of survivors and sufferers. It was then I decided to keep the invitation on my desk, weighted down by Krugerrands in all four corners.

***

With the milestone of our twenty-fifth board meeting on the horizon, Noah, Uzi, David, and I had managed to recover hundreds of millions of dollars from several different banks. Also, Uzi had kept his word—one hundred percent of the recovery funneling into our Krumarkt Partners Fund account. Amazingly, most of the banks accepted me as a blackmailed victim like themselves. One look at Pavlina, coupled with the hint they could be similarly compromised, and they capitulated. My reputation remained unsullied. Even my conscience was clear. My only misgiving was turning the spotlight on my own family. I came from a banking family, a skip from the Swiss borders. My father's banks were likely much less clean than the pristine waters of the lakes bordering Como, Lugano, Zurich, and Zug. Was I just as complicit? Was I one of those bankers benefiting from standing atop the murdered remains of my wife's ancestors, burying the truth and spending the spoils? It was a sickening thought.

Thank God, my very actions were in and of themselves an act of redemption. It wasn't quite what it appeared on the surface, but I had resolved to look into my past before truly committing. Deep down, I didn't think my father knowingly participated in any coverups. Still, I needed proof I could be as proud of him as I was of my wife. Ironically, I would only come to feel truly unburdened with an actual burial, even if the information I could finally admit cleansed my path years before.

***

San Francisco — 2012
Unbeknownst to me at the time, while I was strong-arming alpine bankers, Beryl undertook a new mission. Using her cover as Laila Alisime, she gained an introduction through the Brussels office of Wikipedia to their San Francisco corporate headquarters. Claiming to be a programmer turned marketing manager for SohoMasters, hailing from both Mideastern and European backgrounds, she had the perfect cross-cultural pedigree for the online informational behemoth.

Beryl sat waiting in the modest lobby of a simple office in downtown San Francisco. The non-profit did not strive for either the chic or extravagant campuses of other software titans. The décor of exposed brick and pipes, dotted with cubicles and a few private offices on the fringe, looked like it could have housed any moderately funded start-up. A young man with a ponytail came over and introduced himself.

"Hi, Laila?"

"Yes."

"Welcome. Nice to meet you. I'm Jishnu. Why don't we sit over here." He led her to a small, glassed conference room before continuing, "We're trying to set up some verticals to better categorize content and then exploring ways to drive traffic there. One of our board members is big on the arts, and within our culture mission, we're trying to aggregate, how do I put it, everything art related. So, museums, artists, historical sites, you name it."

"And I understand that's where SohoMasters fits in. Your colleague Monique I met with in Brussels thought we could help organize the data. Plus, as we reach out, maybe get others on board to help you."

"Exactly. We have limited resources and need to reach out to thousands of organizations to help index the space."

"Sounds like a perfect match. As I told Monique, we'd love to help. We already have a database that probably captures half or more of the museums and organizations you want to reach. And if I told my executive committee we're working with you, I think it could even help our own funding pitches. As a side benefit, if we could add some information we index from the project to our database, it would augment our resources. We all need our justifications."

"I get it." Jishnu smiled. "We're pretty flexible, as long as we can stay true to our mission."

"Don't worry. I wouldn't ever suggest doing anything that would compromise you guys. I'm a fan. And a user! There is one challenge, though, that I want to be upfront about."

"What's that?"

"We'll need access to some of your programming links to pull this off. It's a ton of scraping. Source code level."

"I think you know, we let pretty much anyone edit sites. That's the core of Wikipedia."

"I know. It's genius!" Beryl as Laila flashed the green in her eyes, a bewitching ploy. "Just that if we're going to do this right, we need to make sure we're embedded properly so we can also provide metrics back to sites about their data."

"There are certain protocols we still need to follow for security, but let's not get hung up on that. I'm sure our tech gurus can figure out something. Just need to stay within the lines."

"You're not one of those gurus?" she flattered.

"Ah, I know my way around the coding, but lately, I'm focused on the marketing end."

"Clicks not bytes," she laughed. "I'm a bit of an art geek and used to be a programming geek, but here I am helping out marketing." Having done her best to bond, Beryl continued, "I've brought a short presentation. Should I run you through it quickly?"

"Can't wait. Let's get you plugged in," he said, juggling wires coming from a junction box atop the table, miraculously connecting Beryl's computer to a large wall monitor on the first try.

Jishnu was duly impressed by the presentation and shook hands with Beryl on their budding partnership. She now pressed her advantage. "Could I get a quick tour?"

"Sure, not much to see. This is most of it, and then our server and control room. But most stuff is offsite."

"That's fine, love to see what's here. It will be cool to go home and brag to my husband I got to tour Wikipedia."

Beryl had two hidden cameras and recorders, one in her pen and the other in a brooch she wore. As she toured the server rooms, she started recording and made sure to aim it at workers busy on their keyboards. She asked a few pointed questions that she hoped would prompt logins, capturing the keystrokes. Passwords. That was the magic information and the whole reason for her trip. She also had a couple other Mossad gadgets that she managed to implant, distracting one programmer by putting a cup of coffee down on her desk and another by asking if he would mind taking a picture of her with Jishnu in front of a poster.

Beryl might have combat training but fighting in the new millennium required more cyber sleuthing than trigger speed. Back outside, Beryl took a taxi down to the Embarcadero and found a coffee shop where she logged onto their Wi-Fi network. Her encrypted phone would do the rest. She shook her head, looking over San Francisco Bay and out toward the Golden Gate bridge. Why wouldn't one of the biggest websites in the world have tighter security? Then again, who would care about bugging a free, open-source website without any advertising or paying customers? Projecting further innocence, SohoMasters itself appeared remarkably benign, continuing to play its cover role brilliantly. She opened her phone and texted: "We're in. Operational."

***

London, United Kingdom and 25th Board Meeting—2014
Beryl and I left Mateo and Aliza with our nanny. Traveling with kids nearing six years old was challenging. At least packing was becoming marginally easier. Those first few years, with strollers, playpens, toys, diapers, and portable highchairs, before we even

tackled clothes and medicines, were only survived given Beryl's military training. She treated a trip like a logistics supply line, sorting out the packing, transport, cleaning, and replenishment needs. I gained a new appreciation for military coordination and mothers alike. The supply line focus had now been supplanted by the need for military discipline. Beryl's training, reinforcement, and repetition drills far outranked our need to travel with props. I shuddered to think what she had planned for the teenage years. Shackles and prison themes came to mind.

We set the meeting in London because Hamid was living there, and we had agreed to move the location around every few years. It also reminded us of when we had first started out, living in Notting Hill and planning our future strolling through the backyard close. This time we stayed in a quiet boutique hotel on Beaufort Gardens in Knightsbridge. Our rate was fantastic due to it being part of a group owned by Hamid. After settling in, we took a stroll to Harrods nearby, buying some snacks in the food hall, not waiting to pick at them as we walked back to our room. Life felt perfect again—a feeling I seemed to lapse into every few years until something nasty from the past reared up like a ghoul from a monster movie.

Hopefully, those nightmares were behind me. And yet, Uzi's refrain of never forget, though tied to such a different horrible context, periodically haunted me. Beryl told me that was good. We were not meant to forget. As human beings, our history, the good and evil, grounded us. An Israeli soldier's practical perspective, I thought. I kept trying to poke holes, to rationalize—but was that perspective so wrong? Living my life in punctuated bursts of joy and remorse was not so awful. Save for the extremes, it might even be called normal.

Beryl had arranged for a conference room at London's Moultens & Barings headquarters. We arrived at 10:30 the next morning and found Dirk, Pavlina, Hamid, and my Zug-based lawyer Jens already waiting for us. We had finally let Pavlina join the inner circle. She was already privy to everything, and in retrospect, we should have brought her fully into the fold years ago. She gave me a coy smile, and I smiled back awkwardly. Privy to the lascivious pictures and party to the Mossad's shameless scheme, I shifted in my seat and dared not look at Beryl or Dirk. Jesus. I distracted myself pivoting to Jens, a black hole of boring so deep he sucked away Pavlina's allure.

We called the joyous meeting to order. Twenty-five years! It was almost too much to fathom. Beryl and I were in our mid-forties, perhaps close to half our lives behind us. Time, though, was nothing to lament. I remained lucky, wealthy, healthy, and married to the most beautiful Mossad spy in the world—even accounting for Pavlina's oomph. When Beryl walked into the meeting room, her runway model sway had not diminished a bit. The bloom of middle age may have added just enough rounding to her hips to accentuate her walk. All the men turned as she entered and watched until she took her seat. And to think she was a partner in the firm where we were meeting! I was indeed a lucky man.

"Jens," I requested, "Could you please read us the headlines on the accounts. I think we have neared a milestone."

"I would say exceeded." He took off his glasses and directed everyone to a page of the briefing books neatly set out around the rectangular glass table. "I am pleased to announce that the Krumarkt Partners Fund now has approximately $1.2 Billion in its account."

"Wow," Dirk exclaimed. "Marco, I remember when we started this, you joked about getting to a billion, but I, I really thought that was a pipe dream. Even with your background. This is amazing!" He smiled at Pavlina, who remained silent, smart enough as a newcomer to let her husband take the lead.

"Thank you," I said. "It is amazing. And it's a result achieved because of everyone around this table. If you, Dirk, had not been there at the beginning and had not first suspected an art theft ring, we would not be here. Same goes for you, Hamid, if you had not courageously helped us bring down Mullen Antiques and then later matched the fund to double its assets and accelerate its growth. If Beryl and I had not been at this for twenty-five years, if she had not found a way through Uzi's colleagues and Moultens to undermine unimaginable art theft and laundering, if she had not built the Berlinerhaus which has helped uncover so many more lost treasures...and well, I'll indulge a moment and give myself a pat on the back for helping tear the Nazi accounts from Banco ICR, and with Pavlina's help a few others, we would never have achieved this spectacular level. Maybe a bit trite, but this fund today is the result of blood, sweat, and tears."

"And a bit of subterfuge, and couples who are partners in more ways than one," Dirk joked, nodding to Pavlina and then looking toward Beryl and me.

"Absolutely. Happy couple at night, bit of ass-kicking by day," Beryl joked.

I wondered whether she was toying with me, whether she and Pavlina were in on some practical joke. My paranoia runs deep, and I calmed myself watching Jens shuffle a few papers. I took refuge in the belief that after twenty-five years, and with Pavlina's assignments, Dirk had been briefed on all our actions or figured most of it out. As for Hamid, what was not already explicit, we assume he surmised and left it at that. Perhaps as a spy's spouse, I was destined to be teased with hints of subterfuge. I had no idea what Jens suspected yet rested assured he would keep his mouth shut.

"And a bit of surviving a gunfight or two," Hamid joined in, still amazed at what he had stumbled into via his partnership with me.

"I know, I know," I took back over, looking around the table, though averting my eyes from Jens after Hamid's last loaded comment. "It would have been easy for Dirk to keep to the quiet diplomatic cocktail party circuit, for Hamid to spend his free time quibbling over transfer fees for players on his football clubs, for Beryl to quit her little Israeli association and stick to appraising pieces for high-end buyers... She's always joked there's plenty of danger in a Sotheby's auction!" I paused, my meager joke soliciting a chuckle. "Everyone, please raise your glasses. We did it! A toast to the Krumarkt Partners Fund! Now we have the endowment base we dreamed of." I paused, thinking of Ruth, "To our mission of doing some real good!"

"Here, here!" everyone chimed in, clinking glasses, beaming smiles around.

CHAPTER 17

Liechtenstein — 2017

I knew the contact several years back from that weasel Bernhard Alfonso was a trap. The first written request from Banco ICR in almost seventy years! Did they think me an idiot? For several years, the Mossad and I had been engaged in a cat and mouse chase, both knowing the inevitable outcome. By then, I had figured out who my adversary truly was. They would not find me, nor would they cease trying. I was still furious they managed to take my money from the bank. When I first suspected they were behind the meeting, I considered moving the money. By then, though, the risk was too significant, modern technology making it increasingly difficult to hide transfers that I knew they would dissect. I had to forfeit the account. I had plenty more — my investments had continued to grow, the fruit of my father's genius. It was the principle, the insult, that stung. I took solace knowing they were only able to penetrate the fringes, and I reveled in what must be their enduring frustration.

And yet, they continued to annoy me, the Israeli scum enjoying their ability to encircle my freedoms. I even succumbed to battling them in the virtual world. A few years ago, posts started appearing online about Mullen Antiques. A small exposé in a German newspaper slandered Rolfe and Florian, postulating whether they may have been heirs to an illegitimate fortune. I had no doubt the article, and its repetition throughout the Internet, was the work of the Mossad—toying with me and reminding me they would never cease chasing. The article implied that Florian and Rolfe could have been in possession of a cache of stolen art. It even speculated that part of the collection might have been initially acquired by their grandfather, Werner Mullenheim, a German who had lived in France. Worse, the author impudently pondered whether part of the collection could date to the pillage of Paris in wartime. I could find no trace of the supposed author and concluded the Mossad were mocking me. I admitted to some grudging respect. It is what I might have done.

I was forced to engage an army to take down the posts. I benefited from a European privacy law, which the lawyers referred to as the right to be forgotten. The law allowed people to erase news about them if the information was false or no longer relevant. The legislation became quite controversial, as criminals who had served their time could demand search engines purge all mention of past sins. Even a child molester who had served his time could now hide his past; the logic being new neighbors should not be able to learn of earlier fondling and then discriminate against beasts living across the street once debts to society had been paid. If a child molester could demand such a right, I could surely expunge slanderous allegations against my family. I was rich, and it was no trouble for my attorneys to dance with the Mossad, wielding the new law to our advantage. I also considered whether this was a direct betrayal, and after all these years, I should release the file on Marco and Beryl. The articles made no explicit mention of Nazi roots and hinted cleverly enough to stop short of breaching our tacit little pact. I was sorely tempted and once again pondered, what did I have to lose?

This ploy motivated me to think about my father's legacy. Two could taunt. I developed a Wikipedia page devoted to my father, focusing on his military career and changing a few details to prevent direct traces to any of us. The law did not allow for the inverse of its erasure, no rights of authenticity or publicity granted to the departed. I wondered what these games meant for history. I did not want my father forgotten, nor did I want to rewrite his history. The world should know his true story. But what about me? I had spent my life perfecting hiding, and if discovered, I would strive to disappear. I was happy to leave without a trace, magnanimously offering Florian and Rolfe the same destiny if they wanted assistance. I would keep correcting aspersions and glorifying the Reich. I became weary at times, though, the effort enervating with so many people trying to write about events and people when they truly knew nothing.

I tried to put aside the nuisance of ensuring what should be forgotten was appropriately erased and what should be glorified was easily accessible. I spend most of my time quietly, occasionally making decisions about Mullenboess investments. Over the last year, I scarcely ventured beyond the vistas of my mountain villa in Liechtenstein. Nearing seventy, I did not yearn to travel as much, content in my morning and afternoon walks. The cool air was good for my health. I understand why the Fuhrer loved his retreat in Berchtesgaden, although I wondered why he wanted to be so isolated from his people. My father met him once. It was an inspection in Munich where officers were paraded and pinned with medals. I found the medal in my father's possessions when he died, but sadly there was no photograph.

I wondered who I should leave it to — neither Florian or Rolfe, nor Sophie would appreciate the honor. Sophie was married and had two boys; she would have nothing to do with me, and it would be hard to influence her children. Florian married Heidi, a subdued woman from Aachen who worked for a while at Mullen Antiques. Perhaps they would raise the next generation. I have given up hope for Rolfe, who recoiled to his house to live a hermitic existence. At least Florian had the fortitude to move past his youthful failures. He was working for one of the Internet companies I backed, and I have been careful to hide any connection that can lead back to me. I have done my best to fulfill my father's wishes and look after them. There was little else I could do, the boys soon to be descending the other side of the slope of middle age. The thought of carrying on my father's lineage gave me pause to consider whether I was too old to father a child myself. Perhaps not.

I thought about my father's third letter. I would be able to read it soon and sensed much work was still to be done. My waiting was nearly at an end.

The Hague, The Netherlands — 2019

Traveling to our thirtieth board meeting, back in The Hague again, I reflected on my father's recent passing. I was nearing fifty and feeling introspective. I loved my father and was deeply grateful that my parents paved such a privileged path for my life. I might be flippant about it, but I didn't take jumping so many queues for granted. Nor did I feel guilt over my benefits. Few first sons fought the rules of primogeniture, and I would not hesitate to grease the way for Mateo and Aliza.

After my father's death, I was willing to share a secret I had kept even from Beryl. After taking Werner's funds from Banco ICR, and Noah and Uzi's requests that I repeat the scheme with others, I approached my father. We took a boat ride alone out on the Zugersee, and I told him what Beryl and I had done with Banco ICR. I told him about East Berlin. I told him about the Krumarkt Partners Fund. I told him everything. Even about Beryl and Uzi, and without using names, about Noah and David. I skipped Pavlina's role and Aaron with no last name — there are prudent limits, even when confessing. The thought that my father, the lauded banker Anthony Bellagio, could have been as complicit as Bernhard Alfonso, that my life may have been seeded by money derived from unspeakable crimes, haunted me. I needed to know. For myself, for my children — I wanted to know the truth. If I did not have that conversation then, while my father still breathed, I might never know. I hoped my fears were unfounded. However, if the truth was damning, I resolved I would prefer to learn and forget than to never know at all.

"I suspected, but I did not know," he told me. "How could you not wonder about accounts from the war? But I didn't set them up. They were before my time. And when I asked questions, there was always a plausible answer. Were those lies? Maybe, I don't know. Probably in some cases. But I swear to you, on my life, on your life, I never helped anyone hide one of those accounts."

"What about the next generation, the sons and daughters, the grandchildren — did you suspect any of them?"

"Of what? They were just that — the kids. Those kids, the ones that suspected what their fathers or grandfathers did, were almost always shy. Embarrassed. How could they live with that? They wanted to make some amends, live a better life, and were conflicted trying to hide their family's past. I can remember one woman, Elizabeth Becker, coming in and asking me to close an account and donate all of it to charity. She told me about her father, an unrepentant Nazi, and broke down crying in my office. I remember thinking I was lucky my father died young, and I did not have to worry about that type of burden. Can you imagine admitting such a thing?"

For a moment, I was paralyzed, not quite knowing how to respond. There were no acceptable words. "No. I'm sorry. I had to ask."

"I'm glad you did."

I then proceeded to ask him to help me identify other banks and, if possible, even accounts. He felt exactly as I did when Noah first approached me about Banco ICR. To agree would mean betraying his honor, not subtly, but knowingly and bluntly. And yet, if he refused, it would drive a dagger into the relationship with his son. Worse, to refuse in the face of my marriage to Beryl, in light of the atrocities committed and with the knowledge that I had come face-to-face with the perpetrators, would be a denial beyond redemption. He pledged to find suspected banks, knowing what I would do with the names and numbers. I will always remember his deeds. He would be forever my silent partner in the Krumarkt Partners Fund.

***

The Hague, The Netherlands and 30th Board Meeting — 2019
I sat around a table with Beryl, Dirk, Hamid, Pavlina and Jens. As customary, we started with a report on the finances. They were spectacular. We had more than doubled our money in the last five years. The returns were driven by three factors, all intimately linked to the fund's roots and yet having almost nothing to do with each other. First, the Berlinerhaus had become an overwhelming success. Not only had the museum become a world-famous jewel, but our scheme to use it as a front to draw in other illicit dealings worked to grow the collection and our coffers alike. If we had done nothing beyond establishing the Berlinerhaus and using it to augment our endowment, the Krumarkt Partners Fund would have been an enormous success.

Second, when we coerced several banks into liquidating suspect World War II era accounts, we were also able to persuade the banks to make generous donations directly to the Krumarkt Partners Fund. Coercion was a strong term, but what else would I call it? I preferred not to use the word blackmail with Beryl. The Mossad was quite keen on not straying over imaginary lines. If we debated politically tinged nomenclature, then I planned to stick with donations. Characterizing the payments as donations assuaged a certain measure of guilt and made them tax-deductible. That was as close to achieving a win-win as imaginable in persuading a Swiss bank to part with its money.

Finally, David and Noah had introduced me to several Israeli venture capitalists and private equity firms. With my connections, I could have called directly. However, a confidential recommendation from the Mossad tended to go a long way in building trust with local partners. Tel Aviv had become second to Silicon Valley in the growth of start-ups and successful technology ventures. The range of companies was incredible, spanning biotech, information technology, and military hardware. There were companies harnessing the sun's power, innovating solar panels absorbing the desert heat, and others implanting sensors in plants creating efficiencies in agribusiness. Initially, I wanted to focus on the military sector, having seen the Mossad's cleverness firsthand. However, David persuaded me to diversify, arguing passionately that the heart of innovation beats as strongly next to the Negev as in San Francisco and Seattle. Not only was he right, but his introductions proved invaluable. One investment alone of $200,000 became worth $100 Million. I hardly considered it a conflict of interest if I invested my own money alongside these stakes; thank goodness in that instance I had elected to match the bet.

Beyond the ballooning of personal wealth, the net result was my little fund, started with a mere bag of Krugerrands, was now worth well over $2 billion. When two more of our holdings went public, as was expected in the next year to eighteen months, that tally could grow unimaginably higher.

What to do with all that money? More of the same, and good thing we already had a roadmap, or I would be sorely tempted down more hedonistic paths. I had not forgotten Beryl chiding Dirk and me when we joked which type of sports cars to indulge in many years before. Perhaps I could talk to Dirk and Pavlina about buying one of those Bohemian spas? Or what about my own trophy island? Perhaps in the Seychelles with its own tax status? We all have our dreams.

But, no worries, we kept our word. I was not an asshole. I could never give away enough money to atone for the sins of wartime bankers, nor heal the wounds of those who suffered unimaginable fates at the hands of the Nazis. I thought of Ruth, and how between meetings in Israel and Rolf and Florian's family I had come into personal contact with perpetrators and victims. I had a new habit at my desk. Like placing a stone on a grave for remembrance, I weighted down my gala honoring invitation with one Krugerrand for each year that the Krumarkt Partners Fund gave out money.

By the meeting's end, we had formally enshrined continuing grants for counseling and psychological outreach, medical and housing allowances for elderly and funding for restitution claims in a billion-dollar trust for the survivors of the Holocaust and their descendants. We launched another trust to endow remembrance museums and memorials. We also established less conspicuous trusts to fund Nazi hunters and track down other war criminals—acknowledging time was running out. Aaron with no last name was ensured lifetime employment. The Krumarkt Partners Fund had become a full-time global enterprise.

Jens excused himself after the formalities of the meeting. With the five of us left, Beryl rose to make a toast. We were holding our meeting in the Berlinerhaus for the first time, and I could tell she was overwhelmed by the moment. I wasn't the only one moved by the reckoning of what we had faced and by the countless people we had managed to help, and which the trusts would continue to support. For Beryl, the Berlinerhaus was a grander reminder than the pile of Krugerrands on my one-of-a-kind invitation.

She began, "We've held these meetings in a lot of places, but this is truly special. I'm thinking back to when I studied at the Royal College of Art in London. In my wildest dreams, I could not imagine being here, head of a world-famous museum that exists because of all of us. I sometimes cry at night thinking about some of the paintings we managed to return to their homes, to the family members who survived, and that we have managed to do some good and change the tide to produce good memories. I even think of my sister Hannah and a kind of silent pledge I made to her that we would do everything we could for all recent generations of victims," pausing to wipe a tear. "I think of the horrors we've seen and survived to get here. That we created this from that evening after seeing Springsteen, turned it around to, my God, this fund to help heal the past." She paused, fighting emotions. "It's hard for all of you to understand. I'm the only one of you from Israel, the only Jew… And to have given back like this." She paused again. "I want each of you to take a half-hour and walk the rooms of the gallery by yourself. Think about the families and stories behind each one. Think about what you've done, what we've done. Take a moment and be proud." Struggling, she said, "I'm going to shut up now."

I went over and hugged her, her cheeks wet. Hamid, Dirk, and Pavlina followed. Pavlina and Beryl held onto their embrace, understanding secrets none of us shared, squeezing in the rarely acknowledged comfort of solidarity, service, and survival. We then took our tour, walking separately, lost in thought, happy to be alive and silently mourning the unknowing donors. Fuck you, Werner. At least I was expanding my cursing.

***

I was drained from the meeting, and the last thing I wanted was to have dinner with Noah, David, and Uzi. I had nothing more to give them. I prayed they had nothing more to ask. It was rare for Dirk, Pavlina, Hamid, Beryl, and me to be together, and the trio from the full-time Mossad wanted to talk to all of us. Well, all excluding Hamid. I lobbied for including him as there were few secrets left and he had shown more than enough mettle and discretion to be a trusted member of the team. However thin the Interpol ruse had become, though, Noah preferred to maintain the pretense, and Hamid headed home. I did not dwell on Hamid's exclusion, instead focusing on the fact our invitation would have been more foreboding if Aaron was joining. I was promised he was somewhere else, a pledge that gave me hope. Still, I could not recall a time when all of us had been alone and sensed this was no meeting to self-congratulate, no encore to Beryl's toast. Could they have finally located Werner? That would be something.

I booked a room at a Thai restaurant in Scheveningen, not far from the fish restaurant where David and Noah had first broached the notion of uncovering old Nazi accounts at a Swiss bank. There was always something cleansing and safe about sitting by the ocean. It was early fall now, though, and the bite of winter advancing off the North Sea was too strong to allow us to sit outside. We sat around a large circular table, Thai beer poured for all. Beryl had pressed her father in advance to give us a hint of the reason for meeting but was stonewalled. I had expected as much, Uzi always the professional keeping business and family separate. I smiled to myself that he maintained a personal Chinese wall and considered whether I should have chosen Chinese over Thai. The choice had been symbolic for another reason. I simply wanted neutral ground, and none of us had ever been to Thailand. No missions, no vacations. We were free of any haunting memories, free of any memories in fact, free to fantasize and just drink beer. I could hope, right? Jesus Christ, another dinner with the Mossad. I tried not to think that way — otherwise, dinner with Beryl could be like this every night.

I decided to cut to the chase. "Any news on Werner?"

Noah took the lead, saying, "Afraid not. He's pretty shrewd. That Stasi training. Unless he makes a silly mistake, he'll probably manage to stay hidden."

"Even from those posts about Mullen Antiques, the veiled implication?"

"No, for a while we had high hopes because someone was taking down the posts. Even a Wikipedia post was edited to purge what we wrote. But he was clever. We couldn't back-trace the IP address from where the changes were made."

"The mention of Werner Mullenheim didn't even spook him?"

"No, well, at least we don't think so. But it was worth the try," Noah lamented. "Even if a little dangerous. We didn't want to push him to overreact."

Dirk interrupted, "Sorry, but I'm not following any of this."

David took over. "Apologies. I guess we kept that scheme compartmentalized. We tried to sow a bit of disinformation, creating fake posts and articles about Mullen Antiques. Stuck fairly close to the facts, which should have made them nervous—used Florian and Rolfe's real names, talked about the gallery's financial downfall, and then mentioned unsubstantiated rumors of their laundering stolen art. That all seemed quite legitimate, but we then took a risk suggesting they were the grandchildren of Werner Mullenheim. We also made up and dangled that their grandfather had lived in France, and suggested several paintings could have been World War II vintage. We dared not go further as that could have precipitated retaliation. Believe me, I thought about planting that he was a Gestapo officer. So far, he's kept his word about not releasing those files."

"Is there any truth to what you posted? Does such a person exist?" Dirk asked.

"No, we just made up the name. All we have to go on is the first name Werner and last name Mullen, which we assume was changed. So, we combined them and made it up: Mullenheim. Werner, whoever he is, will get the message. We assume he's read everything. And if we're lucky, the name is close and should make him nervous. But so far, no contact. He isn't biting."

"And probably won't," Noah added. "What's his incentive now? Rolfe and Florian are free, and nobody's pressing the local authorities to open charges. He would have already acted—and if we go too far, he still has the file on Beryl and Marco. Maybe more, maybe he really has tapes. I'm sure he feels we wouldn't risk it. What's to gain at this point? And there's a big downside— same stalemate. I think we have to accept we may be at a dead end. Be happy with what we achieved." Grasping his glass and coughing out a soft smile, "We're very proud of all of you. What you've done, the money you've raised, the property you recovered, what we managed to uncover. A toast!" Noah and David raised their beers. We all clinked glasses and took a healthy swig.

I looked at Beryl, and we smiled, genuinely proud. Despite the push for euphoria, I could not escape a sense of unfinished business and fiddled with my chopsticks. I believed there was more to the meeting. Noah would not have brought everyone together simply to thank us again. Beryl's earlier toast was sincere. Here, however, I sensed I was being played. This marrying a spy stuff was exhausting. I asked, "You're really dropping it, letting Werner go? What about this never forget mantra?"

"We won't. I promise we'll never stop looking for Werner. But I also don't want any of you to have false expectations. At this point...." Noah's voice trailed off.

David added, "And the new laws don't help. Privacy laws are getting tougher and allow people to take down posts about their past behavior. It will be harder to research in the future. For now, we have access, but even the law is tilting in Werner's favor."

"Assuming you're looking for him within the bounds of the law," I said.

"Well, there is that," David conceded, smiling. "I don't expect our search will be too inhibited."

Dirk sipped his beer and said, "Well, I'm ready to put it to bed. That's what we diplomats do. If we reach a certain compromise, we move on. We know there are limits, and if we tried to seek perfection, we'd never get anything done." He looked over at Pavlina, squeezing her hand beneath the table.

"And that's why we will continue to take the lead on looking," Noah admonished. "Enough, we need to turn our energies elsewhere and stop hoping Werner turns up."

Everyone nodded, Beryl and I fidgeting more than the others, frustrated over the loose end. In theory, I would have liked to take our wins and move on, putting the hunt behind us. I knew Beryl wished similarly. That feeling did not diminish our pride, just gnawed at us, reminding us of an unfinished task. Then I had a bit of a revelation: I would never forget. I had become a part of Beryl's family, converted by marriage, the bonds cemented with our children. I was assimilated as a member of her tribe. The duty and embrace washed over me.

My epiphany, sadly, was short-lived, my wayward mind ever looking to press the advantage. Marriage entitled me to Israeli citizenship, and I pondered whether I had dismissed that option too early. Perhaps I should apply. But then would I need to serve in the military? Screw that. I would settle for a measure of assimilation. Or would I get a better tax break on my Tel Aviv start-up investments with citizenship? Maybe I should investigate that? Would that override the obligation of military service? Probably not. Same dead end. What was wrong with me? Just needed to be happy that I was married to a beautiful Mossad agent and had been shot at infrequently. Shit. I looked over at Dirk and Pavlina, wondering how he reconciled his conflicts. Probably the same rationalizations. Pavlina was as equally stunning as Beryl, and so far, I had not heard of her being tended to for bullet wounds.

I turned toward Beryl, sitting next to Uzi, joking easily. How did those guys manage to be so relaxed? How did Uzi effortlessly camouflage the tension coursing through him? I was sure there was more to this dinner, yet they could compartmentalize and block out the plotting and scheming as if but a distant dream. I turned to Noah and pressed the conversation. "I appreciate all this and the congratulations. I really do. But something tells me you didn't bring us all here just for a toast. If I'm wrong, great. If not, out with it...Let's get whatever it is over with. Then we can enjoy the rest of the evening. Hopefully."

David and Noah looked at each other, Noah then inclining his head slightly toward Uzi before turning back to me. Noah spoke with the authority of the state, "Okay, there is one thing we wanted to talk about. More a warning. When we planted those articles about Mullen Antiques, hoping to smoke out Werner, we also took some other liberties. We thought maybe we could use the same tactic with a couple of those bank accounts you helped us uncover. We left Banco ICR alone — we had put them through enough and didn't want to raise further suspicions with Werner. For a few of the others, however, we concocted fake articles about the history of accounts and how some from the next generations were still profiting. This wasn't too hard to do because we started with a true article, which then made it easy to draft these fabrications, assuming there were likely similar stories. One woman who was especially cooperative — I believe tied to an account your father helped with, Marco — gave us leeway to use her grandfather's real name. She is bitter about the past and was happy to help expose whatever we wanted. That's what gave us the start, and then it wasn't too much of a leap to point similar fingers at other banks, taking some liberties..."

"To come clean, we actually went a step beyond that," David said, looking at Beryl before continuing. "In addition to seeding fake articles, we also created and doctored Wikipedia pages. Our tech ops were able to get into a backdoor and then index references to Nazis, looking for overlaps with anyone that corrected any of our edits. That has allowed us to trace several of the influencers glorifying these bastards and keep us a step ahead. We've even been able to triangulate a few individuals. Let's just say you won't be reading more vile posts from them. Has also helped clean up things on the bank side."

"Jesus. You broke into Wikipedia?" I said, incredulous. If I had glanced toward my wife rather than staring in disbelief at David, I would have seen her eyes cast down, equally intent on tackling her tiger prawns as averting her gaze. It would be a while before she copped to her involvement.

"And a couple of other key sites. You wouldn't believe what people will post or do. They think they're immune online. And the more innocuous, the more dangerous. Why put something about an individual or store or museum or bank on Wikipedia anyway? Ego? Pride? But there's a trove of information uploaded—a literal encyclopedia of data. Once we manage to tease out a lead, then it's just a matter of patience and tracing in most cases. Unfortunately, though, not with Werner. People seriously expert at covering their tracks can mask themselves. But there are enough that don't. Most, in fact."

Pausing to look at me, Noah cut back in, "Anyway, some of the reactions to our targeted articles and posts were completely different than what we had expected. We anticipated the stories soliciting a few comments expressing indignation and criticism…and hoped for a couple people to come forward with similar stories, and with luck, new leads. We left the author's email to respond to—fake, of course—at the end. But most of the feedback was, well… I'll cut to the chase. To our horror, several people were praising them, and then a far-right site made the link and started attacking the people who had uncovered the accounts. Soon others joined in, Nazi sympathizers, claiming the authorities had no right to close and seize the accounts. We'd mentioned one woman's father, Klaus Becker, and that he had been part of the Gestapo—and two sites then posted flattering portrayals. I don't know what was more disgusting—hailing this Nazi war criminal as a hero or attacking his daughter for besmirching his name. We were stunned. The more we looked, the more we found a resurgence of Nazi and neo-Nazi propaganda and recruitment. The amount of traffic tied to fascist posts is scary. The web has created a whole new underground, a place for the Werners of the world to congregate and scheme."

"Jesus," I said.

"I'm not surprised," Beryl said, her prawns now skinned. "This has been growing for a while. It's disgusting. But I don't know how you fight it."

"It's hard," David conceded. "But we can't ignore it. We'd like some money from the Krumarkt Partners Fund to covertly wage counterattacks online. This is bigger than we first realized, and we're gonna need a lot more resources to keep up. It's a little like whack-a-mole taking these things down, but we can't leave it all to the search engines. Too many people claim free speech, so we can't touch anything. But this stuff is dangerous. Vile. We can't let these messages grow and metastasize. That's how things get out of hand. Everyone says it could never happen again…But how did it ever happen in the first place?"

Noah continued, "We wanted to ask you all in person. You've been witness to the horror of the past reaching out into the streets today. We need to stop this now, not let it grow. And because we need to act quickly, not always follow the niceties of every social media site's terms of service, we need to do this off the books. We wanted everyone to understand and ask if you'd help back it up."

My quick reaction was a tinge of vindication, my intuition about alternative motives for dinner correct. Any gloating, though, was undercut by having to face a dilemma that merely danced around politics, ethics, and family ties. Shit! Did I hear this correctly? Was I being asked to fund a black operation? I thought the whole point of plausible deniability and black ops was keeping it secret, not having conversations like these. If this was a courtesy call, I would have preferred being excluded like Hamid. I looked at Uzi and around the table, waiting for someone to break the stone-faced masks. I was sympathetic to the cause, but I was paralyzed by the request.

"Good for me," Beryl said, then looked over at me. She might as well have changed her name to Laila.

Boxed in by three words. I supposed it was three more words than I managed to muster. Once again, I had no choice. Would I have said no, even if I didn't believe in Noah and David's cause? Of course not, and fortunately, I was on Noah's side and thus spared a further conundrum. Looking into her sparkling green eyes, her soft blue eyeshadow batting out the flicker of blue, I was made a willing prisoner. If I tried to escape the grasp, I would then have to wrestle with the surreal challenge of being besotted by a Mossad spy, one capable of kicking a gun from a Nazi with the precision of a practice drill. I did not want to think about the further complications of a father-in-law named after a machine gun sitting next to me.

Noah's and Uzi's goals themselves were fine, perhaps enlightened, even if the tactics stank. Fucking Mossad! I acquiesced, compromised by a familiar blending of fidelity, panic, and awe. I loved Beryl as much today—no more—than back in the innocent tulip fields of our high school adolescence. "Good for me too," I said, somehow skirting the slippery slope of denuded pride. It helped that I also believed in Noah and David's endgame. I was still a lucky man.

"Me too," Dirk said.

Pavlina simply nodded yes, smiling widely, her vote a foregone conclusion. She would no less betray her employers than her husband on this count and, like me, had the added cushion of wholeheartedly agreeing with the cause.

"Another toast," Noah said, raising his bottle of Singha beer, "To the Kurmarkt Partners Fund!"

"To the Krumarkt Partners Fund!" we all repeated.

***

Liechtenstein — 2019

After the theft of the paintings from our warehouse beside the Flugplatz *Schleißheim, I was afraid the bank trustee would hesitate to release or even refuse to hand over my father's third letter. Those were his final instructions, and without them, I would fail him. It was unthinkable.*

Providentially, the trustee was the same bank in Liechtenstein I frequented, and I knew the managers well. One of them, Herr Mertz, was the acting trustee. I made sure to donate to his favorite charity months before making the appointment. He would make the link, but no reason to punctuate my motives. We were both gentlemen living in the principality and should conduct ourselves as such. I put on a fine silk and deep navy wool suit, a somber tie, and a white monogrammed handkerchief in my breast pocket. I considered accenting myself with a cane, a subtle nudge to having limited time, encouraging cooperation sooner than later. I decided, though, to abandon the cane. It could equally convey feebleness, and I was not ready to cede my vigor. Herr Mertz was privy to Mullenboess Ventures, as well as my controlling stake. If that status was not enough, then I would indeed have to rethink my approach.

After sitting down in a private room, decorated with green and yellow silk wallpaper, gold gilding on the moldings and columns and a renaissance looking fresco, I thanked Herr Mertz for meeting me. I explained that in my father's will, he had entrusted a third letter to the bank, a letter that was only to be tendered upon satisfying conditions. If for any reason conditions were delayed, then another seven years would be added before the letter was tendered. When my father died, I admitted to forgetting to tell the boys about that additional seven-year clause. It had never occurred to us it would be necessary. I did not profess understanding the timing. All I could imagine was that my father expected the art to sell quickly. However, perhaps thinking about how long the art had sat in his bunker, he was building in a failsafe, enough time that yet another generation would be budding when the contents were revealed. That was all I could surmise, the failsafe time to sell the art, seventeen years, roughly corresponding to a generation. Regardless, the full amount of time had passed.

I turned to Herr Mertz, lamenting that the conditions applied to the sale of certain paintings but that the bulk of those paintings, belonging to Mullen Antiques, had been stolen. I produced a criminal report of the warehouse theft and documents about the subsequent bankruptcy of Mullen Antiques. Herr Mertz was, of course, already aware of all these facts, but I nevertheless proceeded with the formalities.

I concluded by advising that the period for selling the works had passed and that I had fulfilled the balance of the wishes in my father's will. I had even waited to approach the bank until after the additional period had matured. I described how, dedicated to my father's memory and instructions, I had personally paid each of Florian, Rolfe, and Sophie the minimum that my father wished them to receive from the proceeds. Herr Mertz was not aware of that fact. He considered me more seriously upon learning I had paid each ten million euros despite not being able to fund their shares from the sale of the art. I admitted it was an extraordinary act, and yet one I would do again to honor my father's wishes.

Having earned Herr Mertz's full sympathy and respect, I then asked for the third letter. It was the last item I would have of my father's, in fact his last words to me I would ever see. The terms of release had never contemplated a theft, creating an ambiguity in what it meant to have sold specific percentages of the paintings within stated times. What did selling a certain percentage of the paintings mean when there was nothing to sell? It would be unfair not to let me see his final wishes or words because of an unforeseen circumstance beyond any of our control. And regardless, since the theft had led to this ambiguity, I had elected to wait the entire length of time to ensure the release was due.

Herr Mertz, ever the formal private banker, still offered some reluctance, reticent to violate bank protocol. In his opinion, the time may have passed, but I had still not sold the paintings. He, therefore, agreed to release the letter if I could prove we had sold all the art we were able to sell. Even if the time period had elapsed, questions could be raised if we had not used our best efforts to fulfill the essential terms — which was to sell the art, not wait years after a failure to sell. I knew bankers were loath to part with money and documents, but his haughty rectitude and excessive caution seemed extreme, if not hypocritical. Nevertheless, I realized it was best to proffer a clever solution rather than fight. It was not as if I could reveal the truth about the collection's theft or origins.

I created a fiction tied to selling the last vestiges of the collection, in essence proving we sold all we could sell. My sacrifice for Herr Mertz was to dispose of a couple pieces from Florian's study; treasures I advised had been moved temporarily from the warehouse, a partly true tale. My father had taken a few pieces and given them to the boys and the gallery, seeding the interest in collecting. I sold the minor Hals and an impressionist drawing, deciding to have a bit of fun. I sold them via a colleague to the Berlinerhaus, profiting $15 million and creating fake provenances. The murky trail would lead the Mossad to chase dead ends for a while. With the transaction completed, plus agreeing to donate the equivalent of a commission fee to the bank as a deposit on silence, I finally had the third letter.

I did not open it with Herr Mertz but tucked it into my briefcase and waited until I was back home. The letter was written in my father's crisp handwriting and was several pages long. It was undated, and I could not discern if he had written it close to his death. I suspected that was the case. I took a breath and started reading, waiting to be enveloped in my father's final embrace. What it contained shocked me.

After a smattering of greetings, the letter included an outline. At the top of the second page an underlined heading read: "Master Plan

For A New Reich." My father, Nazi Obersturmbannfuhrer Dieter Mullenhauer, had lived through World War II, the formation and collapse of East Germany, the reunification of Germany, and the growth of the European Union. He was an avowed fascist, loyal to the Nazi regime long after its ignominious end. He hated communism, enduring the economic catastrophe of its precepts in stifling decades behind the Berlin Wall. He also harbored bitterness towards Russia and its satellites, the Third Reich's fate hinging on Hitler's folly of pushing east and failing at Stalingrad. They had come so close. Nor was he a fan of unbridled capitalism, schooled in the lessons of the US depression and old enough to remember wheelbarrows of worthless money in Germany's streets during the economic collapse wrought by hyperinflation. While he might have supported some policies of social democrats, he was not supportive of social integration; certainly, he did not accept mixed races. He believed in the supremacy of the white race, of men as leaders, and in Germany's destiny to lead mankind. It would be unfair to say he was merely a product of his time, for he lived a long time and became a product of many times. Still, the beliefs of his youth held deepest, and he believed powerful states and strong leaders were necessary. That was the only way society could advance, to achieve greatness for future generations.

His letter made clear that we needed to be patient. Just like he had waited out the suspension of progress in East Germany, we needed to wait through this foolhardy phase in Europe. How could there be equality among Poles, Belgians, Greeks, Portuguese, and others with the stock of Germans? Defeat subjugated the German people into accepting this insulting bundling of races and nations, and one day they would wake up to realize their error. When this happened, there would be a new awakening, a chance again for Germany to be glorious, to take its rightful place. But seizing that opportunity was not a given. The seeds needed planting. As importantly, divisions needed stoking to speed the process.

Once he laid out his vision, it became clear what he hoped for the distribution of his wealth. He wanted the sale of the art to provide funding to the next generation who believed. He wanted me, his only surviving son, the bastard that I may be, to help finance a new wave of right-wing government parties. I had to read his words three times before I believed them. He wanted to use the money to back fascist-leaning governments and leaders — these men would show the world what could be achieved. With this lesson, Germany would be ready to rise again. Could he honestly be asking this of me? Was I to finance the rise of the right? Maybe even the rise of the next Reich? Were these last instructions the plotting of a genius or the ravings of a man desperate to resurrect misguided dreams long since dead?

I shook with the power of knowing what he wanted and that I could, if I chose, work to fulfill his wishes. I also knew what he asked was nearly impossible and that it would be a long road from my Liechtenstein mountain retreat to the backrooms of petty tyrants. People might disapprove of my methods and opinions, but they would have to admit I was not stupid. I was an educated man, a billionaire. I would have to ponder how to exercise my power and still not defy my father's last request. Obviously, I would not share the letter with my niece and nephews. I took a lighter and burned the pages in my fireplace. Like my father's destruction of the second letter, the third letter was too dangerous to remain part of this world. I went to sleep, dreaming of what world I wanted to create.

***

Zug, Switzerland and Tel Aviv, Israel — 2020

I was awakened in the morning by a surprise call from Noah Berenbaum. The sun was rising over the Zugersee, but phoning from a time-zone an hour ahead, Noah was already in his office in Tel Aviv.

He started, "Marco, sorry to call so early. First, is Beryl there with you?"

"Yes, right here," I said, wondering why the urgency to talk to both of us so early. "Do you want to talk to her?"

"No, you can pass along what I'm about to share."

"Well, what is it? Hope it's worth waking us up."

"It is. We've just found a lead on Werner Berlin. His real name is Werner Boesseneker. We know everything. I told you, we never forget."

"Holy Shit." And look at that, I have even expanded my vocabulary. I turned to Beryl and gave her the good news.

THE END

HISTORICAL NOTE & AUTHOR'S PERSPECTIVE

I love historical fiction and was inspired by threads of three unrelated items—the first two worthy of stories unto themselves—to write *Provenance of Ashes*. First, Bruce Springsteen played a famous concert in East Berlin (July 19, 1988) which some argue marked the beginning of the end of the communist regime. Crowds of people eager to see the rock concert, used to suppression and unaccustomed to freedoms, flooded the venue; just over a year later, on November 9, 1989, the infamous Berlin Wall came down. Second, in 2012 a trove of over 1,200 paintings, including from artists such as Monet, Cezanne and Picasso, was found in the cluttered and unkempt Munich apartment of the son of Nazi art dealer Hildebrand Gurlitt. Many of the stashed masterpieces were presumably looted from Jewish families or forcibly bought from them under duress (as they were fleeing the Nazis for survival) and more than 60 years later his son, Cornelius, was living a hermitic existence alone with the paintings and occasionally selling a few when in need of money. The paintings were shockingly discovered after he was stopped on a train traveling between Germany and visiting his Swiss bank. Third, the European Union (EU) has implemented what is often referred to as a "Right to be Forgotten" law (the General Data Protection Regulation, popularly referred to as "GDPR", targets privacy protection and includes an article whereby people may seek the erasure of personal data; see GDPR.eu) which allows individuals to apply for and enforce the takedown of negative information about them on the Internet. The worst of criminals (subject to provisions within the regulation) can expunge their past—at least online.

Drawing on these items, I wondered what if a Nazi officer hid art at the end of WWII, got stuck in East Germany after the war, had a son who became a Stasi officer, and with his son's help started laundering the art in the new millennium after the Berlin Wall came down? What a shocking and yet plausible scenario. I then conceived of pitting the most fabled new world spy agency, the Israeli Mossad, against masterminds of the Cold War.

I won't give away more here, but I loved crafting a story of global intrigue, digging into buried horrors, and spotlighting the risk of past evils reaching into the present—and worse, influencing current events. My first novel, *The Lord's Tusks*, is about the rise and fall of a poaching ring in Africa. Although I did not set out with this goal, I suppose I have a bent for crafting stories about truly awful people, their generational influences, and heroes risking their lives to bring them down.

I want to emphasize that *Provenance of Ashes*, including the story and all its characters, is a pure work of fiction. Additionally, some of the museums, such as the Koninghaus in Leiden and Berlinerhaus in Amsterdam, and all of the firms (e.g., Moultens & Barings, Bauer & Hoffstein) are made up for the story. However, Krugerrands (South African gold coins which once dominated the gold coin market), several of the museums and most locations are real. For example, ASH is an international school located in Wassenaar (Netherlands), the Anne Frank House fronts Amsterdam's Prinsengracht canal, the amphitheater in Caesarea (Israel) holds productions within the old Roman structure, Hebrew University of Jerusalem (HUJ) sits atop Mount Scopus, Jumeirah Beach houses luxury towers and hotels in Dubai, Notting Hill is a lovely upscale neighborhood in central London, and the Mauritshaus in The Hague, where Johannes Vermeer's *Girl With the Pearl Earing* hangs, is a true gem of a museum. Similarly, the Alta Pinakothek and Bayerischer Hof are, respectively, classic/landmark museums and hotels in Munich. Indeed, one can also search for hotels along the Rhine in Germany where Hitler stayed, which are similar to the fictitious Himmelgrun. Although I never traveled to East Germany when the Berlin Wall was up, I have spent time in virtually all the places depicted in the story, with many of the Swiss lakes among my favorite spots. Visiting the former concentration camp Dachau (outside Munich) and the Yad Vashem Holocaust Museum in Jerusalem were obviously more sobering visits, though I encourage people to tour these and other memorials which remind us of past horrors and hopefully inspire us to prevent similar atrocities from ever happening again. Spending eight years working in Amsterdam, including talking to a next-door neighbor who hid as a child during the Nazi occupation, made vividly real to me how closely we live to ghosts of the past. There are too many stories like that of Cornelius Gurlitt that periodically surface. Worse still is the inconceivable (though thankfully fringe) trend toward denial of the Holocaust and other past wartime atrocities. As living links like my former neighbor, those concealing stolen property from victims of WWII, generations that lived behind the Berlin Wall, and other survivors now pass on from the more benign reaper of time, we should remember never to forget the history. And, on a more positive note, we should enjoy and appreciate the amazing works of art preserved in Amsterdam and other great museums and galleries throughout the world — Beryl and Marco urge you to visit and donate to real preservation and restitution funds!

ACKNOWLEDGMENTS

There are a lot of people I'd like to thank. First, I want to thank Black Rose Writing, my publisher, for believing in me and publishing first *The Lord's Tusks* and now *Provenance of Ashes*. I also want to thank my editor, Mary Ellen Bramwell, for her pragmatic and supportive comments and suggestions, striking the right balance to raise the level of my writing. I'd also like to thank Kirsten Schuder and Apex (ALM) for championing the story.

Finally, and always first in my thoughts, I could never have completed this book without the support of my family, whose inspiration is limitless. I had written an outline and tinkered with this story for years, ultimately finishing the book as the pandemic started to hit—writing providing an escape from the surreal reality of the time. I could never have survived those ensuing months without the support and positive outlook of my wife Eve. Somehow we managed to turn the angst and anxiety of that period into something positive, life again proving stranger than fiction.

ABOUT THE AUTHOR

After majoring in anthropology at Harvard, Jeff Ulin became fascinated with other cultures and began traveling the world – capturing and moving an endangered rhino on a rescue project in Africa, visiting Buddhist monasteries on the Indian/Tibetan border, exploring Asia, Russia and the Mid-East, coupled with living as an American expat in the Netherlands, UK, and Spain, all which color and inform his novels. He's braved and enjoyed every conceivable mode of travel (tuk-tuk, atop bus with goats, private planes, Concorde, bullet trains). Jeff's experiences working for George Lucas on Skywalker Ranch, creating *Higglytown Heroes*, and working as a General Counsel also infuse his writing. He relishes very spicy Chinese food, is a dog lover, and now lives and paddles on a Mediterranean island.

NOTE FROM JEFFREY ULIN

Word-of-mouth is crucial for any author to succeed. If you enjoyed *Provenance of Ashes*, please leave a review online—anywhere you are able. Even if it's just a sentence or two. It would make all the difference and would be very much appreciated.

Thanks!
Jeffrey Ulin

We hope you enjoyed reading this title from:

www.blackrosewriting.com

Subscribe to our mailing list – *The Rosevine* – and receive **FREE** books, daily deals, and stay current with news about upcoming releases and our hottest authors.
Scan the QR code below to sign up.

Already a subscriber? Please accept a sincere thank you for being a fan of Black Rose Writing authors.

View other Black Rose Writing titles at www.blackrosewriting.com/books and use promo code **PRINT** to receive a **20% discount** when purchasing.

www.ingramcontent.com/pod-product-compliance
Lightning Source LLC
Chambersburg PA
CBHW051316190726
48290CB00001B/178